DARKNESS IN STONE

A SEVEN FAMILIES NOVEL: WOLF

KAT SIMONS

DARKNESS IN STONE

For my family...
My heroes-in-training and their hero dad.
Love you all a ton.

CHAPTER ONE

From cover of the curtains in his front library, Eric Logan watched the woman sitting in her car out in front of his home. He'd always wondered what he would feel when he finally saw her. After so many years of waiting, centuries of waiting, she was finally here.

And he *still* wasn't sure how he felt.

His emotions were all jumbled, too chaotic to sort out. Need. Possessiveness. Resentment. Fear. Uncertainty. Curiosity. Protectiveness. Anger. Desire.

But one thing was as clear to him as the autumn light reflecting off the hood of her beat up Dodge. He would have Katie Donovan. She was his. His Nam-tar. Promised to him by the old god En millennia ago. And nothing and no one would stand in his way.

Not even her.

Katie glanced one last time in the rearview mirror, making sure her makeup and hair were neat and professional-looking. She hated that she hadn't been able to check into her hotel before arriving at the Logan mansion. Between traffic and a later start leaving the city than she'd intended, she'd have been late for the interview if she took the time to find the hotel.

But this particular interview was more important to her career than any previous assignment, so she couldn't afford to be late.

She ran her tongue over her teeth to make sure there was no lipstick, sucked in a deep breath, and glanced at the front door to the mansion. Something vague nagged at her senses—that damned tingling at the base of her skull, an indication her much hated psychic senses were about to give her some knowledge she didn't want.

One long minute passed as she waited for the *knowing*. But nothing came to her. Just an unfocused sense of foreboding.

Grinding her teeth, she snatched up her purse and checked for her digital voice recorder, notebooks, pens, rechargers, and mobile phone —all the really important stuff. Then she forced herself from the car, locking the door even though the effort seemed unnecessary given the setting.

She scanned the front grounds, memorizing the manicured lawns, the tree-lined, gravel-strewn road leading into the estate, the elegant stone fountain centered in front of the mansion, creating a circular driveway. The trees dotting the property were just beginning to turn, decorating the green lawn in bright reds, oranges, and yellows. This part of upstate New York exploded with color in October, which was worth the trip all by itself. The scent of fresh cut grass gave the cool autumn day an almost spring feel, despite the colorful trees.

As she turned in a slow circle, she spotted a side road which she assumed led to a garage, but Mr. Logan's assistant hadn't given her any specifics about where to park, so the front of the house would have to do for now. Given all the detailed instructions the assistant had given her, that one lapse was a little surprising. They probably weren't expecting her to stay long enough to need the garage.

Or maybe the assistant thought Katie would insult Mr. Logan immediately and get kicked out. Since he was notorious for not giving interviews, that was a distinct possibility.

She faced the front door again, taking in the white stone stairs leading up to the house, the gleaming pillars supporting an arched stone portico, the decorative glass windows that prevented views inside. Her stomach danced a little, nerves and pressure making her glad she'd used the strong deodorant that morning.

Finally, she forced herself to walk up those steps, running a hand down her suit skirt to remove any creases, snapping down the sleeves of her suit jacket. Even as she rang the bell, she mentally practiced the way she'd greet Mr. Logan. Professional, competent, no nonsense. She had to get this right.

Her future depended on it.

As she waited, another tingle along her neck and a slight movement near the house made her glance to the right. Frowning, she leaned back, trying to identify the source of the movement. She could swear she saw something. But the lawn and bushes near the house were still. She hadn't felt a breeze to explain any movement. Nothing even rustled as she stared.

Probably just a squirrel.

An older man wearing a grave expression and a very traditional butler suit—black pants and jacket, white shirt and striped cravat-style tie—opened the door. He was a tall, pale man with light eyes and graying hair cut neat and close to his head. His bearing brooked no nonsense.

She straightened her shoulders, imitating his posture, and pasted on her most professional smile. "Hello. I'm Katie Donovan. Here for the interview with Mr. Logan."

"Come in." The man stepped to the side to allow her entry, then indicated a direction to the right with the sweep of his hand. "This way, please."

She followed silently, attempting to take in the interior of the house at once. Stunning was the first word that leapt to mind.

The main entryway was flanked by large white columns past which opened a huge foyer with a thirty-foot, arched ceiling boasting a colorful mural. Unfortunately, from the ground floor, she couldn't see the subject of the painting. But the gilt accenting the crown molding was impressive even from a distance. Green marble floors against white painted walls, gave more depth and an echoing kind of openness.

Several closed doors stood on either side of the foyer, between which were small shelf insets filled with *object de art* she hoped to study closer at some point this afternoon.

Dominating the area was a huge curved marble staircase with elaborately carved wooden banisters, which led up to a second-floor gallery. She got a glimpse of corridors leading off from behind and to the sides of the stairs, into other parts of the mansion. The overall impression was of an immense space and boundless wealth.

She'd barely had time to take in the grandeur before the butler opened one of the doors to the right and gestured her inside.

"Sir, Ms. Katie Donovan to see you."

She nodded politely to the butler, gave her hands a quick flex and release to relax her nerves, and walked into the room with her shoulders straight and her best reporter smile in place.

The smile and her forward momentum froze when she got her first good look at Eric Logan in person.

Oh. Oh my.

She'd been expecting him to be handsome. There were a few pictures of him out in public, at various charity events, museum openings, and sometimes at business functions. She thought she'd known what to expect. She was used to handsome celebrities. That had been a part of her previous job in London. Interviewing—sometimes ambushing—beautiful people to get quotes and gossip. She'd been in the presence of some of the most spectacularly attractive people on the planet.

None had ever overwhelmed her quite like this.

And it wasn't even that he was handsome. He was, of course. Dark hair brushing his collar, dark eyes, clean shaven, sharp features, tall, broad shouldered. He was dressed for the interview in black slacks and a black button-down shirt, which he carried off without his pale skin look too pasty. But there was something…more to him. Something in his bearing, his aura. Magnetic. Compelling. A little scary. And something that took her breath away. Like electricity. Like lightning. Something… Stunning.

Yes, that was the word. Stunned. She was stunned by him.

And for a long moment, all she could do was stare. Not moving. Not speaking. Not blinking.

When his nostrils flared, she got the distinct impression of being a deer facing down a lion.

Her heartbeat pounded hard enough she was afraid he'd hear even though they were across the room from each other. And for a split second, she wondered if she could run away without getting sacked.

Probably. Her editor wouldn't fire her for losing this interview. But Mona would also never let her write the articles she really wanted to write either, the types of stories that would get her a coveted Pulitzer.

She'd worked her ass off to get this interview, even going so far as to call in a favor from a former colleague in London. The fact that as soon as she'd talked to Logan's assistant her psychic senses assured her that he'd agree to the interview hadn't made the process any easier or more secure. He'd already delayed the meeting twice. She couldn't afford to risk this opportunity or allow him to put her off a third time. Not when her entire journalistic future depended on it. She had to stick this out, get this interview.

Even if he did send her primitive flight instincts into overdrive.

She let out a slow breath, straightened her shoulders again, and crossed the room, determined to see this through.

"Thank you for agreeing to speak with me, Mr. Logan," she greeted, hoping he didn't hear the huskiness in her voice. She cleared her throat. "*Aphrodite's* readers will be thrilled to learn more about you."

Intending to shake his hand, she extended her own, but he held still, making no effort to return the gesture. Letting her arm fall back to her side, she nodded instead and waited for him to say something.

A long moment passed in silence.

Okay. Her nerves were already jumping, from more than just the importance of this to her career. But apparently, he wasn't going to make things easy on her.

Glancing around the large, high-ceiling library, she changed tack. "You have a lovely home."

The furniture was both expensive and comfortable-looking, an eclectic mix of styles rather than matching sets, with a modern leather couch and chairs interspersed with an antique settee and cherrywood tables. The dark wood shelves lining the walls were filled with leather bound volumes, the rugs covering the polished wooden floors were thick and colorful. Heavy green velvet curtains hung alongside the three large windows taking up most of the external wall. The fireplace was smooth gray stone with a green marble base, a stack of wood piled on the grate, and a large, decorative mirror over the mantle. A few paintings hung between the shelves, but otherwise the room was free of knick-knacks. A fine, casual display of wealth.

"Thank you," he responded to her compliment.

His deep, quiet voice washed over her, making her skin tingle in its wake and her stomach muscles tightened. So… His voice didn't help her nerves at all. She needed him to speak, to answer her questions, but since the sound of his voice rubbed against her spine like velvet, she wasn't sure listening to him talk was good for her.

Too bad it was the entire reasons she was here.

She cleared her throat again. "Shall we get started?" She spoke in a brisk tone, making sure none of her internal turmoil leaked out. He likely already knew the impact he had on people. Wouldn't do to let him know she was affected.

"Would you like a tour of the house?" he asked, seemingly out of nowhere.

Well, since he mentioned it. "A tour would be lovely. As long as you don't mind me asking questions along the way. Since we have such a limited amount of time."

She'd only been given a few hours with him today and an hour tomorrow morning. Barely enough for the interview Mona wanted. But Katie couldn't pass up the opportunity to see more of a mansion that reporters had never been allowed into.

Until now.

He extended a hand toward the door, and she preceded him from the room, hoping her slightly wobbly knees weren't evident in her stride. Heels might have been a bad idea, even though they were low and normally something she could manage easily. But this wasn't normal. None of this felt even a little normal.

She waited in the huge foyer for him to lead the way, carefully controlling a need to fidget. When he passed her, another shiver of awareness raced across her skin, as if he'd physically brushed against her.

More lightning and sparks danced along her nerves. Her stomach danced, too. And she had no idea if those feelings were anxiety or… something else.

But whatever the reason for her reaction to Eric Logan, she knew one thing…

That feeling, and the man himself, scared the shit out of her.

CHAPTER TWO

Katie blew out a breath and focused on her reason for being here in the first place. Her job. Her future. Her career. Feelings didn't play into it. And being scared was no excuse to fall apart.

She followed Logan as he led her past the stairway and down a corridor with light wooden wainscotting and pale cream walls. The mansion was gorgeous, something *Aphrodite* readers would want details about—and so would Mona—so she catalogued as much as she could memorize. It kept her attention off the man in front of her. At least enough she could think. Sort of.

But she was supposed to be talking to him, interviewing him. With such limited time, she had to get something Mona would love. She started with basics. "Your home really is beautiful," she complimented again. "Did you grow up here?"

"I've spent a lot of time here, yes," he said, his back to her. "This is my family's primary residence."

"You have properties around the world. Do you have a favorite?"

All her interview questions were designed to be light and inoffensive. The sorts of questions that the magazine's readers would love but that wouldn't get her kicked out of Logan's house early because she'd pissed him off. Her editor wanted primarily the light fluffy stuff of a celebrity interview, with a few potential insights into the mysterious Eric Logan's private life.

And if Katie happened to discover some good juicy gossip along the way… Well, that was how she'd originally gotten the job at *Aphrodite*. Her background in writing gossip for the rags in London. She hadn't come here to dig for it. She didn't want to write celebrity gossip anymore. That was the point of getting this interview. She wanted to write other things. Do serious journalism. But if it helped her reach that goal, she wasn't opposed to one last splash in the gossip pool.

When Eric Logan glanced over his shoulder and met her gaze, she had to repress a shiver. The intensity in his look nearly had her tripping over her own feet. A bad idea in her low heels.

Maybe courting the trouble of revealing gossip about him to the world was a bad idea, even if she uncovered something juicy.

"At the moment," he said, returning to her question as he faced forward again, "I'm very fond of this house."

She took in the arched ceilings decorated with gleaming carved wood and crystal light fixtures. "I can see why."

"This is nothing to the atrium."

"The atrium?"

"I thought we'd start the tour there."

He led her to a large entryway opening onto a lush, green paradise. Warm, humid air brushed over her face as they crossed the threshold and the full grandeur of the enclosure momentarily left her speechless.

Brick-lined walkways twisted and meandered through dense patches of plants and flowers. Overhead, a glass and iron roof filled the massive room with autumn light magnified to feel like summer heat. From her vantage, Katie couldn't even see the outer walls, furthering the impression that the space was large enough to be a house all by itself. At least ten times the size of her tiny sublet in Manhattan.

But what most captured her attention were the sculptures.

Stone and marble works of art seemed to emerge from the greenery like living beings rising from the depths of a mythical forest.

"Beautiful," she murmured.

Without waiting, she wandered down a paved path to the nearest statue—a shockingly life-like rendering of a man in a Victorian era suit walking beside a dog so large its head came to the man's elbow.

"Who's the artist?" she asked, without looking at Logan.

"My mother."

"Really?" She turned to face him. He was staring at her rather than the statue. "None of my research hinted that your mother is an artist."

Laksana Logan was known for being a great patron of the arts both in the U.S. and abroad. Some of the very few available photos of the Logan family came from fundraising events. But the articles surrounding the events never had direct quotes from any of the family, and nowhere was it mentioned that Laksana was a sculptor.

"She's…unappreciated in her time," he said with the barest lifting of his lips.

Katie found herself staring at his mouth for a heartbeat too long and turned quickly back to the statue. "She's amazingly talented." To keep her mind on her job and off Eric Logan's entirely too intriguing mouth, she moved to another statue. "This one looks like you. Another of your mother's?"

"Most of the artwork in here is hers."

"I can't believe she isn't widely recognized. This could be your twin." She nodded to the form reclining under a stone tree with one knee bent and an apple resting in the palm of his hand where he braced his arm on his out stretched thigh. In the tree bark, another shape seemed to be suggested by the curving lines. A dog? Or maybe a wolf?

When she faced Logan, the likeness between him and the stone rendering was even more pronounced, almost eerie. His mother hadn't bothered to idealize her son, down to capturing the slight lump on his nose, an imperfection that only made him more attractive—which should have been impossible. As she studied the living, breathing Eric Logan, Katie had to admit, trying to idealize something that close to perfect probably hadn't even crossed his mother's mind.

She blinked hard and glanced quickly away. "Does she use you as a model frequently?"

"She uses all my brothers and sisters as models. She claims she wants to preserve her family in stone."

A strange expression passed over his face when he murmured the last sentence. Katie waited for further explanation. He was leaving something unsaid, and her curiosity nearly got the better of her. After a moment, she opened her mouth to ask him exactly what his mother meant but stopped when he shook his head, glanced back at her, and smiled.

That smile overwhelmed all her senses instantly. Feral, wild, and so seductive she could barely breathe. Wow. For a full thirty seconds, she completely lost her train of thought. She couldn't even remember why she was standing in this gorgeous setting with this sexy-beyond-belief man.

Then the importance of this interview snapped her back to herself.

She returned her full attention to the atrium, but nervous energy had her curling the strap of her purse around her hand, winding and unwinding the thick leather as she moved on to another statue. When she realized she was fidgeting, she cursed silently and fisted her hands to keep them still.

What was it about him that threw her so far off her game? She'd interviewed dozens of actors and celebrities—some of them without their express agreement to the interview—and come face to face with some of the most beautiful people on the planet. Why was her stomach dancing and her nerves jumping around this particular man? She felt almost like a teenager again, rendered helplessly awed by a handsome face.

Drawn to him in a way she'd never felt before.

The sensation was terrifying and distracting because it didn't make any sense. Such a visceral, immediate response… She didn't have those kinds of instant lust reactions to men. Especially men she also found a little scary. She couldn't explain it to herself. They'd barely spoken, hadn't been in the same room for more than ten minutes, and she was here to ask probing questions he usually didn't answer, even if they were light and fluffy questions. None of that lent itself to these out-of-character lusty longings.

She tried to calm her heartbeat and shake off the bizarre feelings as she continued wandering through the garden.

"Do you enjoy modeling for your mother?" she asked, forcing herself to sound unaffected and professional, interested but not too interested. Still hearing the breathiness in her voice despite her best efforts. "I imagine it can be difficult to stand still that long."

She closed her eyes briefly. Some tough professional reporter she was, getting all discombobulated when a handsome man smiled at her. Good thing she wasn't here for a hard-hitting interview.

She glanced back to see him walking behind her, his gaze still way too intense, focused on her and not the surroundings. She faced forward again quickly, because looking at him turned her brain mushy. Still, she sensed him there, a presence she felt down the length of her spine. And not entirely in a good way. She peeked again. Still staring at her. She turned forward. But she couldn't shake the sense of being stalked rather than accompanied through this tour.

"I've gotten very good at...controlling my movements," he answered her question finally. "Posing for my mother is good training."

"Why would you need that kind of training? As a businessman, is there much call for holding perfectly still?" For some reason, Katie thought of the way big cats could remain quiet and unmoving while hunting, and a shiver scurried up her arms.

"Stillness makes some people very uncomfortable."

She couldn't argue with that. Especially since she was one of those people.

She stopped in front of another magnificent piece of art. This one was of a little girl in a frilly dress with long flowing locks and bat-like wings on her back. She was playing with a puppy whose tongue was lolling out. The strange juxtaposition between the sinister-looking wings and the girl's gleeful expression as she held up a ball for the puppy caught Katie's interest. She tilted her head to one side, taking in the details of the tableau. The puppy rose on its hind legs, a happy grin on its canine lips. The little girl's beautifully flowing, ruffle-covered dress gave her an angelic look at complete odds with the leathery wings on which sharp points rose at the joints along the leading edges.

After a moment of study, Katie started to see the wings differently. Instead of odd and sinister, she found they looked quite charming, almost gothic faery-like on the small girl.

"My youngest sister was the model."

Logan's voice startled her enough she jumped. Then she felt stupid for the reaction. Jesus, Katie, get a grip. She could swear he was so close she felt his breath on her neck. But when she looked, he stood several feet away, too far for her to really feel his breath.

Swallowing, she nodded toward the statue. "It's beautiful. Strange but beautiful. Kind of like a fairytale."

He remained silent, so she turned to face him fully. He was smiling slightly, thoughtfully as he studied the statue. "My sister and mother would like the comparison to a fairytale." He met her gaze. "They're both fond of the strange and beautiful."

"And you? Do you like that combination?"

His slight smile fell away. "It depends entirely on the…object in question."

"Meaning?"

"Some strangely beautiful things can be dangerous."

And wasn't that very very true.

But, she acknowledged after a moment of staring at him too long again, a frustrating answer because it didn't reveal much of his character. The expression on his face also left her with an uncomfortable sensation tightening her stomach, a feeling she couldn't put a name to. Willfully ignoring her reaction, she moved on.

Her psychic senses weren't giving her any concrete reason, any actual knowledge to define her edginess since entering the house either. She started to regret not shaking Logan's hand—though she hadn't really had much choice in the matter. If she touched him, maybe she'd learn if this weird combination of anticipation and fear had to do with him directly. Because the feeling of being stalked as they walked down yet another path was strong enough to make the hair on the back of her neck prickle. And yet he was keeping his distance, answering her questions, not doing anything overtly threatening.

So why did she feel under threat here?

"Do you have a hidden artistic talent, like your mother?" she asked, forcing herself back to the job.

"My talents lie…elsewhere."

"Where, precisely?"

He didn't answer for several moments. Then quietly, "That you'll have to discover for yourself, Ms. Donovan."

Was that innuendo or avoidance? His tone was impossible to interpret.

She decided he must mean the latter and replied, "I intend to, Mr. Logan." Let him take from that what he would. In the meantime, she needed a new direction so she didn't consider the implications of any innuendo in his comment. "In the two hundred years your family has owned this house, has it always looked like this? Was the atrium here prior to your mother's contributions?"

"No. And yes."

She raised her eyebrows at the brief answers. Most wealthy men she'd met liked to elaborate on their mansions and the work put into them. She tried again. "Has a lot of work been done in your lifetime?"

"The family is always making improvements to the place. Old houses require a lot of maintenance."

He was hedging—answering without giving her much insight into his life. What could she do to startle a longer response out of him? As she considered her options, a statue of a wolf curled around two pups captured her attention and she paused. She smiled at the tender scene. The detail of the animals was exquisite. And she was struck once again by the fact that no one had heard of Laksana Logan's artistic skills.

"Why doesn't your mother sell any of her work? She's so talented. Why doesn't anyone know about this side of her?" In reality, there was a lot the world didn't know about the Logans. But a gift like Laksana Logan's going unnoticed seemed criminal.

"Her art is for the family."

Katie turned to face him, waiting for further explanation.

"So she says," he responded with a slight shrug. "She has no interest in fame. And as you can see, she already has fortune."

"True." But she didn't really understand Mrs. Logan's logic. She was desperate to achieve more with her career. She had Pulitzer dreams. If she'd had a talent like this, she'd find it hard not to share her work with the world, even if she had plenty of money.

"You disagree with her decision? To keep her art to herself?"

His question surprised her. "It's her decision to make, of course," she said. "I'm just not sure I'd have made the same one."

He frowned, and she felt as if she'd disappointed him in some way. The thought bothered her enough she wanted to apologize. And then irritation gripped her. She wasn't here for his approval. She didn't care whether he liked her or not. She was here to do a job, plain and simple.

So she got back to it. "Besides your mother," she said, forcing a smile, "who's your favorite artist?"

"I'm fond of the Impressionists. For sculpture, besides my mother, I quite like Rodin. His realistic approach to the human form has always appealed to me."

His tone when he stated this last caught her attention. She got the feeling there was underlying meaning to his comment, but she couldn't identify anything specific in his neutral expression. "Any Rodin piece in particular?"

"The Kiss has a lot of power," he murmured.

Katie nearly tripped on an uneven brick. Clenching her purse tightly to control her reaction, she chose once again to ignore even the possibility of innuendo in his statement. Though his kiss probably did hold a lot of power.

Do not even think about that.

But it was hard not to. He paced behind her, his expression closed, his mood impossible to read, but his attention was fully focused on her. She could feel his stare all along her back, raising goose bumps over her skin. An odd mixture of sexual excitement and intimidation tightened her muscles, and her primitive instincts played havoc with her common sense.

Damned inconvenient time for her *knowing* to have up and abandoned her. Not that it had ever been very useful. Still…

"You don't like this piece?"

His question brought her back to her surroundings, and she focused on the statue she'd stopped in front of without thinking. It was of a man with a wolf crawling out of his torso. The wolf's front paws were forward, head low, ears back, as if leaping through the man, except that the man's back was unmarred. She glanced up and realized the man looked like Logan.

"You were the model for this one, too?"

He nodded.

"It's as impressive as all the others. What's it supposed to represent?"

"The animal spirit in all of us."

"You believe we all have an…animal spirit?" She kept her attention on the statue as she asked. Something about it called to her, drawing her closer. She couldn't explain why, but this piece, more than any other, felt so real. Like a real wolf was leaping from the living Eric Logan.

Without thinking, she brushed her fingers over the cold marble, lightly touching the man's torso just above where the wolf emerged. She gasped quietly as a tickle of energy vibrated along her hand, similar to a psychic reaction, and yet the sensation was unique. More intimate. Almost…erotic.

"Perhaps," Logan answered, his voice deep and quiet.

She felt him close the space between them. For no good reason, her heart started to pound. She swallowed as the air thickened. "Interesting idea," she breathed.

Unable to stop herself, she swiveled around to face him.

He took a single step closer, and Katie's pulse jumped, though whether from fright or anticipation she wasn't sure. His gaze dropped to her mouth, and her throat dried.

What the hell was the matter with her? Why did she suddenly want him to kiss her so badly she thought she might scream if he didn't?

His nostrils flared, as if catching her scent, and a subtle curve of his lips made her think he could sense her very thoughts. Which just pissed her off. She took a deliberate step away from him and flashed him an icy smile.

"So your mother thinks you're a bit of a wolf? Mrs. Logan sounds like a very perceptive woman to me."

To her utter astonishment, he dropped his head back and laughed. The sound was dark and throaty, rubbing across her skin like a velvet caress. Leaving her breathless and once again…

Stunned.

"She's not the only one," he said as his laughter eased. "Are you afraid of me, Ms. Donovan?"

She raised a brow. "Should I be?"

He held her gaze for a long moment. Then almost thoughtfully, said, "Probably."

CHAPTER THREE

Katie swallowed and turned her back to him, despite every self-preservation instinct screaming at her to keep him in sight at all times. To give herself some room to breathe, she walked down a smaller path and into a different section of the atrium.

The light darkened and she glanced up. Clouds moved over the sky, cutting off the bright October sunshine. Until that moment, the light pouring through the glass ceiling had made the atrium cozy and warm, almost hot. The gray clouds brought a chill to the air.

She rubbed her palms over her arms to warm them, despite the long sleeves of her suit jacket. "So," she said, once again trying to refocus on the interview, "does your mother keep all her art here? Or is it scattered around the family properties?"

"She has pieces in all our homes."

"Do you have a favorite sculpture of hers?"

"Ms. Donovan, wait."

She rounded a sharp corner in the path without watching her step, half turning to see why Logan sounded so urgent, and bumped into something on the ground. When she glanced down to see what she'd hit, shock sent her stumbling backward. She came up hard against a solid wall of muscle. Warm hands caught her shoulders and held her steady, the gesture much more reassuring than it should have been.

For a moment, the physical contact with Logan captured her full attention. His heat seeped into her back, warming her all the way to her toes. Her stomach danced as fire raced through her blood stream, pooling low in her belly. Her skin tingled with awareness and a need for more contact.

But the horror of what lay on the ground kept her from wallowing in those delicious sensations.

"Are you all right?"

He murmured the question near her ear, the hot brush of his breath raising goosebumps along her skin.

"I'm fine. Just…startled." She nodded toward the statue as she stepped away from him.

His grip on her shoulders tightened for an instant, as if he intended to keep her close, before he dropped his hands. Katie sighed, surprised to find she missed the physical contact more than she was relieved to be free of his touch.

"I should have warned you about this…"

When he didn't finish his sentence, she said, "This isn't one of your mother's sculptures, is it?"

A stone man lay writhing on the ground with a six-foot silver pole sticking out of his chest. His face was clenched tight but barely recognizable as human. A muzzle, like a dog's nose, distorted the skin of his cheek. A canine ear and eye were visible through the stone skin of his forehead, the ear just poking out. A paw thrust out of his side. Another animal leg burst from his thigh. The skin covering the parts of the body still obviously human seemed to be rolling and buckling. Several large tears opened up the statue's skin and spilled things out Katie didn't want to look at too closely. And his human mouth gaped wide in a silent scream.

She shuddered and turned away.

The statue was horrific in and of itself. But the worst part was the expression on the man's face—terror and pain like nothing she could imagine. And anger. Rage. She could practically feel the rage pumping from the figure. The face didn't look like any of the others in the atrium. She only hoped if Logan's mother had created this…piece, she'd used a model from outside the family.

"I should have had that removed before you arrived," Logan said. "I'm sorry I didn't think to stop you sooner."

"Yeah, I'm kind of sorry I made that last turn." She kept her back to the statue. "The model isn't one of your siblings?"

"This is not one of my mother's sculptures." His nostrils flared as he looked past her at the stone monstrosity. "Come on."

He gripped her elbow and led her back the way they'd come. His touch shot a spark of electricity through her system. And for just a moment, she wanted to lean into him for comfort. How could he do that with just a simple touch?

Even more disturbing, the contact didn't give her any psychic understanding. She got…nothing. Frequently, physical contact sparked some *knowing*. But with Logan, all she felt was heat and want. Nothing that either eased her discomfort or gave her a source for the danger she sensed.

The tumble of emotions and strange needs left her feeling vulnerable and edgy. She hated feeling vulnerable.

"I can walk on my own," she said sharply, then cringed at how unprofessional she sounded. He was only being courteous. But she had to get his hand off her. Now. "Thank you," she added in a more measured tone.

His eyes darkened. "I wouldn't want you to take another wrong turn."

"I'm sure that won't be a problem," she replied, hoping for smooth but afraid she came off churlish.

Damn it, she didn't want to offend him and risk getting tossed out of the house before she finished the interview. But she didn't want him getting the wrong idea either. She wasn't here on a date, even if her hormones wanted her to be. She was here to get a job done. And touching Eric Logan was too much of a distraction.

It crossed her mind that he was doing this to her on purpose, subtly seducing her, muddling her thinking so he could more easily control her story. She'd dealt with that tactic from a few celebrities in the past. If that was Logan's plan, she intended to disappoint him.

But first, she had to get his hand off her.

"Now that statue looks more like your mother's work," she said, pulling out of his grip.

A tremor of discomfort moved through her, a cold shiver tinged with disappointment. She rubbed her arms again, and made a concerted effort to ignore everything that had just happened.

ERIC WATCHED KATIE DONOVAN RETREAT AND COULDN'T PREVENT HIS slight smile. Did she realize what she did to him by running away? Probably not. Or she wouldn't have dared. Not that it mattered. This was a chase his predatory nature couldn't resist, even if he'd wanted to.

"All your mother's work focuses on a single person," she said. "Did she every use more than one sibling at a time in a single piece?"

"No." He tried to provoke her into facing him with his one word answer, but she refused.

"Why not?"

"Too hard to get more than one of us in the same place at the same time for very long," he said. Something of a half-truth, but she'd know the real reason soon enough.

He moved up close behind her and breathed in her spicy scent with that hint of vanilla in her shampoo. He flexed his hand, making a fist before releasing the tight grip. He could still feel the imprint of her lush body pressed tight against him, and it took a great deal of willpower not to reach for her again.

Swallowing a low growl, he watched her rub her hands along her arms. He knew the temperature in the room wasn't cool enough to warrant her chill, even with the cloud cover. His smile widened. Her scent gave her away. Oh, she did a good job of hiding her interest, her attraction, a good job of keeping her distance and attempting to maintain that professional air. But she couldn't hide from him.

The only thing he didn't regret about her finding Jason's remains was that her shock had given him an excuse to hold her. One of the very few things he might ever thank Jason for.

"Do you get along with your family?" she asked as she started walking again.

Given what she'd just seen, and what he'd been thinking, her question was more ironic that she could know. "Most of them."

He still smelled the blood soaking the soil and stones around Jason's remains. Thankfully, Katie's all too human sense of smell wasn't as good as his or she might have guessed that sculpture was more than simply a grotesque carving. She'd have to know eventually. To survive in his world, she'd have to understand it. Which was why he'd started the tour of his home here, in this virtual shrine to what he and his family were. If she had a hint, even in her subconscious, of what to expect, she might not run away.

"Who don't you get along with?" she asked.

Well, he hadn't been very fond of Jason in the end. "We have a huge family. There are always some personality conflicts."

He only half paid attention to the answers he gave her. He was so overwhelmed by having her here, it was hard to focus on anything else. After all these centuries, his Nam-tar, here in his home. His fated one. The woman who could break his curse and bring him peace.

He needed Katie Donovan. To avoid Jason's fate. To put the horror of that kind of death behind him forever. The god En had made that promise to the Seven Families millennia ago. But Katie had to stay of her own free will. He couldn't force her. That would break the covenant and Ne's curse would remain intact.

Nothing said he couldn't seduce her into staying, though. And with her desire so strong in her scent, he thought he might have a pretty good chance of doing just that.

He edged closer as they strolled toward the middle of the atrium, wanting to wash the residue of Jason's death from his nostrils. Breathing her in, he tasted her need, her fear, her leeriness and reluctant want. The flavors mingled on the front of his tongue like a heady wine, leaving him drunk. And a little more desperate than he'd ever been in his long long life.

"Gently," he heard the echoed memory of his mother's voice whisper through his mind. "She can't be forced."

Gently was the last thing he wanted. He flexed his hands, his need to take hold of Katie again strong. But his mother was a wise woman. To ignore her warning was foolishness he wasn't prepared to embark on, even after more than three hundred years.

So he resisted the lure of his Nam-tar, so close but still just out of his reach. He couldn't afford to mess this up. Couldn't risk letting her get away.

He did give in to a little temptation, though, and allowed his gaze to move across her long legs, to skim over the lushness of her curves in her fitted skirt suit. The dark maroon color suited her pale gold skin tone and the cut was good for something not specifically made for her figure. But he couldn't help resenting the suit, just a little bit. Hers was a figure made for nudity. Like the lushest of love goddesses. It was a damned shame to keep those curves hidden behind clothes.

"Did any of the family refuse to pose for your mother?"

He barely heard her question he was so caught up in his study of her. "No," he answered. Dragging his gaze higher, he wondered what her hair would look like free of the loose bun. Was it long or short? He couldn't tell but he suspected long, a rich brown color that reminded him of dark silk.

When she flashed him a slight frown, he shifted his study to her face. Her bright blue eyes were surrounded by dark lashes. Her lips were plump and a muted plum color from her lipstick. She had high cheekbones, and a stubborn jawline his mother would admire. Her neck was long, elegant, and he found himself following the curve of her throat down to the top of her blouse, wondering what she'd do if he edged the top of the material aside to kiss her shoulder.

"So somewhere in here there's at least one statue of every member of your family?" she asked, clearing her throat.

He watched her swallow visibly, and a faint hint of color crept across her collarbone, up her throat. "No."

"Who's missing?"

"All of my immediate family is represented here. And some of the extended family." He paused, glancing back in the direction of Jason's body.

He noticed Katie staring in the same direction and she gave a little shiver. The scent of her disgust rose and overpowered the more pleasant scent of her desire. No part of him liked that.

He frowned. He'd intended to leave Jason's body there, as a reminder of what happened to those who betrayed the Family and their duty. Jason had been a friend centuries ago, when they were children, cousins of close enough age to form a bond. But Jason had joined the monsters. That choice carried consequences in their world. Consequences Eric didn't regret enforcing.

The statue disturbed Katie, though. Maybe he should move it. He wanted her comfortable in his home—needed her comfortable—as he intended to keep her here.

A sound from overhead caught his attention pulling his thoughts away from his dilemma. Rain fell in thick sheets against the glass panes, darkening the atrium until it was more night than day. When he turned back to Katie, she was staring up at the glass ceiling, watching the rain, her mouth curved down and a small crease forming between her brows.

"Is there a problem?" he asked, joining her, because he didn't like being too far away from her.

KATIE SHOOK HER HEAD, RESISTING ANOTHER SHIVER. "NO. NO problem," she said. "I just don't have an umbrella. Wasn't expecting rain."

And her borrowed car leaked. She sighed, thinking of her clothes still in the trunk. Maybe the hotel would have a laundry service. She really didn't want to come back for her one short hour of interview time tomorrow in damp, wrinkled clothes. This would teach her to try and save money by borrowing a friend's car instead of just renting one.

"I'm sure by the time we're finished the rain will have stopped," she said, forcing her professional smile.

That smile was harder to maintain when Logan stood so close. She was much too aware of his heat, and the memory of his hands on her shoulders, her back to his chest. The sensations seemed to have imprinted themselves on her skin and she couldn't shake the desire to have him touching her again.

But more than Logan's intimidatingly sexy presence had her edgy and uncomfortable in that moment. The sudden, unexpected storm made her nerves jump. She didn't like rainstorms. Not anymore.

A tingle on the back of her neck snapped her attention to Logan's face. Lightning flashed overhead in that moment, and the bright light cut sinister shadows across his handsome features. For an instant, she thought his eyes were glowing. But the illusion faded as the room plunged back into darkness.

A clap of thunder made her jump. It sounded like it had hit the ground just beyond the atrium's glass walls. She laughed, or tried to, at her own reaction. Five years ago, she'd loved the sound of thunder. The flash of lightning. Now, the crack and sizzle made her skin crawl.

Funny, the weather report that morning hadn't mentioned rain or the possibility of thunderstorms today. She'd have mentally prepared for it, if she'd known to expect it, so she didn't screw up this interview with her jumpiness.

Speaking of the interview... "So will you admit to having a favorite sibling? Or would the answer get you into trouble?"

Before he responded, a chill swept through her and she hugged her body to keep a shiver at bay. She glanced up at the pelting rain. When the first pebble of hail hit the glass, dread crawled along her skin.

Knowing pushed past her vague unease.

Without taking her gaze off the ceiling, she said, "Mr. Logan, we should get out of here."

"There's no reason to worry. The glass is designed to withstand worse weather than this."

The hail hit harder, the size of each chunk larger than the last. Katie forced her breath in and out once, very slowly.

"Mr. Logan. We have to leave. Now."

"What is it?"

From the corner of her eye, she saw him look up, caught his slight frown, but most of her attention stayed on the hail, falling fast now. She could barely hear above the noise and her heart pounded so hard she thought it might burst.

For a second, she couldn't move, could only stare at ice chunks hammering the glass.

And then the first crack appeared.

CHAPTER FOUR

"Run!" Paralysis gone, Katie bolted toward the main house. Shattered glass showered the ground where they'd been standing. She screamed.

An instant later, a strong arm circled her waist, pulling her toward safety almost faster than she could run. She stumbled alongside him, scrambling to keep up and protect her head at the same time as glass and water pummeled the paved stones. Logan lifted her off her feet as he sprinted the last few yards.

They cleared the archway and skidded into the protection of the mansion. Her pulse thumped hard, and she could barely catch her breath.

Turning back, Katie was horrified to see the once stunning atrium now a storm-whipped, glass-strewn death zone.

"Bloody hell," she murmured and dropped her purse from limp fingers.

Logan took her into his arms, holding her close to his body heat. She didn't even think to protest, to find the gesture weird and strangely familiar, as she watched rain, wind, and hail continue to beat the lush jungle. Her heart hammered against her ribs so hard she was sure he could feel it.

"Are you okay?" he asked, his breath warm against the top of her head.

"Yeah. You?"

"I'm fine. Now."

His strength and heat felt so good, so comforting, she wanted to stay right where she was for the next few hours. Which was strange and inappropriate and scary. She barely knew the man. Escaping catastrophe with him didn't mean she should be standing here with his arms around her. Especially because it felt easy and weirdly natural. Like they'd been here before.

She straightened away from him, though a part of her whimpered in protest. Too much of the last half hour had left her edgy and off balance. She needed to get it together. Stop acting like an idiot. Definitely needed to take a few steps away from her host and interview subject.

She didn't get far, though, before he took her by the shoulders. His fierce scowl had her sucking in another sharp gasp.

"You're not okay," he growled. "You're hurt."

Frowning, she followed his gaze down to her leg. A nasty-looking gash seeped blood down her calf. "Oh. I didn't notice. Doesn't look pretty, though, does it?"

Memory took her so fast it clogged her throat, filling her vision with blood and rain.

Helpless terror swamped her as she raced down the dark city sidewalk, knowing she was already too late. The flash of a knife, her sister's last gurgling breaths, the sound of an ambulance too far away, rain and tears streaming over her cheeks, landing on her sister's face. And blood. So much blood washing into the gutters.

Katie wobbled, her knees weakening. She blinked fast to clear the memories even as her chest ached with five-year-old pain. Breathing slowly in and out, she forced herself back to the present. Slowly, slowly, her surroundings came back into focus.

She took a quick peek at Logan through her lashes to see if he'd noticed. She'd gotten good at hiding her reactions when the memories hit her like this, but he'd been watching her so closely since she arrived. Had he seen her lapse?

Fortunately, his full attention was on her leg. With a last deep breath, she released the remaining dregs of memory to concentrate on her injury. A blessing and a curse when the reality of her own blood sunk in.

"You know," she murmured, "that didn't hurt until I looked at it."

"Sonofabitch," Logan cursed and let go of her shoulders.

She swayed forward, only then realizing he'd been holding her up more than she'd noticed. That was embarrassing. He caught her again before she lost her balance. Thankfully. But damn, she'd hate to pass out in front of him. Bad enough she was starting to shiver. Nausea rolled through her stomach and black spots danced in front of her eyes.

He took in her expression, cursed again, and in a swift, violent gesture, he ripped the already torn sleeve off of his black shirt and dropped to his knees in front of her. Katie gasped, nearly falling over when he gently lifted her injured leg. With his free hand, he gripped her hip, helping her to remain standing. Seeing no other option, she rested her hands on his broad shoulders. When she was steady, he removed her shoe, then set her foot against his thigh and gently probed the area around the cut.

"I'm sure it's not as bad as it looks," she said. Her teeth started to chatter so she clamped her lips shut.

Logan wrapped the torn shirt sleeve tightly around her wound. It stung like hell, but at least it would stop the bleeding.

She realized as she watched him work, he hadn't escaped the cascade of glass unscathed either. There were nicks and cuts on his hands, slices through his clothing, including the sleeve he was using to bandage her wound, and one thin line of blood on his right cheek. Her own hands, when she looked, were also covered in little nicks. No doubt she had rips in her clothes as well. Bugger. This was one of her favorite suits.

But since she didn't feel blood dripping anywhere else, she had to assume she didn't have any other serious injuries. Though her leg hurt so much just then she couldn't be sure.

Logan leaned back and frowned at his rough bandage. He looked so fierce she might have been nervous if she wasn't still in shock.

"See, all better," she said, trying to lighten his mood.

"Not even close." He tugged a thick, sharp piece of glass from where it stuck out of her skirt and tossed it toward the atrium where the storm was still pummeling the greenery.

Katie cringed at the sound of ripping material, but at least the shard hadn't cut her. He set her foot carefully on the ground, waiting until she got her balance on only one high heel before he stood. Then he stalked a small circle around her.

"Your suit is ruined."

"I figured," she said, trying very hard not to scowl.

She hated shopping. Well, except for shoes. But none of that was his fault. Maintaining her professional demeanor was a lot more difficult, though, when standing around in only one high heel, her suit ripped to shreds, and a huge gash in her leg hastily bandaged with Logan's sleeve.

The butler came rushing up to them, his footsteps tapping quick over the hardwood floor. "Sir, what happened?" he said, his grave voice edged with urgency. "We heard the noise. What was it?"

"There was an incident in the atrium."

The butler looked into the rain lashed remains of the room, paused for a moment, then nodded. His reaction was very stoic and understated to Katie's mind. Was that his training kicking in? She'd be freaked out if her employer's atrium full of priceless art work had just been destroyed.

She *was* freaked out, and she didn't even know Logan.

"Are you hurt?" The butler faced them again, taking in the black "bandage" around Katie's leg. "The lady is injured. Shall I contact an ambulance?"

"I'll see to Ms. Donovan." Without warning, Logan lifted her into his arms.

"Whoa. What are you doing?" She gasped and would have struggled out of his grip, but he glared and tightened his hold.

"Don't. We need to get the cut cleaned and properly bandaged. There might be glass in it."

She hadn't even thought about that. The idea made her nauseous again.

He nodded at the butler. "Make sure the atrium is closed off." He started down the corridor, deeper into the mansion, then paused and faced the butler again. "Secure the rest of house, too."

He held the butler's gaze long enough that Katie was sure some unspoken message passed between them. Then he turned back down the corridor, moving fast despite her weight. She watched the butler over his shoulder. The older man's expression was grim as he faced the atrium.

"You think the storm might cause damage to other parts of the house?" she asked.

"Gregory will make sure everything is secured." He glanced at her for an instant before averting his gaze and muttering, "No one else will get hurt today."

Her instincts hummed. She couldn't have said precisely what was making her suspicious, but she was positive there was something more going on with Logan than just worry about the storm. Though the massive damage caused and the possibility that many of the priceless works of art had been destroyed would be enough to upset even the most laidback person. And Logan didn't strike her as particularly laidback.

But there was an undercurrent of tension, something unspoken that had passed between him and the butler. What was it?

The fact that her miscreant psychic skills were silent on the matter came as little surprise. When she could really use the help of some foreknowledge, when it might do her some good, she got nothing. She hated the *knowing*. All that extra sense had ever done for her was cause her pain.

She turned her mind back to the problem at hand—a serious looking cut on her leg and a nagging suspicion that there was more going on than met the eye.

"I'm sorry about your mother's art," she said, hoping to draw him out. "That's going to be a real mess to clean up. Your insurance will cover it?"

"I'm not worried about the mess," he grunted.

"But the statues…"

"She can sculpt more," he snapped.

So… Her instincts were right. Something else was bothering him. "She'll be devastated, though, won't she? Having something she invested that much time in destroyed."

"Wouldn't be the first time." He spoke so quietly she almost didn't hear him.

"But…"

"Katie," he said, catching her gaze. "Stop worrying about the art."

He was definitely hiding something. She didn't need her *knowing* to see that.

Her mind spun as the possibilities played out, the old instincts for digging up dirt rising to the surface without much effort. What was it? Why wouldn't he be concerned with the loss of all those valuable statues? What could be more important? Were there counterfeit works in the atrium? Did the storm open the house up to unwanted inspections by contractors and insurance people? Why would that be a worry unless there was something else in the atrium he didn't want others to find? Maybe something under the room?

And maybe she was just making up a lot of stories. She needed answers. Real answers. Not speculation. This wasn't for a gossip column after all. Real answers might mean a scoop, an article to make her name. But how? How to niggle out the secrets? What could she ask that wouldn't get her kicked out of the house?

She was so caught up in the possibility that she'd stumbled into a deeper story, or at least some juicy gossip that would get her her coveted promotion at work, she nearly missed the fact that he'd called her Katie instead of Ms. Donovan.

CHAPTER FIVE

They turned into a bathroom, moving through a door seemingly at random. And Katie only then realized she hadn't been studying things as they walked through the long corridor. Shit. Well. They had to leave again. She could study the house more then.

Logan set her gently on a long marble countertop. She glanced around as she took off her ruined suit jacket, while he dug through the cabinet beneath one of the two sinks. The room was huge, tiled in blacks and dark, spotted gray, accented with silver. The towels, soap dish, empty toothbrush holder and small bin near the toilet were all bright spots of red in the dark room. A Jacuzzi bathtub took up one corner, a separate shower another, and a window looked out onto the storm-tossed wooded area at the front and west side of the mansion.

Hail and rain battered the reinforced glass. She watched the havoc outside a moment, before deciding she felt safe enough here. No warning tingles predicting another imminent glass failure.

"Has anything like this happened before?" she asked. "Storm damage, I mean. You said your mother lost other sculptures prior to this. Was that to accidents as well?"

She tried for a casual tone, not her interviewer's clipped patter, hoping he'd answer without censoring what he said. Most normal people would wonder about these things after what had just happened, even if they weren't members of the press. Seemed a logical topic of conversation.

Logan pulled a large red, plastic box out from under the sink and set it on the countertop next to her. "A house this old takes its fair share of weather damage over the centuries," he said.

"And the atrium?"

"Has never collapsed before, no." He pawed through the plastic box, pulling out bandage tape, antiseptic spray, non-stick wound pads and some unmarked bottles.

"That's some first aid kit," she commented. It was the biggest, most well-stocked kit she'd ever seen. He looked to have a virtual hospital's worth of medical gear in that one box.

"Lot of kids in this family."

"Must have been a lot of scrapes and cuts." She knew from her own childhood with an older brother and a younger sister just how much damage kids could inflict on one another in the name of play.

Even vague thoughts of her sister left her feeling too vulnerable. Especially after the earlier memory. So she focused on his family, his siblings, his life.

"Your parents must have had their hands full with six boys and four girls."

"Actually, there are eight boys and five girls."

"Really?" How had she missed three siblings? Scowling, she shook her head. "Your family's habit of using the same names over and over again complicates things. How do you keep straight who's who?"

She was embarrassed to have gotten that simple fact wrong. She'd poured through birth and death records, made a chart by dates, and been confident of her final conclusion. Obviously, she'd still managed to miss a few records. And that was just mortifying. Even when she was working the gossip beat, she'd prided herself on her research.

Of all the people to screw up in front of, it had to be Eric Logan.

Logan knelt in front of her. "The names are an old family tradition," he said. Then he gently lifted her leg, set her bare foot on his thigh again, and removed his make-shift bandage from her calf.

Katie swallowed hard, once again thrown off balance by him. The position was so intimate, his touch so gentle, she felt a flood of heat race through her. How the hell did he do that? Why did she go so addle-brained at his touch?

She gripped the countertop tight and tried to keep her foot relaxed in his lap. Probably wouldn't send the right message if she ran her toes up his thigh to his crotch. Though the idea was tempting.

And the fact that it was tempting was just baffling. She didn't react so fast to men like this. He was sexy, yes. He was gorgeous and mysterious and a puzzle she wanted to crack. But for *professional* reasons. She wasn't here for personal reasons. She wasn't here to let herself get confused and distracted by a gentle touch. To get turned on by having him kneel in front of her.

The fact that she had to keep reminding herself they didn't know each other and she was here to do a job was… It was just so strange.

He hissed when he got the shirt sleeve free, calling her attention away from her thoughts. She focused on the wound, then wished she hadn't. The cut was an ugly, jagged slice through the side of her calf. She was lucky the glass hadn't cut deeper across her shin or she might be seeing bone.

The thought made her swallow hard. "Could have been worse," she said aloud, proud when her voice sounded normal.

"That doesn't make me feel better. You need stitches."

Damn. She didn't want to call the interview short just because of a little cut, not after all it had taken to get this far. Especially since she suspected there was a deeper story here, something juicy and powerful beyond a man-behind-the-mystery exposé. Plus, she hated hospitals with a passion.

"Don't you have anything in that massive first aid kit you could use?" she asked, a little desperate to avoid both leaving early and having to go to a hospital.

He glanced up, his eyes dark, and Katie stopped talking. From that angle, the intensity of his gaze wiped all thought of hospitals and news stories away.

The intimacy of his position sent heat coiling through her stomach.

What if she was naked and he was kneeling at her feet like that, staring at her just as he was now?

She'd probably have an orgasm just from the look in his eyes.

"Why don't you want to go to the hospital?"

His question broke her out of her daze, and once again, she felt stupid for her reaction. If he wasn't affected by their close proximity, she shouldn't be. "We only have a few hours to talk today. I can go to the hospital when the interview is over."

He continued to stare at her for long enough she had to concentrate on not fidgeting.

Finally, he said, "I have butterfly stitches. They'll due for now. But tomorrow, you go to the hospital."

"Sure. After we talk in the morning, I'll go to the hospital and have the cut looked at."

She had absolutely no intention of following through on that. She'd rather a scar than a hospital visit. But he didn't need to know that, or her reasons for avoiding emergency rooms. Besides, an argument over this would only take time away from her job.

He acquiesced with a sharp nod and turned his attention to her injury, beginning the process of cleaning the cut.

Because his ministrations hurt, and because she wasn't sure how much longer he'd continue to answer her questions after what had happened, she said, "You mentioned your mother had lost sculptures before but you didn't say how. What happened?"

He shrugged. "Over time, stone and marble can get damaged."

"We weren't talking about simple damage." She hissed when he pulled a small piece of glass from her cut.

"I'm sorry," he said, his tone gentle and sincere. "I know that hurts, but I'm almost finished."

Swallowing, she nodded and said, "So your mother's statues?"

"Stubborn," he mumbled. Then louder, "As you mentioned, we have a lot of homes and her art work is scattered around the houses of our entire extended family. Even valued family heirlooms get damaged in house fires, inadvertent children's play, fluke accidents. She's produced so many sculptures in her lifetime, some of it is bound to be damaged or destroyed."

Well, that was an answer as far as it went. But not the whole truth, she was sure. "Has any of her art been stolen?"

"No," he said firmly. "Okay, the cut's clean." He held up a spray bottle. "This is going to sting, but it'll keep infection out and I need to use this kind of antiseptic treatment if we're going to apply the butterfly stitches. Otherwise, I'd use something gentler."

"Do what you have to do. I'm fine." She focused on the tiles over his head, trying to think past the ache radiating through her calf. He was right, the spray stung. She gritted her teeth and waited for the pain to ease. When it did, she sucked in a deep breath.

Glancing down, she caught him staring up at her. With a half-smile, she said, "See, no problem."

He shook his head and turned his attention back to her leg but not before she saw his hand clench and unclench in a quick fist. What was that about?

She struggled past the pain in her leg for her next question, but he beat her to the punch.

"How did you know the glass wouldn't hold against the hail?"

"What are you talking about?" She feigned confusion easily and instinctively after years and years of hiding her psychic intuition.

"You were very insistent we leave. What made you think we weren't safe?"

"Giant chunks of ice were slamming against a thin pane of glass. Anyone would have worried." Which was true.

"There was more to it."

"No. I saw the glass crack, and I panicked. Good thing I did, too, or we might have been more seriously hurt." She held her breath when he rose to his full height in front of her. He couldn't know she was lying. She'd been telling these same types of lies for most of her life. She was very very good at it now. But something in his expression belied her assurance.

"What other UK idioms did you pick up besides 'bloody hell'?"

The question was so different from what she'd been braced for, she blinked. "Huh?"

"You said 'bloody hell' when you saw the damage to the atrium. I just wondered what other colorful terms you picked up."

"Did I?" She half-laughed, half-grimaced. The first slang she'd adopted during her years in London had been the curse words. "I don't remember."

"Even the accent was good. You were only in the UK for three years, right?"

"My father's English." She was sure he knew that. She couldn't imagine he hadn't researched her as thoroughly as she'd researched him. But at least he wasn't pushing her on how she'd known the atrium glass would break.

He collected more of the supplies he'd set out on the countertop—the stitches she thought—and returned to kneeling at her feet. His touch when he lifted her foot was a gentle caress that sent a shiver up her spine.

Interview, Katie. Back to the interview.

But since she didn't want to focus on the atrium for the moment, so he wouldn't ask any more of his own questions, she changed tack again, going to one of her original questions for the fluffy celebrity interview angle.

"You spend so much time outside the US, what's your favorite country?"

He kept his head down, his attention on applying the stitches. She felt a tugging on her cut but resisted the urge to look. She really wasn't good around blood anymore.

"Outside of the US," he answered, "I love Austria, Ireland, Argentina, Turkey, and Jordan."

"That's some list." She winced at whatever he'd just done to her leg and tried to ignore the sharp stab of pain. Blinking away the spots dancing at the edge of her vision, she said, "I've been to a few of those places, but never Jordan. What puts it on the short list?"

"Beautiful country."

"Travel there a lot?"

"When I can."

She waited for more, some insight about what in Jordan drew him. But he remained silent, so she asked, "Have you been to Petra?"

He kept his attention on her leg. "Yes. Several times."

"It must be amazing." She glanced down long enough to see him squeeze some of her sliced skin closer together and had to look up at the wall tiles again. She let out a long stream of silent air to push back the rising nausea.

"It is," he said, even as he continued to work, "I can't help but admire a city carved of stone."

"Because of what your mother does?"

He paused, long enough that she couldn't tell if he was concentrating on the stitches or considering his answer. Finally, he said in a half-distracted tone, "Yes. Stone creations have always attracted my interest."

Interesting, though not unusual since his mother sculpted from stone and marble. "I've always wanted to see Petra, too. But the timing never seems to be right."

"I'm sure you'll get there one day." His tone was more promise than prediction, as if he knew she'd travel to Jordan in the future.

"How about Turkey?" she said, because she needed to keep talking and ignore that tone in his voice. "Been to Ephesus?"

"Of course."

She tried to smile. "You make it sound like everyone should have been to Ephesus before. I got to Turkey once for a holiday and we never made it there."

"We?"

"Friends." And why did his tone go so sharp? She had her eyes half closed because he seemed to have stopped torturing her calf, but the ache emanating from her wound was still very unpleasant. At the bite in his question, though, she glanced down at him.

He was staring at the bandage around her wound. He slid his hand in a slow caress down the back of her calf, then stroked back up to the soft underside of her knee. The gesture made her thighs clench and her heart rate thump faster. She sucked in a breath, unable to prevent the telltale reaction as he brushed his fingers against one of her most sensitive erogenous zones. He couldn't possibly know what touching the back of her knee did to her, yet she got the feeling he'd hunted out that spot on purpose. And despite her aching calf, the touch still affected her.

"Your mother isn't living here," she squeaked, then cleared her throat, feeling like an idiot. "Where is she living at the moment?" She tightened her grip on the counter, trying to stamp down the edgy desire rushing through her body. Shouldn't the pain in her leg prevent this kind of thing? She was sure it would under normal circumstances.

But Eric Logan's effect on her was most decidedly not normal.

"Europe," he murmured, his fingers still lightly teasing the soft skin along the back of her knee. "Mostly Vienna, but she travels a lot."

Katie pulled her gaze back up, focusing on the wall tiles again. Looking at him as he studied her leg and touched her in just that way was going to make her combust.

She made a pretense of studying every other thing in the bathroom. "And you just returned to the US from where?"

"Most recently, I was in Vienna with my mother and two of my brothers. Before that..."

He paused, and she was sorely tempted to look at him so she could read his expression. She risked a glance out of the corner of her eye and realized his was focusing on her injury again. She couldn't see his face but that was probably best while he still had his hands on her.

"Before that?" she urged. The color of his hair captured her interest. In the bright bathroom lights, she could see all the various shades of brown and black that made up the thick mass. There were even a few strands of gray at his temples, not many, but enough to give him a distinguished charm. Given her reaction to him up to now, charming wasn't the word she might first use to describe him. But then everything about her reactions to him had been contradictory and strange.

"Before Vienna," he continued, "I spent a lot of time crisscrossing Europe and the Middle East."

"The Middle East? Jordan or the whole region?"

"The whole region." He rose and started placing things back into the first aid kit.

"For fun or business?"

"Mostly business."

"Why so much travel?"

He glanced at her briefly before returning to his tidying. "One of our businesses misplaced some valuable cargo. I spent the better part of a year tracking it."

Well, that was a big fat lie. The story sounded rote, like he'd memorized it to use as an explanation for his real purpose. She didn't need her psychic senses to figure that out. The part about tracking something, *that* had a ring of truth to it, though.

And something about the timing of all that travel…

Wait, a year? His father had died a little over a year ago. That's when Eric took over as head of Logan International. Did his travel have something to do with that? Maybe he'd inherited business trouble. The company employed thousands around the world. If the Logan business was in trouble, that would be a big scoop.

Or maybe it was something more nefarious?

Shaking her head slightly, Katie reigned in her imagination. Seeing something nefarious, that was the gossip columnist in her talking. The business trouble part, though… That was more plausible. But guessing wouldn't get her answers. Investigation would.

"Did you find the cargo?" she asked.

"I took care of the situation."

Her next query jumped to her lips, but he stopped her by shaking one of the unmarked bottles.

"You need something for the pain."

Since she'd completely forgotten about her wound in the last minute, his comment caught her off guard. She held her calf up to inspect the new bandage. "You do good work."

"You'll still need to see a doctor, but that should do for tonight."

He twisted the top off the bottle, tapped out two pills and held the round pellets out to her. She stared at his hand a moment, not sure she should take any drugs he was offering. Especially since the bottle didn't have a label to indicate what the tablets were.

Sliding off the counter so she felt more in control, she realized immediately that wearing one shoe wasn't going to work. She kicked the remaining high heel off and bent to retrieve it. Barefoot was better than toppling over.

She nodded at the pills. "What are they?"

"Aspirin." When she still didn't take them, he frowned. "Do you have an allergy?"

"No. But…" She grimaced.

He scowled. "You think I'd drug you? To what end?"

"I don't know." She scowled back. "But that bottle isn't labeled. And you're not a doctor. How do I know what you're giving me?"

"Actually, I do have some medical training." He dropped the pills back into the bottle.

She blinked at both his comment and how quickly he'd acquiesced on the pills. "You have medical training?" Another fact she hadn't come across in any of her research. How the hell much had she missed? She'd been certain she'd done a thorough job of researching what was available on him and his family. "What kind of training?"

"I was a medic." He pulled out another bottle that had been hidden beneath some rolls of gauze. This was a small, sealed bottle of generic aspirin, the bottle clearly labeled. "If you need them later." He handed her the entire thing.

She took it absently, going back to his first comment. "You weren't in the military. At least, not here in the US."

"No. Not in the US."

Before she could ask where, he closed the space between them. The move was so fast she didn't have a chance to avoid him. When she finally recognized the danger, she tried to take one step away and came up against the counter.

"You do that a lot," he said, his voice quiet. "I scare you."

"No." He terrified her. On several levels. But she wasn't about to admit it. "I just like my space is all, and you keep invading it."

His gaze dropped to her mouth. Katie licked her suddenly dry lips.

His eyes darkened and again his nostrils flared, like he was scenting her. Sucking in a breath, she started to say something sharp to put this back on a professional level. But then he leaned forward and rested his hands on the counter, caging her. Her heart raced.

"I can't seem to help myself," he murmured. "I like being in your space."

She swallowed. His scent, some rich, subtle cologne she couldn't place, teased her until all she wanted to do was bury her nose against his neck and breathe him in.

He leaned a fraction of an inch closer, and Katie's stomach tightened. His breath brushed her lips. She realized she would only have to move forward an inch or two, no more, and their mouths would touch.

What the hell was happening to her? Why wasn't she pulling away? His presence seemed to pin her in place, holding without actually touching. She was acutely aware of his single bare arm brushing against her ripped sleeve. Heat, anticipation, and something darker, a need she could barely comprehend, washed over her. He edged closer, closing the distance between their mouths in painfully slow increments.

He would kiss her. If she didn't stop him, he would kiss her.

And she couldn't afford to let that happen. Not now.

Not with this man.

CHAPTER SIX

L eaning away from Logan, Katie forced an impersonal smile. "Thank you for bandaging my leg. We should get back to the interview."

He didn't back off, but he no longer pressed forward either. "Are you sure? We can wait until you're feeling better."

"No, no that's not necessary. I'm fine."

Her leg still ached like hell, but she wasn't going to let something like a little pain get in the way of finishing this interview. Being in Logan's presence was difficult enough. Extending that time so she could "feel better" and risk letting things get…unprofessional, seemed like a bad idea. Worse, not getting the interview at all!

No, she'd soldier on, as her father would say. And then get as far away from Eric Logan as she could get.

"You don't want to at least change first?" Nodding to her torn shirtsleeve, he raised his brows.

Bugger, he was right. She didn't want to waste what limited time she had left today, but trying to keep up a professional conversation while wearing clothes with holes in them seemed a little desperate. She was a little desperate but she didn't want *him* to know that.

He probably wanted to change too, she realized, embarrassed that hadn't occurred to her. She glanced at the cut on his cheek. It didn't look as bad as she'd at first thought. In fact, there was barely even a line marring his skin anymore. That was fortunate.

Still, he'd been through a lot in the last twenty minutes. She wasn't the only one who'd been hurt or who was sitting around in ripped clothing. Being rude and pushy in this instance probably wouldn't earn her any points with him, and she couldn't afford to have him send her away yet.

"I have spare clothes in the car," she said. "It shouldn't take me but a few minutes to clean up. Then we can get back to work?"

She'd meant the last to be a statement, but the question slipped out. She was terrified he'd call an end to their time today, and she'd have one scant hour tomorrow morning to get as much information as possible out of him. They'd barely scraped the surface so far. With an hour, she'd be able to pull together something for Mona. But she'd have a hard time prying the deeper story from him.

And she was absolutely positive there was a deeper story here.

"There's no hurry," he said without moving away from her.

"I know your time is limited. I won't waste it."

"Time with you could never be a waste."

She frowned. Since he didn't know her, and she was a member of the press, the comment was…odd. And suspicious. What game was he playing at?

It occurred to her again that maybe he was attempting to seduce her to control her story. To ensure she didn't dig too deep or reveal anything damaging about him or his business. The thought was like a lovely, well-timed bucket of cold water.

No one, and nothing, got between her and the story. He could play games all he wanted. She intended to get her interview.

"I know how valuable your time is, Mr. Logan," she said in her professional tone, with her small, professional smile. "I assure you I won't let this…incident interfere—"

"Why are you so concerned with time, Ms. Donavan?"

"Your assistant made it quite clear—"

"Ah. Margaret." He nodded and his mouth quirked up at one side. "My cousin. She's very…protective of the family. She didn't approve of my giving this interview."

That caught her attention. "Why not?"

"Because the Logans don't give private interviews."

She knew that well enough. The fact that he'd agreed had been her bargaining chip with Mona. "Why did you grant my request?" She'd *known* he would, in that way of hers, but the *knowing* never gave her a *why*.

He held her gaze, still so close she could feel his body heat wrapping around her, somehow both comforting and disconcerting. She could practically see him thinking, considering how to answer her, and she was tempted to lean just a bit to her right so their arms would touch, to see if her psychic senses actually gave her some information this time. But touching him so far hadn't given her any insights. Only thrown her more off balance. Any physical contact right now would be infinitely more dangerous to her peace of mind than the information she might get.

His stillness reminded her of his earlier statement about how remaining unmoving could make people uncomfortable. She understood well in that moment how he could use the trait to intimidate a roomful of businessmen. Just holding his gaze was taking all her resolve.

Finally, he lifted one shoulder in a barely perceptible shrug. "The time was right."

"For breaking the silence?"

"Something like that."

Not even remotely an answer. So she asked the question in a different way. "Why me?"

"I thought you'd do a good job."

Another half-truth, mostly lie. He had some other reason for allowing her, specifically, into his life. The initial fear she'd experienced when facing him for the first time wrapped around her throat again. She put a tight clamp onto her imagination before it even got started on possible scenarios. Whatever he wanted from her, she'd figure it out soon enough.

Meanwhile, she intended to get her job done.

"We'd better get changed now so we don't waste any more time."

"Katie," he said, his voice a low caress.

The sound of him saying her name, in just that tone, left her breathless. That was the second time he'd dropped the formalities. And for some reason, having him use her first name left her feeling exposed. Vulnerable.

"You can have as much of my time as you need," he murmured. "As much as you want. Margaret's limits were…exaggerated."

"But—"

"Stop worrying. I'm at your disposal."

Oh the things her imagination wanted to do with that.

In a hurry to change the subject, she bumped past him, careful to touch only enough of him to get his big body out of her way. He moved back reluctantly, but he moved.

She snatched up her abandoned suit jacket and said, "Thank you for offering your time. I realize you'll have a lot to take care of with the atrium, though."

He waved that away as she proceeded him out of the bathroom, back the direction they'd come. "Nothing can be done until the storm passes."

Katie conceded the point as she limped along, barefoot, to the atrium to retrieve her purse and other shoe. She felt him staring at her and raised her brows in question.

He scowled and nodded at her bandaged calf. "You shouldn't be walking on that leg."

"I'm fine," she assured. "Besides, how else will I get around?" She'd meant the comment as a joke, but the expression on his face made her worry he might actually try to carry her again. That was absolutely the last thing she wanted.

Right?

Right.

To keep him from getting any ideas, she attempted to walk a little more normally. "Perhaps we should conduct the rest of the interview sitting down, though," she conceded.

"You're hurting?"

"No. No, I really am fine," she hedged, still clutching the pain meds she had no intention of taking. "But I don't want you to be preoccupied with my injury."

"Too late for that," he muttered.

Huh. Was he worried about a lawsuit? That hadn't actually occurred to her before this, but she'd been injured under his roof, and he was extremely wealthy. Some people would take advantage of that. She wasn't one of those people, but was it better for him to know that, or would she do well to keep her mouth shut?

As she needed him to open up to her as much as possible, she decided, in this case, honesty would be best. "Don't worry, please, Mr. Logan. I'm sure it'll be mostly healed by tomorrow anyway. I won't think any more about it, and this won't come back and be an issue for you."

Again, she came up against his unreadable expression, but she got a sense that he was surprised by her comment. He'd probably been expecting her to parlay her injury into some personal gain. But the only thing she wanted from him was this interview. If he continued to cooperate and answer her questions, he'd be giving her more than he could possibly understand.

When they reached the point in the corridor outside the atrium, Katie frowned. A wood-paneled wall covered the spot where she knew the atrium entrance had been—because her shoe and purse where still where she'd dropped them. If not for that evidence, though, she would never have guessed the glass room was there.

"Nice trick." She pointed to the wall with her shoe.

"Thank you."

Her gaze narrowed. "Any other secret walls in this place?"

He raised his brows but didn't answer. She'd bet money there were. Unfortunately, thanks to the stupid cut on her leg, she couldn't risk a long tour of the house anymore. And she wasn't likely to be left to explore on her own—she'd definitely go hunting for some of those secret panels, if given the chance. Not likely now, though. Shame.

She shook her head and continued her limping walk to the front door.

Logan followed silently, but she could feel his gaze on her. Tension prickled between her shoulder blades, an awareness heightened by the adrenaline still trickling through her blood. She concentrated on making sure she didn't limp too much and on keeping her hands from shaking. But she was going to have to sit down soon. She hadn't realized how wobbly she was still. She didn't need Logan to know either.

The butler, Gregory, appeared as they reached the front door. Impressive. How'd he managed it? Cameras? Was he stationed near the door? A butler sixth sense?

"I fear the weather is still too severe to go out, madam," he said, his hand on the door knob. "Perhaps waiting another hour or two?"

"Thank you, but I won't be a minute. Just running out to get my bag," she said, gesturing at the ripped remains of her suit and blouse.

With a glance behind her to where Logan stood, Gregory shrugged and opened the front door.

Rain slashed inside bringing a cold, biting wind so strong it knocked her back a step. Logan's hands were on her shoulders instantly, steadying her. Disturbed by how reassuring that gesture was, she shrugged off his hold, put her head down, and pushed into the wind.

She made it two steps out the door and looked up at her car. Narrowing her eyes against the rain, she gasped.

Then nearly broke down and cried.

Shattered windows and windshield. Dents the size of fists in the hood. What might have been a hole in the driver's side door. And the trunk buckled in half so rain poured unchecked onto her bag.

For a long moment, she stood staring at the damage, letting the cold rain soak her to the skin. Only shock held her burning tears at bay.

This was not turning out to be a very good day.

With a sigh, she stepped back into the house. Logan's hand landed gently on her shoulder. She glanced up long enough to see him scowling at the remains of her car. Following his gaze, another sigh that sounded suspiciously like a whimper escaped. Just then, a flash of lightning and the booming clap of thunder rent the dark skies. Logan pulled her limp body farther back into the shelter of the entryway as Gregory forced the door closed, cutting off the wind and rain, and the sight of her borrowed vehicle.

Logan cleared his throat. "I'm sure the rental agency's insurance will—"

"It's borrowed, not rented," she interrupted. "And I'm not sure what kind of insurance my friend has."

Knowing Jess, whatever insurance she had would probably only cover towing the wreck to the scrap metal lot. Jesus, how was she going to tell Jess about this? She'd have to call her as soon as she had a minute. That'd be the last time any of her friends loaned her a car.

"We'll take care of it," Logan murmured, his hand still resting lightly on her shoulder. And for some completely illogical reason, his statement comforted her.

Until she realized she was now, officially, stuck.

She had no way to leave his house, no way to get to the hotel— even if she'd been able to get there through the storm. She was very literally stranded. What the hell was she going to do?

She blinked at the closed door, the reality of her situation settling in.

She was stuck. In Eric Logan's house. With *the* Eric Logan. No way to leave…

He'd have to let her stay, at least until the storm calmed.

She swallowed her smile, but a jump of adrenaline surged in her veins. He couldn't kick her out. Even if she offended him, he'd have to let her stay.

This could actually work in her favor.

"Ms. Donovan," Gregory said, pulling her out of her thoughts, "you should get out of those wet clothes. You'll catch a chill."

Some of her newfound excitement drained away. "All my clothes were in the trunk." She sighed. "I don't think this storm likes me very much."

Her comment brought a harsh inhale from Logan, and his grip on her shoulder tightened just a little. She looked up in time to see him and Gregory exchange one of those looks.

Then Gregory said, "Ms. Tanya's clothes will fit you. I'll show you to—"

"I'll show her Tanny's room," Logan interrupted. "Would you check the weather reports, see how this is affecting the area, please."

Gregory nodded and headed back into the heart of the mansion.

"If the storm's as bad as I fear," Logan said, "you'll have no choice but to stay the night."

She worked really hard not to show her journalistic excitement at that comment, or to jump too quickly to agree. She wasn't sure how he'd take it. Especially after that near kiss in the bathroom—or… whatever that had been. She was supposed to be upset, given her borrowed car was totaled. He needed to think she was upset about that.

But staying in the Logan mansion overnight offered up so many opportunities, she could hardly contain herself.

She must have made some physical gesture or sound, despite her efforts, because he squeezed her shoulder, gentler this time. "You'll be safe enough. My youngest sister is here, remember. She can act as your chaperone."

His misinterpretation of her reaction was both a relief and disturbing. Why wouldn't she be safe here? Why would she need a chaperone? Because he really did intend to try and seduce her?

That part was a little worrisome. While he couldn't kick her out, she also couldn't leave.

Then he did something that dried whatever response she might have made. He touched a gentle kiss to the top of her rain-soaked head. She was sure the gesture was meant to be comforting, placating even. A calming gesture you might use on a distraught child.

But she wasn't a child. She was a full grown adult who'd been inches away from letting her hormones get the best of her only a few minutes ago. And she felt his gentle kiss all the way through her body.

Brief though it had been, his lips touching any part of her sent heat coiling through her, sent her heartbeat thumping. Blood rushed to parts of her that weren't supposed to be involved in this interview.

She took a slow, careful breath.

Maybe staying the night wasn't such a brilliant accident after all.

CHAPTER SEVEN

"Let's get you those dry clothes," Logan said and turned her from the front door.

Katie allowed herself to be led through the huge foyer, between the white columns, and straight up the huge curved staircase. Still a little shaken by her reaction to his comforting kiss to the top of her head, she had to force herself to study her surroundings.

Once on the second floor, a climb made that bit slower by her injured leg, she saw the stairway on the opposite side of the gallery which led to the third floor. She glanced up again at the ceiling mural but even from the second floor she couldn't make out the details. Would it be clear from the third?

They turned right at the top of the stairs and continued down yet another long corridor, walking slowly to accommodate her sore leg. She was still making an effort not to limp, but the longer she stayed on her feet the harder that got. The rain had soaked her so thoroughly that a chill was starting to grip her, further hindering her efforts to appear in control.

The new corridor Logan led her through was lushly decorated with thick red carpets and wooden wainscoting, pocketed with cubby holes full of what looked to be expensive knick-knacks. She was pretty sure that pretty vase was Ming porcelain, but she'd have to ask about the art. She was a little worried if she asked at that moment, though, he'd hear her voice shake or her teeth chatter, and the last thing she needed was for Logan to see her weak. Instead, she concentrated on cataloguing her surroundings so she could make note of everything and ask him about the details when she was warm and dry again.

She spotted a framed photo of some ancient stone ruin in a desert setting which caught her attention. Egypt maybe? Didn't look like a pyramid, but what did she know about Egyptian architecture. The photo seemed out of place among the other décor, yet for some reason, she could see Logan liking the scene. She had no idea why. Maybe because he'd placed Turkey and Jordan so high on his list of favorite countries.

The wealth surrounding her was a little overwhelming. She'd met any number of rich people over the years and even managed to see into some of their lush homes. But this place was unlike anything she'd encountered outside of a museum. Palatial. Yet, there was a hominess to it she found surprising. Well, homey if you happened to have more money than god.

Must be nice not to worry about money. She could pay her rent at the moment. And she could afford her two good business suits—well, one now—and the occasional nice pair of shoes. But she wouldn't be buying any precious art or expensive jewelry anytime soon.

Money had never been her motivator, though. That was her older brother's driving goal. And her sister had only wanted to have fun and revel in life. Katie was driven by acknowledgement, by doing a job well and having other people notice, by being the best at what she did. She'd want that Pulitzer even if she never got paid to write.

They turned a corner which opened into a huge, brightly lit corridor. The walls here were painted white and lined with multi-colored glass balls of light interspersed with shelves at various heights, each holding a profusion of plants.

"Wow. This is…not exactly what I would have expected," she said, managing to keep her voice steady. She stopped to grin at a ceramic fairy peeking out from one of the green ivy plants, ran a hand down her face to wipe away dripping rain water, realized she was leaving a puddle on the floor, and winced

"My youngest sister, Andrea, is responsible for the decoration in this part of the house," Logan said. He glanced around the corridor and shook his head.

Katie chuckled. "Not your taste, I take it?"

"Not exactly."

He shrugged and let one hell of a killer smile loose on her. She tried very hard not to react to that look or the heat it generated in her blood. Fortunately, her soaking wet state was keeping her nice and chilled. She shivered and hugged her arms around her stomach.

His gaze sharpened. "Come on. You need to get dry." He took her hand and hustled her down the hall.

Her palm felt small and fragile in his larger grip. But the warmth of his touch traveled up her arm, chasing away the cold.

He pushed open one of the many doors they passed and ushered her into a huge sitting room. It was decorated with overstuffed furniture in pale yellows and creams, plush Turkish rugs on hard wood floors and a large green marble fireplace against one wall. Floor to ceiling windows would flood the room with light on a brighter day. With the storm still raging outside, the room was dim before Logan flicked on an overhead light.

Katie glanced longingly at the fireplace. Sitting in front of a roaring fire sounded heavenly at that moment.

Logan tugged her hand, pulling her through an arched doorway near the fireplace into the bedroom. Through another open doorway she spotted a bathroom. The bed was thick and tall and covered in more creams and yellows, accented with darker oranges and reds. The colors were very autumnal, bright and cheery on the dark afternoon. There was another fireplace in the bedroom and Katie nearly groaned. What she wouldn't give for a fireplace in her bedroom. But she was lucky to have a full bathroom in her miniscule studio apartment in Manhattan. An actual working fireplace was beyond her current economic status.

"Your hands are freezing," Logan said.

"I just need a towel to dry off."

"And clothes that aren't soaked."

Without releasing her hand, he walked her into a closet—another huge space, nearly the size of her studio. It was one of the most impressive dressing rooms she'd ever seen. How did one person manage to accumulate so much clothing?

"These are my sister Tanya's rooms," Eric said with a gesture toward the area outside the closet. "She's about your size, so feel free to use anything in here you need."

"Are you sure she won't mind sharing her clothes with a stranger?"

"By the time she decides to flit through this house again, she'll probably feel the need for a whole new wardrobe anyway."

Though the comment was sardonic, Katie couldn't miss the affection in his voice and took a mental note. He talked about his family with the same sort of affection she might use when talking about her brother and sister. Everyone but his father, who hadn't come up in conversation yet.

His assistant—cousin, she reminded herself—had forbade Katie from mentioning Alexander Logan. But if Eric's time wasn't as limited as the cousin had stated, maybe bringing up his father wouldn't be an interview killer either. She was very curious to know how he felt about his father, and his father's death.

"But she's very generous," Logan continued, breaking into her train of thought. "She'd be forcing clothes on you herself if she were here."

She glanced around the massive room. Tanya probably wouldn't even notice if something was missing. How could anyone keep track of all that clothing?

"Okay, then." She gave in with a shrug. When he just stood there, holding her hand, she raised her brows. "I won't take too long. You'll want to change, too?"

"What did you mean when you said you didn't think the storm liked you?"

She blinked. Bit of a non-sequitur. "I meant that a lot has gone wrong in the last hour, since the storm started. Don't worry. I don't think Mother Nature is out to get me." She smiled to prove her point.

He nodded but still didn't move.

"Mr. Logan?"

He took a step closer and brushed a strand of wet hair behind her ear, startling her. The gesture was so personal, so intimate coming from a virtual stranger. Being trapped here was turning into both blessing and curse. Because the longer he stared at her, the harder it was for her to remain focused on her job. She could barely comprehend what a disaster it would be for her—professionally and personally—to get involved with this man. A man being any kind of threat to her career was usually enough to dump cold water over her libido. Hell, she had quite literally been drenched in cold water not fifteen minutes ago.

So why was she still feeling that curl of heat in her belly and a fluttering of nervous anticipation? Why was she thinking about the beautiful shape of his mouth and the way her hand felt small and safe in his?

"You can use these rooms if you like, during your stay," he said finally.

"You said your younger sister was here. Her room nearby?"

"Two doors back the way we came."

"And yours?"

His expression remained serious but a dangerous light brightened his dark eyes. "Just across the hall."

That was a little too close for her sanity. "Where is your sister now, by the way?"

Seeing him with his sister would be fascinating, and getting a chance to talk with one of the other elusive siblings could only add to her interview. But that wasn't the only reason she wanted to know the younger sister's whereabouts.

And to think she'd scoffed at the idea of a chaperone.

"Probably in her workshop," he said. "She takes after our mother, only she works with wood."

"Do you think she'll let me see some of what she does?"

"Maybe after you dry off. I doubt she'd want you dripping on her art."

Katie glanced down at the clinging material of her shirt. "Right."

She stepped away from him. "Where will I meet you when I'm changed?"

"Do you want some help? Drying off. Warming up."

"No," she squeaked. Clearing her throat, she tried for a less panicked tone. "I'll be fine."

He brushed his knuckles lightly down her cheek, another of those casually familiar gestures that left her breathless.

"When you're ready," he said, "meet me in the library, where Gregory brought you when you first arrived." Pausing on the threshold of the bedroom, he faced her with a faint frown. "Stay away from the windows. Just in case."

With that ominous warning, he left.

Katie waited until she heard the outer door close. Then she puffed out a breath. Her brain kept repeating the phrase "blessing and curse" as she turned back to Tanya's closet.

CHAPTER EIGHT

After digging through Tanya's clothes for something to wear, Katie hurried to the bathroom to dry off and change. She stared at the huge, multi-jet shower for a full thirty seconds before deciding to jump in quickly to warm up. Her cut was wet already anyway and needed a new bandage.

Despite her hurry to get back downstairs, after the one minute flat shower, she did take a few minutes to blow dry her hair and pin the mass of waves back into a loose bun. She also found another huge first aid kit in the bathroom and used some gauze to rewrap her wound, making an effort not to study the cut too closely. Logan had done a good job on the butterfly stitches and cleaning her up, but she still didn't want to look at the jagged rip in her skin too closely. It reminded her too much of the damage a knife could do.

When she was finished, she studied herself in the mirror. The loose-fitting black trousers, button up maroon silk shirt and black tank top—a stand-in for her too-wet-to-wear bra—weren't as polished as the suit had been. But she looked respectable enough. At any rate, it would have to do for now. She didn't have time to dig further into Tanya's mounds of clothes for a business suit that might fit.

She returned to the closet to find a pair of shoes to borrow, mulling over the questions she still needed to get to today.

The sight of someone sitting on the bed made her squeak in surprise.

"Sorry," the woman said with an apologetic shrug and a small smile.

Dark hair and dark eyes, pale skin, and petit. Outside of the size, the woman bore a striking resemblance to Eric, though at least fifteen years younger. She also looked like several of the statues in the atrium.

"I'm Andrea," she said, jumping off the bed and crossing to take Katie's hand. "You can call me Rea."

"It's very nice to meet you. I'm Katie Donavan. I'm here to—"

"I know. Eric told me. That's why I'm here. To see if you need anything."

"No, I think I'm good. The shower really warmed me up."

"But your leg? Did you get it wet? Eric said you were cut when the atrium exploded."

"Well, it didn't exactly explode…" She trailed off when Rea dropped to her knees and lifted the loose-fitting pant leg covering her wound. The younger woman removed the bandage Katie had put on after her shower so expertly Katie didn't even have time to protest.

"This doesn't look too bad. But you should get to a hospital in the next couple of days and get it checked out." She poked gently around the cut. "Probably be too late for proper stitches by then, unfortunately. Does it hurt?"

"Not much," she lied. She'd dropped the bottle of aspirin Logan had given her into her purse but hadn't taken any. She'd ignored the pain medicine in Tanya's first aid kit, too. She was sort of hoping the ache in her leg would keep her focused and less distracted by Logan's…presence.

Rea rewrapped the bandage much better than Katie had, then stood. "Good. Do you need some painkillers?"

"No. Thank you."

"Be sure to steer clear of the windows until the storm passes. Eric would never forgive himself if something bad happened to you."

Katie frowned. Probably because he'd worry about getting sued. "I'm sure the rest of the house will hold against the weather."

Rea glanced at the windows with a slight frown, then shrugged and hopped back up on the bed. "So you'll be staying the night, then?"

"I…"

"You can't go anywhere. Weather channel says this storm is down for the night. And your car was totaled. I'm afraid you're stranded."

Katie tried not to show her dismay at the term stranded. Having access to Logan and his house was a good thing. But for some reason, in that moment, being "stranded" in an old mansion with a storm outside conjured up images from old horror films and gothic novels. She'd better be sure to avoid wearing anything that resembled a white nightgown while she was here.

She smiled to hide her sudden nervous adrenaline spike. "Thank you for your hospitality."

"Of course! I'm so glad you're here."

Katie couldn't begin to think why. "Your brother mentioned you're an artist like your mother. In wood?"

Rea grinned. "I am. Not nearly as good as my mom. But I like to tinker." She glanced down and her eyebrows rose. "You need shoes." Sliding off the bed again, she disappeared into the closet. Her voice floated back out. "Tanya's not nearly as curvy as you, but I think you have the same shoe size. I'm sure she's got something in here."

"Thank you."

"Oh, don't thank me," she said, returning with a pair of ballet style flats. "I miss having sisters around."

"Your family is very scattered."

"Lot of work to do in a lot of different places." She handed the shoes to Katie. "Try those on and see if they fit."

Katie sat down on the edge of the bed and slipped her feet into the flats, which were maybe a half size too big but close enough to serve. "Perfect," she said. Then, "Most of your brothers and sisters work for Logan International?"

Rea settled into a chair opposite her. "You could say that."

"Do you work for the family business?"

That brought out a huge, charming grin. "Why, yes, I do."

"And what's your role?"

Rea's grin dropped and her eyes narrowed slightly as she considered Katie. Finally, she tilted her head to one side and said, "I work on defense."

"Corporate security? Or defense contracts for the government?"

"Oh no, I don't work for governments." She stood in a fluid, graceful burst, and put her hands on her hips. "Eric likes red. That shirt was a good choice."

The quick change of both position and subject caught Katie by surprise and left her momentarily speechless. "Ehm…"

"Gregory said your suit got ruined." She gave a sympathetic grimace. "I'm sorry."

"It's nothing."

"But it was our atrium that exploded and ruined it. Eric will make sure the suit is replaced."

"That is absolutely not necessary—"

"Oh, but it is." She turned her back on Katie and trotted to the closet again. "Maybe Tanya has a suit you could take in the meantime. She's got some good things in here she'll never wear again."

Katie wasn't sure whether to be grateful for the woman's generosity or offended that she thought Katie needed hand-me downs to get by. Then she caught sight of a series of dark lines across the girl's lower back, where her shirt had risen away from her low-slung jeans and left a gap of skin. The lines looked like part of a tattoo, but she couldn't see enough of it to identify the design. It was definitely large and extensive, though, covering most of the visible skin.

"Rea," she called, "really, I'm fine. I do have another suit. I need to get back downstairs anyway."

Rea reappeared. "Your interview?"

Katie nodded. "Would you mind if I asked you some questions, too? To flesh out the article?"

"About Eric?" She chuckled. "He'll tell you to ignore anything I say about him."

"Like?"

"Like…he's in desperate need of a woman who can keep him on his toes."

"I'm sure *Aphrodite's* readers will be interested in that fact."

"I wasn't thinking about your magazine's readers." She headed toward the bedroom door. "Don't make things too easy on him, all right?"

"In the interview?"

Rea chuckled. "Sure. Also in the interview."

She disappeared before Katie could question her further, which was probably for the best because the woman's last comment had once again left Katie speechless.

When she managed to recover, she realized Rea hadn't agreed to answer questions for the interview. Bugger. She'd have to try again. She was absolutely positive Logan's younger sister would have some very juicy things to say about her brother. If Katie could get her to talk.

In the meantime, she didn't want to keep the subject of her interview waiting much longer. She stood and shook off the strangeness of the unexpected meeting. Rea seemed like a very nice woman, but their conversation made Katie feel like she was missing something. Something important.

Whatever it was, she wasn't going to find the answers hiding in this bedroom. She snatched up her purse and pulled her notebook and voice recorder out, relieved to see nothing in the bag had gotten wet. She ensured her phone was okay, checked the recorder was working properly, then took a deep breath, straightened her shoulders, and headed down to the library.

Where Eric Logan waited.

CHAPTER NINE

Eric stood at the fireplace, fighting the urge to check on Katie, to assure himself she was safe. Rea had already grilled him on their guest then hurried off to meet the woman who controlled his future. He hoped his little sister didn't overwhelm her. Or scare her off.

He glanced at his watch again. What was taking Katie so long? Impatience and worry were emotions he wasn't used to. After three hundred years, he'd developed a great deal of patience. And he'd thought his worst fear had already come to pass when his father was murdered. He'd been wrong. Losing Katie, after only just finding her, was a lot more terrifying. If his Nam-tar was killed before he had a chance to win her, he didn't think he'd be able to remain sane.

He looked out at the storm. Beyond the atrium, there hadn't been any indication this was anything more than extremely bad weather. Still, with Katie in the house…

He faced the door, willing her to walk through. He wanted, *needed* to see her again. Changing clothes couldn't possibly take this long. Maybe she'd taken a shower. The idea made his pulse jump. He glanced up at the ceiling. The thought of Katie, naked and wet in the bedroom just across from his left him a little breathless.

Despite everything both his father and his mother had told him over the centuries, he hadn't been prepared for just how intense his feelings for his Nam-tar would be. Or how much fear he'd feel. The lust was… well, expected. A pleasurable tension.

But the fear…

A flicker of lightning pulled his attention back to the storm. Wind lashed the windows, tiny bits of twigs and leaves splashing against the thick glass along with the heavy rivulets of water and the steady plinking of hail.

He'd known his cousin was in league with the monsters, but he hadn't found out who had lured Jason to the enemy camp before he'd had to kill him. He wasn't sure which monsters he'd been working with. What Eric did know was that regular hail didn't shatter safety glass or pummel cars into scrap metal. And all of that happening right after Katie arrived was an awfully big coincidence.

Had he put her life in jeopardy by bringing her here? The monsters couldn't possibly know who she was to him. Not yet. The only people who knew Katie was his Nam-tar were Gregory, Mrs. Patterson, and Rea. And he'd only told them after Jason was dead because they'd be meeting Katie. None of the rest of the family knew yet. Not even his mother. For Katie's sake as well as his own. He didn't want his immediate family interfering or getting involved as he tried to win his Nam-tar.

So it was unlikely the monsters had any idea Katie was important to him. But even without that, Katie was still officially under the Logan Family protection. To kill her would be a definite strike at the Family, payback for Jason.

And if the monsters found out who she really was…

Eric's hand fisted against the fireplace mantle. He'd protect her with his life if he had to. But knowing he might have to, because of Jason, stretched his patience thin. He didn't want a death like his cousin's, and he needed Katie to stay with him of her own free will to avoid it. Until that happened, they were both vulnerable.

The door behind him clicked open. He didn't have to turn to know it was her. Her presence filled him with a tense sort of awareness. Anticipation. And having her here, where he could protect her, allowed him to relax, just a little.

"That's coffee on the table. Help yourself. After your walk in the rain, I thought you'd like something warm."

"Perfect," she said. "Thank you."

He waited until she'd finished pouring, listening to the coffee splash into the heavy porcelain mug. Then he turned to face her.

She'd pinned her hair up again, but a few tendrils curled against her neck, drawing attention to the elegant length. The borrowed clothes gave her a more casual look that he liked very much. As if she was at home, as if she belonged here. And the color of the shirt highlighted the lovely tone of her skin and hair. She looked soft, comfortable. And tempting beyond belief.

Carefully, he paced toward her, watching her pupils dilate. She took two steps away before stopping and holding her ground. Her instincts were good. Running from him now would be more dangerous than remaining still.

He stopped very close, letting her scent fill him. "How's the coffee?"

"Good." She gulped. "Just what I needed."

"You showered." She smelled clean and fresh, the vanilla in her scent stronger now.

Shrugging, she settled on the couch near the fire. "I was already wet."

He tried not to read double meaning into her words, but he groaned inwardly. "Did you get your stitches wet?"

"The rain took care of that. I changed the bandage. The stitches stayed in place."

He didn't immediately sit, watching her shift uncomfortably as he stood next to her. Despite the signs of discomfort, he picked up the scent of her reluctant attraction, watched her steal glances up at him before hiding her face in her mug. She might be a little afraid of him, but she also wanted him. A fact he had every intention of using to his advantage.

"You're not having any?" She raised her steaming mug.

"I'm not the one who got drenched in the rain."

She chuckled, but it sounded forced. "The fire is nice."

He finally took some pity on her and sat. But he settled close to her on the couch, near enough he could still breathe in her scent. "The way you were staring longingly at the fireplaces in Tanya's room, I thought you'd appreciate one. Warmer now?"

"Uh huh."

At the slight squeak in her voice, he allowed a smile. "Good."

She nodded and took a gulp of coffee he was sure was too hot for that.

He eased even closer, until their thighs could touch with only a slight shift in position from either of them. He wanted to touch her so badly he ached with the control it took to resist. Instead, he remained where he was, savoring her scent and listening to her breath speed.

"How long do you think the storm will last?" she asked quietly.

"The news says through the night and into tomorrow."

Although, he wasn't sure the weather stations could reliably predict this storm. Not if it was what he feared. It would end when whatever or whoever was fueling it decided to calm the elements again. Now that he had Katie safe in his home, though, and away from breakable windows, Eric was more worried about the storm ending than continuing. Once the weather calmed, there would be no way to predict when, where, or what kind of attack might follow.

"Are you hungry?" he asked in an attempt to keep his hands to himself. The bouncy little curls of hair on her nape were calling to him. Would they be as soft as they looked?

"I don't expect you to feed me," she said.

"You're a guest in my home. I won't have you go hungry." And in fact, the thought of feeding her and ensuring she was comfortable appealed to him in a way he hadn't expected. Taking care of her felt...right.

"An unexpected guest." She nodded toward the windows. "Not likely to end before tomorrow, huh?"

"No. You're stranded. And you need to eat."

She frowned briefly when he said the word "stranded" but cleared her expression almost instantly and smiled. "Thank you. I do appreciate your hospitality."

He watched her face closely as he murmured, "I like having you here."

She shivered, despite the heat of the fire. A thrill of triumph coursed through his blood.

"I met your sister," she said suddenly. "Andrea. She's very nice."

"When she wants to be," he said sardonically.

That earned him a soft chuckle. "Spoken like a big brother."

"Siblings of your own?"

"An older brother and younger sister." Her mouth tightened slightly and tension creased the skin around her eyes. She took another sip of her coffee then set the mug onto the table with a firm click. "But we're here to talk about you and your family." She snatched up her notebook and voice recorder from where she'd placed them next to the tray with the coffee pot.

The flash of pain in her eyes made him frown. Something about her family had caused that. He wanted to ask what. But some pain took time to reveal. They barely knew each other. She wouldn't be ready to discuss those kinds of private things. Yet. They had time, though. He wanted to know everything about her, but he didn't want to push and risk her closing up.

As she flipped through her notebook, she said, "Andrea said she works in defense but didn't get a chance to elaborate. Does she handle corporate security?"

He raised his brows. "Something like that."

"She's quite young for such a position."

"She's a true Logan."

Katie stopped staring at her notebook and looked up at him. "Meaning?"

He held her gaze. Part of him wanted to tell her everything. The newly discovered impatient part of him. But fear of her disbelief and rejection held him back. She wasn't ready. He didn't want to lie to her either, though. He had a feeling she wouldn't look kindly on that when she did learn the full story.

Until he could be sure she wouldn't run, he had to walk a fine line. "We've all grown up in the family business and started working as soon as possible." A half-truth that would do for now.

The wind outside blew so hard the windows across the room shivered. Glancing over, he studied the panes.

"Why don't we eat before we get back to work," he said. "You've had a tough afternoon. And we have all evening for the interview."

She shrugged. "If you're ready to eat." At that moment, her stomach growled and she cringed. "Guess I am a bit hungry."

"You should have said." He rose, took her hand, and pulled her to her feet. The contact sent a pulse of heat through him. "Leave the notebook and recorder."

He didn't let go of her hand as she set her paraphernalia aside. Then he tugged her toward a side door which led to a small he'd had Gregory turn into a dining room. The space was more intimate and cozy than their overly large formal banquet hall, yet provided more privacy than eating in the kitchen, as the family liked to do when they didn't have company. It had the added benefit of being without windows. Given the tenor of the storm, a windowless room was the only way he could guarantee some peace for the meal.

That and keeping his little sister away. He'd specifically told Rea to eat somewhere else. But to guarantee she couldn't interfere he'd made sure there were only two chairs at the round table.

"Your sister isn't joining us?" Katie asked.

"She won't eat until later. She doesn't eat while she's working, and she said she was going back to work after introducing herself to you." A little fib. Rea probably had gone back to her workshop, but not because she wouldn't have joined them for dinner given the chance. She just didn't know he'd planned dinner so early.

He held Katie's seat for her, lingering a moment longer than necessary to fill his lungs with her scent, then he forced himself around the table to his own chair. With his sensitive hearing, he caught her stomach growl again. "You are hungry."

Color suffused her cheeks.

"Don't wait on propriety. Dig in."

He nodded to the covered dishes on the table. Mrs. Patterson had prepared steak, roast vegetables, and garlic potatoes with a side of beef gravy, leaving everything on warmer trays and covered so the food would be ready when he and Katie were. Katie hesitated to lift the lids, so he did, revealing the full meal.

"Looks good," she said, a slight frown putting a little crease between her brows.

"Are you a vegetarian? Have some allergy? I'm sorry, I should have asked beforehand. Gregory can arrange…"

"No. No. It's not that." She smiled. "It looks lovely. I just… I'm not sure what I was expecting."

"Something more elegant?"

With a half-laugh, she dropped her napkin onto her lap. "Maybe. Several courses. Each only big enough to qualify as a bite."

He snorted out his own laugh. "Not in this family. In this family, we eat."

Her blue eyes glittered when she glanced up at him and grinned. "Good," she said, then dug in.

Her expression made his pulse jump. He loved when she smiled. He'd die a happy man if he could see that look on her face every day for the next hundred years.

As she ate, he tried not to stare. He wanted her to enjoy the meal, not feel uncomfortable. But it was hard not to get caught up in the sight of her. This woman he'd been anticipating for so many years. In his home. Eating his food. Across a candle lit table from him. He could get used to this. Other evenings spent just this way, eating dinner together and talking about their day. His parents had had that kind of relationship. Comfortable with each other.

He'd never thought of himself as a man to want comfort from his mate. But maybe that's exactly what he'd been missing. Especially over the last year, since his father's death.

"How long are you planning on staying in the country?" she asked.

"I don't know yet. It will depend." When she raised a brow, he said, "On business." On his business with her.

"Do you mind if I ask about your business here?"

"I thought we were waiting until after dinner for the interview."

She ducked her head and a lovely pink suffused her cheeks. "Just making small talk."

"No, you weren't. Tell me about you."

"Why?"

"Because I'm curious."

"I'm not sure…"

"Katie." When she looked up, he said, "I'd really like to know more about you."

She blinked hard a few times, then glanced down at her plate, pretending to a casualness her scent belied. "What do you want to know?"

He set his fork and knife down, put one elbow on the table and rested his chin in his hand. "Why did you move to London?"

"I just wanted to live somewhere else for a while. England seemed like a good option given it's my father's native country. Not that hard to get all the paperwork and immigration stuff sorted out so I could work there."

She wasn't telling him everything. But it was a start. "Are you from New York?"

She shook her head. "This was just one of the places we lived."

"Why did you move? Your father wasn't in the military?"

"No. My mother just liked to move. She got…restless staying in one place for too long."

"She's American or English?"

"American. Mexican American. Very proud of her heritage." She smiled a little.

"Do you look like her?"

"Actually, I look more like my father. My brother looks like my dad, too."

Katie wanted to bite her tongue after that comment. She knew what question would come next. It was natural to ask about her sister.

But Katie didn't even want to think about her sister at that moment, with the storm outside bringing past events a little too close to the surface. If Eric asked who her sister looked like, all she'd be able to picture was the way Ana had looked that last time, wet from rain, soaked in blood, dead on a New York City sidewalk.

She did not want to share that image with him.

But to her complete surprise, he didn't ask the question.

"You like to move," he said instead, "like your mother? Are you restless staying in one place?"

"No," she answered with complete honesty. "I like traveling, don't get me wrong. But I prefer a stable base, a home to come home to. So to speak." She smiled faintly, then shoveled food into her mouth.

She was starving and the meal was excellent. But more than anything, she wanted a minute to collect herself after yet another memory flash of her sister's death. She didn't want Logan to see her vulnerable.

Glancing around the small dining room, she noticed something she hadn't right away. "There aren't any windows in here."

He shook his head. "Given the events of the afternoon, I thought we'd have a more relaxing dinner away from glass."

And wasn't that very considerate of him. She wasn't sure why that surprised her. He'd had a glass ceiling fall on him as well. He probably didn't want to be around breakable windows at the moment either.

"When do you think you'll be able to get people in to fix the atrium?" she asked.

"Depends on how much damage the storm does in the area."

And how long it lasted. Reality intruded on the excellent food, once again reminding her she was currently trapped in this house. How was she going to get a car and get home? She still hadn't even called Jess. She'd have to do that as soon as they ended the interview tonight.

"Have you decided to make New York your base?" he asked, returning to their earlier conversation.

She'd prefer to discuss the atrium rather than anything to do with herself. "I'd like to. Maybe." She shrugged. "Actually, I'm not sure. I haven't decided."

"Why come here from London, then? Testing run?"

"Mostly, this is where the job offer came from. If I'd landed a job in San Francisco, I'd have moved there."

"Then I guess I'm a luckier man than I thought."

She frowned. "Why?"

"If you'd moved to California, it might have taken us longer to meet. I'm rarely on the west coast."

"You say that like our meeting was inevitable." She tried to make a joke out of it, but a tiny shiver of *knowing* tickled her neck, whispering that meeting Eric Logan *was* destined.

He echoed her thought by saying, "It was."

The devilishly curious part of her wanted to ask why he thought they were supposed to meet. And what their meeting meant to him. But she wasn't sure she wanted the answers to those particular questions. Talk about opening a Pandora's Box. No, sticking to questions that didn't involve her being a part of his life was safer.

"Tell me more about your travels," she said to change the subject and turn the focus back onto him.

They finished their meal, discussing innocuous topics like traveling, and trains, and living in New York. They seemed to talk about food a lot as well—did he like bagels? What kind of pizza did she prefer? Did he hate the food in England as much as she did? But every time he tried to steer the conversation towards more personal information about her, she dodged his efforts. One of the benefits of doing all the interviews she'd done was she knew all the ways to spin away from a direct response to anything she didn't want to answer.

When she'd cleaned her plate, she sat back and sighed. "That was delicious. The only thing missing was a glass of wine."

"I wasn't sure if you'd taken those painkillers or not, or I would have offered."

"Do you drink?"

"I do. But not tonight."

His response caught her attention. "What's special about tonight?"

He wore his inscrutable expression as he contemplated his equally cleaned plate. "The storm. The power could go out. I'd rather have all my senses intact if that happens."

Suddenly nervous, she frowned. "You think the power might go?"

"Never know in weather like this."

"Maybe we should go back to the library. And the fire. Just in case."

He studied the door leading out of the dining room for a moment, then shrugged. Rising, he came around the table and held her seat as she stood. Her wounded calf muscle protested the change in position at first, so she had to lean into him to get her balance. But she quickly straightened, afraid of the ease with which she'd relied on his strength to hold her upright.

Taking her elbow, he ushered her back to the fire. The physical contact started her nerves humming. She still couldn't sense anything from him, though. The black hole in her *knowing* was weird enough to momentarily distract her from the feel of his hand on her.

For almost two seconds.

Then her body grew painfully aware of his heat and the strength in his fingers. As unobtrusively as she could manage, she pulled out of his grip and sat on the couch near her notebook. She needed to get back to work because anything else just wasn't acceptable.

She flipped to a blank page and said, "Are you ready to continue the interview?"

Not that she hadn't already been asking him a lot of questions, but those were filler and technically off the record, if he wanted to declare his food preferences and love of train travel too private for her to print. She wouldn't offer to keep that part of their conversation private, but she wanted to make sure that now, in this moment, he was aware they were going back on the record.

He shrugged and sat on the couch next to her—entirely too close. She'd managed to deal with that closeness before they ate. Sort of. But she would never be able to focus like this.

She snatched up her voice recorder and moved around the coffee table to a chair facing the couch. He'd have to sit on the chair's armrest to get close to her now. She was pretty sure he wouldn't do that.

Okay, so she was a coward. Given the circumstances, just this once, she could fully embrace the epithet.

When he raised his brows in question, she said, "It's better having the voice recorder between us." As far as explanations went, it was a good one. Even if it wasn't the real reason.

His lips turned up slightly, as if he knew she was making excuses. Unable to hold his gaze and not blush, she flipped open her notebook again and jotted down a few details: Twelve siblings: seven brothers, five sisters; Favorite food: blueberries; Favorite pizza topping: anything meat; Traveled to Vienna and Middle-East in last year; Missing cargo? Atrium?

She included another few details to jog her memory later, then leaned forward and turned on the recorder. She studied his casual posture, one arm resting on the back of the couch, his legs stretched out and crossed at the ankles. He'd changed his shirt to another dark button up. Both sleeves were intact, but they were rolled up, revealing strong forearms. He looked at ease, comfortable.

She flipped to her list of questions and tapped the notebook. "Since I haven't already, I need to ask the question my editor is most interested in."

He raised his brows.

"Are you seeing anyone special at the moment?"

His gaze darkened and that seductive little half-smile of his flashed. Then, to her utter surprise, he laughed. The sound was deep and full of masculine amusement, the sort of satisfied chuckle she'd expect from a lover, not a virtual stranger she was interviewing.

"So that's a no?" she asked.

"That's not why I'm laughing."

"I'm missing the joke, then."

"Your timing is impeccable. Because I have just started *seeing* someone special."

He held her gaze as he made the statement. She didn't miss the emphasis on the word "seeing." She narrowed her eyes. What kind of game was he playing? He was involved with someone? Why not just say yes? And if he was, why did he seem to be hitting on her? She wasn't imagining those looks he kept giving her. Was this a game to him?

But before she could ask, the library door burst open. Slamming against the wall with a loud snap.

CHAPTER TEN

Katie startled and only barely kept from screeching by clenching her teeth tight. Her pulse thudded so hard she could feel it in her neck. The adrenaline rush nearly had her coming out of her seat. Until Rea sidled into the room, eyeing her big brother, like she hadn't just given Katie a heart attack by slamming open the library door.

"What's going on in here?" she asked, her eyes narrowed at her brother.

The young woman looked much as she had earlier, but there was a fresh coat of sawdust covering her black t-shirt and low-slung jeans. And between her shirt and jeans, Katie caught another glimpse of her tattoo—it curved around onto her abdomen as well. She could only make out the dark lines, though, and still couldn't discern the actual design.

"Business," Eric told his sister, without actually looking at her.

"The interview?" Rea asked.

He nodded.

"Why are you smiling?" She flopped onto the couch next to him.

"I do that occasionally."

Rea looked at Katie and shook her head. "Only when he's up to something. What did you just ask him?"

Katie shrugged, fascinated by the interplay between brother and sister. "Just if he was seeing anyone special?" When she saw the look on Rea's face, she elaborated. "My editor and the readers of *Aphrodite* are very interested in your brother's personal life?"

"And you're not?"

Katie coughed. "Only in relation to the article I'm writing."

"Fair enough. Why are you smiling at that question?" She turned her attention back to her brother.

Eric just raised his brows. Rea mirrored the expression so exactly there was no mistaking they were siblings. They stared silently for a full minute before Rea broke the standoff and grinned. "So you decided not to tell me you were eating early, huh?"

"You were busy." He nodded to her shirt and the wood chips.

"Right. That was your only reason."

"And you eat too much."

"Ha!" She punched him in the arm and flowed up from her seat. "Actually," she said to Katie, "he's right, I do eat a lot. And speaking of which, I'm going to find some food. Enjoy."

Katie watched the young woman leave, a bit bemused by the interruption. All that drama in her entrance, she sat there for a full minute giving her brother grief, and then she was gone.

When the door closed, Katie said, "She doesn't sit around much, does she?"

"Never. Probably why she can eat more than a linebacker."

The comment made Katie chuckle. The idea of that little body taking in more food than a football player seemed pretty farfetched. But she was glad she'd caught the comment on her still-running voice recorder. It showed a great deal of family affection.

"That tattoo on her back and stomach is extensive." She faced him again. "What's it of?"

Eric's slight smile flattened and his expression returned to its unreadable state. The change sharpened her attention. Why would he go on guard after such an innocuous question? She waited several beats for an answer.

Finally, he said, "Folded wings."

"Wings? Like the statue of her as a child playing with the puppy?"

He tilted his head as if surprised by her comparison. "Similar, yes."

"Do you think she'd let me see the full tattoo at some point?"

"You'll have to ask her."

She made a mental note to do just that. And to ask why Rea had chosen folded wings. There was a story to body art most of the time, and Katie had the feeling there was a story here too. Given the statue, probably a fascinating story at that. She jotted a few words in her notebook, then returned to her questions for Eric.

She focused on things her editor wanted to know first, the sorts of tidbits that would fascinate *Aphrodite* readers. And he answered easily and, as far as she could tell, with complete honesty. She scribbled the occasional sentence as they talked but let the voice recorder log the details of his answers. She made notes on the feel of the room, the sound of the fire crackling and the window panes shivering against the force of the storm.

A few more questions about the house revealed there were basements, and lot of rooms, a very large kitchen, and a level specifically for Rea's workshop. But when she brought up the possibility of hidden passageways again, he dodged the question.

She was about to bring up the forbidden subject of his father and his father's death, testing how amenable he'd be to the taboo subject, when the lights flickered and threatened to go out. Katie held her breath as she stared at the overhead light fixture. Everything dimmed. A moment passed. Then the lights brightened and settled back to normal. She let out her breath in a whoosh.

"Do you have flashlights nearby?" she asked. "In case the lights do go out."

"Gregory would come find us with one. The fire will give us some light in the meantime." Even as he spoke, he rose to feed the flames with more wood.

She caught him glancing towards the window, frowning. Unable to resist, she followed his gaze. Sometime while they'd been eating, the curtains had been drawn, but through a crack in the thick green fabric she saw the jittery flash of lightning. A moment later, thunder crashed.

Katie nibbled her bottom lip. "Some weather."

"Maybe we should call it a night," he said, nodding at the clock over the mantle. To Katie's surprise, it was nearly nine p.m. "I have a few phone calls to make. And I'm sure you're exhausted."

He was right, she was tired enough that the thought of bed actually sparked an involuntary yawn. "Oh." She covered her mouth. "Guess I'm pretty beat. And I have a few calls to make as well. Obviously, I'm not going anywhere tonight."

"Tanya's room is yours for as long as you need it."

"I'm sure the storm will ease tomorrow."

At least, she hoped it would. While having such unprecedented access to Logan was a boon to her story, she did want to leave this house eventually.

She flicked off her recorder, mentally reminding herself to plug it into its charger when she got upstairs. Fortunately, the contents of her bag had survived her brief moment outside better than she had.

Clutching her paraphernalia, she stood, stretching her back a bit to work out the kinks. Then she reached out with her free hand to shake Logan's. "Thank you very much for the lovely dinner. And the warm fire."

He took her hand, but instead of the goodnight shake she'd intended, he pulled her close and tucked her hand around his elbow. "I'll walk you to your room."

"Not necessary," she said in a hurry. She needed time to think and plan. To go over her notes. And she wanted a little unsupervised access to the house. If he accompanied her back to Tanya's room, she'd have no excuse for wandering the halls, pretending to be lost.

She could do without him touching her, too. The contact started her miscreant hormones churning. Heat tingled down her arm from his fingertips, flowing across her breasts and down to her stomach. Suddenly the room felt warmer, the lighting more intimate, the situation entirely too personal.

And she simply couldn't afford this attraction. "Really, I can manage on my own," she said, keeping her tone light and firm so he wouldn't know how he was affecting her. "I don't want to keep you from your business."

"I'll feel better seeing you back. In case the lights go out. Wouldn't want you to get lost in the dark."

She'd be safer alone in the dark. She swallowed the retort and let him lead her from the library. If she were too insistent, he'd realize she was affected by his touch. Something he really didn't need to know. He also might realize she wanted to be alone to sneak around the house without his watchful presence. Something else she'd rather he didn't know.

"How's your leg?" he asked as they slowly climbed the stairs.

"A little sore at the moment but not too bad." Actually, the cut was a low ache she hadn't noticed until they started walking. Now, the pain was bothersome. Nothing she couldn't limp through, but damned inconvenient.

"Tanny should have some more painkillers in her bathroom. Take a couple before you go to sleep."

"I will," she lied. No drugs, even painkillers, while she was in a stranger's house. "I already had to borrow her first aid kit to rebandage the wound after my shower."

"Would you like me to take another look?"

"No," she said, a little too quickly. Clearing her throat, she said in a more reasonable tone, "No, thank you. I'm sure it's fine. Rea checked it."

"The hospital is probably out of the question tomorrow if this weather keeps up. So I do want to have another look in the morning. If the butterfly stitches are sufficient, we'll leave them. But if the wound needs more, I can suture it myself."

"I'm not sure that's a good idea."

"I've done plenty of them before," he said, squeezing her elbow. "Medic, remember? I'll even make sure the stitches are small so there's less of a scar."

She was more worried about having his hands on her leg again than she was a scar. "I'm sure the butterfly stitches are good enough." They reached the door to Tanya's rooms, and Katie turned to face him.

"I'll feel better if I check the cut tomorrow," he said.

He was so serious she relented. "Fine. But no stitches."

"We'll see."

He leaned in and Katie leaned back, but the closed door got in her way. Her heart started pounding, that combination of fear and anticipation clogging her throat. The switch from concerned doctor to invading her space was so sudden, her mind went completely blank. She couldn't seem to find a single word. She should say something. Push the tone back to business. Push him back a few feet to restore her personal space. But none of those things happened. Her gaze dropped involuntarily to his lips and her stomach tensed.

"Are you going to be all right tonight?" His voice was quiet and deep. "Strange house, strange room. Storm outside."

She nodded, still not quite verbal. His mouth was so close to hers. He would kiss her if she didn't stop him. Except she wasn't stopping him. Why wasn't she stopping him?

"I could join you, make sure you're safe."

A nervous snort escaped before she could stop it, and she finally found her voice. "Having you around is not going to make me safer."

"True." His head dipped closer.

Say something, damn it! Stop this now. "What about this special person you're seeing?" She pressed closer to the door, trying to put some space between their bodies. The mouth she couldn't seem to stop staring at curved upward subtly.

"I'm *seeing* her right now," he murmured.

His words snapped her out of her daze, and she finally got the joke. Scowling, she shook her head. "You knew that wasn't what I was asking earlier."

"But that was the answer to your question." He leaned in another inch and braced his hands on the door frame. "I'm not sure I'm comfortable letting you sleep here alone tonight. What if the power goes out?"

She raised her chin, irritation giving her back some sense. At least enough to fend him off while still maintaining her dignity and professionalism. "I'll be asleep so I won't notice."

"And if you wake up?"

He angled his face close to her neck, and Katie tilted her head to the side, a move which actually gave him better access to her throat. The position left her shockingly vulnerable. Why the hell was she doing this? Only the instant before she'd been ready to send him packing. Now she was savoring the feel of his breath on her skin.

She felt like a completely different person around him in moments like this. Not like herself at all. Like someone who knew him better. Like this was a normal way for them to be.

She swallowed. "I…" But the words trailed off when she heard him inhale and his lips brushed the air just above her skin—not quite touching but so close he might as well have been. Her heartbeat hammered. The almost contact left her knees weak and wobbly. If the door hadn't been holding her up, she wasn't sure she'd still be standing.

"Katie," he murmured her name, his lips close enough to her skin to brush the barest of kisses against her throat.

She gasped as heat zinged through her body, pooling between her legs. No. This could absolutely not happen. Not with him. Desperate and clumsy, she reached for the knob and fumbled the door open, nearly falling on her butt as she stumbled back into the room.

"Goodnight." She used the door to support her shaky knees.

He bent down and scooped her notebook and voice recorder off the floor, then handed them back to her. She hadn't even realized she'd dropped them. She snatched her things out of his hands, careful not to touch him, and started to close the door.

He stopped the swing with one finger. "Let me know if you need anything. I'm just across the hall. And I have excellent hearing."

"Goodnight," she said again and closed the door in his face.

Leaning her forehead against the cool wood, she tried to steady her racing pulse. Was that last comment a threat or a promise? Did he guess she might try to sneak back out again? Or was he just promising the things her body wanted and her brain refused to indulge in?

Damn the man anyway, he knew what he was doing to her. He was teasing her on purpose, playing some game she wanted no part of. She cracked the door open again, absurdly wondering if he planned to keep watch, guarding her so she didn't go wandering around the house alone. She felt like a fool when she saw the empty hallway. Glancing at his door, she realized she hadn't actually heard him go in. He might have gone off to an office somewhere else in the house.

She looked up and down the corridor. No sign of anyone. Then she considered his door again. What if he *was* in there? Listening.

Easing her own door closed again, she frowned. This was ridiculous. He wasn't lurking in his room waiting to pounce on her if she ventured out. He had work to do. He was probably already on the phone.

Rolling her eyes, she crossed to the couch and dropped her notes and recorder, then she went to the bedroom for her purse. She had calls to make as well. And her leg hurt. She needed to get off it for a little bit. Then she had her own work to do.

And in an hour or two, when she was sure no one was around, a little unaccompanied tour would be in order.

She yawned on her way into the bathroom. She didn't want to get caught snooping. As accommodating as he'd been so far, she was still treading a fine line between investigation and offending him and getting sent away. Or put under guard since he couldn't actually send her anywhere just yet. She'd have to have a decent excuse for wandering around the house if she was caught. Maybe looking for the kitchen?

She hunted bathroom cabinets until she found some toothpaste. After finger brushing her teeth—because she felt weird taking one of the unopened toothbrushes—and washing her face, she headed back toward the sitting room. The bed loomed comfy and promising as she passed through the bedroom. She really was exhausted. The day had taken a higher toll than she'd realized. She might actually have to go in search of the kitchen and some coffee if she wanted to get anything more done tonight.

After a moment's consideration, she went into Tanya's closet and found a pair of pajama bottoms to sleep in. The tank under her button up shirt would continue to serve for sleepwear. She wasn't about to sleep in only the tank top, though. And any nightgown she might borrow reminded her too much of her earlier thoughts of being trapped inside a gothic novel. No white nightgowns for her.

She changed out of the borrowed pants and laid them out neatly on a chair in the bedroom. Then she took her purse back out to the couch.

After a quick call and voicemail left for her editor and another more difficult call to Jess, she turned to her notes. Before she was halfway through the last part of the interview, her eyes were drooping closed. She forced herself to continue but exhaustion dragged at her.

She startled awake sometime later and realized she'd actually fallen asleep on the couch for nearly half an hour. With a groan, she set her things aside and went in to bed. She'd sleep for a few hours and then get up and snoop around. That was actually a better plan, she decided as she crawled beneath the heavy comforter. Everyone else would be asleep by then and she'd be less likely to get caught.

After a bit of consideration, she got back out of bed and went to the window. If the power went out, she didn't want to get stuck in pitch blackness in an unfamiliar space.

Fingering the thick curtains, she watched rain water dribble down the window. This room looked out onto the back of the house, across an expanse of lawn to the woods. She hesitated, wondering what the chances were of another window shattering around her. Her *knowing* wasn't bothering her so having the curtains open was probably safe. She pulled them apart enough to leave a foot of glass exposed. When she switched off the bedroom light, ambient light filtered through the window to prevent total blackness.

She hadn't heard any thunder in a while, and no lightning flashed. Maybe the storm was dying faster than anticipated. As she crawled back into bed, she hoped for a bright sunny morning.

She really hated storms.

CHAPTER ELEVEN

A flash of lightning woke Katie from a deep, dreamless sleep. She blinked in the dark room, wondering what time it was. Several seconds passed before thunder rumbled in the distance. She stared at the window, waiting for more lightning and listening to rain pelt the glass.

Tink, tink, tink.

The patch of sky visible between the curtains was glowing gray, but below the sky, the night was blackness. She continued to stare outside as the steady tinking noise filled the otherwise silent room. Something about the sound… She'd never heard rain sound exactly that way.

The hair on the back of her neck prickled.

She stared harder, trying to see through the thick gloom. Was there a tree that close to the window? She didn't remember one. She couldn't hear the wind blowing either. Wouldn't there have to be wind to blow a tree branch against the glass?

A shiver of awareness crawled through her belly. Her breathing flowed faster. And the nerves along the back of her neck tingled with the first hints of *knowing*.

She held perfectly still, her gaze focused on the black space between the curtains. Waiting. Listening.

Tink. Tink. Tink. Tink.

The next flash of lightning brightened the room.

Outside the window, a gray-skinned horror smiled at her with a mouthful of sharply pointed teeth, as a gray tentacle tapped against the glass.

Katie screamed.

And darkness closed around her.

Still screaming, she scrambled out of bed, blind terror making her limbs awkward and clumsy. She got tangled in the blanket and hit the floor hard, but the jolt didn't stop her from struggling to get away. Desperate, animal fear forced adrenaline through her blood stream. She pushed to her feet and ran toward the sitting room, only to hit up hard against something solid and warm.

She screamed again and struggled as if her life depended on it.

"Katie. Katie! It's Eric. Calm down. I've got you. What's wrong?"

"Eric?" She shuddered against him as his arms came up around her, strong and solid. But she still pushed to get away from the window, too terrified to stay in the bedroom. "Something... There was something outside... I saw it..."

Giving in to her struggles, he led her into the sitting room. Light from the hallway illuminated the otherwise dark space. Katie noticed the door had been slammed open so hard, it had pulled free from the top hinge. If she wasn't trembling so much, she might have been impressed by the strength required to do that. As it was, she couldn't think beyond the impossible thing she'd seen at the window.

Eric sat her on the couch and turned toward the bedroom. She clutched his hand. "Where are you going?"

"I just want to take a look."

"No. What if it's still there?"

He knelt in front of her, covering both her hands with his. "Tell me what you saw."

She swallowed and glanced toward the bedroom. "It was horrible.

Gray everywhere. With tentacles. Lots of scaly tentacles. And its face was all gray and thin, skeletal but not a skeleton. It had flesh but the flesh was…just gross looking. Like melting leather. Does that make sense? There was hair, I think. But maybe that was just more tentacles. And it had clothes on, but they were rags, the same grey as its skin. Its teeth were really sharp and pointy." She looked back at Eric and squeezed his hands, panting as she tried to drag in air. "And it smiled. It smiled at me." Panic constricted her lungs so she could barely breathe.

"Calm down, Katie," he said, his tone soothing and gentle. "It's okay now. Breathe. That's it, baby. Good. Just relax. I've got you."

She gulped in air, struggling to control the fear. Holding his gaze, she focused on the concern in his eyes, the steady grip of his hands, the warmth of his body near hers. Slowly, very slowly, she pulled herself together. After a few moments, her lungs opened, and she felt the panic receding. She dragged in a long, slow gulp of air.

"Better?" he asked, pushing a lock of hair from her face.

She nodded, working now to calm the shaking that still wracked her body. Her gaze jumped to the bedroom then quickly away. She could still hear the rain on the living room windows, but it no longer sounded like fingers tapping against glass.

"I wasn't dreaming," she said, defensive now that she'd calmed a little. "I did see something. I didn't imagine it."

"I believe you, baby." He rose to his feet, still holding her hands. "I'm just going to take a quick look, make sure the windows are closed. I won't be gone long."

She clung to his hand for another moment, reluctant to let go of his steady presence. But finally, she relaxed her grip. He strode to the bedroom and disappeared from view. Katie held her breath, realized what she was doing, and let the air out again slowly. She hadn't been dreaming. She'd really seen something impossible. A monster unlike anything she could have imagined.

Shivers raced up her arms and down her spine, chilling her. She rubbed her palms along her biceps, trying to warm her cold skin.

When Eric stepped back out of the bedroom, she nearly sagged into the couch. She didn't even think to question her relief. All she knew in that moment was that he was big and strong and real and there. And she was beyond any terror she'd ever experienced before—basic, animal terror that bypassed her higher brain functions and hit her in her most primal instincts.

"Did you see anything?"

He shook his head as he crossed to her.

"I did see something. I wasn't dreaming," she insisted.

"I believe you, Katie." Without another word, he leaned over and scooped her into his arms.

"Wait. What are you doing?"

"I'm not leaving you in here alone tonight."

Again, that irrational relief swept through her and without hesitation she clung to him, her arms wrapped around his neck. Part of her noticed he wasn't wearing a shirt, just dark pajama bottoms. She probably should be embarrassed. Mortified by her own clinginess and both their states of undress.

She wasn't. She needed his heat and strength in that moment too desperately to care about a little thing like being in pajamas. She rested her head against his shoulder and held tight to the only solid thing in her world.

Rea waited just outside Tanya's door. "Is she okay? What happened?"

"She's not hurt. Just scared," Eric said, his voice low.

He didn't say anything more, but Katie saw the look on Rea's face as she locked gazes with her brother. Rea must have seen something in his expression because she nodded, looking grim.

"If you need me, call," she said, before she turned back toward her own bedroom.

"What was that about?" Katie asked as he carried her into his room.

"She was worried about you. Your scream woke the house. Took years off my life," he muttered.

She wasn't sure she was supposed to have heard the last sentence but his obvious worry for her made something insider her soften dangerously.

"I really am okay, now. Just..." She glanced passed his shoulder, across the hall and shuddered. "I doubt I'll be able to sleep in that room again."

"Don't think about that tonight. You'll sleep in here."

She looked up at the side of his face. "Where will you sleep?"

"On the couch. Unless you say otherwise."

He nodded to the massive piece of furniture taking up one section of his room, and Katie finally glanced around. Unlike his sister's room, his wasn't divided into a living room and bedroom. He just had one huge space divided into a sitting area, with a couch and a couple of chairs set before a fireplace, and a bedroom area. Two large wooden columns were the only dividers between the areas. Book-filled shelves lined two of the walls. A dresser and a free standing, full-length mirror took up a corner near the bed. A couple of doors led off from the room, resumable to a bathroom and a closet. And windows covered with dark curtains took up most of the outside wall.

The space was massive, the ceilings high, the floors and wainscotting all dark wood, the walls above the wainscotting painted a pale color she couldn't quite discern in the darkness. His bed was even larger than his sister's, framed by more dark wood and covered with dark blankets.

The blankets were askew, thrown back and falling half off the bed. Katie realized he must have rushed out of the room when he heard her screams.

"I don't want to kick you out of your bed," she said. "I can take the couch." And the fact that she was even considering sleeping in here with him showed just how rattled she was. All logic and professional self-preservation subsumed under absolute terror. She did not want to be alone.

"Not very gentlemanly of me if I let you do that," he said with a faint smile. "My mother would box my ears if she found out."

The thought of anyone scolding Eric Logan made her chuckle.

"Ah, that's better," he murmured. "You scared the hell out of me earlier. I thought someone was killing you."

He sat on the couch, keeping her in his lap. A part of her

recognized she should move off him and sit on her own, at the very least, but that part was very quiet.

"Not something I'm going to recover from any time soon," he said. "So for my peace of mind, you will sleep in my bed, and I'll stay on the couch where I can make sure you're safe."

"I'm okay. Really. I'll be fine."

But she didn't stand up, and she made no pretense of leaving. Alone in a bedroom with Eric Logan sounded infinitely safer than alone with…whatever that was she'd seen in the window. She doubted she'd be able to sleep anymore tonight anyway, but at least she'd feel better having someone else in the room with her.

"Do you want a drink to help calm your nerves?"

She shook her head. "Do you want a drink?"

"Yes," he said. But he didn't get up and his arms tightened around her.

"I'm sorry I scared you."

"I'm sorry you were scared." He brushed her hair back from her face, then cupped her cheek. "Will you be able to sleep?"

"Probably not." She shrugged, unconsciously rubbing her cheek against his palm.

For a long moment, they sat in the dark, quietly holding each other. Katie could feel his heart thumping against her side where they were pressed together. The steady beat was reassuring, helping to calm her further. She took in the planes of his face, the dark arch of his brows, the shape of his eyes, the sensual curve of his mouth, the dark shadow of his beard stubble—fixing those images in her mind in an attempt to block the memory of the thing she'd seen looking in her window.

Finally, he dropped his hand from her cheek and stood, still keeping her cradled in his arms. "You should try to sleep."

He walked her to the bed and gently laid her down, pulling the covers up around her shoulders. Sitting next to her, he stroked his fingers down the side of her cheek. "If you get scared, just say my name. I'll be right here."

"Thank you," she murmured.

He held her gaze for a heartbeat. Then he leaned over and brushed his lips against hers, gently, briefly. The gesture was so surprisingly comforting, she sighed. He straightened and stared down at her a moment longer.

"You're safe now, Katie. Try to rest."

She nodded, but she didn't look away as he rose and walked back to the living room area. He pulled a blanket off one of the chairs and stretch out on the couch, disappearing from view behind the high back. But she knew Eric was there and that was enough to make her feel safe.

She stared at the couch until her eyes closed and sleep finally dragged her back under.

Katie opened her eyes again before the sun rose and glanced around the dark room. A soft noise caught her attention. A wolf came out of the shadows from the direction of the fireplace. It padded toward her, staring. But before it reached her, it turned toward the window nearest the bed and laid down at the base of the curtains. The large animal settled its head on its forepaws and watched her.

She smiled and drifted deeper into sleep, comforted by the wolf's protective presence.

CHAPTER TWELVE

The next time Katie woke, dim morning light filtered in through a crack in the curtains. The first thing she did was look at the bottom of the window nearest the bed. The space beneath was empty. She touched a finger to her lips, then she glanced at the couch. The blanket lay neatly folded along the back.

"Eric?" she called just to be sure. But she already knew he was gone.

At some point last night, she'd stopped thinking of him as Logan or even Mr. Logan… He was Eric now. Dangerous, that. Very dangerous.

Sliding from beneath the covers, she crossed to the two doors leading off the bedroom area. One opened onto his closet. It was almost as big as Tanya's, a full apartment in her world, but filled with Eric's scent. Katie stood there for a moment and breathed in the warm, masculine smell. Then she closed the door and crossed to the other. This one led to his bathroom. The colors were once again dark and masculine, like the outer room. Splashes of maroon brightened the browns and creams, reminding her of Rea's comment that Eric liked red.

She smiled at the new toothbrush sitting on the cream marble counter next to the sink beside a not-so-new tube of toothpaste. She brushed her teeth and finger combed her hair as she looked around the room. His shower wasn't as large as Tanya's but his separate bathtub was actually bigger, looking more like a Jacuzzi than a tub. The countertops were clean but for a can of shaving cream. She picked it up and sniffed. Part of Eric's scent, but not all. She opened the mirrored medicine cabinet. Razors, shaving cream, deodorant, soap, his toothbrush, a comb. No medicine or pills. Considering the first aid kits this family kept in every room, he probably didn't need to store medicine in his medicine cabinet.

When she finished her business and stepped back into the bedroom, she noticed for the first time the hoodie lying across the foot of the bed. A note was folded on top of the garment. She ran her hand over the cotton material then lifted the paper.

The house is a little chilly in the mornings. I didn't think you'd want to go back into Tanya's room for a sweater. My sweatshirt is too big for you, but it'll keep you warm. Come down to the kitchen when you're ready.

  ~Eric

At the base of the note was a little hand-drawn map with an arrow directing her from his room to the kitchen. She set it aside and picked up the sweatshirt. It zipped in front and was a deep purple. When she slipped into it, she was immediately surrounded by Eric's scent. Breathing deep, she wrapped the edges close, savoring the warmth.

Unable to resist being alone in his room, she did a turn around the area. There were pictures tucked away between the books, photos of his family she guessed. Over the fireplace mantle hung a large, abstract painting. And here and there, flat surfaces were decorated with small wooden or stone statues.

One corner of the room was dominated by another of his mother's pieces—one she hadn't noticed the night before as it was tucked between a window and a bookshelf. It was a full-sized sculpture of Eric standing with his arms folded over his chest looking very stern and domineering. She grinned at the way his mother had captured that expression so perfectly. The woman was incredibly talented. Katie still couldn't believe she'd never heard of her work before this.

She turned back to her investigation. The entire room was neat and tidy but for a pair of slippers carelessly tossed close to the couch. There wasn't a desk so she didn't have drawers to riffle through. And given what he'd done for her the night before, she wasn't sure she wanted to invade his privacy that blatantly.

Not right now anyway. Later…probably. But at the moment, she was feeling too indebted to him.

And, if she were being perfectly honest with herself, she'd admit that she didn't want to uncover his secrets by snooping. She wanted him to tell her everything there was to know about his life. She wanted him to trust her with his secrets. Even though he had no reason to. Even though she was here as a reporter and he had every reason to worry she might reveal those secrets to the world. That didn't stop her from wanting his trust.

But it was early in the morning. No doubt that irrational desire would fade as soon as she had her first sip of coffee.

For some reason, she thought of the wolf she'd dreamt about and the security she'd felt with the large animal guarding her. Strange. She'd never dreamt about wolves before. She certainly wouldn't have expected it to make her feel safe. Her brain probably pulled the idea from all those images of wolves in Laksana's statues in the atrium.

With a final glance at the windows, Katie pulled the sweatshirt more firmly closed and left Eric's room.

In the hallway, she contemplated the closed door across from his. It didn't close properly, the top hinge was off kilter still, but it covered the entrance. She stared for a long moment. Her notes, her cellphone, her purse were all still in there. She'd need her gear.

Licking her lips, she crossed to the door and pressed her hand against it. No psychic warnings rose up to worry her. She concentrated on keeping her breathing slow as she pressed the door open. Despite the dim morning light brightening the space, she hesitated on the threshold. With an irritated snort, she stalked inside and snatched her up purse, notebook, voice recorder, and mobile off the couch where she'd left them the night before. Then she glanced toward the bedroom and despite the light, fear tightened her stomach muscles. She backed out of the room, not wanting to look away from the windows.

In the hallway again, she closed her eyes and shook her head. She was an idiot. But knowing that didn't seem to quiet the irrational terror still lurking just below the surface. She hurriedly dropped her things into her purse, slid the long strap over her head and across her chest, then left to find the kitchen.

She needed caffeine.

She followed Eric's map out of the family wing and down a set of stairs she hadn't used the day before. She tried to take in as much of the house as possible as she went, but in broad daylight, she had no idea who was around and didn't want to get caught searching the place. Shame she hadn't gotten to explore last night. But then her night hadn't turned out at all as she'd intended.

When she neared the kitchen, the smell of coffee and cooking bacon guided her more than the map. She stepped through an open double doorway into a large, bright space filled with wonderful scents. A small, plump woman stood at an industrial sized stove, turning sizzling slices of bacon, her back to the rest of the room.

Katie wondered if the woman could hear her stomach growling from such a distance because she didn't turn away from her task as she spoke.

"Coffee's fresh. If you want any, you'd better pour quick. When Rea gets here, you'll be lucky to get a drop."

Smiling, Katie moved from the doorway toward the high-tech coffee machine. "Thanks. I could use some caffeine." She poured the dark liquid into one of the red ceramic mugs sitting on the granite countertop. "My name's Katie, by the way. Katie Donavan."

"I'm Geraldine Patterson. I cook for the Logans. And I know who you are." The woman finally faced Katie, looking her over with her lips pursed and a frankly assessing expression. She adjusted her glasses and sniffed. "Reporter. Never allowed one of those in here before."

"Guess I'm just lucky."

The woman snorted. "We'll see if you're calling it good luck or bad in a few more days."

Katie blew on her coffee before taking a sip. "Something I should know?"

"Nothing I'm willing to talk about. The Logans are good people. Just remember that, missy."

Raising a brow, Katie nodded and carried her cup to one of the windows flooding the room with light. From here, she could see out across the grassy lawn in the back of the mansion that led down to the woods. This time of year, the flower beds were bare, decorated with evergreens, ivy and bark chips. She wondered what the area would look like in the spring when the flowers bloomed. Rain still sheeted down outside and gray clouds blocked most of the sunlight.

Sipping her coffee, she watched the rain and listened to Geraldine putter around the kitchen.

"I'm surprised you can stand so close to a window this morning."

She glanced over her shoulder to see Eric standing in the doorway. She hadn't heard him enter. He was dressed in a cream, button up shirt and dark slacks. His hair was still damp from a shower which made her wonder where he'd taken it. She was sure she wouldn't have slept through the sound of running water. And his bathroom had shown no signs of him having bathed there anyway.

She smiled a little and said, "Things look a lot less scary in the light of day." Things outside of Tanya's room that is. She turned fully to face him. "About last night… I'm sorry for all the fuss. I mean, obviously, I was dreaming." She frowned. "It seemed so real at the time, but obviously, it had to be a nightmare." When he didn't comment, she shrugged. "I guess I feel a little silly this morning."

"Don't. You were scared."

"Still…" She took a drink of coffee. "Funny, but that monster wasn't the only strange dream I had last night."

"Oh?"

"Back in a minute," Geraldine said from across the kitchen and left through a side door.

"What was the other dream?" Eric asked when they were alone.

Katie glanced in the direction Geraldine had gone. Suddenly alone with Eric, she became very aware of what had passed between them the night before. The security she'd felt in his arms, the gentle kiss he'd brushed across her lips. Her mouth tingled with the memory, and she had to take another drink to cover the heat rising in her cheeks.

He must have noticed her sudden discomfort, though, because he closed the space between them, his expression intent. Without touching her, he stood close enough to make her aware of every hard inch of his body, ever muscle she'd been pressed up against last night. She'd been too scared to give more than a passing notice to his state of undress then, but this morning, memories of his near perfect torso surfaced and made her stomach tighten with desire. Her gaze settled on his mouth as a flash of his kiss flitted through her mind.

"Your other dream," he prodded when she continued to stare.

The reminder made her shake off her distraction. "There was a wolf. It was strange. This huge wolf was in your room, and it laid down next to the bedroom window. After the other dream, you'd think the wolf would have scared me."

Eric went very still. "It didn't?"

"No. I actually felt safe. Like it was watching over me. Weird, huh?"

"Do you dream of wolves often?"

"Never have before." She took a gulp of her drink. The coffee was excellent, but it was also just good to have something to do with her hands while she talked with him, while he stood so close. "But I have a friend who dreams about whales all the time. She says she considers them like her guides. Maybe that's what the wolf is, my guide." She shrugged and smiled a little. "Or maybe I just saw too many wolf statues in the atrium yesterday."

"But you weren't scared? Of the wolf?"

"I guess after that other thing, something as normal as a wolf seemed safe." She glanced down at her empty mug. "I need another cup. Do you want some coffee?" Any excuse to put some space between them. His steady watchfulness made her want to fidget. She crossed to the coffee machine, trying to ignore her discomfort. "Thanks for the sweatshirt, by the way," she said as she poured. "I would have been a bit cold without it."

Before he could respond, Gregory came into the kitchen. "Good morning, Ms. Donavan. I hear you had a scare last night. I'm very sorry."

"Probably just my brain trying to work out the trauma of the day. Pretty scary nightmare, but what can you do?"

"Well, I don't know if this will help, but your clothes have been cleaned and dried. I was able to salvage your suitcase from the trunk of the car and most everything survived the soaking. Since I didn't think you'd be in a hurry to go back into Ms. Tanya's room, I've laid your things out in Mr. Logan's. When you settle on another room, or if you decide to return to Ms. Tanya's room, let me know and I'll have the clothing moved."

Katie set her cup down, crossed to the butler and gave him a big kiss on the cheek. "Gregory, you are a star. Thank you so much. I can't tell you how much better I'll feel in my own clothes." She grinned at the butler's smile, then glanced back at Eric. "Save me some breakfast? I'll be back down in twenty."

CHAPTER THIRTEEN

Eric watched Katie hurry from the kitchen. Then he raised his brows at his butler. Gregory raised his brows back.

"I run to her rescue in the middle of the night," Eric said, "get a century scared off of my life, sacrifice my bed, and spend most of the night awake protecting her. And you get the kiss."

"I can't help it if my natural charms have enchanted the lady."

"Well try, Gregory. Try. Because if she kisses you again, I will not be pleased."

"Perhaps you should try some charm yourself. Sir."

Before Eric had a chance to retort, the butler left. Scowling, he crossed to pour himself a cup of coffee. Being even a little jealous of Gregory was ridiculous. Katie had obviously kissed him in a friendly way, nothing romantic involved. But Eric couldn't seem to stop the rush of anger. And jealousy. Why the hell wasn't she kissing him this morning? Considering the scare she'd given him, a little kiss on the cheek in thanks didn't seem too much to ask.

"What's that mug ever done to you?" Rea asked as she hip butted him from in front of the machine and filled her own cup.

"Just thinking."

She took a long gulp, sighed, and faced him. "So, what are we looking at?"

Eric studied his youngest sister for a long moment. Finally, he said, "We've got a grinluk on the property."

Rea took another gulp of coffee and set the empty mug back on the counter. "I'll go make sure my swords are sharpened then. Don't eat all the food." She left without another word.

Eric sat at the large, wooden kitchen table where the family usually ate casual breakfasts and waited for Katie to return. Mrs. Patterson entered moments after Rea left, refilled the now empty coffee pot, and started it brewing again. She ignored Eric as she went back to cooking up enough bacon to feed an army. With Rea in residence, the quantity was necessary.

As he sipped, he considered Katie's reaction to the wolf. Her lack of fear was a huge relief. If she considered the wolf safe, even a guardian of sorts, there was hope she'd be able to accept the truth about him and his family when he finally told her everything. Her reaction gave him a small rush of satisfaction too, though he was a little embarrassed to admit as much, even to himself. She'd turned to him when she was scared, and she'd found security in the presence of the wolf. That settled something in him.

The fact that she'd had cause for fear dampened his satisfaction considerably, however.

A grinluk at Katie's window. Why? Why her window and not his or Rea's? Could it possibly know who Katie was to him? He wasn't sure how.

More likely this was the monster Jason had been working with. Grinluk could be very loyal to their associates. Up to a point. Tormenting Katie was almost certainly just the monster's revenge for Jason's death. Anyone else in this house would know what they were facing and fight back.

He still didn't like the situation. Katie was in danger merely by being here. But as long as the monster didn't find out she was important, it might confine its efforts to just scaring her. If they were lucky. Unfortunately, in his experience, luck was never a very reliable option.

And then there was the storm.

Grinluk couldn't control the elements or conjure rainfall. Which meant the grinluk wasn't their only problem. He was positive now this weather was no coincidence. A sorcerer, an Elemental, a weather witch, certain members of the Fae, and a number of other species of monsters were all capable of this. Any of them would be deadly foes, especially working with a grinluk.

Normally, Eric wouldn't worry about the threat. In fact, he'd welcome the monsters into his home where he could kill them more easily. It was his job, and he'd never hesitated to do it. But with Katie in the house, these threats took on a sudden gravity he'd never had to consider before. He wasn't sure he'd be able to forgive himself for placing her in harm's way. He'd tried to protect her, keep her safe. Canceling their meeting several times, until he made sure Jason was dead. But he should have uncovered the monsters first, before bringing Katie anywhere near his home.

He was still trying to decide what to do about keeping her safe when she returned. She'd changed from Tanya's pajamas into a pair of dark grey trousers and a long-sleeved, purple blouse which hugged her curves. He liked the silhouette the shirt created. But he was sorry to see she'd left his sweatshirt upstairs. He'd enjoyed seeing her wearing something of his. He'd enjoy seeing her wear nothing at all even more.

Some of his thoughts must have shown in his expression, because her gaze danced away from his almost as soon as she'd entered the room.

"More coffee," she said, making a beeline for the carafe. "Great."

"How's your cut?" He noticed she didn't seem to be favoring the injured leg, which was a good sign.

"Not bad, actually. I haven't taken the bandages off to check yet, but it isn't hurting as much so that smust be good."

"I'll check the stitches after breakfast."

She gulped coffee that was obviously too hot because she quickly covered her mouth and made a waving gesture with her hand as she swallowed convulsively. He rose to try and help but she set her cup down and shooed him away with her now free hand. "Just burned my tongue," she said.

"Do you need some water?"

She shook her head. "It's nothing. I think my leg is fine, too. You don't need to worry about it."

"We had this conversation last night," he said, settling back into his seat. "I'm checking your wound. Period. There will be no gangrene in this house."

She rolled her eyes at his dramatics. "Fine, but I'll have to change again. These trousers aren't baggy enough to roll up over my calf."

"Whatever it takes. Although, you could just take the pants off and not bother with anything else."

"No."

Her tone was so absolute, it sent a rush through his blood. The thrill of the chase. He'd have her naked soon. The delay only added to the anticipation.

"Sit," Mrs. Patterson ordered without looking at either one of them. She dropped two overflowing plates of eggs and bacon on the table. "If you don't eat now, Rea might think you don't want it and finish it off for you."

As Katie settled in front of one of the plates, Mrs. Patterson set down another piled high with toast next to a selection of jams.

"It looks wonderful," Katie said. "Thanks."

With his sensitive ears, Eric heard her stomach growling. Good appetite. She fit in well with his family.

Rea banged through a side door in the next instant. "You haven't eaten all the food, have you?"

Mrs. Patterson put two full plates in front of her and gave her a separate plate filled with toast.

"You're going to eat all that?" Katie asked in obvious disbelief.

"To start. Might have to have seconds." Rea grinned as she shoveled a forkful of eggs into her mouth.

Katie turned to Eric and raised her brows. He shrugged. "Rea can eat."

"Where does someone so small put it all?"

Rea laughed and swung one leg up onto the table, a move that made Mrs. Patterson hiss in protest. "Mom always said I had a hollow leg." Rea tapped the limb in question, dropping it back beneath the table seconds before Mrs. Patterson's towel snapped out in warning.

Katie smiled, and Eric felt a funny little flutter in his chest. She liked his sister. A good sign.

When they'd finished breakfast, he insisted on looking at Katie's cut. "I'll give you a complete tour of the house afterward as a bribe," he said when she continued to hesitate.

That captured her interest and she relented. Faster than he would have expected. Obviously, she wanted to see the house.

They returned to his room so she could change into something that would allow him access to her calf. She hurried into the bathroom and closed the door with a solid click and when she reemerged, she had Tanya's pajama pants on again.

"On the couch," he ordered with a shake of his head. He made a point of brushing against her when she passed him and reveled in her sharp intake of breath. Teasing her was more fun than he could have imagined. Not as much fun as the ultimate result of all this teasing, but still a nice appetizer. "Roll the material up over your knee," he said as he ducked into the bathroom for his first aid kit.

"Yes, sir. Whatever you say, sir."

Her mumbled, sarcastic response lacked only the salute. He was also positive he wasn't supposed to have heard her. He shook his head, continually surprised by her ability to amuse him. She was going to be an excellent partner.

So long as she willingly stayed.

KATIE ROLLED THE COTTON MATERIAL OF THE PAJAMAS UP OVER HER knee and waited on the couch for Eric to return. The thought of his hands on her leg made her head spin, but there was no avoiding it. He'd badger her until he got his way. And since she didn't want the cut to get infected and slow her down any more than it already had, she knew she needed it looked at again.

Then she'd get the rest of the tour she wanted. And hopefully more questions answered. The whole nightmare thing had thrown her off her game this morning. She'd spent breakfast observing him and his sister, the way Mrs. Patterson puttered around them and ruled the kitchen with an iron fist. But Katie hadn't really asked much.

Now it was time to get back to work. The storm was still too strong. She couldn't go anywhere yet. But that could end at any time. She couldn't afford to waste this opportunity. Or forget why she was here in the first place.

She was bouncing her still covered leg impatiently when he returned and kneeled down in front of her. That position again. Her imagination veered into dangerous territory, things she really didn't need to be thinking about when the memory of his naked torso was still so fresh in her mind. Maybe if he sat on the couch next to her, her leg in his lap…

Nope. That would be just as bad.

Nearly groaning out loud, Katie had to admit, no matter what, having Eric touch her was never going to be easy on her libido.

He removed the bandage with care and gently probed the wound. To her surprise, his touch was efficient and detached, the touch of a doctor. Her shoulders relaxed a fraction.

"How's it look?"

"Good. But I'm going to replace the stitches since you got these wet yesterday. There doesn't appear to be any infection, no swelling or reddening." After removing what was left of the butterfly stitches, he sprayed disinfectant over the cut again.

Katie clenched her teeth but there was remarkably little sting. She glanced down. The injury did look better. "You do good work," she commented.

"I'm glad you approve."

He didn't look up as he started to apply new stitches, so Katie stared at the top of his head. He had nice hair. She was sure it would feel soft and thick as she ran her fingers through it. The fantasy kept her so occupied, she nearly jumped when he finally looked up from his work.

"Finished already?" She cleared her throat when her voice squeaked.

"All done."

Her heart thumped wildly. His expression was dark and tempting and entirely too knowing.

"I'll just change, shall I?" she said. "And then we can take the tour."

Geez, her English phrasing was creeping out. She'd made an effort to squash that tendency since moving back to the US because she didn't want people to think she was putting it on. But after three years in London, and all the years before that with her father, that accent was the flow of language she reverted to when she was edgy.

And Eric Logan made her edgy.

She returned to the bathroom. Being in pajamas, even pajamas that covered her completely, made her feel a little too…relaxed. Especially in Eric's bedroom while Eric was there. She wouldn't have thought the tension she felt in his presence yesterday could get any more intense, but somehow her adventurous night had left her even more aware of him. In the light of day, she couldn't help remembering the sheer power it must have taken to slam Tanya's door nearly off its hinges. And the thought of him coming to her rescue was doing shocking things to her system, turning her on in a primitive way she'd have been embarrassed to admit even to her sister. What the hell would she do if he actually kissed her for real?

Probably combust.

She buttoned the top of her slacks and tried not to think about that possibility. Right now, she was due a full tour of this mysterious mansion and would continue the interview. If she could just keep her mind on that, she might get through the day *without* falling into bed with him.

She stepped back into the room and looked at Eric, big and strong and sexy, and let out a sigh. Or maybe not.

CHAPTER FOURTEEN

The tour actually was very distracting in the end. Eric led her up to the third floor and into another wing of the house. These corridors were still lavish but much more conservatively decorated than those in the family wing. She studied the art and décor, asking about different pieces as they passed, and questioned the different feel to this floor.

"On the rare occasion we have parties that include people outside the family, we bring them here," Eric explained. "So we couldn't let Rea do the decorating."

She chuckled and followed his outstretched arm through a pair of large double doors, stepping into a huge open space. "An actual ballroom?"

She paced around the hardwood floors, polished to a reflective shine, admiring the three giant crystal chandeliers, beautifully carved coving and gold detailed wallpaper. At evenly spaced intervals along the interior wall, floor to ceiling decorative mirrors added to the spacious feel of the room. French doors took up the entire outer wall, adding light and spectacular views of a lushly landscaped garden. The wrought iron railing lining the white stone balcony glistened in the slashing rain.

"In the summer, we leave the doors open," Eric said, "to keep this place from getting too hot."

"That must be beautiful." She crossed to the windows, glancing out at the gray day and taking in a new view of the surrounding woods. The thick collection of trees was closer to this side of the house, starting at the base of the wide ridge that made up the garden. Off to her left she spotted a three-tiered ornamental waterfall cascading down a natural rocky hill into a decorative pool. Statues she couldn't quite see in detail filled the center of the pool, spewing ribbons of water against the rain.

Such a shame the weather was so rotten or she would have loved a tour of the grounds. If he'd give her one. Though, if the weather wasn't so rotten, she might not still be here. More mixed bag luck.

"When was the last time you entertained here?" She wandered over to the bar taking up one side of the room, curious to see if they kept it stocked.

"A while ago. Maybe six, seven years."

"Why so long?" Behind the bar she saw glasses and spigots for pouring beer, but no actual bottles of anything. Good evidence that either the room hadn't been used in a while, or the Logan's kept their alcohol elsewhere.

"We've been traveling a lot in recent years, and most of the family is scattered. If we all got together in one place at one time, we'd probably have another party."

"Did you have parties a lot in the years before everyone scattered?"

"Often enough. A few times a year. Mostly for birthdays. Occasional solstice and equinox parties."

She made a mental note of the fact they celebrated the turning of the seasons. But no mention of more typical American holidays. Since the Logan's were a very international family, she supposed that made sense.

"Lot of birthdays to celebrate with so many siblings," she said. "Does everyone get a separate party?"

In her family, separate parties had been a requirement despite the fact that she and her brother had birthdays quite close to each other.

"Most of the time," he said, his expression softening with memories. "Combining them rarely worked out well."

She could relate. "Where is everyone now?"

"My mother is in Vienna, as I mentioned. Three of my brothers are in Europe. I have a sister living with her husband in Canada. One sister and one brother are in China this month, but they'll be heading back to Europe before the winter solstice. Tanya is in South America, Brazil the last time she was in touch. My sister Rebecca is somewhere on the west coast, but I'm not sure where. One brother is in Oregon. And my other two brothers are working as rangers in Yellowstone National Park."

"Wow, they really are scattered."

"We tend to roam. Rea's only been back in the US for about six months."

"How long will she stay?"

He shrugged as he crossed to an electronic panel against the wall near the bar. "Depends on how long she can stand to be in one place."

"And you're here until your business is done. Then where?" Curiosity had her following him to the panel.

"I don't know yet. It will depend on…some things." He pressed several buttons and turned a knob. Quiet, classical music filled the room.

He faced her and Katie was suddenly aware of the mistake she'd made getting this close to him. She'd been thoroughly distracted by the room, the interview. Suddenly, she was aware of *him* again.

"Do you dance?" he asked in a quiet voice.

"A little. I can waltz. My father taught me."

"Would you dance with me, Katie?"

She must have nodded, although she hadn't intended to, because Eric wrapped one arm around her waist and took her right hand in his. The first few steps were awkward as she remembered how to move through the pattern—it had been years. But then they fell into a rhythm, sliding in slow, measured circles around the room. With each turn, Eric pressed the small of her back a little tighter, easing her closer until their bodies were flush, thighs touching, her breasts flattened against the hard planes of his chest.

Katie's heart pounded. The logical part of her brain was screaming, *Too close! Too close!* But the irrational part was whispering an insidious chant of its own. *Not close enough. Not close enough.*

Eric stroked his fingers in tiny circles against the small of her back, somehow managing to move her shirt aside enough to give him access to skin. That hot touch shot need straight through her, making her stomach tighten. She tilted her face up to his, savoring the brush of his breath across her lips. When his hand spread across her back so he spanned a large expanse of her skin, she shivered.

Ask him something. Get this back to business! "Two of your brothers work as rangers? I thought all the siblings worked for Logan International?" She was appalled to hear how breathy her voice sounded. But at least the questions were focused and to the point.

And not, *How soon can you get me naked*?

"Everyone works for the family business in some capacity. But most of my brothers and sisters have other interests as well."

His voice was deep and his answer distracted, as if he weren't really thinking about his response. His gaze never wavered from hers.

She swallowed. "Do they all have outside jobs?"

"No."

She tried to concentrate, to hold his stare and remain unaffected. But the feel of his hands on her, his body against hers, his warm breath so close to her mouth, was too much. She couldn't think.

She looked over his shoulder, hoping that would help. "Did you have another job before taking over Logan International?" She caught their reflection in the mirrors as she spoke. They looked good together. That surprised her enough to make her miss a step. She recovered with an embarrassed apology. Then asked her question again to cover her blunder.

"I've had several…interests outside the business."

"Of course, you were a medic. What else?"

"Archeology. Mythology."

"You worked in those fields? Or just pursued them as a hobby?"

She tried again to look him in the face, to pretend the feel of his hand on her back wasn't driving her insane. But the heat in his eyes only made matters worse. And when their hips bumped, she realized she wasn't the only one affected by their dance.

"I've studied both extensively," he murmured, his voice gravelly deep now.

The sound raised tingles all along her skin and made her pulse speed. When he tightened his hold, pressing her even closer so there was no way she could pretend he didn't have an erection, she caught her breath. She had to stop this, had to end the dance. But her feet kept sliding through the pattern. She clenched her hand on his shoulder, thrilling in the feel of hard muscle beneath her fingers.

Enough. Think of something else. Now!

In the ballroom mirrors, she focused on the reflection of rain rivulets running down the French doors, trying to regain some control of her thoughts. What had they been talking about? She had to think of something else to ask.

Instead, she watched the rain dribbling down the windowpanes, watched one particularly thick line of water creep across the glass, slowly elongating. Slowly getting thicker. And darker.

Awareness pricked the skin along her neck and chills shivered over her spine.

She blinked. A gray tentacle inched over the window. Joined by a second. And a third. Breathing hard, Katie stopped dancing, her gaze stuck on those three tentacles. When one tapped the glass, she gasped and spun around to face the French doors, dislodging Eric's hold.

"What? What is it?"

She ignored his urgent request as she caught a glimpse of gray disappearing above the door.

And then there was only rain.

"Nothing," she said after a moment. "Just my imagination."

"What did you see, Katie?"

His hands gripped her shoulders and she started to tremble. She couldn't have seen what she thought she saw. It was the middle of the day. And the thing she'd seen last night was a nightmare. Not real.

She'd just imagined the rain rolling along the glass looked like tentacles. That was all.

But as she stared at the slashes of water, she knew she hadn't confused those for something thick and solid. Something that moved to tap against the window.

Another prickle of apprehension, a moment of *knowing* teased her senses. Danger.

She didn't understand why or what posed the threat, but she knew they were in danger here. They had to leave.

"Just seeing things," she whispered when Eric's hands tightened.

"Like last night? Did you see the same monster?"

"No. Yes. No. Tentacles. Must have been the rain." She faced him, though it took a great deal of willpower to turn her back on those doors. Her stomach rebelled at the effort, but she swallowed and forced herself to breath calmly. "We should get moving, finish the tour."

He stared at her for a long moment. "Whatever you saw scared you," he stated after several long moments.

"Residual of the nightmare, that's all." She tried to smile and failed miserably.

He studied her a few beats longer, then he walked past her toward the French doors.

"Where are you going?" Panic bubbled up in her throat.

"To check outside."

She knew, in that nanosecond of time as she watched him step toward those doors, she *knew* if he walked outside, he'd be hurt, maybe even killed.

"No!" Rushing forward, she grabbed his arm. Despite his superior strength, her adrenaline and his confusion gave her an advantage, and she physically pulled him away from the doors.

His confusion didn't last long, however. He stopped allowing her to drag him and stood stubbornly still. "What's wrong?"

"You can't go out those doors, Eric. Please. Let's just finish the tour." She started tugging him again, pulling him reluctant step by reluctant step away from danger. He glanced back once, but she jerked harder at his arm to keep him moving.

Her heart was pounding so hard it hurt when she finally got him back into the hall. Fear so overwhelmed her, she continued to drag him farther and farther down the corridor until he finally stopped, refusing to take another step. He glanced back toward the ballroom, which sent another rush of terror through her, but when she opened her mouth to protest, he raised a hand for silence.

"What just happened in there, Katie? And don't tell me that had anything to do with a residual of your nightmare."

She dropped her hold on his arm. "Nothing," she lied. "I just wanted to finish the tour."

"Katie…"

She licked her lips at the warning in his voice. "I didn't want you getting wet. That's all. Not over a blip in my imagination."

He gripped her shoulders and gave her a little shake. The move irritated the hell out of her, snapping her out of some of her shock.

"Hey! Stop that." She swatted at his hands and scowled.

He dropped his hold but not his intensity. "Was it the same as in the atrium?" he asked, slowly, with a great deal of deliberation.

"What the hell are you talking about? I didn't see glass cracking, if that's what you're asking?"

"You know what I mean. You knew before the glass cracked that we were in danger."

"No." She straightened her shoulders.

"Yes. And just now… Your reaction was too extreme. Tell me the truth, Katie. What just happened in there?"

"Nothing, damn it. I got a little freaked out by my imagination. That damned nightmare must have left me more edgy than I thought. And now I'm embarrassed about it. Okay? Are you happy?"

"That wasn't embarrassment making you pull me from the room."

"Of course it was. Can we just drop it?"

"No."

"Why?"

"I want the truth."

"Tough," she spit out before she realized she'd just given herself away, as much as admitting to the fact that she was lying. She snapped her mouth closed, pressing her lips together. But too late. And she was too flustered to cover her lapse.

Damn him. Damn him and that nightmare and this house and her interview. And damn her fucking psychic sense.

She spun away from him, blindly stalking back down the hallway, in the opposite direction from the ballroom. Trying to escape her own foolishness.

He caught her before she'd gone ten steps and swung her around to face him, his hands clenching her shoulders again. "Enough of this. You're in my house, under my protection. If you lie to me, I can't keep you safe. Tell me what happened in there."

Anger, frustration, outrage, fear, and confusion all rose up to choke her. "You want to know what happened? I'll tell you what bloody well happened. I just saved your fucking life. That's what happened. Now let me go."

"How did you safe my life?"

She ground her teeth together and turned her gaze to the corridor walls, refusing to look at him. "If you'd gone outside, in that moment, something very bad would have happened to you."

"How do you know?"

She crossed her arms and refused to speak.

"Katie. How do you know?"

"I just knew all right," she snapped, shaking off his hands.

"You're psychic?"

She glared at his chin, then turned to stare at the wall again.

"You are, aren't you?"

"Don't be ridiculous. There's no such thing."

"And there's no such thing as monsters either," he said, his voice quieter now. "But you just saw one."

"No, it was…"

"If it was a nightmare, then how could it hurt me?"

"I don't know. Maybe you would have been struck by lightning and that's what I was—" She cut off the rest of her sentence, but she might as well have just said, *Yes, I'm psychic.*

She shook her head and turned her back on him. Years of lying and keeping this secret, years of learning how to hide her *knowing*. And in less than twenty-four hours, he had her admitting to something no one but her immediate family and one or two close friends actually knew. And her family mostly chose to pretend her psychic sense didn't really exist. How the hell had she gotten into this mess? How did this all get so beyond her control so fast?

She dragged in a shuddering breath and hugged herself. She felt him close behind her, near enough to touch but not actually touching.

"Katie." He whispered her name, both plea and reassurance in his tone.

She shook her head again and closed her eyes. "I just know things. Okay. It's not a big deal. But… Sometimes… Sometimes, I know those things before they actually happen." There it was, stated starkly and with no more lies. He could think what he wanted about her now. Did she really care if Eric Logan thought she was a crazy woman?

She opened her eyes and let out a low sigh. Unfortunately, yes, yes she did.

A long moment passed in silence. The tension drew painfully on her nerves and had her clenching her teeth and hunching her shoulders. She didn't want to face him, to see his derision and disbelief. But that made her feel like a coward. So she turned to confront him head on. He could think what he wanted of her. She'd just saved his stupid life.

Instead of the scorn she'd expected, though, he was looking at her with a strange expression she couldn't interpret. He wasn't smiling, or scowling, or mocking her. He stared, and she almost thought maybe that was wonder in his eyes.

Still trying to understand what his silence meant, she was startled into a gasp when he lifted a hand and cupped her cheek.

"You saved my life," he whispered.

And then he leaned down and kissed her.

The gentle brush of his lips stopped Katie's breath for a heartbeat. Unlike the night before, however, he didn't pull back after a teasing touch. In the time it took Katie to suck in a gulp of air, Eric wrapped her in a tight embrace, angled his head so their lips were perfectly aligned, and deepened the kiss. She had one moment to consider that this was a supremely bad idea. One instant to try and remember why she wasn't supposed to be kissing him. But the feel of his mouth against hers and the strong arms circling her waist, coupled with her emotional upheaval, pushed all other thought aside.

She surrendered with a sigh.

Her acceptance seemed to spur him on, encouraging him to deepen the kiss further. Her lips parted willingly, eagerly under his urgings. And when his tongue swept into her mouth, she met him in a kind of desperation she'd never known before. Like she'd been waiting for this man and this kiss for her entire life.

She wrapped her arms around his waist and squeezed against him, needing to feel his heat and strength, needing to assure herself he was all right. And she was all right. Not crazy. Not a fool.

He groaned, a sound she swallowed, and tightened his hold. Their tongues tangled and clashed, their mouths devouring each other. Katie savored every second. Her hands rose to his shoulders, then she burrowed her fingers through his hair, tightening her hold as need rushed through her. She'd never experienced a kiss this potent before. She wasn't sure anyone had ever kissed her with such intensity, such urgency. And she didn't want it to end.

So when he eased back, leaving her panting and disoriented, she pulled his mouth back to hers and kissed him again. He didn't resist. In fact, he grew even more desperate, raising one hand to the back of her head to hold her more firmly in place. His arm around her waist tightened, fusing their bodies together. She thought she might have moaned, but she was too caught up in the passion he'd sparked to care. Her head spun, her body was on fire, and her entire being focused on the taste and texture of his lips, the play of his tongue against hers, and the sweet strength of his embrace.

She was weak-kneed and dizzy by the time he lifted his mouth again. For a long moment, the only sound filling the hallway was their harsh breathing. She watched his desire churn in the dark depths of his gaze and wondered if he saw the same thing when he looked at her.

Then abruptly, he stepped back, dropping his hold and letting cool air swirl between their bodies. She swayed at the sudden change and had to brace a hand against the wall to keep from falling. She raised her brows in question. She'd have been offended if not for the continued sound of his ragged breaths.

"We should continue the tour," he said.

His voice was raspy and deep. At a glance, she could tell the erection she'd felt against her stomach hadn't subsided. He was quite obviously still as affected as she was. Yet he wanted to finish the tour? Disoriented and still combating the heat racing through her blood stream, she couldn't think clearly enough to argue with him.

Frowning slightly, she nodded. "Sure. Lead the way."

Eric worked at slowing his breathing as he escorted Katie toward the music room. One kiss. All it had taken was one kiss.

And he was hers to control.

He'd thought he was the hunter in the game they'd been playing, chasing her toward his trap. Only she'd turned the tables on him. And now he was well and truly caught.

Since the first time he'd heard her voice, in that instant when he'd known what she was to him, his only thoughts had been to convince her to stay, so he would no longer have to face the horrific death he was cursed to experience if he couldn't keep this one woman with him. He hadn't considered how his own feelings might get away from him. It never crossed his mind that she would end up having such power over him. Oh, he recognized her power to break his curse. He just hadn't considered the sway she would hold over his very soul.

Now, with just a single kiss, he was finished. He was hers, plain and simple. In the space of five minutes, she'd saved his life and captured him completely.

For reasons beyond all logic, he wasn't bothered by this abrupt change in their positions. Glancing down at her profile, seeing the flush in her cheeks and the slight frown tugging at her luscious lips, he accepted that this woman would control his life from this moment on.

There were worse things that could happen to a man.

CHAPTER FIFTEEN

As Eric ushered Katie into the music room, he caught the scent of her hair and found himself breathing deeper, just to hold the smell with him longer. She made a show of looking around the instrument-packed space, but he could tell she wasn't really seeing the splendor before her. Her distraction pleased him on a very basic level.

It also made resisting another kiss more difficult.

But there were windows in this room, and it was on the same side of the house as the ballroom. So he stayed near the hidden panel by the door, the one housing a range of weapons suitable for killing monsters. Similar hidden panels were in almost every room and corridor of the house. The Logans were monster hunters. You never knew when you might need a handy sword.

He alternated between watching the window and watching Katie, though it was difficult looking away from her. But he didn't want her hurt or even scared again. Not now. There'd be time later for her to learn the grim reality of his life. Right now, he wanted her thinking about his kisses.

The knowledge that Katie was psychic helped settle some of his worries. If she was used to the unusual, she'd be more likely to accept his real nature and that of his family. She'd hated admitting to her talent, and he couldn't blame her. Society was frequently unkind and derisive to people with her abilities. Little did she realize she'd stumbled into a family whose own unusual attributes made a small thing like being psychic seem normal.

With another glance at the window, his gaze moved inevitably back to her. She reached out and ran her finger over the strings of a violin. The gesture caught his full attention. Images of her stroking that same finger over him made his heartbeat quicken. A fantasy he couldn't resist played out in his imagination as he watched her circle the room —Katie naked, in his bed, her fingers teasing down his chest, over his abdomen, and up the length of his cock, her gaze hot and focused as she licked her lips. At that moment, Katie did lick her lips, and Eric groaned quietly.

She wandered back in his direction, flashing him a distracted smile. "Beautiful room. Who in your family plays?"

"We all play something, some of us better than others."

"Which instrument is yours?"

"The violin."

Her eyes widened, and he knew she was remembering the instrument she'd stroked just moments ago. He'd have given up all the money in his sizable estate to know what she was thinking in that instant. Because if her thoughts were even remotely close to his own, he was going to drag her into the nearest room and fuck her until neither one of them could move.

Her proximity made his pulse pound. He caught her scent the closer she got and it sent a hot rush of excitement through him. The memory of her lips against his, the taste of her mouth, the teasing dance of her tongue with his. He tried to look away to check the windows again and couldn't. She was getting closer and he couldn't think of anything else but touching her, kissing her one more time.

He forced himself to look at the windows, to do his job and protect her. Nothing but water slid over the glass.

When she started to pass him, heading back into the corridor, he caught her arm and jerked her against his chest. He couldn't stop himself. He needed the contact more than he needed breath. One hand tangled in her thick hair, as soft and silky as he'd anticipated, and his other arm tightened around her waist.

"I just need… One more…"

He dropped his mouth to hers again, teasing her lips apart with his tongue as he kissed her. She moaned quietly, the sound charging his system. Tightening his hold, he kissed her deeply for another few moments, then released her and walked back into the hall.

She tripped out after him, looking mussed and confused as she blinked rapidly. Her lips were red from their kisses, and her eyes were slightly glazed. She looked so deliciously rattled.

The hunter in him recognized another game. Though he'd lost the first round to her, and it wasn't a loss he regretted in the least, the thrill of playing again fired his blood. As a distraction from her earlier fear, he couldn't think of a better, or more enjoyable, plan. And if he won this round, he'd be able to make some of his earlier fantasies come to life a lot sooner than he'd anticipated.

She might have captured him body and soul, but he intended to make her so desperate for him, she'd have no choice but to stay.

KATIE FOLLOWED ERIC DOWN THE HALL INTO ANOTHER ROOM, THIS ONE held a small stage and chairs. A performance area of some kind. Under ordinary circumstances, she'd be fascinated, but at that moment, all she could think about was Eric's mouth on hers. And all the other places on her body she wanted his mouth.

Flicking a glance toward the windows, she moved around the room. Rain still slid across the panes, but she was careful not to stare too long. She forced herself to take in the rich carpets, opulent chandelier, polished wood of the stage. She felt Eric following her around the room with his gaze, but he remained near the door, waiting. Something about the gesture was reassuring, though she couldn't put her finger on precisely why.

"Did your family put on performances? Or was this for invited artists?" she asked, trying to force focus.

"A little of both."

"Concerts or theater? Or both?"

"A little of both."

She wanted to roll her eyes, but instead asked, "Did you ever perform?"

"I did. In a few concerts."

"For more than family?" She'd have liked to have seen that.

"No. Just family."

She wasn't surprised by his answer. For some reason, she had a hard time picturing him putting on a show for others. He was too controlled, too still. Rea, on the other hand, she could picture on stage. "When was the last time this room was used?"

"Years ago. I can't remember exactly."

So she wouldn't be getting a showing any time soon. "Before or since the last ball?" She hated bringing up the ballroom because the thought of the windows, the rain, the tentacles rose up to color her vision. But she couldn't let fear prevent her from doing her job.

"Well before the last ball."

"So more than six years at least."

"At least."

She did a final turn around the room, avoiding even looking at the windows. Then she walked back to him. Her heart started pounding a little harder. Fear might not interfere with her job, but lust was definitely causing her problems. As she neared him, she wondered if he'd try to kiss her again. Try? She snorted under her breath. No trying necessary. If he pulled her in, she'd go willingly. She should probably attempt to resist, but the closer she got, the harder it was to remember why.

"What do you think?" he asked, gesturing her back into the hallway.

"Impressive."

He nodded and led her to another room. Masking her disappointment took effort. Stupid to think he'd start kissing her every time she left a room.

This time he kissed her going into the room.

One moment he was holding a door open for her, the next she was in his arms with his lips demanding response from her. She pressed close, kissed him eagerly, and then found herself released and freed to explore. She looked around without actually seeing a single thing. For the span of several minutes, she simply could not think.

They left and headed to yet another door.

Halfway there, he spun her around, and muttered, "Again."

He kissed her quick and hard, his lips the most delicious temptation. She responded instinctively. She didn't have much of a choice. When his mouth covered hers, she fell headlong into his kiss. Then as suddenly as it had started, he let her go and ushered her forward with a hand at the small of her back.

Dizzy, Katie stumbled along as he continued the tour and she continued to stare at the various rooms only half seeing them. She had vague impressions of a sitting room, a library, what she thought might be a smoking room. And she did attempt to ask questions in each place. But by the next room, she barely remembered what she'd asked or the answers he'd given. Eric's randomly timed assaults kept her distracted and on alert.

He stopped and kissed her suddenly, unexpectedly, again and again, each time releasing her and continuing on as if unaffected. Except she knew he was. She could feel his erection every time he pulled her close. Somehow, though, he managed to continue a regular conversation, answering her questions, pointing out features in the various rooms, even asking a few questions of his own. She made an effort to continue with her job, and waited on edge for his next kiss.

Sometimes, he went several rooms, drawing out the suspense until she thought she might scream. Then he'd dive in for an embrace that left her weak and wanting. Before walking on.

Torture. He was torturing her.

She gazed around yet another room, this one filled with exercise equipment, and realized just how precisely torture described this game. Like dripping water torture, only with kisses. Her stomach bunched in anticipation and impatience, waiting for his next move. Not knowing when the next erotic attack would come was enough to make her crazy.

He kissed her again on the way out of the weight room, walked another few feet down another hall and pulled her close. The taste of him was like a drug. She wrapped her arms around his neck and held him close as her body wound tighter with need. He groaned into her mouth and his hands clenched her waist. A moment later, she found herself pressed up against the wall, standing on her toes as he ground his hard cock against her lower abdomen.

Oh yes, that's what she wanted. Him out of control and as desperate as she was. She rolled her hips against his, satisfaction sweeping through her when he made another guttural sound and took her ass in his hands, holding her in place.

Yes, yes, yes! Her body screamed for more. What logic she'd had earlier in the tour had abandoned her completely. His torture method had worked. She was beyond desperate now. All she could think about was finding a room with a bed and tumbling him onto the soft mattress, and doing all the wicked things his kisses promised.

His hands clenched tighter on her ass, and Katie moaned. Much more of this and they'd have to stumble into the nearest room, bed or no, because she wanted to touch more of that hot, firm skin she'd come into contact with last night. She wanted to explore every inch of him, first with her hands, then with her mouth. But she wanted privacy, not a corridor where anyone could come across them.

And yet, even knowing they could be caught at any moment, she couldn't stop kissing him, couldn't stop running her hands over his back and shoulders, into his hair, over his chest. She was a woman possessed, and Eric Logan was her possessor.

Then abruptly he pulled away, took her hand, and continued the tour.

Katie couldn't believe it. She could barely walk, she wanted him so badly, and he was moving on as if she hadn't pulled his shirt from his trousers or mussed his neat hair. His gate was a little stiff, understandably so given his very obvious arousal. But he seemed able to ignore the state of his body and return to the convivial host at will.

And that just infuriated her! Why wasn't he about to burst? Why wasn't he dazed and needy and confused? How could he just…stop?

She opened her mouth to demand answers but held her tongue

when the absurdity of her situation sank in. Less than twenty-four hours ago, she'd been determined to turn down any effort on his part to seduce her. Now she wanted to demand an explanation for why he wasn't pushing her clothes aside and fucking her against the nearest convenient wall? How utterly embarrassing.

And, she realized suddenly, likely exactly what he wanted. Her begging him to take her to bed. She'd have no excuse then, would she? Her professional objectivity would be compromised, and she'd have no one but herself to blame.

Not that her objectivity wasn't already a faint memory.

Her gaze narrowed as he ushered her into yet another room, this one a guest suite. She had to put an end to this now. Be firm and say no. She could resist him.

Or so she thought right up to the point that he pulled her close and kissed her again. Her brain turned to mush, her body melted, and her hands clung to his shoulders. God, this was so good, he tasted so bloody good. Her knees actually started to tremble, and she knew the only reason she was still standing was the hard arms holding her upright. A guest suite. Was there a bed in here? Could the torture be over? She sure as hell hoped so.

Then to her utter amazement, he lifted his mouth again, stepped back and said, "Are you ready for lunch?"

Her legs gave out and only his quick reaction kept her from hitting the floor hard. He gripped her arms long enough for her to get her footing, though she still trembled in reaction, then he released her and raised his brows. Not a seductive, knowing expression. A bloody polite, inquisitive look! When she didn't answer because she was too stunned to get past his lack of reaction, he tilted his head down in inquiry.

"Lunch? If we don't get there before Rea, there won't be much food left."

"Yeah, sure, lunch."

The last thing she wanted was food. She wanted Eric! She wanted to feast on him for the next several hours, and then maybe a few more hours after that. What had he done to her? She couldn't think straight.

She couldn't remember why she had to maintain distance between them. Hell, she could barely remember why she was in his house.

He set a hand to her lower back, the gesture causing her body to quiver again, and ushered her from the room. She let him lead her to the kitchen without paying any attention to her surroundings.

Why was she here again? As they neared the kitchen and a delicious aroma reached her, her brain turned back on. Bugger it, she was here to do a job, to study his house and learn as much about him as was necessary to write a compelling article. She wasn't here to bed the interviewee.

But his touch kept her so aware of him, his heat washing over her back, she couldn't force her thoughts back to work. Warmth suffused her face as they entered the kitchen and Geraldine Patterson pursed her lips. The woman could not possibly know what they'd been doing on their tour, but their close proximity, Eric's touch, must have given her a hint.

Mortified, Katie stepped away from him and mumbled, "Something smells good."

Geraldine grunted. "Rea's been here already. I'm working on a second batch of stew and the bread rolls are nearly done." She gestured to the long wooden table where they'd eaten breakfast. "Sit. You'll want to eat before Rea comes back."

"She'll be back? I thought she ate already?"

"That's never stopped her before," Eric said. He stepped around her and took a seat at the table.

When she hesitated, he gestured to the seat across from him with a polite nod. She sat quickly, diverting her attention from Eric's barely perceptible smile to the big windows dominating the kitchen. They sat so they were both at the end of the table farthest way from those windows. She finally realized that in the time he wasn't torturing her with kisses, Eric had also been keeping her away from windows. She'd been so distracted she'd stopped noticing them.

Now, the image of those gray tentacles came back to haunt her. Swallowing, she watched the rain for a long moment. Waiting.

Nothing happened. She took a deep breath and tried very hard to convince herself the whole thing had been her imagination. After her nightmare last night, after the entire day yesterday, it was only reasonable for her to have strange daydreams. But as Geraldine put bowls full of meat and potato stew on the table in front of them and a plate stacked with warm rolls, Katie couldn't shake the sensation that she really had seen something. She knew in that way of hers *something* had been on the balcony outside the ballroom. And that something was a threat.

She caught Eric staring at her as she dipped her spoon into her bowl.

"Are you okay?" he asked. "You went a little pale just now."

"Did I? I guess I was just remembering my nightmare."

"You were thinking about the ballroom again," he said without hesitation.

"What happened in the ballroom?" Rea asked as she bound into the room and dropped into a seat at the table. She snatched a warm roll before Eric could bat her hand away and turned a charming grin on Geraldine. "Don't suppose there's a little more for me, Mrs. Patterson?"

Geraldine grinned indulgently and placed an already full bowl of stew in front of the petit woman. Katie realized that was the first time she'd seen the cook smile.

"So what happened in the ballroom?" Rea asked again as she started eating.

"Nothing," Katie said.

"Katie thought she saw something," Eric said at the same time.

Katie glared at him. The last thing she needed was for another Logan to think she was crazy. She realized suddenly he might tell his sister about her psychic abilities too and her stomach dropped. For some reason, she had assumed he'd keep that to himself. He hadn't been surprised. He hadn't even seemed to mind. But she sure as hell didn't want to share the news with the entire world. Admitting the truth to him had cost her more than she'd ever wanted to pay.

"Like last night?" Rea was unfazed by Katie's glare and Eric's comment.

"No. I just… The rain… I'm just tired," she said, unable to come up with a reasonable excuse. Sister and brother exchanged a long look, another one of those that seemed to convey a multitude of information without a word being spoken.

Not that again. If he was allowed to have one of her secrets, she bloody well wasn't going to allow him to keep one of his own. Especially when it involved her nightmare.

But before she could speak, Rea said, "You shouldn't stay alone tonight."

"She won't be," Eric answered.

"I'll be perfectly safe on my own," Katie said, meeting both their gazes without flinching. "Maybe not in Tanya's room, but I'll be fine on my own in another room."

"No," Eric said.

"Yes," Katie returned.

"You think Katie will be staying in your room again tonight?" Rea asked. "Why?"

The suspicion in her voice made Katie frown. That better not be smug pleasure or her opinion of the younger woman was going to drop significantly.

"Because that's where she stayed last night and she was safe," Eric said. "She'll be perfectly safe there again."

"With you?" Katie and Rea asked at the same time.

Eric scowled. "If Katie prefers, I'll sleep in Nick's room next door. But it would be safer if I stayed with her."

"I doubt that," Katie mumbled.

"She'd be just as safe with me," Rea said. "Maybe even safer." She turned to Katie. "We could have a slumber party. We'll stay up all night talking. And then you won't have to worry about…nightmares. That'd be great fun, huh? I haven't stayed up all night talking girl-talk in ages."

Katie found it hard to be annoyed with Rea for long. Her enthusiasm was catching. The idea of getting no sleep wasn't quite so appealing. But she could probably get a lot of dirt on Eric from his sister.

She raised her brows. "That might not be a bad idea," she said after a moment. "But I really don't need a babysitter. I can sleep on my own."

"You'd be happier with company," Rea interjected. "We can camp out in the sitting room with wine and a fire and gossip all night."

Oh, she could definitely warm to that idea. Getting gossip about Eric and the rest of the Logans could make up for her disastrously unprofessional behavior this morning. And Rea was a fascinating subject all on her own. There was a lot of potential in having the young woman all to herself for an evening.

"No," Eric said, cutting into her thoughts.

Katie turned to stare at him. There was wariness in his gaze. He didn't want her "gossiping" with his sister. She was sure.

To stir the pot a little, she said, "Why not? It sounds like fun. And Rea's right. I probably shouldn't stay alone. I'm sure I won't have any nightmares if I have company."

"You will be staying in my room, and that's final."

"No. I will stay where I want to stay. If I want to camp in Rea's living room, I'll camp in Rea's living room. If I want a room to myself, I'll either have Gregory show me a room, or I'll find a way to get to my hotel."

She didn't want to leave yet. She still had a lot of information to gather. But she couldn't afford to let him order her around. If he thought he could get away with it in something as minor as this, he might think he could control other things she did—like what she included in her article. He had to know now she wasn't a pushover. Even if she had gone crazy for his kisses.

"You can't leave in this weather," he pointed out. "There's flooding everywhere."

"She's already decided, bro. She's staying with me."

"Rea." Eric's voice dropped half an octave in warning.

"Eric," she mimicked, not the least intimidated.

Katie watched the two siblings trying to stare each other down, the tension between them winding tighter. Finally, she puffed out a frustrated breath and said, "If it's such a big deal, I'll have Gregory point me to an empty room."

"No," they said in unison.

And they were so deadly serious, Katie was momentarily taken aback. They weren't playing games. They were adamant. Neither had any intention of leaving her in a room alone tonight.

Suspicion crawled along her spine. Were they simply worried about her having another nightmare? Or was it something more? Did they want to keep an eye on her so she couldn't search the house alone, as she'd intended to do last night? Or maybe there was some other problem they weren't admitting to her.

"Any reason I shouldn't be alone?" she asked, watching them both carefully.

"The storm," Rea said.

"You've been scared twice now," Eric said. "I want you comfortable here, not afraid to fall asleep."

"Why?"

That question made him pause and lean back in his chair. Katie guessed it wasn't the kind of question most people asked when given a reasonable and polite explanation. But why did he care if she was comfortable in his house or not? She was only here as long as the storm lasted, long enough to get her interview done. Then she returned to Manhattan, most likely never to see the man again.

"Because you're a guest," he said finally.

She *knew* that wasn't the real reason. He was hiding something. But what? The only way to find out was to dig, and to do that successfully, she had to go along with his excuse for the moment. When he wasn't on guard, she'd learn the truth.

"Fine," she said. "If you're both going to insist I have a babysitter, I'll stay with Rea and we'll gossip all night."

"Ha!" Rea grinned at her brother.

Eric scowled, Rea gloated, and Katie rolled her eyes. Brothers and sisters.

"I need to call my editor." She rose. "I'll be back in a minute."

"Are you gonna finish your stew?" Rea asked hopefully.

Katie glanced at her half-empty bowl. She'd been eating during the conversation but barely remembered. Since her stomach wasn't growling and she hadn't really noticed being hungry before lunch, she said, "Help yourself. I'm full."

She went to find a quiet corner of the house to make her call, somewhere without windows. Shivering, she settled into a corner next to a painting she suspected was a Monet and pulled out her mobile phone. Between Eric's kissing torture, the strange things she'd seen, and *knowing* there was more going on here than met the eye, her body was on high alert, waiting for the next shoe to drop.

Or the next tentacle to appear.

Suddenly, having company tonight seemed a very good idea.

CHAPTER SIXTEEN

Katie slid the disconnect on her phone and sighed. Her editor was thrilled at having one of her reporters stuck in a house with Eric Logan for the foreseeable future. As far as Mona was concerned, Katie had hit the motherload. She was expecting the best article to ever cross her desk.

Katie intended to deliver. But she had to figure out a way to get him to tell her more about the atrium. And the reason he and Rea didn't want her alone. She knew in her bones those two things were connected in some way. It could be as simple as they didn't want her searching the house tonight, getting lost, or stumbling across some big family secret. But her psychic senses were telling her it was something else. Something a lot more dangerous.

And where did her nightmare come into all this? Daymare, too, she reminded herself as she hugged her arms across her stomach. That was part of this as well. Eric hadn't been surprised by her seeing her nightmare in the daylight. And he should have been. He also hadn't been surprised by her psychic ability. What normal man didn't even blink at finding out a stranger in his home claimed to have psychic skills and was seeing monsters?

There was a lot more to Eric Logan than the billionaire businessman and playboy. She had to find out what.

Since no one had come looking for her yet, she took a moment to check her purse, ensuring her all her gear was where she'd left it, no missing notebooks or missing voice recorder. She couldn't take anything for granted at the moment.

When she returned to the kitchen, Geraldine was busy putting dishes in the dishwasher. Eric and Rea were gone.

"He said to meet him in the library where you were talking yesterday," the cook said without looking up.

"Thank you." Katie turned and went back the way she'd come, finding her way through the curving hallways to the library with only one wrong turn. Probably good her sense of direction wasn't horrible. They'd have had to send out a search party for her sister. The thought made her smile and her heart ache all at once.

Eric was standing with his back to her when she entered the library, looking out the window at the storm.

"What did your editor say?" he asked without turning.

"She said to come back when it's safe and not to rush."

"She's thrilled you're stuck here, isn't she?"

Katie smiled even though he couldn't see it. "Delighted."

He fell silent for a long moment. She waited where she stood, clenching her purse strap and wondering what had happened in the last twenty minutes to leave him so pensive. Surely he wasn't that upset about her staying with Rea. He could hardly expect her to actually sleep in his room again. Despite what happened this morning. Especially after what happened this morning!

There was no way they'd be able to sleep in the same room and not let something happen. Now that she wasn't so off balance from the bombardment of kisses, her sanity had returned, and she was determined—yet again—not to sleep with him. She couldn't afford the slip. And not just because it might influence her article or because she thought he would be using her. She couldn't go to bed with him because she was afraid more than her body would be affected by the experience.

After the silence stretched out longer than she could stand, she took a seat on the couch and set her equipment out on the coffee table. Then, "Are you okay?" As good a place to start as any. "Do you need to take a break from the interview? For work?"

"No, I've the whole day for you," he said, still without facing her.

"Then, should we get started?"

He nodded but continued to stare outside.

Though she wasn't getting any psychic sense of danger, watching him stand so close to the glass panes made her nervous. Telling him that would be entirely too revealing, though, so instead she asked, "Are you sure you're okay to continue right now?"

He finally turned. "Stay in my room tonight."

Her eyebrows rose. "Ehm…"

He crossed the room and stood over her. Katie found her heartbeat pounding hard for no real reason that she could pinpoint.

"Stay in my room tonight. I know you'll be safe there. This isn't some play to get you into bed." His lips twitched just a little. "Though if you invited me to share your bed, I wouldn't refuse."

Heat crept up her neck.

"More than anything," he said, his tone intense, "I want you close so I know you'll be safe."

"From what?" She narrowed her eyes as she studied him. "You weren't surprised upstairs when I said I'd saved your life. You believed me. But I don't even know what I saved you from. How can you accept so easily?"

He pursed his lips and glanced toward the cold fireplace. "I'm not sure how to answer that." He faced her again, a furrow between his brows. "My family… We're not… Something like psychic ability is not unusual to us."

Well, that was a tantalizing bit of information. "You have psychics in your family?"

If not for her own talents, she would have been more cynical of the claim. There were a lot of charlatans out there. But she had a hard time denying what she'd lived with all her life. She might not admit to it out loud or to other people, but she'd been forced to acknowledge her differences years ago. And that ensured she was at least a tad more open-minded about such things.

"Not quite," he said. "Although, there have been a few in the past. We're just…different."

"How?"

"Always the journalist."

"You brought it up. What makes your family so different from every other family? Besides bucket loads of money."

"Let's just say we have an easier time believing in things that other people refuse to accept."

"Why?"

He took a deep breath and walked back toward the window. "Why don't we get back to the interview?"

"I never went away from it. You're not going to answer this question?"

"Not yet. Soon. But…not yet."

Again it was on the tip of her tongue to ask why. Frustration gnawed at her. How could he start this conversation and not finish it? "You will tell me, though? Eventually."

He tilted his head in a slight bow, agreeing to her request. "I'll tell you everything eventually. In exchange for one concession."

Here it comes. This was where he asked her to keep his secrets out of her article.

"Stay in my room tonight. I'll sleep on the couch or in the next room. But I want you there tonight."

Since that wasn't the concession she'd thought he'd ask for, she didn't answer right away. Straightening against the couch back, she held his gaze for a long moment. He was serious and sincere. There was no seductive glint, no teasing curve to his mouth. Nothing but intensity and a degree of coiled watchfulness that reminded her of a caged animal.

She still wanted to know why, though. Why was she safer in his room than with Rea? What was he worried his sister would tell her? Then she realized if she agreed to his request, he was promising to answer those very questions. He said he'd tell her everything. Eventually. But still everything.

Not an opportunity she could afford to pass up.

"Okay. If you insist, and can convince your sister this is the right decision, I'll sleep in your room. But I'll take the couch." When he opened his mouth to speak, she held up a hand. "I'll explain the lack of chivalry to your mother if she ever finds out." That comment earned her one of his heart-stopping smiles.

"Fair enough," he said. "It goes against the grain, but if you insist, I won't argue. So long as you're there and I can watch over you."

The thought of a man as powerful and mysterious as Eric Logan watching over her sent a tiny shiver down her spine. Not from fear but from excitement. He made the act sound so intimate, like there was something more between them than just a job and lust.

Breaking eye contact before he could see her sudden need, she picked up her notebook. "Now that's settled, I'll just turn on the recorder."

He sat on the couch next to her as she flicked on her recorder. She refused to move away again, but the temptation was strong. After their morning, she was painfully aware of him physically, and that made concentrating on the job at hand infinitely more difficult.

Then she noticed him glance at the window. The gesture was subtle and swift, but in that instant, she knew he'd positioned himself so he'd have a full view of the windows. And she realized there was no way she'd be able to sit with her back to the storm after seeing those gray tentacles in the ballroom. The itch between her shoulder blades, the urge to keep glancing behind her, would be more of a distraction than trying to sit next to Eric.

She took a deep breath and settled sideways on the couch, facing him and putting a little more space between them in the process. When their gazes met, Katie's voice froze. The heat in his eyes made her pulse race. He looked dangerous and much too sexy. Suddenly, all she could think about was the torturous series of kisses he'd laid on her that morning.

She couldn't believe she'd actually agreed to share a room with him again. She was crazy. Had to be. Because she couldn't imagine sleeping in his room without crawling into bed with him. She'd agreed to share the lion's den. And the fact that she wasn't more afraid of that was enough to terrify her.

Clearing her throat, she switched on the recorder and started, asking things her editor had nudged her to uncover, mostly about his social life and wealth. She could tell by his slight smirk he knew those weren't her questions. But he answered nonetheless, for which she was grateful.

And she tried to ignore the way his gaze kept flicking to the window.

As the clock on the fireplace mantle chimed half past three, Katie flicked the recorder off, leaned back in her seat and sighed. "Why don't we take a little break?" She motioned to the blinking red light on her recorder. "I need to plug in the recharger."

Then she wanted to ask about his father. Those questions, the deeper, personal stuff she wanted to know, kept getting pushed off as other things came up during their conversation. But her journalistic instincts hinted that delving into his relationship with his father would open up a lot more about the real Eric Logan. And maybe even take them into some of those "eventually I'll tell you everything" topics.

"Do you want a drink?" he asked as she reached for her recorder.

"Don't go to any trouble." Even as she spoke a sneaky yawn escaped. She covered her mouth and grimaced. "Sorry. Busy night last night."

"How about some coffee?"

She gave in very easily. "Probably a good idea."

With a sound that might have been a chuckle, he rose. "I'll be right back."

She watched him leave, unable to resist staring at the way he filled out his trousers. When the door closed behind him, she blinked and shook her head. Staring at Eric's ass was not a good way to keep her mind on business.

Digging through her purse, she pulled out the recharger and cord, then plugged in and ensured her recorder was charging. Unconsciously, she glanced at the windows when the panes of glass trembled. The storm still raged, water slashing across her view of the manicured front lawns. A flash of lightning brightened the dark gray clouds. And Katie realized how dark the room had gotten in the last half hour. This time of year the sun would be going down in a couple of hours, but the clouds had left the afternoon extra gloomy.

She dragged her attention back to the task at hand, but even as she set her recorder and recharger back on the coffee table, her gaze returned to the window. A shiver crept along her spine, tingling the fine hairs at the nape of her neck. She swallowed.

Maybe she should go find Eric, help with the coffee?

A clap of thunder made her jump. Cursing under her breath, she glowered at her shaking hands. This was ridiculous. Now she couldn't be in a room alone without scaring herself? No wonder Eric and Rea were concerned about her staying by herself tonight. They were probably more worried about the state of her mental well-being than any real danger. She was starting to doubt her mental well-being, too.

She continued to tell herself she was acting silly even as the first tentacle slid across the windowpane she stared at. Stupid imagination, she thought. Nothing more. Another tentacle slithered into view, rising from beneath the windowsill and tapping against the glass.

Maybe this was post-traumatic stress. The therapist she'd seen after her sister's murder warned her PTSD could come back if she didn't deal properly with her feelings.

The tapping sound set her teeth on edge, even as more tentacles and gray, raged material climbed across the glass.

Katie stared, frozen in place, her brain almost numb. Not real. Things like that didn't exist. She was just seeing low lying clouds or thick fog. That's it, it was probably just fog.

A gray, skeletal face appeared from amidst the writhing tentacles covering an entire window. Sharp gray teeth flashed as a thin-lipped mouth pealed back into a rictus of a grin. A hissing sound filled the library, muted by the glass but still discernable. Two hands tipped with long sharp nails clicked at the glass on either side of the face. The grin widened impossibly, revealing a mouth full of dagger-like points. Black eyes stared at her, never leaving her face.

"Katie."

The sound of her name whispered through the air, making the hair on her arms rise. It's not real, she repeated over and over to herself. Just a hallucination. She needed to get back into therapy, that's all. Her imagination was creating a horror to compensate for repressed emotions about her sister's murder, emotions resurfacing because of the storm.

There was no such thing as monsters.

Three of the tentacles pointed toward the glass. The tips blinked open. Revealing black eyes.

Staring right at her.

And Katie screamed.

CHAPTER SEVENTEEN

Katie screamed again, the sound ripped from her throat, as she scrambled over the back of the couch. She heard the door behind her slam open, heard Eric call her name, but she couldn't look away from the eyes on the ends of those tentacles. The shear horror of it overwhelmed her.

The creature finally looked away, all of its eyes turned toward a spot over her shoulder. The eyes in its face narrowed, but its grin widened even more. It tapped the glass, as if in greeting, and then it was gone, so fast Katie gasped.

Breathing hard, she continued to stare at the window. Even when she felt Eric come up behind her, she couldn't look away. Terror swamped her mind.

"You saw that," she said, her voice harsh with fear. "Tell me you saw that."

"Katie…"

His hands landed on her shoulders and she jumped, then pulled free, scrambling to get farther away from the glass.

"Tell me you saw that!" She could feel another scream tickling her throat as hysteria raced through her blood stream.

He looked resigned but not surprised.

For just an instant, Katie thought she really had gone insane. His expression meant he knew she wasn't well and needed help. For just a split second, she thought, *He didn't see the monster. I am crazy.*

Then he said, "I saw it."

Her knees weakened, whether from relief or more horror she wasn't sure. She reached out and grabbed the nearest thing to her, a section of wall without bookshelves, to hold herself upright.

Eric took a step toward her, but she shook her head, warning him off. All her senses were on overload. She couldn't take one more thing or she would snap. With what remained of her strength, she stumbled from the library and ended up collapsing on the bottom step of the curved staircase in the foyer.

She stared at the marble columns dividing the foyer from the entryway as her breathing came fast and hard. Her heart hammered, her vision started to blur, and she couldn't seem to drag in enough oxygen. Dropping her head between her bent knees, she closed her eyes and concentrated on filling her lungs so she didn't pass out.

When she heard footsteps nearing, she opened her eyes. Eric's shoes stepped into view in front of her, but she didn't raise her head.

"So," she said, swallowing against her dry throat, her breath still coming out in pants. "So. There are real monsters in the world, then. Not just human monsters but actual…monster monsters."

"Yes," he said quietly.

"You knew last night that thing was real when I told you what I'd seen."

"Yes."

"And I'm not having nightmares or going insane."

"No, you're not."

She nodded and finally raised her head to meet his gaze. "Mind explaining how you knew all this?"

He sat on the step next to her and tried to take her hand in his, but she pulled away. She didn't need his touch right now. She needed answers.

"You look like you could use a drink," he murmured.

"I could. But you're going to explain this to me first."

"It has to do with my family's differences."

"The reason you were able to accept my…ability so easily?"

"Exactly. As you might have guessed, I've seen much more extraordinary things."

She snorted. "What was that?"

"It's called a grinluk. And it's a particularly nasty species of monster."

Her gut tightened. She wet her lips. "There's more than one species?"

"There are a lot of monsters in the world."

She stared at the inlaid marble floor. "I knew that already," she mumbled. She just hadn't known about…this.

When she glanced back at him and saw his narrowed gaze, she rushed to fill the silence, to keep him from asking questions of his own. "And how do you know about these creatures when the rest of the world doesn't? At least outside of nightmares and horror novels."

"My family hunts and destroys monsters. It's what we do."

He made the statement so simply, so starkly, that for a long moment Katie wasn't sure what to say. How did you respond to someone who'd just told you the world was a much spookier place than you ever thought it could be?

She kept silent for long enough that Eric reached for her again. "How about we go to my room, I'll get you a shot of whiskey, and you can ask me all the questions you need to?"

"Why?"

"Why…what?"

"Why are you going to tell me everything? I know you agreed to, but… Why? Aren't you afraid I'll write all this up in my article? Expose your family to the world?"

"The only place you'd be able to sell that article is to the tabloids and most people would assume you were crazy or making it all up."

She huffed out a breath, not quite a laugh. He was right. Hell, she'd come to that conclusion herself while she was trying not to pass out. "So then why go through all this with me?"

"You deserve an explanation after what you've just been through."

More half-truths. He'd agreed to tell her all this before she'd seen the…whatever the hell that was just now. So if he was going to tell her anyway… "Why not tell me last night? Why let me believe I was dreaming?"

He paused. Long enough Katie started to doubt he would answer.

Finally, he said, "You weren't ready to know yet."

"I thought I was losing my mind."

"Now you know you're not."

She launched upward, stood for a second, and then her knees wobbled and she nearly collapsed back to the stairs.

"Fuck," she hissed and grabbed the banister for support at the same time as Eric rose and gripped her around the waist. She tried to shrug away from him again, but he didn't release his hold this time.

"I didn't want you to have to deal with this yet," he said, his voice quiet and rough.

"Yet?"

"Let's go upstairs. You don't look very steady."

"I'm not. You've just told me fucking monsters are real!"

"The whiskey will help."

She frowned, frustrated at having so many questions still unanswered and yet knowing he was right about sitting somewhere comfortable for the long conversation they were about to have. And there was no way she was going back into the library.

"I hate whiskey," she said, wincing inwardly at the pout in her voice.

"Good. You won't have more than one."

"So not going to get me drunk tonight?"

His lip twitched as if he wanted to laugh but knew the timing would be bad. He was right, too. If he laughed in that moment, she would slug him.

"You need color in your cheeks, but you still need a clear head," he said.

"Fine. A shot of whiskey and then answers."

He nodded and stepped closer, his grip shifting from her waist to her shoulders. When he started to lift her up, she pulled back. "No. No carrying me around again like I'm some damsel in distress."

Looking her over with heat in his eyes, he said, "How about a dame in a dress?"

The bad joke and his blatant desire were almost enough to distract her. She let loose a short snort. "Ha, ha. Don't change the subject." She was a little worried if she laughed at his attempt to relieve the tension, her laugh would turn into hysterical tears. "I can walk up the damned stairs myself. You just lead the way and get me that nasty ass whiskey."

He nodded and stretched his hand out for her to proceed him. She didn't miss the worry in his eyes. As she used the banister to haul herself up the stairs on her still unsteady legs, she wondered what he was more worried about—her questions, his answers, or her sanity.

Personally, she was most worried about that last bit.

CHAPTER EIGHTEEN

Once settled on Eric's bedroom couch, Katie accepted the shot of whiskey Eric handed her, downed it in one burning gulp, and handed the glass back to him as heat charged through her blood stream. Within moments, the awful tasting liquid had done its job, chilling her nerves ever so slightly and warming her cold skin.

She sat on the end of the couch farthest away from the window, careful not to look outside. But Eric saved her the trouble by turning on a few lights to chase away a gloom that was close to nighttime anyway, then flicking the curtains closed.

"That thing, it's still out there. Why are we safer here than anywhere else in the house?" she said because she had to ask this question first.

"We're safe everywhere in the house. It can't get in. But it won't try to…scare you here while I'm with you."

"Why?"

"Because then it would have to fight me. And it's been avoiding that."

Katie closed her eyes, took a deep breath, and let it out slowly. When she opened her eyes, she said, "Okay, let's start from the beginning because none of this makes sense. Your family hunts monsters? Since when? And why?”

“For more than sixteen thousand years and because we were created to.”

Her eyebrows popped up at the date. “You…you haven’t been around that long. Have you?”

“Personally? No, thank the gods. I’m not sure I could take living for sixteen hundred centuries.”

“Yeah. I’d have to agree.”

“My family traces its roots back that far.”

“And who created your family?”

“The god En, with the help of his mentor and uncle, the god Pah.”

“Never heard of them.” She shifted to lean against the armrest so she could better see him as he explained what sounded more like a fiction plot than a real family history.

“Those are the earliest names we have for them. Those names were…eventually lost and the gods renamed, given different roles in different cultures. Pah became Enki in Mesopotamia for example. We were created thousands of years before those early civilizations developed writing for documenting their myths. Before that the Families’ story was recorded in…carvings. Bas relief. Have you heard of Göbekli Tepe? In Turkey?”

“Vaguely.” Nothing she could remember, though, since she’d heard the name on documentaries on science channels she’d kept on in the background after her sister’s murder. Shows she didn’t have to think about, but the sound comforted her.

“Some of what they’re uncovering there… The archeologists won’t realize, but they’re seeing some of the earliest records of our existence. The bas reliefs of the animals carved in stone…” He shook his head. “Anyway, we’ve been around a long time. The names of our gods were passed down through our Families, so these are the names we have for them. But you won’t find them recorded anywhere. They were assimilated into other cultures and their original stories lost. On purpose.”

“Why on purpose?”

"To protect us. And to protect humans."

"From the monsters?"

"In a way."

"Why did En and…Pah? Why did they create your family?"

He pursed his lips and glanced at the picture over his fireplace mantle. "There was a god called Ne. He was En's brother. Both children of the Earth Goddess, we call her Gia. Ne came to be known as a demon god, although he wasn't from a demon realm or anything like that."

She bit her lip, because she didn't want to derail him, but the question, "Demon realm?" crossed her mind.

Eric gave his head a distracted shake, as if pulling himself back to the story, too. "Ne led an army of demi-gods against humans. The Families referred to these demi-gods as demons back in the day. So Ne came to be known as a demon god. When Ne became Asag in early Mesopotamian mythology, he was still often referred to as a demon god."

"Sure. Of course." As good, if incomplete, an explanation as any for the demon god part. She was still curious about the demon *realms* stuff, but since that felt like a digression, she asked, "Why did Ne go after humans?"

"Jealousy. At least that's what we've been told. Humans were beloved by his brother En, and his mentor Pah. Ne thought they were a plague on the planet, and that Gia should never have allowed them to come into being."

"Harsh. Not…undeserved. But harsh."

Eric smiled a little. "En wanted to protect humans, so he led an army against Ne and conquered the demons. In retaliation, Ne resurrected the Slain Heroes and used them to create a multitude of monsters."

"Slain Heroes? How do you turn heroes into monsters?"

"That was just the name used to refer to them in mythology. They were actually a group of monsters who had been destroyed by En before the start of the war with his brother. When Ne resurrected them, they were eager for revenge and were happy to create more monsters to overrun the god's beloved humans."

"Okay…" Katie let that sink in. This all sounded more like a mythology lesson than anything relating to modern times. But Eric was answering her questions, so she'd keep asking more. "So, to fight the monsters, your family was created? Right? You said that's your job. Fight monsters. What's so special about you? You have superpowers or something?"

His mouth quirked up at one corner. "Not quite. But we are stronger, faster, more agile, and have better senses than an ordinary human. We live longer. If we aren't killed, of course."

"Of course," she said dryly.

"And we know monsters exist, which is a big advantage."

"Yeah." She narrowed her eyes at him. She could tell he'd left some things out of his explanation, but she wasn't sure what exactly. She wasn't even sure how to feel about this story. But monsters existed, at least one did anyway, so she'd keep asking questions. Hopefully, if she kept digging, she'd uncover the missing facts.

Her gaze strayed to his arm where it rested on the back of the couch. For a moment, the strong muscles and lean strength of his hand captured her full attention. It would be very easy to pretend none of this was happening. Monsters didn't really exist, Eric was telling her a story that had nothing to do with reality, and if she kissed him now, he would take her to bed. So easy to ignore what she'd seen downstairs and lose herself in passion.

But she needed to face this. She *knew* she had to, damn it. For her future, for her very life, she needed this information.

"Okay, you're faster than the average bear." She watched his eyes widen in a moment of shock that was quickly masked, and her own gaze narrowed. Interesting reaction. What did she say to cause it? "Any other special skills? Or is speed and strength it?"

"Mostly speed and strength. Some Family members have specific talents beyond that. But most of us, no."

He hadn't been looking directly at her when he answered. Another hint something was going unsaid. "For sixteen thousand years, your family has been hunting monsters and killing them. Is it like killing vampires or werewolves? Do you need special weapons? Silver?" Had she really just asked those questions in all seriousness?

"For the most part, we just have to remove a monster's head for it to die. Sometimes that's easier said than done."

She watched his face closely. He'd made that statement very carefully and his eyes had flickered at the mention of werewolves. And silver. Curiouser and curiouser. "How long lived are monsters?"

"Some species live for several centuries, some for a lifetime equivalent to a human being."

"And how many species are there?"

"Over the past few millennia, a lot. No one's sure exactly how many. We've driven some earlier species to extinction, but monsters evolve, interbreed. Some of the creatures that exist today didn't exist in the time of my ancestors."

"The…what did you call it, grin luck?"

That earned her a faint smile. "Grinluk," he pronounced. "That's a newer species, around for about a thousand years. They were one of the monsters who…used humans to evolve."

"Used?"

"Interbred. Mostly through force."

Katie shivered. "Ew." Bad enough creatures with dagger pointed teeth and tentacles with eyes on the tips existed. To be raped by one… She shivered again. "Have a lot of monsters…evolved this way?"

He shrugged. "A few. Though, the added humanity to the different species has had unexpected consequences."

"Like what?"

"Like some monsters aren't monsters anymore. They don't hunt, terrify, kill, and eat humans. They've evolved…compassion."

She tried to ignore the part about eating humans when she asked, "How do you know the difference? I mean, when you hunt one, how do you know if it's a 'good' monster or not?"

"We hunt the ones that are preying on individuals or communities of humans. The other kind, the 'good' ones… Most of them stay out of our way. A few of them even fight with us."

"Why haven't I ever heard of this? I've heard of werewolves, vampires, fairies, goblins, but nothing in any bedtime story even hints that there's a family of monster hunters out there. And most people would consider creatures like the grinluk nothing more than a nightmare."

"A state of affairs we go to a great deal of trouble to perpetuate." He raised his hand, palm up, and shrugged. "After what you've seen, what you've experienced in the last day, how do you think people would react if they knew the truth?"

She was going to have trouble getting near windows from now on. A constant undercurrent of fear would haunt her for years. She'd faced the human kind of monster before, but this... This was beyond horror, something she really would have preferred not to know about. Now, she'd never see the world the same way again. And she thought her world view couldn't get any bleaker.

"You're right," she said. "People would spend so much time living in fear, they'd never get anything done. Although, they might also help you kill these things. Make your lives easier."

"They would assume they could kill them all and then be safe. That's not possible. And if some still exist, there's always something to fear."

"Do you live in fear?"

He tilted his head to one side, holding her gaze this time. "Not of the monsters."

"What then?" Something in his voice, his expression caused her heartbeat to speed and her breathing to deepen. Intensity and desire mingled with something so surprising she was sure she was imagining it. She wanted to reach out then, touch his arm, see if she could read him and *know*. But he'd been a brick wall to her from the beginning. If she touched him now, he might misinterpret the gesture, and she'd never get the rest of the story. Hell, *she* might misinterpret the gesture and forget she had other things she needed to ask.

She waited in silence for a long moment before she realized he wasn't responding to her last question. "You don't want to tell me what scares you? Bit needlessly macho, that, don't you think?"

He huffed out a half-laugh. "I'll tell you all about my fears eventually. But right now, we're discussing the monsters. And I'm not afraid of them."

"Fine. Don't assume I'll forget to ask again."

"Never thought otherwise."

Flashing a reluctant grin, she searched for another good question about the creatures. The personal nature of the grinluk's behavior made her frown. "Why the hell is that thing trying to terrorize me? It must know who you are, right? You said it was avoiding a fight you. But it's not running away from the house of a hunter. It's busy trying to drive one of your guests nuts. Why me?"

"That's one thing I'm not entirely sure about. You're under my protection in this house. Scaring you could be a way to get at me, keep me off balance before an attack."

"But why attack? Isn't that a little suicidal given what you do? Shouldn't these things be avoiding members of your family?"

He sighed. "Yes, they should. And usually do."

"But...?"

"But recently, I might have given the grinluk reason to retaliate."

"What reason?"

"They have been known to be quite loyal to their allies. And their allies include more than just other grinluk. Recently, I had to...kill someone. I believe he might have been working with the grinluk."

"Another monster?" Katie hadn't actually thought about the fact that Eric was a killer. Somehow, destroying monsters didn't seem like "killing" the way her sister had been killed.

And, technically. it wasn't. This was his family's job essentially. They'd been created to do this by a god, according to his story. And they were protecting innocent people by doing that job. According to him. But she realized the aura of danger surrounding Eric came from this part of him. He was a hunter.

No wondered she'd frequently felt like prey in his presence.

"Not another monster," he said. "But someone who'd done monstrous things and deserved to die." His voice was hard and unrelenting, without a hint of apology.

"Was this person a human?" she asked warily, watching his expression carefully.

"He was a member of my Family."

Katie sucked in a sharp breath and slid back against the arm rest. "But… I thought… Your family…"

"He was a cousin. He broke the covenant with En. Joined with the monsters and initiated a series of events that resulted in the murder of my father. He didn't kill him personally, he just arranged for it to happen. In our world, that earned him a death sentence. And it was my duty as the new head of the Family to deliver that sentence."

CHAPTER NINETEEN

Katie blinked rapidly a few times and had to close her gaping mouth. Eric's expression hardened into a mask of stern authority, a look she'd never seen before. She could practically feel the power radiating from him, and her heart pounded loudly in reaction. He didn't regret killing his cousin. He wasn't ashamed or bothered by his actions. As far as he was concerned, it was justice.

And maybe it was, she realized as the rest of his story sank in.

She leaned against the couch armrest, the low bedroom lighting cutting shadows across his face as she considered him.

This cousin had been responsible for the murder of Eric's father. Hadn't Katie done everything in her power to make sure her sister's murderer was brought to justice, to make sure he received the maximum penalty New York could dole out—a life sentence in jail. She'd even used her psychic ability to ensure that outcome. If New York had allowed a death penalty punishment, she was pretty sure she'd have advocated for that.

Her *knowing* hadn't been enough to save her sister's life. She'd never been able to stop much of anything even when she did know about it in advance. But she had been able to point to her sister's killer with confidence, first in a line up and then in court, even though she'd never seen him clearly that night. And she'd been able to tell her story on the stand with such convincing detail, the jury had no choice but to convict the man.

Could she blame Eric for wanting a similar justice for his father?

Granted, he hadn't gone through the courts and legal system as she had. But that option probably wasn't even open to him given his family's unique situation.

"You were sure he caused the murder of your father?" she asked quietly.

"Yes. He admitted as much to my face in the end. And he would have murdered my mother and me if he'd had the chance."

She nodded, absorbing his story. Slowly realizing she wanted him to hear hers. For this conversation to continue without Eric going on the defensive over his actions, he needed to understand her past.

"My sister was murdered." She said those words starkly, bluntly. But it didn't deaden the pain.

His gaze narrowed in on her face as his entire body coiled. She had his full attention.

"Five years ago," she continued. "On a Manhattan street, in the middle of the night. During a rainstorm."

His jaw tightened visibly when she mentioned the storm. "Why didn't that come up when I looked into your background?"

"She was using our mother's second husband's last name. Trying to be a model. She liked his name—Alvarez—better, liked the way Ana Alvarez sounded. During the trial, I used my step-father's last name, too. I was writing under Donovan and didn't want this following me." She shrugged. "It did anyway." Closing her eyes briefly, she murmured, "I didn't get there in time to stop it."

"You knew it would happen?"

"Not soon enough. I never seem to know in time to prevent most of these things. But I saw her murderer, standing over her. And I was able to hold her as she took her last few breaths." Everything in her ached, clenching tight around her chest, making it hard to speak above a whisper. Five years and the memories still hit her like this. She doubted that would ever change.

"The person who killed her?" Eric murmured.

"Ran away when he saw me. Later, I learned he was a serial rapist. He carried a knife. My sister fought him, and he stabbed her multiple times. She bled out quickly. There was nothing anyone could have done." She watched Eric's fist clench against the couch. But he held himself still as she spoke, and for that she was grateful.

"What happened to him?"

"Serving life in a maximum security prison. I identified him in a line up, testified against him in a court of law, along with some of his other victims, and spoke at his sentencing hearing. I wanted him dead. Life was the best I could do."

"I would have killed him for you."

A half-smile actually lifted one side of her mouth even as five-year-old grief brought moisture to her eyes. "I wanted to kill him myself. But I needed to have his crimes made public." She shrugged. "And I didn't want to go to jail for his murder."

"Understandable."

"Are you worried you'll go to jail for your cousin's death?"

"No."

"Why not? Won't someone miss him?"

"Everyone who might have reported his death knows exactly what happened to him and why. None of them want to call attention to the Family by going to the human authorities. And almost every single one of them supports my actions."

"Almost everyone?"

"We've a big family. There are always those who resent being made to adhere to the rules. Unfortunately, as the head of the Family now, I might have to hunt some of those in the future. But for now, the order is maintained."

She nodded. "I told you about my sister because I want you to know I understand, on some level. Not completely. Yours is a very different world to the one I know. But I can't judge your actions because I understand where they came from."

All the coiled energy in his body seemed to seep out at her words, and she realized just how tense he'd been holding himself.

"My opinion mattered to you?" she asked, slightly awed by that realization. She told him her story so he'd continue to answer her questions honestly rather than trying to justify himself. She never thought her acceptance of his actions would be important to him.

"Yes," he said.

"Why?"

"I don't want you to think I'm little better than the monsters I hunt. My Family is built on a code of honor and a duty to protect humans from their nightmares. I didn't take the killing of my own cousin lightly. But I don't regret it."

"I know. And I don't think you're like the monsters—human or otherwise."

"Good."

"I'm still not sure why you care, though? We haven't known each other long enough for my opinion to be that important to you."

"Yes, we have. Your opinion matters a great deal to me, Katie."

"Why?" she murmured, unable to catch her breath as emotion swirled in his eyes.

He leaned forward, cupping her cheek in his hand. "You're important to me. More than you can know."

"How is that possible after only twenty-four hours?"

"I knew the minute I spoke to you on the phone. I've been waiting a long time for you, Katie Donovan."

She shook her head, unable to believe him despite the sincerity of his tone and the intensity of his gaze. She didn't believe in love at first sight or destined soul mates or any of that. "This is just lust," she said, trying to deny the growing sense that he was telling the truth.

"Oh, there's definitely lust here." He stroked a finger across her jaw and down her neck.

She shivered at the touch and arched forward instinctively, reaching for more.

"But that's only part of what's between us. And with a little more time, you'll realize that."

She didn't want to listen to him, didn't want to admit he could be telling the truth. Because if she did, she'd have to believe that Eric Logan might have real feelings for her. And thinking that would only make her fall in love with him. She could picture that happening. Not quite a *knowing* but an awareness of the possibility. The potential.

But he would break her heart when he left her, when he admitted all this talk of waiting for her and her being special was just an excuse to get her into bed. She wasn't normally a naïve woman. She was a realist who accepted that the world was hard and lasting love was rare.

"Please, Katie," he murmured as he leaned in close.

The change in position brought his mouth near to hers. "What do you want from me?"

"Time," he said. "Trust." He cupped the back of her head, drawing her closer. "And this."

His lips closed over hers, soft and seductive, taking what he wanted even as she succumbed to the temptation. All the tension he'd built earlier in the day came roaring back through her system. She wrapped her arms around his neck and opened her mouth to deepen the kiss, flicking her tongue along his in an erotic play she couldn't resist.

Kissing him felt so natural, so wonderfully right. Why deny this? Why resist? She wanted him and had from the very first moment they met. She didn't have to fall in love. She could hold her heart back and take the comfort and passion he offered without risking more.

She needed this, almost more than she'd needed his answers earlier. Vulnerable and shaken to the core, she needed something solid, something real to hold onto. And Eric Logan was as real as a man could get.

She clung to him, arched against him, and abandoned herself to the inevitable. There was no denying her need any longer.

And she just couldn't bring herself to pull away now.

CHAPTER TWENTY

"Katie," Eric breathed her name, his voice harsh and desperate.

She loved hearing his desire, knowing he was as hungry for her as she was for him. Needing to feel his skin against her palms, she fumbled with the buttons on his shirt, spread the material, and ran her hands along his chest. The contrast between course hair and hard muscle, taunt skin and heat fed her desire. Pushing the shirt over his shoulders, she let her fingernails trail along his biceps back up to his shoulders and then down his chest. He groaned and she smiled against his mouth.

In the next instant, she found herself flipped beneath him on the couch, the solid length of his body pressing her into the cushions. He moved one hand to her breast, massaging her through her shirt, and she arched into the touch. He raised his head and shifted to one side, enough to watch her as he pulled her shirt free of her trousers, then trailed his fingers underneath, along her bare abdomen. Breathing hard, she rolled her head back and closed her eyes. The rough texture of his fingertips felt like heaven against her skin. Now she didn't have to wonder where a businessman got calluses. He hunted monsters. The man was a warrior. And feeling the quiver running through his body as he touched her filled her with power and desire.

When his fingers skimmed over her bra, she moaned and opened her eyes. He unbuttoned her shirt, exposing her breasts to his hungry gaze, and toyed with her nipple through the thin purple lace of her bra. Then he closed his lips over her straining peak, suckling and nipping lightly with his teeth. Katie's body exploded with heat. The contrast between the rough lace and the wet heat of his mouth drove her wild.

She buried her fingers in his hair, holding him to her and savoring that feeling. She might have protested when he lifted his mouth, but he didn't give her time. Slipping her bra cup beneath her breast, he brought her to his mouth again, this time with no material between his lips and her skin. A current like electricity raced through her bloodstream, tugging tighter the line of need between her breast and her pussy. She closed her eyes again as sensation tingled over her skin.

"Does that feel good?" he asked before taking her into his mouth again.

"Yes. Oh, god, yes."

He swirled his tongue around her peak, flicked her nipple with the tip, then switched to her other breast, moving the cup of her bra out of the way before inflicting another wave of erotic torture on her. She trembled when his hand passed over her abdomen, sliding across her skin to the top of her slacks. His pinky dipped beneath the band, nothing more, and Katie thought she might jump out of her skin. The tease of that touch tightened her muscles and forced a gasp from her. Another brief sweep of his fingers left her panting.

He popped open the top buttons of her slacks, then the sound of the zipper lowering joined the sound of her pulse pumping in her ears. She opened her eyes as he lifted his head from her breast and stared down the length of her body. Following his gaze, she watched his hand slide into her trousers, under her panties to skim through her curls, then lower until he brushed one finger across her wetness. Her hips jerked against his hand. He sucked in a breath and his finger settled more solidly against her folds.

"You smell delicious," he murmured as he stroked over her most sensitive flesh, drawing more moisture from her. "I can't wait to taste you."

The thought of his mouth replacing his finger made her entire body shake, pushing her closer to orgasm than a single whispered comment ever should.

"You want my mouth here?" he asked, rubbing a little harder.

"Yes." She barely recognized the husky, desperate sound of her own voice.

"Yes," he echoed. Then shifted positions to pull her slacks and panties down her legs.

She backed up on the couch, giving him more room, and watched him settle between her thighs. The look of intensity on his face took her breath away as he stared at her, now exposed and open to him. A combination of vulnerability and eroticism pulsed inside her. Then his mouth closed over her, his tongue licked into her, and Katie cried out as anticipation turned to relief.

But that sense of relief didn't last long. He kissed and sucked at her tender flesh, building the pressure. She writhed beneath him, and his fingers clenched tight on her hips, holding her in place as he feasted.

She watched him until sensation overwhelmed her, then she closed her eyes and dropped her head back against the couch. Moaning, she brought her hands to her own breasts, squeezing her nipples even as the growing tension in her core neared breaking point. He growled against her, the sound vibrating through her and raising the hair on her nape. She glanced down again, saw him watching her as she pinched her nipples even while he continued to suckle her, and the heat in his gaze pushed her over the edge. She cried out as her orgasm broke, her hips jerking against his firm hold.

Only after she started to return to the present, as he moved from between her legs to kiss his way up her stomach, did she realize she'd screamed out his name.

He settled over her, his hands cupping her face, and kissed her long and hard. He was still almost fully dressed while most of her clothing had been pushed aside. The rub of material against her popping nerves was an erotic torment that left her hungry for more.

But as he rose to finish shrugging off his shirt, a shiver danced along the base of her neck and trembled through her gut. That tingling of awareness that let her *know* something was wrong.

"Eric?" She'd barely said his name when someone knocked at his door, hard and demanding.

His gaze narrowed and he cursed, violently enough she nearly smiled. Sweat gleamed on his bare chest and his erection strained against his trousers. As he stared down at her, she could see him debating whether or not to answer the door. Finally, with another viscous curse, he stood and pulled his shirt back up over his shoulder, though he didn't bother to button it as he stalked across the room.

Katie scrambled to readjust her clothing, but he glanced over his shoulder and stopped her with a look.

"Don't," he growled. "I'm not finished with you."

His comment sounded like both promise and threat. She swallowed hard against another wave of desire. But that nagging tingle at the base of her neck, the *knowing* that something was wrong refused to be quieted.

Eric barely cracked the door to the intruder, keeping the entire room and most of his body blocked. From his actions and his state of undress, whoever was outside was sure to know what was going on in the bedroom. Katie's cheeks heated despite the fact that she was hidden from view. She heard him mumbling something to the person in the hall, but the conversation was too quiet for her to hear.

After he closed the door, he kept his back to her for a long moment. Then he turned, his head bowed and his hands on his hips. With his mussed hair and shirt hanging open he looked sexy as hell. But when he raised his head and met her gaze, she saw frustration and anger rather than lust.

"What's happened?" She pulled her bra back into place and started buttoning her shirt. Since he didn't object, she knew whatever the news was, it was serious.

The muscles in his jaw tightened visibly. "We've had a security breach. Finish dressing. I'll be right back."

"Wait. What...?"

But he'd already disappeared into the bathroom. She heard the water running in the sink. Quickly reordering her clothing, she stood to wait for him. When he came back out again, his shirt was buttoned and damp tendrils of hair clung to his forehead. Without glancing at her, he went to his bedroom door. But rather than opening it as she'd expected, he hit a section of the wall next to it.

To her surprise, a secret panel opened, revealing two long swords, a half dozen knives and daggers, and a semi-automatic rifle.

"Jesus," she whispered, not realizing she'd spoken aloud until he turned to face her.

"We like to be prepared," he said, pulling out one of the swords.

"Why not the gun?"

"A gun won't stop a grinluk. You have to cut its head off to kill it. Anything less and it'll just keep coming."

Katie nodded, too shocked to comment on the information. "That thing is in the house." She wasn't asking. She could tell by his expression.

"Come on. We'll meet Rea in the main foyer."

Fear had her heartbeat pumping hard as the realization set in that she might have to see the creature again. That nightmare thing that wasn't just a dream. A real life monster.

She scrambled to be closer to Eric, feeling like a child but too scared to fight the impulse. He was the one with the sword and the experience fighting monsters. She was safer by his side than anywhere else in the house.

"What are you going to do?" she asked, embarrassed by the slight squeak in her voice.

"Go hunting."

CHAPTER TWENTY-ONE

Eric had never wanted to kill a monster so much in his entire life, despite several centuries of hunting them. Frustration was a living thing in his gut. If the grinluk appeared in front of him at that moment, he'd likely rip its head off with his bare hands.

He could still taste Katie on his lips, feel her warm skin against his. That monster had a lot to answer for.

Although, he had to admit, he probably wouldn't have been able to seduce her so quickly if the grinluk hadn't forced his hand so he had to tell her at least part of the truth about his family. He hadn't told her everything yet. Once he had her trust, once he'd made love to her again and again until she never wanted any other man in her life, he'd tell her the rest. Right now, for her to know monsters were real and he destroyed them was enough.

He held her hand even as he kept the sword ready in his right hand, scanning the corridors with his heightened senses for any sign of the grinluk. He wasn't sure how it had managed to get into the house, but he wasn't going to rest until he'd personally severed the thing's head from its neck.

Rea was waiting with her swords strapped to her hips, gunslinger style, and two huge rottweilers flanking her. As Eric approached one of the animals, the male, growled quietly and lifted his lip in a snarl. Rea quieted him with a hand on his head. Most of the Logan Family couldn't be around dogs for very long. Rea was the exception.

Katie tugged him to a stop. "Are those things…trained?"

Rea grinned. "Don't worry. They listen to me. They're actually really sweet and harmless unless I tell them to be otherwise."

"Uh huh."

He glanced at Katie as she licked her lips and stared at the animals. "Afraid of dogs?"

"No. No. It's just… Those two are the biggest bloody dogs I've ever seen."

Rea patted the male again, proudly. "I've been breading rotties for years. Bella and Bain are the result of all that effort. I was going for larger, stronger animals."

Since they didn't have time for this conversation, Eric interrupted. His sister could discuss dog breeding with Katie later. "You ready?"

"Yeah," she said, though she didn't remove her swords from the scabbards. Her gaze darted between him and Katie before finally settling a serious stare on him. "Did you tell her?"

"She knows what we do. She knows the monsters are real."

He watched his sister's eyes narrow and stopped her comment with a barely perceptible shake of his head. Now wasn't the time to discuss how much he'd admitted to Katie either.

"Okay. The breach was in the back of the house, near the old nursery." To Katie, she said, "We haven't really used that part of the house for ages."

"Did you get a time stamp from the alarm?"

"Almost exactly three thirty. Took Gregory and me some time to locate the breach and verify it wasn't a false alarm."

"Three thirty?" Katie said. "That's around the time I saw the grinluk at the library window."

Katie voiced aloud what Eric had been thinking. "Shit. We might have more than one."

"Or whoever is causing the storm used the grinluk as a distraction to break in," Rea said.

"Causing the storm?" Katie said, her voice rising. "What do you mean causing the storm?"

Eric sighed. He'd gotten distracted by his need to touch her and forgotten about his suspicions that the grinluk was working with another creature. "The monster you saw, while it's dangerous and deadly, can't manipulate the weather. Something else is doing that."

"How do you know this isn't a normal storm?"

Even as she asked, he watched understanding rise in her expression.

"The atrium," he said quietly. "Your car. The constancy and severity of the rain. Despite what the weather satellites revealed before it started. This isn't natural. And it's tied to the appearance of the grinluk."

He didn't want to tell her the storm had coincided more directly with her visit. She was already pale, and he could feel a fine tremor transferring through their joined hands. The last thing she needed to hear was that he worried all of this had to do with her.

He squeezed her hand and said, "We'll talk about it all later. Right now, we have to find the monster in the house."

Rea nodded. "Gregory's been scanning the video screens, but he hasn't found it. We'll have to hunt through the entire house." She glanced at Katie. "You want to put her into one of the safe rooms first?"

"No!" Katie said before he could answer. She gripped his hand tighter. "I'm sticking with you. There's no way I'm being left alone with that thing running around unchecked."

"You'd be with Mrs. Patterson and Gregory. You won't be alone." He didn't want her leaving his side either. But the truth was he'd be able to concentrate on the hunt better if he knew she was safely locked away behind impenetrable steel doors.

"I'd feel safer with you," she murmured.

Unable to stop himself, he let go of her hand and cupped her cheek. "I won't let anything happen to you. I promise. But I'll be able to track the creature better knowing you're safe."

She nodded, despite the shiver that shook her shoulders. "Okay. Okay. But just… Promise not to get yourself killed."

Her concern twisted his heart. "You're not getting rid of me that easily. We have unfinished business." He leaned in and kissed her, ignoring his sister.

When he lifted his head, Katie looked steadier, her color returning. Without taking his gaze from hers, he said to Rea, "I'll take her to the safe room. You start the hunt in the east wing. When Katie's safe, I'll take the west."

"You got it, big bro." Rea let loose a series of sharp whistles, and Bella and Bain took off toward the eastern wing of the house. Rea pulled her swords from their scabbards and followed.

"Come on." Eric took Katie's hand again and led her toward the kitchen. He didn't relax his vigil, continuing to scan their surroundings for any sign of the grinluk. Or any other monster that might be working with it.

Given the skill it took to breach the house security, Eric had a good suspect for the monster's ally now.

A sided Water Elemental.

Elementals were supposed to be neutral in the ongoing battle between the Seven Families and the monsters. But some of them had chosen sides over the millennia. Those who sided with the monsters were more dangerous than anything Ne had bred.

If they had an Elemental in the house, he was going to need more than a simple sword.

"So," Katie murmured as they moved into the kitchen, "is this what your sister meant when she said she works in security for the family business? She hunts monsters, too?"

"Yes."

"Guess she's stronger than she looks."

Katie had no idea. He led her into the pantry and the safe room behind it.

The room was built to be virtually impenetrable. A panic room created before panic rooms came into vogue. The Logan Family had fully embraced technology in their fight against monsters. Though they couldn't rely on it, they used it wherever it was useful. The clean, brightly lit room was created to keep the staff safe in case a monster got past all the initial household defenses. Gregory and Mrs. Patterson would have gone there immediately after the security breach.

Both were waiting patiently when Eric arrived with Katie in tow.

"Any word, sir?" Gregory asked.

"Not yet. I'll be back to let you know when all's clear."

"I've been watching the screens." Gregory motioned to the wall of monitors displaying views from the security cameras scattered throughout the public parts of the house. There weren't any cameras inside the family suites or staff quarters, but just about every other inch of the house was covered. "Nothing."

"Did you scan the video from the time of the breach?"

"Yes. The camera short circuited just before the alarm sounded." Gregory's gaze darted to Katie, then back to his. "There was water damage around the camera, sir."

"That's what I was afraid of." He crossed to the weapons' panel next to the door and pressed it open.

"Is there a trick to that?" Katie asked, coming up behind him. "A special place you have to press? A code?"

He showed her the pressure point at eye level. "All the panels work the same way. If you need a weapon at any time, there's one of these hidden storage closets in just about every room of the house, behind the door."

She nodded, nibbling her bottom lip as she studied the array of swords, guns, two compound bows, and other implements.

"But," he added, turning her to face him, "I don't want you taking chances with something you're not familiar with. Only go for one of these in an emergency. Understand? Gregory and Mrs. Patterson are both proficient with a sword and have used most of the guns. Mrs. Patterson is also an expert with knives. Gregory can use the compound bows. Let them take the lead."

Her eyes widened as he spoke and she glanced over at the butler and cook. He wasn't sure if she was surprised, impressed, or just in shock. But she nodded again, so he'd take that as acceptance.

"Good."

He let her go and reached into the cabinet for two fire daggers. The weapons were specially made by his brother, Benjamin. They were difficult to forge and not to be used casually when a normal blade would do. In this case, though, the possible presence of a Water Elemental made fire daggers absolute necessities.

"Sir?" Gregory said quietly. He knew what the daggers meant.

"Just keep the door sealed." He held the butlers gaze for a long moment until the man nodded understanding.

Eric closed the panel then faced Katie. She looked worried, frightened and pale, but somehow still steady. And all he could think about was keeping her away from any more tragedy.

But he had to ask because he'd never been one to overlook a possible advantage. "Are you…sensing anything?" he murmured.

"No. I know something's wrong. I have since the knock on the door. But I'm not getting anything specific."

"Okay. Stay here. Follow their lead." He nodded to the two members of his staff. "They know what to do."

She grabbed his arm, her grip tight. "What if something does come to me? What if I suddenly *know* something and can't warn you?"

Frowning slightly, he looked around the small room. They had one set of two-way radios, but he hadn't planned to take one with him as it usually just got in the way. Katie was right, though. He'd be a fool to ignore her psychic instincts. After three centuries of hunting monsters, Eric was no fool.

"I'll take one of the radios." His announcement earned a raised brow from Gregory, but he didn't have time, nor did he care, to explain his actions. He crossed the room and selected a radio. "I'm on channel 1." He handed Katie the second. "Only use this if you have to. A distraction at the wrong time could be…bad."

She dropped her chin back and gave him a "no, really?" look that might have made him chuckle if he wasn't so worried about her.

"You can watch the screens and track most of our progress. If you happen to spot the grinluk, let me know. But you likely won't see it."

"It doesn't show up on video?"

"They move too fast. By the time a gray flash registers for a human observer, the monster is long gone from that location."

She nodded, holding his gaze.

And he couldn't leave without one more taste of her. Ignoring his small audience, he pulled her close and kissed her soundly. "Stay safe," he whispered against her mouth.

"You, too," she said. "If you get hurt, I'm gonna be pissed. We're not done with the interview yet."

Her comment finally pulled a chuckle from him. "Trust me. I've been doing this a long time."

"We'll discuss that when you've gotten rid of this thing."

With one last quick kiss, he turned toward the door. "Remember, don't leave until either Rea or I come back to give you the all's clear."

He glanced over the three humans in his care, his gaze settling on Katie. He took a brief moment to memorize her face, then headed out.

He had a monster to kill.

CHAPTER TWENTY-TWO

Katie stared at the video screens as if her life depended on it. The room she and the others were in felt perfectly safe, so she wasn't actually worried for herself. She was worried about Eric. And the fact that she wasn't getting any specific psychic nudge was driving her mad. Not that her psychic skills had helped her much over the years. But if they were ever going to be an advantage, now would be the time for them to work.

Still, all she felt was a vague sense of unease, the knowledge that things weren't right and danger lurked nearby. But that was it. Nothing that could help Eric and Rea.

She watched Eric come back into view, after he'd gone into one of the rooms not monitored by a camera, and released a breath. She found herself holding her breath every time he was out of sight, only to relax a fraction when he reappeared. Rea and her dogs were making quick work of the eastern wing, the dogs taking the lead into rooms more often than not. But Eric was on his own, with no help from animals with heightened senses.

She trusted he knew what he was doing. He'd survived until now, hadn't he? Wiping her damp palms on her trousers, she tried to convince herself all would be well. But there was more going on than just the grinluk. There was the "other" monster that was causing the storm. He hadn't clarified, which frustrated her no end even though she knew there hadn't been time for lengthy explanations. And when she'd pressed Gregory—who she was sure knew exactly what the "other" monster was—he told her to ask Eric.

But she got the feeling from both Eric and Gregory that whatever this other thing was, it was more dangerous than the grinluk. That was not a comforting thought.

As she watched Eric ease into yet another room, she allowed a quick glance at some of the other screens. Both Gregory and Geraldine were following the progress of the hunt, too. They would tell her if something happened. But she still found herself studying the other screens whenever Eric was out of view. She held the two-way in a tight grip, ready to alert him if she saw or felt anything at all. She glanced back at the camera showing the door Eric had walked though, then scanned the other screens again.

And something, a movement maybe, or maybe just a changing in shadows, made her stare closer at one of the screens. She pointed to the location. "Where is this in the house?"

Geraldine answered. "Third floor, corridor outside our two largest guest rooms."

"Which wing?"

"West."

Where Eric was searching. But he was still on the second floor, working his way back toward the front of the house.

"Did you see something?" Gregory asked.

She continued to stare at the screen. "Not sure. Maybe not."

But that tingling along the back of her neck had started. Her other senses quieted, leaving her psychic one open and buzzing.

Just then, Geraldine gasped, breaking Katie's concentration. She glanced at the cook, then followed her pointed finger. Rea's dogs were running at high speed after something Katie couldn't see on camera. Rea followed them moving faster than a human woman should have been able. So fast, she blurred on the camera.

Katie swallowed hard. Eric said his family had skills that helped them fight monsters. Speed was one of them. But she never guessed he meant that kind of speed.

Suddenly, one of the dogs broke off from the chase and headed in a new direction.

"She's sent Bella to get Eric," Geraldine said before Katie could ask.

Katie's gaze snapped back to the camera where she'd last seen Eric. He was just immerging from the room, his head tilted as if listening to something. His entire body was tense, the sword held firm but low, ready to be used. He raised his chin, almost as if he was sniffing the air, and then he took off running. She watched Bella bark at him on another screen, then both dog and man charged toward Rea.

"There!" Gregory pointed to a view of the front foyer.

Katie gasped.

The grinluk in full view with Rea and Bain flanking it. The monster looked huge as it rose above woman and dog. It seemed to have thousands of tentacles thrashing out, its sharp teeth gnashing together as it followed Rea with its black eyes. Skeletal hands tipped with razor pointed nails hung at its sides. Its legs and feet—which she'd never seen before—were actually lifted off the ground as it balanced on thicker tentacles. Its feet looked a little like gorilla feet, with an opposable big toe resembling a thumb. But the grinluk's toes were tipped with thick talons that looked like they could rip through most things with ease.

As she watched, the creature struck at Rea with those feet, swiping at her chest. She leapt out of reach with ease and swung both swords in alternating circles, swaying back and forth as she watched the monster's flailing limbs.

Just then, Eric and Bella appeared at the creature's back and the grinluk's attention was divided. All four spread out, circling the thing, keeping it in one place so it couldn't easily escape. The monster responded by opening its mouth wide and throwing its head back as its tentacles slashed at the hunters. There was no sound. Katie couldn't hear the noise the monster made. But the hair on her arms stood anyway.

Then the thing looked directly at the camera. And smiled.

Katie shivered and stepped back. For reasons she didn't understand, her gaze snapped to the screen she'd been studying earlier, the one on the third floor that had caught her attention. The tingle on the back of her neck intensified.

Suddenly she *knew*. "There's a second one! It's in the house, too."

"Are you sure?" Gregory asked.

"I haven't seen anything," Geraldine said at the same time.

She ignored them both and glanced back at the fight in the foyer. Rea and Eric looked like they had their hands full with just one monster. If that second one snuck up on them…

She lifted the radio to warn Eric, watching and waiting for a moment when the monster was distracted by an attack from Rea or the dogs. When she saw her moment, she pressed the button and said, "Eric, there's—"

But before she could finish, she watched the grinluk lash out with two tentacles, ripping the radio away from Eric's belt, where he'd hung it, and throwing it against the wall. Pieces of metal and circuitry scattered uselessly across the floor.

Despite the monster's speed, Eric used its attack to sever a tentacle. He'd lost the radio, though, and Katie had no other way to warn him.

"Fuck!" She slammed her now useless radio on the console beneath the screens. Then she looked at the hidden weapons closet. She was halfway across the room when Gregory stopped her with a hand on her arm.

"No, miss, you can't. You'll only distract him."

"Gregory, there's a second grinluk in this house. I know it. And I know with absolute certainty that if I don't warn Eric and Rea, the second monster will turn this fight against them. One of them could die, Gregory. Both of them."

"They've faced these things before. You have to let them do what they do."

"You don't understand. I *know* this fight will go bad for them if they aren't warned. I have to tell him. If I don't, he'll…"

She couldn't finish the sentence. But it was there, hovering in that part of her brain that knew things. Eric would be seriously injured, maybe even killed, if she didn't do something.

"How can you be so sure?"

She held his gaze, not admitting anything out loud. But Gregory had been working for the Logans long enough to have developed some skill with a sword. He was used to things that normal people scoffed at. She let him see just how serious she was and watched as acceptance filled his expression. His hand loosened on her arm.

"Be very careful, miss. If there's a second, it could find you before you reach Eric and Rea."

Katie nodded, turning back to the storage closet so Gregory wouldn't see her rising fear. She knew the risk, that other monster was on the third floor, or had been a few moments ago. But it moved fast. And she didn't have the same speed as Eric and Rea.

She opened the closet, removed the .38 she'd seen earlier, checked the magazine in the gun, which was full, then took three additional magazines and stuffed them into her two front pockets. Eric had said a gun wouldn't kill a grinluk. But maybe it would slow the monster down. And she knew how to use a gun.

She glanced at the screens. Eric and Rea seemed to have the advantage in the fight. But they weren't getting anywhere near the creature's head and Eric said that was the only way to kill it. The third-floor screens showed no disturbances. The second monster wasn't there any more, she was sure of it. But she also *knew* it wasn't near the foyer yet.

She took a deep breath and opened the steel doors sealing the safety room. With a quick glance to make sure no monsters lurked just outside, she slipped into the corridor leading to the kitchen, letting Gregory relock the door behind her.

He murmured, "Be careful, miss."

Then the steel clicked back into place and for a heartbeat, Katie felt as vulnerable as she'd ever felt in her life.

Letting out a slow breath, she gathered what courage she had. Eric was in trouble. There was no turning around and hiding now.

She crept through the hallways, keeping her back to solid walls and the gun low against her thigh, her finger along the edge of the barrel so she didn't accidentally shoot her own foot off.

Each step seemed to triple her anxiety. Would she get to Eric in time? Would the other grinluk find her before she got to the foyer?

She wanted to rush but was afraid of running headlong into the second monster, so she shuffled as fast as she dared while still keeping her senses alert.

She purposefully opened her psychic sense as well, something she'd spent a lifetime avoiding, and paid close attention to her gut and the back of her neck, waiting for the tingles.

The closer she got to the front of the house, the clearer she could hear the battle. The snarl of a dog, the roar of the monster, the cursing of both humans.

When she finally reached the foyer and the actual fight came into view, fear clogged her throat. The anxiety of getting here had left her unprepared for the actual scene before her.

And only profound terror kept her from screaming.

Eric lunged at a mass of writhing tentacles just as Rea leapt back from a frontal attack by the monster. Blood sprayed across Eric's chest as three of the tentacles hit the ground. The grinluk squealed a high-pitched sound that made Katie want to cover her ears.

Then it turned back to Eric and she lost sight of him behind the creature.

From her position, just inside a corridor to the left of the fight, she had a clear view of Rea and the two dogs who were circling the monster, lunging in and out of its reach.

She wanted to shout, to warn them about the second monster. But she was afraid to disrupt their concentration. How was she going to tell them? She scanned the area before creeping along the corridor wall, edging toward the columns that separated the foyer from the front entryway. From there she hoped to be in a position to catch either Rea or Eric's attention without forcing them to take their focus off the monster for long.

Each slashing snap of the grinluk's limbs made her jump. The thing stood at least six feet above the two human fighters. How the hell were they going to get at its head?

Holding in a screech she wasn't sure she had the breath for anyway, Katie's gaze darted between the marble columns and stairway. She had to be quick. The second thing could be here at any moment.

To reach her target, she crossed in front of two doors but both were closed, so she wasn't worried about the monster jumping out at her when her back was exposed. Finally, she positioned herself so she could see both Eric and Rea. And because she knew she was going to draw the attention of everyone when she cried out, she raised her gun.

"Eric!" She shouted to be heard above another scream from the monster.

His gaze flicked to her and his eyes widened. "Get out! Now."

"There's a second monster. Somewhere in the house. It's coming."

Though she was focused on Eric and the monster, from the corner of her eye, she saw Rea slash out at the thing again, trying to draw its attention. But the monster flicked out a tentacle in a way that forced Rea to retreat. Then it turned its full attention on Katie.

And smiled.

Katie swallowed a scream. Its black eyes held hers as its grin widened to unnatural proportions, showing a mouth full of deadly teeth. She backed up another step, coming up hard against a marble column. A column positioned too close to the wall to allow her to slip behind it for cover.

The monster's gaze held her captive. She wanted to shout, to close her eyes and pretend it didn't really exist. But she couldn't look away.

Even when she heard Eric shout her name. Even when she heard the sharp squeal of an injured dog. Katie couldn't turn from the grinluk.

Her body trembled as the thing inched toward her. After the way it had moved earlier, a part of her wondered why it approached so slowly, but she was too terrified to concentrate on that thought.

She heard both Eric and Rea shouting again, was aware of the monster's tentacles thrashing out to its sides as more tentacles reached toward her, boxing her into her corner.

She continued to stare at the thing as it rose over her. Its sharp teeth clicked together. Taloned fingers stretched closer.

And Katie knew she stared into the black eyes of death.

Arching her head back to hold the monster's gaze, Katie let out a long, slow breath. Raised her gun in a two-handed grip. And fired.

Right into the grinluk's face.

CHAPTER TWENTY-THREE

K atie didn't bother to aim. She'd practiced enough with a .38 that she didn't have to.

She emptied her magazine into the monster's head, released the empty cartridge, and reloaded without looking away from the grinluk.

Blood sprayed over the floor as the monster roared and thrashed. She tracked the movement, making sure her bullets landed exactly where she wanted them too. Despite the creature's speed, her surprise assault with the gun seemed to have caught it off guard and slowed it enough that she emptied her second magazine into its face, leaving a bloody mess she tried not to see.

She was so focused on its head she missed the movement from below. A tentacle lashed out, catching her on her thigh. She flew across the foyer, hit the floor on her side, her back slamming up against another column, and the gun slipped from her fingers. Her lungs burned as the air was knocked from her, and for several seconds, she struggled just to breathe.

When she looked up, Eric stood over her, facing the monster, his body between her and those deadly limbs. The damage to the creature's face was so extensive its eyes were useless, but the eyes on its tentacles faced Eric. Its other limbs lashed the air and a sound like a bubbling scream escaped what had been its mouth.

Then faster than a human man should be able to move, Eric swung his blade in circles as he lurched forward, severing limbs before jumping straight into the air and slicing his sword through the grinluk's neck.

He landed in a crouch as the head dropped to the ground with a sickening thud. The tentacles, hands, and legs of the monster continued to convulse and whip through the air, but without purpose.

As Katie watched in fascinated horror, it sank to the floor, still writhing. She looked past the monster to see Rea, bloodied and still gripping her two swords, with her back to the stairs.

Above her, at the top of the stairway, stood the second monster.

"Rea!" Katie's shouted warning echoed in the large foyer.

Rea swung around to face the new threat as the second creature cried out in a strange hissing screech. Then it turned and fled back into the east wing of the house.

"Take care of Katie," Rea called as she charged up the stairs.

One of the dogs followed her but the other remained in a crouched position off to the side, and Katie realized that one might be hurt.

"Go with her," Katie said as Eric stood and turned to face her. "She'll need help."

As if he hadn't heard her, he stalked close, grabbed her arm and hauled her to her feet with a strength that shocked her. No human man was that strong. He was covered in blood, his sword actually dripping red onto the marble floor, and his eyes were glowing with a feral light that made her heart thump.

For the first time since coming into the fight, she got a good look at his expression. He looked furious and dangerous and wild. And suddenly Katie wasn't so sure she was safe with him.

"What the hell were you doing?" he ground out. "You could have been killed."

"I had to warn you about the second monster. If I didn't, you and Rea could have been killed." It took most of her remaining courage to face his anger. "The radio was smashed before I could tell you that way."

His jaw muscles flexed and the grip on her arm tightened reflexively. "You could have gotten us killed by diverting our attention."

She shook her head. "I knew, Eric. I *knew* you'd be in trouble if the second monster got to you before I could."

His gaze narrowed, the only change in his otherwise lethal expression. He held silent for so long, Katie thought he'd ignore her reasoning. Her entire body shook from shock and adrenaline. The fear that had carried her this far was taking its toll. Her knees wobbled, threatening to drop her to the ground. Only Eric's hold on her arm kept her upright, but his grip was so tight she knew she'd have bruises.

When he still didn't speak, she said, "Go help Rea. I'm fine now."

"No. You're not."

He released her bicep and wrapped his arm around her waist before she sank to the ground. She knew he was getting blood all over her clothes and she couldn't seem to care because she was still too terrified of what had happened and what could have happened. With little ceremony, he ushered her limp body toward one of the drawing rooms off the main hall, kicking the closed door open. Katie glanced back once at the dead monster, its limbs still moving in spastic jerks, then she turned away, unable to face the bloody mess anymore.

He led her to a seat. Her legs wobbled so much she collapsed into the chair the moment he released his grip. Fortunately, she landed on the side of her body that hadn't hit the ground earlier. Her entire right side felt bruised. She straightened to face him, realizing too late that she'd gotten blood on the leather seat. Since he'd put her in that chair, if he didn't care about its upholstery, she supposed she wouldn't either.

"Go help Rea," she said again. Her teeth were starting to chatter. But sitting helped.

"Rea is fine. That second monster will run rather than fight now. She'll either chase it from the house, or catch it and kill it."

"They didn't look that easy to kill." Katie had to speak through clenched teeth to make her words clear.

"They're not." He dropped into another seat opposite her and let his bloodied sword finally slip from his grip, the weapon landing with a clatter on the hardwood floor. "But its running, which gives Rea the advantage."

She nodded and wrapped her arms around her stomach to ward off the shivers now wracking her.

"You're in shock," Eric said, almost matter-of-factly.

"Wonder why?" she muttered.

"Are you hurt badly?"

"Bruised. But nothing feels broken."

He nodded, remaining where he was.

The fact that he was sitting rather than standing over her and giving her a lecture suddenly caught Katie's full attention. She looked more closely at him.

"Some of that blood is yours," she breathed as she noticed the gaping hole in his shirt and the angry-looking set of gashes beneath. Four deep cuts sliced sideways across his chest from his left shoulder to his right hip.

Without thought, she left her seat and dropped to the ground in front of him, pushing the ragged edges of his ruined shirt aside to get a better look.

He gripped her hands in his before she could do more. "I'll heal. Quicker than you will."

She met his gaze.

"Another gift from En when he created us."

"Shouldn't you...clean it or something?"

"Later."

"Is that my fault?" she murmured as her gaze dropped to the wound again. It had obviously come from either the monster's taloned feet or clawed hands.

"No."

But she didn't believe him. She hadn't seen an obvious injury on him before she'd been attacked by the grinluk. Of course, she could be mistaken. She hadn't noticed his injury immediately after the creature had been killed either. Still, the instinct that gave her knowledge whispered his wound was her fault.

"I'm sorry. I…" She turned away and looked at the door as tears gathered in her eyes.

Despite her intentions, he'd still gotten hurt. All her effort, all her supposed psychic foresight, and she still hadn't been able to prevent him from being wounded. Oh, she'd warned him about the other monster, but by doing so, she'd gotten him injured anyway.

"Damn it," she muttered as the first few tears leaked down her cheeks.

He caught one of the tears on his finger and wiped it away. "Don't cry, Katie," he murmured.

"You don't understand. This, this knowledge I get… It doesn't stop things. It never seems to help. I try to keep you from getting hurt, and you're hurt anyway because of me." More tears tracked down her face. She roughly wiped them away, ignoring the blood on her hands. "I couldn't stop my sister from dying. I couldn't fix my parents' marriage. I know all this stuff, but I can't do a fucking thing about any of it."

"You kept us from serious injury in the atrium. You saved my life this morning and probably just now." He cupped her cheek and turned her face back toward him. "You do help."

"Yeah? That's why you were so happy to see me in there?"

"Katie," he sighed. "You scared the hell out of me. I thought the grinluk was going to kill you." He paused as his thumb rubbed a soothing pattern along her cheekbone. "Where did you learn to fire a gun?"

"Shooting range, the last time I lived in New York."

"After your sister?"

"During the trial. I practiced a lot."

"Did it make you feel safer, having a gun?"

"I never bought one of my own. I rented them at the range. I got so I could shoot with a great deal of accuracy. And then I moved to a country where most guns are illegal."

"Why?"

"Because it didn't help. I didn't feel better, stronger, safer. I just felt hollow." She shrugged.

"I've never seen a human able to shoot a monster with such accuracy."

"I obviously surprised it. It wasn't moving as fast as I thought it would."

"Your aim was perfect. If you'd shot it in the chest, it wouldn't have slowed down much. Shooting it in the head left it more vulnerable and slowed it significantly."

"You said removing the head was the only way to kill it. I didn't think I'd be able to shoot its head off, but…" She made a vague gesture before letting her hand drop back to her lap.

"You did good."

She sniffled and nodded. She didn't feel particularly good since he was sitting there bleeding. But he was alive. Rea was alive. And she was alive. That had to count for something.

"Please stop crying," Eric murmured.

She hadn't realized her tears were still flowing. "I can't seem to help it." She rubbed at her face again.

"You're breaking my heart."

His simple statement made her throat close. She rubbed her cheek against his palm where he still touched her. For a long moment, no words were necessary. She set her hand gently on his thigh and took comfort in the fact that he wasn't worried about his wound.

The moment was interrupted by Rea's abrupt entrance. "Damn thing got away," she said. "Ran out the same way it came in."

"How're your dogs?" Katie asked, as she turned to face Rea.

The woman was covered in blood as well, but she'd resheathed her swords and was standing with her hands on her hips as if being covered in blood was an everyday occurrence. Katie realized belatedly that, given what the family did, maybe it was.

"They're fine. Bella took a thump from a tentacle. Her leg seems to be a little sore. But she's not broken, so she'll be fine with a little rest and a lot of food." Rea's gaze narrowed. "That was some fine shooting in there. I never would have guessed you could fire a gun."

Katie shrugged. "Long story."

"You'll have to tell me about it sometime. For now, I'll get the security breach locked down." She glanced at herself. "Then I'm gonna take a shower. You okay?" she asked her brother. "It got a pretty good swipe at you with its claws before you got its head."

"I'll heal."

"Be sure to—"

"You should get to that breach. Before the second grinluk gets brave and comes back."

Katie frowned at Eric's interruption. She looked back at Rea in time to see her raised eyebrows. But rather than argue, she shrugged and turned to leave.

"And don't forget about Gregory and Mrs. Patterson," he called to her.

"On my way there now. I want Gregory's help with the security hole." She poked her head back into the room long enough to say, "You two should get cleaned up too, by the way. You look like hell." Then she was gone.

For some reason, Katie found that last statement particularly funny. She started to giggle. The giggle turned into a full-blown laugh. But the laugh sounded a little crazed so she covered her mouth to hold it in.

With effort, Eric rose from his seat, taking her hand to help her up. "Let's go tend our wounds."

She nodded, still trying to stifle her giggles. "Why do you call Geraldine, Mrs. Patterson? Seems pretty formal."

"Habit." He moved his shirt aside to look at his injury, shook his head, and let the shirt fall closed. Then he wrapped his arm around her waist and headed out of the room, leaving the bloody sword where he'd dropped it.

Katie peeked at his chest. "I get to bandage you this time."

"If you insist." He glanced at his wound again as they stepped back out into the foyer. "Mostly, I just need to clean it. There'll be nothing but red lines left by morning. If that."

"I don't care how fast you heal. I'll feel better if you've been bandaged."

"Worried about me, are you?"

"Yeah, well…" She wasn't sure what to say. Of course she was worried about him.

And yet, she'd only known him a little over twenty-four hours. How was it that she felt so close to him already? That the thought of him hurting made her ache physically, too? She knew more about him now, thanks to the interview and his own revelations. But still, she felt as if she'd known him for years. And that shouldn't be possible after a single day.

As they headed slowly up the stairs and toward his bedroom, Katie realized her life would never be the same after this.

And she couldn't tell if that was a bad thing or not.

CHAPTER TWENTY-FOUR

When they reached his room, Eric allowed Katie to inspect his wounds. Between their earlier session on the couch and the battle, his blood was hot and running fast—despite his injury. The fear he'd felt when Katie had stepped into that foyer was still strong in his system, which wasn't helping his state of mind. It was all he could do not to rip her clothes off and throw her on his bed. But she was obviously too shaken by her encounter with the grinluk. And he wasn't ready to show her his true animal side. Yet.

He had to bite the inside of his cheek when she stripped his shirt off and ran her hands over his chest. Fortunately, her investigation of the claw marks stung enough to help keep his lust in check. Because the pain helped his control, he didn't complain as she washed and bandaged his injuries, even though it hurt like hell.

"You're just going to get these bandages wet when you take a shower, aren't you?" she said when she'd finished, frowning at his chest.

"Don't worry, I'll take a sponge bath." He wasn't going to need the bandages in another hour anyway. "Your turn now," he said. "I want to check your leg and make sure getting tossed around didn't reopen your cut."

Katie hedged. "I'm not sure you'll be able to see the cut through the bruising."

The very idea of her beautiful skin being black and blue from bruising made him crazy. "Let me have a look anyway."

She nodded. And to his surprise and pleasure, she removed her pants without insisting on getting something to cover up. The events of the afternoon had either left her too shaken for modesty, or she was now more comfortable with him and trusted him. He hoped it was the latter, though he suspected there was a lot of the former involved.

He ignored the temptation of having her half naked and focused on her injuries. A renewed surge of anger rushed through him and he wanted to kill the grinluk all over again.

"Could be worse," he said to make her feel better. As far as he was concerned, this was bad enough.

The cut on her leg had managed to survive the abuse without reopening, thanks to the bandage. There were bruises along her right hip and thigh, bruises he was sure extended to her shoulder. He tenderly moved her arm to make sure she hadn't broken anything.

When he was finished, he nodded. "Okay. You take this shower. I'll use my brother's room next door."

She grabbed his arm, her grip tight. "Is that a good idea, us separating?"

He couldn't resist a slight smile. "Are you inviting me into your shower?"

"That's not what I meant."

Her scowl helped relax his tension somewhat. Teasing her made him…happy. Such a strange reaction.

"Shame," he said, tweaking her nose to see if it would make her frown fiercer. It did. "We're safe for the moment. And Gregory will alert us immediately if there's any more trouble. But the second grinluk ran away, so I think we'll be okay for a few hours."

She sucked in her bottom lip, nibbling it as she continued to hold his arm. "You shouldn't get those bandages wet," she said at last, repeating her earlier concern.

"I won't."

"I'm going to take a full shower. We can redo my bandage after, right?"

"I'll take care of it."

She continued to hold his arm.

"Do you want me to stay with you?" he asked. He needed a little time alone, time to let his wolf out so his wound would heal faster. But he needed to reassure and protect Katie more.

She finally dropped her grip and shook her head. "I'm sorry. I'm being silly. I'll be fine. And you're just next door, right?"

"Right. I can be here in half a second if you need me."

She nodded, but her gaze flickered to the windows.

"Remember, I have excellent hearing. You'll barely have to make a noise, and I'll be here."

"Your hearing is really that good?"

"It is."

"Hmm. I'm not sure if that's good or not. There are some things I might not want you to hear."

"I'll only listen for emergency sounds."

She smiled reluctantly. Then surprised him by leaning in and kissing him lightly on the lips. The contact was over much too quickly. And it took a lot of willpower to stay on the couch and not follow her when she stood.

He watched her disappear into the bathroom, waited until he heard the shower water running before he left the room.

On the way out, he stored the two fire daggers he still carried in the weapons closet by his door. He wanted the daggers close, just in case. But he didn't want them out in plain sight. Also just in case.

Next door, he didn't bother starting the shower yet. He'd do that after, so his hair would still be wet when Katie saw him again. For the moment, he needed something more than fresh water and clean clothes.

Because the grinluk could still be on the property, though, he couldn't simply sit down. He would have to pose his body so it looked like one of the many statues around the house. He removed his tattered shirt and unwound the bandage Katie had carefully tied. That tell-tale cloth would give him away. Then he went to stand in a corner near a stone statue of a small dog. Rea had given it to Nick for his last birthday—a kind of joke since he hated little dogs. But he still kept it in his room—probably because he was rarely in this room anymore.

Eric stood next to the dog and looked down at it, a pose that would make it appear he was part of a larger piece. Then he pulled in a deep breath and touched his wolf. *It's time to jump.*

The familiar, cold sensation moved through his limbs, his vision blurred and distorted, as if he was looking out of two different sets of eyes at two different views. His human eyes still registered staring at the stone dog. His wolf eyes took in the far side of the room. He resisted the urge to close his eyes, despite the disorientation, and waited for the shift to complete.

When it was done, the wolf stood a few feet away from a life-sized stone statue of Eric's human form. His human consciousness took a moment to orient to the wolf's physical form, four paws, a perspective closer to the ground. Already heightened senses increased tenfold and he could smell the blood, sweat, and grinluk on his shirt.

He could also smell Katie. Both wolf and human essence reacted to that scent.

With one final look at the stone figure of his human body staring down at the stone dog, the wolf edged out into the hall and padded to his own bedroom. He'd left the door cracked to allow easier entry and exit. Paws made manipulating door knobs tricky.

He went directly to the bathroom door, his ears twitching forward as he listened for Katie through the sounds of running water. What he heard made the wolf whine quietly. She was crying, a muffled sound like she had her hand over her mouth, but he could clearly hear her sobs. Lying down on the floor, the wolf rested his head on his paws and stared at the door. His human awareness felt helpless and guilty. The wolf felt concern and the need to guard.

He waited, unmoving, until he heard the shower shut off. Then he rose to his feet. But he didn't immediately leave, instead listening to her towel off, hesitant to go until absolutely necessary. When she neared the bathroom door, he sprinted from the room, slipping out an instant before she emerged.

Back in Nick's room, he crossed to his statue body and stared up at it. That form would heal faster the longer he stayed in his wolf shape. But Katie needed him. Whatever healing had been done in the last half hour would have to be enough.

The wolf took a few steps back and leapt into the statue's chest. Another few moments of disorientation swept over him and the sense of cold limbs and warm fur blurred for an instant. As the process finished, he sucked in a breath, feeling the pull of his human lungs and the stretch of human muscles.

Blinking, he listened for sounds from next door. He could hear Katie moving around. Time to clean up and get back to her. He took a quick shower, removing all the blood still covering him. Then he wrapped his chest in a bandage again, though the wounds were now just angry raised welts covered with thick scabs. Thanks to at least some time in his wolf form, in another couple of hours the injuries would be little more than red lines. By tomorrow, even the lines would be gone.

He was tempted to go next door in his towel so he could dress in his own clothes, but he wasn't entirely sure how Katie would take that, so he borrowed from his brother's limited wardrobe—a pair of sweats and a college t-shirt. In his bare feet, he went back to his room, unable to stay away from Katie any longer.

She was sitting on the couch, her legs pulled up to her chest as she stared at his fireplace.

"How was your shower?" he asked, making enough noise as he entered the room to keep from scaring her.

"Good. I needed it."

She glanced at him and smiled. He noticed the red around her eyes and a slight splotchiness around her mouth, the only hint that she'd been crying.

"How about you?" she asked. "Feeling better after getting clean?"

He nodded. "I'm starving now, though."

As if his comment was a summons, there was a knock on his door followed a moment later by Gregory pushing a tray overloaded with food into the middle of the sitting area.

"Sir. Miss," he greeted.

Katie looked at the food and raised her brows. "You can eat after what happened?"

"Actually, I *need* to eat after what happened. Fighting monsters leaves us pretty hungry."

"Rea is currently eating Geraldine out of a month's worth of supplies," Gregory confirmed. The butler looked at Katie and frowned. "Are you okay, miss? We saw the fight, your…part in things. Were you hurt when that thing threw you? Do you need any medical attention?"

Katie smiled. "I'm just bruised. My cut didn't even open. Eric checked." Her smile faded. "Not sure I can eat, though."

"Oh but you really should have something. Maybe something simple?"

"I don't want to put Geraldine to any trouble when she has to feed Rea. A can of chicken noodle soup would do me."

"Perish the thought," Gregory said. "Geraldine wouldn't hear of feeding you soup from a can. She does have some mushroom soup ready. Would that suit?"

"I haven't had mushroom soup since the last time I went to Ireland. That sounds perfect, Gregory. Thanks so much. And thank Geraldine."

"But of course. You just relax there, and I'll be back in a few minutes with your meal."

She nodded. Once Gregory left, she said, "He's very sweet."

"I think he's developing a crush on you." Eric wasn't sure if he was joking or not, and not entirely sure how he felt about the attention his butler was heaping on Katie.

She snorted. "I doubt that. But he's being very kind to me in the middle of all this."

Eric sat on the couch next to her, but she stood immediately and paced away.

"I need some answers, Eric. We need to finish the conversation that got interrupted earlier." She settled into a chair beside the couch and motioned to the tray of food with a hand gesture. "Go ahead and eat while we talk. You need to renew your energy."

He did. But the fact that Katie didn't want him next to her

disturbed him. He held his concerns in check and said, "Ask your first question." He kept his back to her, filling his plate as he waited.

"How old are you?"

"Right to the sensitive topic," he joked. When she didn't laugh, he shrugged. "I'm three hundred and thirty-four years old. Living a long time is one of the benefits of our arrangement with En. It takes time to train and educate a monster hunter." He decided to explain why later, when he told her about the curse.

"How old is Rea?"

"She's a hundred and fifty-six, but don't tell her I told you. She's touchy about her age."

Again his humor went unappreciated. He gave up and sat down with his plate of food. His body was screaming for sustenance now that the adrenaline of his earlier activities had worn off.

"Okay. Okay. So you've all been around a while. You can be killed, though, because you killed your cousin. Does it take some special… technique? Like a stake and garlic or silver bullets?"

"Yes. But it depends."

"On what?"

"On the Family."

"You mean which part of your family?"

"No, which specific Family of hunters."

"There's more than one family of monster hunters? How many?"

"Seven."

She leaned back in the chair and stared at him. "What makes the families different? I mean, if there are different ways to kill you, there must be some other differences between families, right?"

Here it was. A part of the story he had been delaying telling her. He still wasn't sure how to explain this. Because it wasn't like anything she would have come across before. And he wasn't sure how much to tell and how much to keep for a later time, when she was less freaked out by the grinluk fight.

He was saved from an immediate answer by a knock at the door. Gregory came in with a tray and the scent of warm mushroom soup and heated bread flowed in with him.

Eric raised a brow. "You only brought one bowl?"

"You do not need soup, sir," Gregory said as he set the tray down on the coffee table.

"Maybe Katie will want more," he said, trying not to sound defensive.

"Will you be wanting more than one bowl, miss?"

She smiled at Gregory. "I think this'll be all I'm able to eat. But thank you, Gregory. It smells wonderful. Thank Geraldine again, too."

"I will, miss. You just let me know if you need anything further." He straightened and faced Eric. "Will you be needing more food, sir? Rea has left a few scraps."

"No. I'm good for now. Thank you."

Gregory nodded and left without another word. Eric continued to stall, waiting for Katie to settle with her soup and take a few sips before he started a roundabout version of the truth.

"Each Family is associated with an animal."

"Like a mascot or heraldic-type symbol?"

"We do consider the animal a…signature of our Family."

"What's your animal?"

"The wolf."

Katie straightened, her soup forgotten. Was she remembering the "dream" she'd had just last night of a wolf guarding her? She was too smart not to make the connection.

"Are you a werewolf?"

Her tone was both worried and disbelieving. "No," he said without any hesitation. "We're not werewolves."

"I just have to ask, *are* there werewolves?"

"Yes."

"That is beyond weird." She titled her head and snorted. "Although, not nearly as weird as a grinluk, so I don't know why I'm surprised." She took a sip of soup before saying, "So what are you then? How does the wolf come into things?"

Again, how much to tell? He hedged, telling a partial truth again. "Each Family is…imbued with the spirit of their associated animal. That animal spirit gives each family unique talents. In ours, we've got a heightened sense of smell and hearing, our night vision is better than normal, and we're very fast and strong."

"That part I noticed."

He liked her dry tone. It meant she was recovering.

"What are the other animals, for the other six families?"

"That's very private for each Family."

"Not like I'm going to meet another one of these families. I promise not to tell."

He was tempted to argue with her. As his Nam-tar, hopefully his wife, she would meet the heads of the other six Families eventually. But since she didn't know her place in all this—and he wasn't prepared to tell her just yet—he simply said, "Fine, but I'm not going to tell you which Family is associated with which animal. That's up to the members of the Family."

"Fine. What are the animals?"

"Lion, Eagle, Snake, Dragon, Griffin, and Bear."

"Wait. Dragons? As in fire-breathing, gold-guarding dragons? Do they breathe fire as their added talent?"

"Some. Others breathe mist. Actually, more breathe mist as there's been more of an Asian influence in that Families' evolution."

She paused with her spoon halfway to her mouth. "You're serious?"

He nodded and took a bite from an apple slice.

"And griffins? Real griffins with bird heads and lion bodies?"

"That's the animal associated with one of the Families. There's also a monster, a demon-griffin, which is something different."

Katie's spoon dropped back into the bowl. She stared at him for a moment. "I'm not sure I can take much more of this."

"We can talk about something else. I'm sure there are other things you want to know. The other Families… You can learn more about them later, if you like."

"You know what I find truly unbelievable about all this?"

He shook his head.

"I can't write about any of it. This is amazing, newsworthy stuff. And I can't write a single word. Truly tragic."

He felt his lips twitch with a smile and squelched it. The last thing she needed was encouragement. She might just go out and write about everything he told her. No one would believe her, and she'd likely be put away in a psychiatric hospital. That wouldn't suit either one of them.

"I suppose I could always start writing fiction," she murmured, mostly to herself. "I mean, this is the stuff of novels, isn't it? I could write a bunch of horror stories."

"I wouldn't try. We don't like people to even suspect we exist. We'd work very hard to keep those novels from being published. Even if they were disguised as fiction."

"Would you succeed? In preventing the publication?"

He held her gaze without speaking, leaving her to come to her own conclusions. It would be much safer if she believed the Families were capable of anything. They kept their secrets not so much to keep other humans from knowing about them, but to prevent the monsters from learning too much. And even disguised as fiction, the monsters would know her novels held truths. That would be bad for the world.

And extremely dangerous for her.

CHAPTER TWENTY-FIVE

After a quiet moment, Katie shrugged. "I'm not a great fiction writer anyway. Better at non-fiction."

Eric went back to the ham sandwich on his plate, trying not to look pleased by her decision. She was just stubborn enough that she'd try it anyway if she thought it would irritate him.

Something about that stubbornness really appealed to him, though. While he didn't want to tempt her, he was drawn to that part of her personality. Under some circumstances, her stubbornness would be a real asset.

"Okay, let's move on to something else for the moment," she said with a slight head shake. "I'll get back to the other families when I think my brain can handle the information."

"Fair enough."

She went back to spooning up soup. Between bites, she said, "You mentioned something else working with the two grinluk, and I got the feeling Gregory knew exactly what you were worried about. I think it's only fair you tell me what you're worried about, too."

"Ah. That." He glanced toward the windows and the closed curtains. "Have you heard the term 'Elementals'?"

"As in the elements?"

"Elementals are beings that are the elements and part of the elements. It's hard to describe. They're both of those elements and the reason those elements exist and continue. They're…a personification of nature. But not just a mythical idea. They are actual beings."

"Like a wind spirt or something?"

"Sort of. Each element has its associated Elementals. Water, fire, air, earth. And Elementals are supposed to be neutral. In all things. But particularly in the war between the Seven Families and the monsters."

"But some of them aren't."

He tipped his head to acknowledge her correct guess. "Some have sided with the monsters. Others with the Families. Most are still neutral. But even one sided-Elemental can wreak havoc."

"And you think there's an Elemental working with the grinluk."

"Specifically, a Water Elemental."

"The storm," she said with a nod as understanding sank in. "You think this rotten weather is caused by the Elemental."

"I'm positive it is now. It was only a guess when the storm started."

She looked away and stared at the cold fireplace for a long moment. She was so still and quiet he started to worry. Opened his mouth to fill the silence.

Then she faced him again. "That explanation *feels* right. I *know* the storm's not natural."

"Have you known from the beginning? About the storm?"

"No. Guess there were too many other things to be worried about. My psychic senses couldn't take it all in at once."

So, there were limits to her skill, more than just the last-minute nature of her awareness. That was useful information. He wanted to press her to learn more about her own talent, but she interrupted with her next question.

"What does the Elemental want? And what do we do to stop it?"

"More difficult to say." He finished the last hunk of cheese on his plate and stood to get his next course. "What it wants probably has to do with the cousin I killed. The Elemental is obviously working with the grinluk, and the grinluk were working with my cousin. I don't know what they were working on exactly, except that it required the death of my father, myself, and my mother. Since there's an Elemental involved, and it was able to bring my cousin onto its side, there has to be a bigger plan. I just don't know what it is."

He returned to the couch with a large bowl of pasta covered in Alfredo sauce and topped by blackened chicken. When he glanced at Katie with his first forkful halfway to his mouth, he caught her raised eyebrow. "What?"

"You're still hungry? You just ate a huge plate of food."

He snorted. "That was just the appetizer. I wasn't exaggerating when I said the fights required a lot of energy from us." He left out that the injury and the jump from his human body added to the drain.

"What happened sixteen thousand years ago when food wasn't so readily available? How did your family survive?"

"Apparently, there were helpers who hunted for us when we were busy hunting things we couldn't eat. And I understand from some of the oldest stories that some of the monsters were edible."

"Ew. That's really gross."

"You asked." He shrugged as her nose crinkled in disgust then shoved some food into his mouth. "Now, where were we?"

"What the Elemental wants and what do we do to stop it."

Her use of "we" had a spark of hope leaping into his blood. "The only explanation I can think of for its current attack is revenge for my cousin's death." He paused, frowning. "Or else it's still trying to kill me. Which means it may still be after my mother, too."

He made a mental note to check with the guard in Vienna and to warn them about the Water Elemental as soon as he'd finished eating. He wasn't really worried about his mother at this point. After his father's murder, she'd been put under such protective guard even he had trouble getting through to see her. His brother Richard was the one in charge of that security, and he trusted him implicitly with the safety of their mother.

"Are you worried about her?"

Katie's question followed his thoughts so exactly he wondered if it was a psychic reaction. Then he realized it was a reasonable question for any person to ask. Especially a reporter used to asking follow-ups.

"One of my brothers is looking after her," he said. "She's safe. But I'll make a call after dinner to warn them of the Elemental's involvement."

"So, revenge or just finishing the job your cousin didn't. Both options don't bode well for your survival."

She said that off-handedly, but he heard the catch in her voice, caught the whiff of worry in her scent, and it made his heart jump. She cared. He'd known that when she faced down the grinluk to help him. But knowing his death really would bother her gave him a great deal of hope for their future. Hope that she'd stay.

"I'm difficult to kill," he said.

"But it's not impossible."

"No."

"So what do we do? How do we stop this thing first?"

He loved that she kept saying "we." "We may have to face the Elemental."

"You can do that? And not get killed? I mean, can they be killed?"

"No. Can't be killed. They're…nature itself. You can't kill water. Elementals are as immortal as the planet."

She released a snort-huff filled with cynicism. "Until we kill the planet with global warming."

"Even if humans make the planet uninhabitable for humans, the planet—and things like fire, water, air, earth—most of those things will continue in some form. At least until the sun eats the planet in a few billion years."

She gave him a contemplative nod as she nibbled on her warmed bread.

"But Elementals can be scattered," he continued, trying not to get distracted by her mouth. "Essentially turned into non-cohesive particles that take time to reassemble into a being. The reassembly can take a very long time, depending on the weapon used and the area of the wound."

"I take it you have weapons to use against an Elemental?"

He nodded. "Each one requires a different type. Against Water, we need fire."

"What like a flame-thrower?"

His sudden snort of laughter sounded loud in the room. He swallowed and said, "Actually, that would probably work for a short-term effect. But unfortunately, it wouldn't disperse the Elemental for long enough. Creates quite a visual, though."

"If you say so. How do you use fire, if not just throwing it at them?"

"We use what we call fire daggers. They're created in a very unique way, with unique materials, and then treated with a final chemical that…reacts badly with a Water Elemental."

"So. Not magic, then."

She seemed so relieved he decided not to tell her there was some magic involved. It was a rare smith capable of forging such weapons. Special talents, beyond the forge, were required. Talents his brother Benjamin wielded, fortunately, which meant they could increase their supply of fire daggers if needs be.

Instead of mentioning the magic, though, he said, "The weapons are difficult to make and so aren't used lightly."

"You have some here though?"

He nodded. Taking a final bite of his pasta, he set the bowl down and rose, crossing to the weapons storage closet beside his door. He pressed the wall, opened the panel, and pulled out the two fire daggers he'd stored there earlier. He returned to the couch and handed her one, hilt first, to inspect.

"It doesn't look special," she commented as she stared at the metal. Then she paused, her movements going utterly still. "Oh. It feels different. And…there's a red glow if you look at it right. Though, that's pretty hard to see."

"Feels different?"

"Part of my psychic sense. I get more specific flashes of *knowing* through touch."

He froze, staring at her. "With me? When we touched, did you… know anything specific?"

"You, unfortunately, are a blank wall." She cringed. "I wasn't going to admit that. But I suppose it would be rude to let you think I know more than I do. And given the circumstances, dangerous."

"True."

"So I don't know anything…well, much about you that you haven't told me."

"That's probably a good thing."

She snorted, as if not entirely agreeing with his statement. Carefully, hilt first, she handed the knife back to him. "So that thing can…scatter a Water Elemental. For how long?"

"Long enough to prevent it from being a threat for at least one human lifetime."

She straightened a little. "That's brilliant."

"But only if you hit the Elemental in exactly the right spot. The dagger to their leg will scatter them, but not for as long."

"Where do they have to be hit?"

He tapped his head with a finger. "Center of the forehead. When they take a form that presents a forehead."

"So, an easy shot, then," she said dryly.

"Exactly. It takes incredible aim, accuracy, and luck to get an Elemental between the eyes. Hitting them anywhere in the head or around where a human heart would be will disperse them for a pretty decent length of time, though. Years."

"Years are good." Her voice got quieter when she said, "I've never used a knife before."

He realized belatedly that a knife was the weapon used to kill her sister, and cursed under his breath. "I'm sorry if this is dredging up bad memories."

"Maybe a little. But I'm more concerned with survival at the moment. I can get over my issues with knifes."

She still shuddered at the word, and Eric silently cursed again.

"Don't worry," he said. "You won't have to use the knives. I'll take care of the Elemental."

She didn't respond but her eyes narrowed. What he wouldn't give for a little of her talent in that moment so he could know exactly what she was thinking. Rather than interrogate her and risk her closing up, he set the two daggers on the coffee table and got the next part of his meal.

He noticed she'd finished all her soup and a good hunk of the bread. That was good. "Do you want more?" He nodded to the empty bowl.

"No, I'm full. Thanks." She shook her head at his next plate full of food, but didn't comment. "Should we put the daggers away, like you did before?"

"No." Now that he wasn't busy healing, he wanted them close to hand.

"Thought you said we wouldn't have a problem with that thing tonight."

"With the grinluk? We won't. I'm just being overly cautious." He weighed up the timing and decided this was the right moment to broach something he'd been thinking about all evening. "And speaking of caution, you're still staying here tonight. With me."

Part of him expected her to argue. She had already agreed to sleep on his couch, but a lot had happened since then. Including their heated session on this very couch. He was afraid she'd resist sharing his room now, after all he'd told her, all that had passed between them. She didn't seem to be afraid of him, but her scent was clouded by her exhaustion and confusion. All the revelations about his family's work, as well as the fight with the grinluk, had to have her shaken. And he couldn't help but remember that she hadn't wanted to sit next to him while they ate. He held still as he waited for her response afraid any movement would scare her off. If she insisted on sleeping anywhere else in the house, he'd never rest tonight.

"I already said I'd sleep on the couch. Now I'm definitely insisting you take the bed. You've been through a lot today. You need to sleep well."

Her easy acquiescence flooded him with relief. "Katie. You're bruised from top to toe. You are not sleeping on the couch."

"Neither are you," she said firmly.

He had to work very hard not to react to her challenge. "You realize that leaves us with only one option. To share the bed."

Color rose in her cheeks, but she didn't look away. "I'm well aware of that. If you don't mind sharing, then neither do I."

He held her gaze for a long moment. Did she expect him to sleep next to her and not make love to her?

Or had she just issued him an invitation?

CHAPTER TWENTY-SIX

Katie refused to turn away even though she could feel her cheeks heating. After what had happened that day, that afternoon, she didn't want to sleep alone. She wasn't sure she was ready for sex—despite the sheer quantity of stuff they'd been through in the last thirty hours, it had still only been thirty hours since they met.

But the events of the day made it feel as if she'd known him for so much longer. And he'd trusted her with information about himself and his family. He was giving her so much more than she expected, even if she couldn't use any of it in her article. Still. His honesty was pulling her in, winning her trust.

She was sure they wouldn't be able to sleep in the same bed without the chemistry between them getting the better of her common sense. She was also sure that sex with Eric was exactly what she wanted, whether she was ready or not.

The tense moment broke when the door abruptly swung open. Rea stood there looking curious and not the least repentant for the unannounced interruption. "Have you finished eating? We should talk."

"I'm not finished yet," Eric said.

He continued to stare at Katie for a moment longer, making his meaning clear, before turning to give his sister a dry look.

"Katie's finished," she said.

"Fine. Come in."

Gregory strolled into the room after her, as if Eric had given permission for the full invasion. She nearly laughed out loud at the exasperated look on his face.

Gregory came straight to her. "Did you enjoy the soup, miss?"

"It was wonderful, Gregory. Please pass on my compliments to Geraldine."

"And you've had enough?"

She patted her stomach. "I'm plenty full now."

"Very good. Shall I start a fire? It's quite chilly this evening."

She hadn't really noticed until he mentioned it. Only a moment before, she'd been feeling too warm. Now the chill in the air registered and she was grateful yet again for Gregory's thoughtfulness.

As the butler got a fire going, Katie noticed Rea and Eric having a very quiet conversation. They glanced her direction once or twice, but despite how close they were to her, she couldn't hear any of what they said. She did see their lips moving, she knew they were talking. Strange she couldn't hear them.

By the time the fire was blazing, Rea had turned to Katie. "So you know about the Water Elemental and *some* of our Family history."

Her emphasis on the word "some" caught Katie's attention. "What don't I know yet?"

"Nothing that affects the current situation," Eric answered, giving his sister a quelling look.

Rea opened her mouth, but Eric cleared his throat to shut her up. She made a face and said, "She needs to know everything eventually."

"Rea," Eric warned.

Now they really had Katie's attention. But it looked like Eric was winning the battle of wills, because Rea sighed and flopped against the couch back.

"Fine," she said with a huff.

"Ehm…" Katie started.

But Eric interrupted. "We can discuss this later. Now we need to talk about a strategy for dealing with the current threat."

Rea opened her mouth again and got another quieting glare. She shrugged and sank deeper into the couch cushions.

"Tell Katie what you learned," he said.

"Okay." Sitting up again, Rea leaned in toward Katie. "So the Water Elemental was responsible for getting past our alarm system and letting the two grinluk into the house."

"How can you be sure?"

"Water doesn't normally move like that."

"The part of the system that was disabled was nowhere near anything that could have leaked," Eric clarified. "It had to travel through cracks in a door that were so small even dust doesn't usually get through, and then it moved up along a wall, through a vent and into the alarm circuitry."

"Ah. So not a simple leak. And not something the grinluk could have done on their own."

"Exactly," Rea said with an approving nod. "So Gregory, Mrs. Patterson, and I have…waterproofed the house. So to speak. We have a system in place just in case. But it sucks up a lot of electricity, so we don't keep it on most of the time. We are now living in as dry a house as is possible."

"Can't the Elemental move through the water pipes, or get in through the showers?" Even as she said it, Katie shuddered at how unguarded she'd been in the shower earlier.

"No, we have an enclosed water system," Eric assured her. "No way to access it from outside the house. And since it can't get in the house now, that's safe, too."

"You're sure it wasn't in the house when you sealed things up?"

"We checked," Rea said. "We ran tests on all the water to make sure it wasn't hiding inside before we dried up the house. Don't worry. We covered the bases. No unauthorized water is getting in."

Katie nodded without being completely reassured. She was going to look twice every time she turned on a faucet. And sitting on the toilet was going to take an act of courage.

"So we're safe in the house," Eric said. "But we can't stay here forever."

"Is the storm still blowing?" With the curtains closed, Katie couldn't tell.

"Even worse than before," Rea confirmed. "I think it's throwing a temper tantrum at being thwarted."

"Well, that's not good."

Rea chuckled. "I think it's very good. Means we're getting under its skin. Metaphorically speaking."

"Yeah, well, I'm not sure pissing off something immortal and as strong as an Elemental is wise. Especially when we still have no idea what it wants."

"Something to do with Jason no doubt," Rea said. "Wish you'd been able to find out what he was up to before you killed him."

Eric frowned. "Next time you can interrogate the homicidal traitor."

Rea snorted. "Would have done a better job than you?"

"Oh, really?"

"Hey," Katie interrupted the growing sibling argument. They sounded just like her and her own siblings, and she was starting to understand why her mother moved to Spain when she remarried. "Can we get back to the issue of what we're going to do?"

"Not sure we can do anything offensive," Rea said. "I mean, we don't know what it wants, were it is, or what it intends to do now. And outside the house is its domain at the moment."

"Plus, we still have the second grinluk running around," Eric said with a sigh.

"We can at least hunt that," Rea said to Katie. "If it's still on the property, we can track it down. But the rain and the unpredictability of the Elemental make hunting impossible right now."

"So we wait it out," Eric said. "It's angry. It won't be able to keep from attacking again. And when it does, we'll be prepared."

"Sounds like this could take a while," Katie said warily.

Rea shrugged. "Might. Elementals are patient bastards."

"But grinluk are not," Eric said. "And that second one is going to be really mad now that we've killed one of its own. The Elemental won't be able to keep it in line if it doesn't agree to help the monster get revenge sooner rather than later."

He sounded very sure of himself. So sure, Katie believed him. "But this could still drag out for days. Weeks?"

"Maybe. But not much longer."

She sighed. "My boss is never going to understand this." At least she didn't have to worry about getting Jess's car back to her. Since the car was totaled and useless now anyway.

"I'll call her," Eric said, "and assure her you're getting an in-depth interview that will ensure a huge increase in circulation."

She thought her editor's head might explode if he called her, but Katie didn't argue with him. A call from *the* Eric Logan would definitely smooth the waters. So to speak.

"Okay," she said, nodding. "I guess we're settling in for a siege then."

"Exactly," Rea said, not the least bit bothered by the idea.

Actually, Eric didn't look upset by the prospect either. Either they were both gluttons for punishment, or they both wanted her to stick around for a while. She had an idea why Eric might want that—and that had to do with the bed on the opposite side of the room. But why would Rea care? Maybe she didn't. Maybe she just didn't consider a few weeks of waiting that big a deal. Did weeks even have meaning to someone who was over a hundred and fifty years old?

Rea and Eric started discussing supplies and defenses, so Katie settled back into her chair to listen. She had nothing to contribute to this part of the conversation, but she wanted to know what they intended to do so she could be prepared. The heat of the fire warmed the side of her face as she listened to the quiet drone of their voices, Gregory also contributing a comment here and there. She smiled at the occasional bickering between brother and sister that never turned into anything serious. Despite the topic of discussion, it was nice listening to a family conversation again. She hadn't had this in a long time.

She sighed and settled farther into the chair as the heat dropped a warm blanket of lethargy over her. She closed her eyes, still listening to the sound of voices and the quiet crackle of the flames.

.   .   .

KATIE WOKE SOMETIME LATER, TUCKED INTO ERIC'S BED. SHE blinked at the dark, quiet room. The fire had died out completely so several hours must have passed. She took a moment to assess her state. She felt quite good actually. The fear and exhaustion of her afternoon had calmed, leaving her more clear-headed than she'd been all evening. She also realized she was physically comfortable. A quick peak under the covers confirmed she was in a t-shirt and panties. Nothing else.

Rolling over carefully, she looked at Eric, sound asleep next to her. He was a warm, reassuring presence, lying on his side facing her. The blankets only came up as high as his waist and he wasn't wearing a shirt, which left that lovely, muscled chest temptingly open to her touch. And she was very tempted. He'd removed the bandage that had wrapped his wounds. There were four small red lines left. No other evidence he'd been injured. Her fingers itched to slide over those red marks, to reassure herself he really was okay.

She turned her attention to his face, studying the handsome planes in the relaxation of sleep. He was breathtakingly gorgeous this way. Almost unreal. In a way, he wasn't real, though, was he. He was a mythic warrior. A more than three-hundred-year-old mythic warrior. That was some age difference. The thought almost made her laugh. She swallowed the sound so she wouldn't wake him.

There was so much more she wanted to know about him. So much still unsaid. But she supposed, given their current situation, she was going to have time to get to know him much better. Depending on how long the Elemental held out, she could be here for quite a while. Being perfectly honest with herself, she wasn't really upset about that. This was likely the only time she'd ever have with Eric. And she wanted the time. To have him all to herself, even if just for a few days. She'd probably get her heart broke into little tiny pieces.

But after what had happened yesterday, she was willing to take that chance. The fight with the grinluk had reminded her how short life could be. Something she'd somehow managed to forget in the years since her sister's murder. She'd been too busy trying to protect herself from that kind of hurt. But she wasn't living. She was biding her time.

She had to start living again.

She stared at Eric's sleeping form. His hard jaw, the sharp cut of his cheekbones, his slightly crooked nose, the dark fan of his eyelashes against his pale skin, and that perfect perfect mouth. Her gaze wandered over his muscled shoulder and down his arm where it rested on his waist. The flat plane of his abs looked firm even in his relaxed state. Her gaze dropped to the blanket over his hips. Was he wearing anything under there? She licked her lips. It would be very easy to run her hand under the blanket and find out.

The idea that he might be completely nude made her pulse thump hard. How would he react if she drew her hand down his stomach, over his hip to cup his firm ass? She could pull him close, feel the rise of his erection against her thighs.

The sensory memory of their extensive make-out session on the couch came back to her, and she could almost feel his mouth on her again. She had to press her knees together as a wave of lust wash through her at the thought of returning the favor.

She could wake him up that way, take his cock into her mouth and suck him until he was hard and trembling. Her fingers inched across the mattress, closer to his chest, and her gaze rose to his torso.

He'd fuck her if she woke him. And they'd both enjoy it. But her fingers froze on the sheets as she stared at his chest, at the red lines still visible through his dark hair.

She couldn't wake him. He might have healed amazingly fast, but the fight had to have done more than just increase his appetite. How could he not be exhausted? If she interrupted his sleep, he'd welcome her advances and willingly sacrifice rest he had to need. If they were going to survive, he had to fully recover physically.

And that wasn't going to happen if she woke him.

The temptation to touch him was so strong, she closed her eyes. But the sight of him, warm and sleeping, stayed with her. Bugger.

As carefully as she could, she rolled over. Maybe if she wasn't able to open her eyes and see him, she'd be less tempted. Still, sleep felt a long way off. With a sigh, she buried her face in the pillow and tried to think of something that wouldn't turn her on. When images of the grinluk flashed through her mind, she corrected herself. Something not sexy and not scary either.

Eventually, replaying one of her favorite comedy movies in her head helped and sleep dragged her back under.

ERIC WAITED UNTIL HE WAS SURE KATIE HAD GONE BACK TO SLEEP before he opened his eyes. He stared at the back of her head, reaching out to touch a lock of her hair where it draped across her pillow. It took every ounce of his willpower to remain still and seemingly relaxed as he felt her looking at him. Her scent filled his head. Every nerve screamed for her. He'd waited, tense inside, hoping, willing her to touch him.

When she rolled over, he could have ripped the mattress in half in frustration.

But she was probably exhausted after everything that had happened that day. He couldn't blame her for going back to sleep. Hell, she'd practically passed out in front of the fire. He was being selfish, wanting to roll her over and finish what they'd started on the couch that afternoon.

He blew out a silent breath. At least she hadn't gotten out of bed to go sleep on the couch. She had to know he'd undressed her. If that had upset her, she wouldn't still be next to him, would she? That was promising. He knew she wanted him. They just needed a little more time.

And it looked like the grinluk and the Elemental were providing that time. Unfortunately, they weren't the kind of distraction he'd prefer.

He closed his eyes again, leaving his fingers resting on that single, soft lock of her hair, and breathed her in. He needed to sleep, too. His lack of rest last night was wearing, and the injury today took a lot out of him. He couldn't afford to be slowed down by exhaustion. Not with the current threat.

But he couldn't stop imagining taking Katie into his arms. He could almost feel her warm curves pressing up against him, and a soft groan bubbled in this throat. Not a good image for getting back to sleep. Reluctantly, he let go of her hair and rolled onto his back.

Exhaustion pulled him back toward sleep. Tomorrow, he promised himself. He'd seduce Katie tomorrow.

CHAPTER TWENTY-SEVEN

Katie woke the next morning to an empty room. She wasn't really surprised. But she was disappointed. If Eric had still been in bed beside her, she wouldn't have felt at all guilty about seducing him since he would have had a full night's sleep.

She glanced at the closed curtains, a faint line of gray light filtered in around the edges, but otherwise the room was dark and the potential for a scary view blocked.

Was she ever going to be able to look out a window again without a faint hint of fear? Not likely anytime in the near future. Time to get thicker drapes in her apartment.

She looked away from the window when the door from the hallway opened. Eric walked in carrying a tray. She sat up to greet him, keeping the blanket across her lap.

"Cereal, eggs, toast, country potatoes, bacon, and orange juice," he said, bringing the tray to the bed. "Courtesy of Mrs. Patterson. She's concerned about you and thinks you need food to recover from yesterday."

"Geraldine is worried about me? I thought she didn't like me because I'm a journalist."

"You atoned for that sin by coming to help me and Rea yesterday." He sat down next to her on the mattress, settling the tray across her lap.

"This is a real treat. I'm not sure I've ever had breakfast in bed—at least not a breakfast I didn't have to make first."

"No ex-boyfriends thought to do this?"

She glanced up at his tone. He looked as if the question was casual, a teasing joke. But there'd been an undercurrent of extreme interest. So he wanted to know about her ex-boyfriends? Well, he was just going to have to ask directly if he wanted details. Besides, she had serious doubts that after more than three hundred years, he was in any position to comment.

"No, the ex-boyfriends never served me breakfast in bed. I'm not sure any of them knew how to make cereal, nonetheless cook eggs and bacon."

His brow creased at her mention of multiple ex's, and she had to hide her smile behind a sip of orange juice. "This is perfect. Though, I could do with some coffee, too."

"I told Mrs. Patterson not to include any. I figured I'd need the lure of coffee to get you to continue the house tour."

"You're willing to show me more?"

"Did you have anything else in mind for the day? We can't go out. The storm is worse, if that's possible. There's been reports of tornados."

"Wow, the Elemental must be really pissed. But aren't tornados wind?"

"Depends on the kind of twister. Eat your food."

She scooped up some potatoes and groaned when the glorious flavor hit her palate. "What does she do to these? They're gorgeous. I've never had country potatoes this good."

"Secret recipe. She won't tell us what she adds. Rebecca's been trying to figure it out for years—she's the family foody."

Katie chuckled and gobbled up more. The eggs and bacon were just as yummy. Though she was a little self conscious eating while he stared at her. "Did you eat?"

"Wouldn't have been able to get out of the kitchen if I didn't."

"How're Rea and the dogs this morning?"

"Patrolling the house. I spent the morning on the phone to Europe."

"Your mother?"

He nodded. "Everyone's been warned. Family's on high alert."

She ate a bit more before saying, "Thank you for getting me to bed last night. I would have had some crick in my neck if I'd stayed in the chair."

"It was my pleasure," he murmured.

And she knew he was talking about getting her undressed. "You're lucky I'm understanding." She hoped she wasn't blushing. It wasn't as if he hadn't seen her nearly naked already. At her own urgings!

"You're lucky I'm a gentleman. You were pretty hard to resist."

"I was so sound asleep I didn't notice you undressing me. I wouldn't have been much fun even if you weren't a gentleman."

"Then I'll be sure you're not even a little sleepy when I drop this guise of being one."

Promises, promises.

But in the light of day—what light there was—she was glad she hadn't given in to her lust last night. Well, the part of her that still hoped she could protect her heart was glad. Most of her thought it might be fun to set aside the tray and pull him in for a little morning nooky.

She wondered why she was still hesitating. Okay, so they hadn't known each other for very long. But he'd told her so much about himself, things that few people outside his family knew. She felt like she knew him far better than the time they'd spent together suggested. She'd even told him about her sister, something she hadn't talked about since leaving for England. Even the people she'd been close with over there didn't know the details. He knew her secret too, her psychic ability. And he accepted it without question or derision.

After less than two days, they probably knew each other better than most couples did after weeks or months of dating. And the more she knew about him, the more she admired him. The more she felt herself falling for him. Hard. That small part of her trying to save herself from heartbreak was fighting a losing battle. She wanted Eric. And she was going to develop feelings for him, whether she wanted to or not.

Unfortunately, she could only picture one outcome to that—and it wasn't a happily-ever-after ending. She wasn't a part of his world, either the billionaire business world or the monster hunter world. She was a journalist living in a small studio apartment in New York, trying to move away from writing gossip. Her life, her goals, didn't seem to mesh with his very well. Which meant there wasn't much of a future for them. Even assuming he'd want one. And that was a huge assumption.

No, casual sex and a bit of fun because they were trapped together... Maybe. But anything more? Anything involving feelings...? That probably wasn't meant to be.

As she finished her eggs, she thought about how it would feel, having him for a short time while she was here and then leaving, knowing she wouldn't likely see him again. It would hurt but... It would hurt more to *not* give in to all these desires. She could live with the consequences, the heartbreak. Because it would be so much worse to never have him.

And really, she didn't have much choice at this stage. She wanted him too much to walk away. She'd accepted that truth last night.

With the acceptance came a growing idea that had her considering him.

"What?" he asked, raising his brows.

"Just thinking." Thinking about seducing him. It seemed only right, since he'd been trying to seduce her for the last two days. Fair was fair and it was her turn. She smiled at him as she considered when, and where, she might make a move. She wasn't feeling quite confident enough at the moment, though the place and the time were both pretty appropriate. But she really wanted to brush her teeth first. Maybe another opportunity would arise over the course of the day.

"I'm not sure I like that look," he said.

"No? You might rethink that later."

His eyes darkened, and she knew he'd picked up her innuendo. If she wasn't careful, the tray was going to end up on the floor and they were going to end up tangled in the sheets. But she didn't want to rush this. He'd been torturing her. It was his turn to suffer a little.

She handed him back the tray, effectively keeping his hands occupied, then pushed the blankets back and climbed out of bed. She didn't bother covering up. He'd seen her already. She strolled into the bathroom in her t-shirt and underwear, knowing he was watching her. "I'll be out in a few minutes."

She closed the door and grinned. Would he be tempted to follow her? Since that would take the situation out of her hands, she went ahead and turned the lock. Her hearing wasn't as good as his so she couldn't be certain, but she'd swear she heard him groan. That made her chuckle.

When she finished showering, she realized she didn't have a fresh set of clothes in the bathroom. Going out there in a towel which barely covered her butt would definitely torture him. It might also land them in bed immediately. But then there were all those bruises along her left side, standing out in sharp relief against the white towel. Actually, she realized as she stared at the bruises in the mirror, those had been on display on her trip into the bathroom, too.

That robbed her of some of her confidence. How sexy could she look with a patchwork of greening purple running down her thigh? So much for teasing him senseless this morning.

She did her best with her hair, taking the time to blow it dry. Then she rebandaged the cut on her leg, checking the stitches. The cut seemed to be healing. She'd have a scar, but she'd accepted that as better than a trip to the hospital anyway, so she wasn't too bothered. She realized as she finished wrapping the clean bandage that Eric had stopped nagging her about stitching the wound up himself. That lapse of memory was a bonus.

Although it meant she couldn't ask him about his experience as a medic without reminding him of his intentions. A little irritating. Now that she'd remembered that detail about his past, she was really curious about the answer. Especially knowing he was over three hundred years old. When exactly *had* he worked as a medic?

Bugger. Maybe in a few days when it was too late to bother

stitching her up she could bring it up. She made a mental note to come back to the topic. Then she faced herself in the mirror. She actually looked more rested than she had the day before. That was something anyway. It would have to do. There wasn't enough makeup in the state to cover her bruises.

Tightening the towel, she left the bathroom. Eric was still sitting on the bed, though he'd set the tray on the coffee table so he'd obviously moved. She went right to her bundle of clothes, sitting on a chair in the corner of the bedroom, and grabbed what she needed.

Eric didn't speak but she could feel his gaze on her. "Is it the towel or the bruises that have your full attention?" she asked without looking at him.

"Both."

She snorted.

"And I forgot about stitching your cut."

She squeezed her eyes shut. Dammit. "Can you read minds? I was hoping you'd continue to forget that."

"Don't worry. It's too late to be much help now. What's there will have to do. You'll have a scar."

"I know. I don't mind."

"I do."

She finally looked at him. "Why?"

"Because you got the scar here. When I was supposed to be looking after you."

"Eric. You've saved my life and are continuing to protect me. I think a scar is a small sacrifice."

"Still."

"Stop. You're no longer allowed to blame yourself. I mean it. Enough."

His lips crooked up at one side. "You sound like Mrs. Patterson. Ordering me around."

"Ha. Well, Geraldine is a smart woman."

"I agree." He huffed out a breath. "Fine, I won't mention the scar again."

That didn't mean he wouldn't keep blaming himself. She shook her head and took her gathered clothes in her arms, heading back to the bathroom.

"You can change out here," he said. "I promise not to attack you."

She smiled. "Right. But what if I attack you?" She closed the door again, laughing aloud this time at the look of interest on his face.

She immerged in jeans and her spare t-shirt. She didn't have a huge range of clothes with her. And between exploding glass and blood, most of what she'd brought was ruined. This interview was supposed to have ended yesterday. She should be driving home today.

"I'd better call my editor again," she said, collecting her mobile from side table beside the bed.

"Meet me in the foyer when you're done," Eric said, standing. "We'll explore some more."

She nodded, frowning a little. Facing the foyer was going to be tougher than she thought. The idea of being in that area of the house made her skin crawl. But it wasn't exactly an area she could avoid. Having a hang-up about going there would be a pain.

Occupied with her thoughts, she missed Eric's approach until he stood in front of her, invading her space. She jerked her gaze up to his, startled by his sudden nearness.

"Next time you walk into the room wearing only a towel," he murmured, "I will not leave you wearing that towel for long." He leaned in so his mouth hovered over hers. "You've been warned."

He kissed her hard, with only their mouths touching. Katie's head spun. She eased closer, wanting to press her body against his, but he broke contact before she could.

He ran his knuckles down her cheek in a brief touch, then left without a backward glance.

She scowled at the closed door. How had he done that? He'd managed to get the upper hand when she was the one who was supposed to be torturing him. Shaking her head, she hit the fast dial for Mona. Her stomach danced at the deliciousness of his threat. Eric Logan did not play fair.

She liked that about him.

CHAPTER TWENTY-EIGHT

When Katie finally reached the foyer, after the call with her editor, her stomach muscles tightened and she had to take a deep breath before stepping out into the open. She expected to see the body of the dead grinluk still there with its twitching limbs and blood splattered everywhere.

But the marble floors were spotless. The entire area cleaned and sparkling. Empty of any corpses. If she hadn't lived through it, she would never have known a major battle went on in this very area only yesterday afternoon.

Eric joined her from the direction of the kitchen. "Ready?"

She nodded.

"Are you okay?"

Sighing, she shrugged. "I'm not sure I'll be able to look at this part of the house again without seeing dead monster."

"I'm very sorry this is happening to you."

"It's not just happening to me."

"But we're used to it. I don't really think about the monsters after they're dead." He touched her cheek with one finger. "Though I'll never be able to get the image of you flying through the air out of my head."

"Yeah, that was fun." He didn't laugh at her sarcasm, but the angry tension tightening his shoulders eased.

Taking her hand, he nodded. "Let's go. I want to show you some of the more exotic parts of the house."

"Exotic? I thought the atrium was pretty exotic."

"The basement garden is even better. And the swimming pool is pretty nice."

"Indoor swimming pool?"

"Yes. The outdoor pool will have to wait."

"Uh huh."

She followed him through the house to a stretch of wall in what looked to be a perfectly ordinary hallway. Eric opened a hidden panel, entered a code onto a small keyboard, then set his eye to a retinal scanner as he pressed his hand against a palm print analysis pad.

She should have known nothing in this house was ordinary.

A door in the dark paneling slid sideways into the wall, revealing a well-lit corridor. The floor was carpeted in thick burgundy, the walls painted a soft sand color and covered with a hodgepodge of paintings and posters. The hallway looked…lived in. Like an ordinary corridor in an ordinary house.

When they'd passed through the hidden door, it slid closed behind them. On this side, it was an obvious wooden door. "Guess there's no reason to camouflage it from this side, huh?"

Eric shook his head. "We like to have parts of the house completely reserved for family."

"I thought a lot of this house was that way."

"Some areas are more guarded than others."

They walked down a small flight of stairs at the end of the hallway and turned left. She looked to the right to see another branching corridor. "What's that way?"

"You'll see later. Don't worry, you'll get to explore everything."

There was a hint of wickedness in his comment. She had a feeling he wasn't just talking about the house.

The first open door they came to held an actual movie theater.

"Holy cow. You've got a cinema here?" A full-sized screen took up one wall in front of stepped rows of couches. The seats looked big and comfortable, softly cushioned and perfect for watching a movie.

"Just a small one for the family."

"This house is even bigger than it looks from the outside, isn't it?"

He nodded. "We had it designed that way."

"How the hell did the grinluk even find its way around this place?"

He made a sound she'd swear was a growl, and the small hairs on the back of her neck rose. His wolf side coming out, she thought, now that she realized why she reacted so strongly to that noise.

"Probably Jason," he said.

"He told them how to get around your family home? That's pretty low."

"He had my father killed. Revealing family secrets is a small sin to that. Though I'd kill him again for this if I could."

"You guys really take your privacy seriously."

He held her gaze for a beat. "You understand why now."

"And I can't blame you." But it did beg the question, why was she here? He'd been evasive about the answer the last time she'd asked. What would he say now? "Still, you brought a reporter into your home?"

He stared at the cinema screen as he said, "That was…different." He tugged her out of the room.

Still evasive. Would he ever admit his reasons for granting this interview? He'd trusted her with so many other secrets, his silence on this point didn't make any sense. Though, to be fair, his trust in her didn't make a lot of sense either.

She'd try asking again when he was off guard. Because she had a feeling the answer was important.

In the meantime… She glanced back at the door to the theater. "Think we can watch a movie later?"

His hand loosened around hers a little. "If you like. A regular date."

She grinned. "Yeah, just dinner and a movie. All in the comfort of your enormous house."

"Makes things easier."

"But you can't kiss me goodnight at the door this way." She cringed the moment the words left her mouth. If that didn't sound like a come on… Not that she didn't want him to kiss her. But subtlety did not seem to be her friend this morning.

His eyes darkened. "We can still arrange a kiss at a door. I just won't be staying on the opposite side of the door after."

Yesterday, she would have contradicted him on that point. Today, she was thrilled by the prospect. So thrilled, in fact, she was tempted to kiss him right then. But curiosity about the house kept her from acting on the impulse. If they started kissing now, they wouldn't stop. She wouldn't want to stop.

She wondered if he was thinking the same thing. Given the way his gaze dropped to her mouth, she was going to say probably.

"Sounds like a nice date," she said. "What time are you picking me up?"

"Seven?"

She laughed. "I'll be ready." Then to keep from attacking him, she walked on, forcing him to follow.

He grabbed her hand again and they strolled side by side while he showed her more of the underground sanctuary. There was a huge game room, complete with classic video games and a basketball hoop. A couple of smaller living rooms, another library—this one had shelves overflowing with paperbacks—and what looked like a fifties-style diner.

"Can I get a chili dog and chocolate shake?" she asked.

"Absolutely. In fact, we can have dinner here if you like."

"I don't want to make Geraldine come all the way down here to cook."

"I can take care of a chili dog and shake," he said.

"You?"

"Don't look so surprised. I don't always have Mrs. Patterson around to cook for me."

"I just never imagined you having time to cook."

"It's rare," he admitted with a shrug. "But after three hundred years, a man picks up a few things. I can boil up a mean pot of water."

She laughed. "I'll look forward to my chili dog, then."

As they continued the tour, Katie realized the corridors seemed to lead in a big circle. When she asked, he confirmed they were walking a loop. "Are there any short cuts if you want to get to something specific?"

"There are. But you see everything this way."

He gestured and she turned to see a beautiful set of stained-glass doors. The pictures on them were intricate and stunning. Whatever was behind the door was well lit, setting the various colors of glass aglow.

"Beautiful," she breathed as she touched the image of a hummingbird hovering over an open red flower.

"This is the garden." He pushed the glass doors inward.

Katie gasped. The room looked as if it was bathed in daylight. Since the rain was still heavy outside and the skies a dark gray, this was obviously artificially lit. But it was so artfully done her internal sensors assumed daylight and a break in the storm.

"How do you do that with the light?"

He pointed to the ceiling. It was a bright, cheery blue. As she watched, a lazy white cloud drifted past. Whatever the ceiling was made of allowed it to glow, almost exactly like sunshine. The artificial sky appeared so real her senses were fooled into believing she was outside. She even imagined feeling the warmth of sunshine on her skin.

"It's a combination of sunlamps, LED lights, and a few experimental gadgets my sister Sarah is working on."

"Experimental gadgets?"

"She's our inventor. To be honest, I don't understand it either, but it has to do with holographic projections and a special polymer coating the ceiling. Sarah's ahead of her time. If the people at MIT ever got wind, she'd never have a moment of privacy again."

Katie chuckled. She wandered into the room and was struck immediately by the thick, earthy scent and the heat like sunshine radiating from the ceiling. The garden itself was as impressive as the special effects. Layers of thick greenery lined stone paths. Within the darker green, flowers bloomed in colorful array. They scented the air in a heady perfume that somehow managed not to overwhelm.

There were no statues here, no little figurines, just plants, flowers, a few small palms and the stone path. She thought she heard running water in the distance and followed the sound, amazed at how large the garden felt.

"This place is like a jungle," she commented over her shoulder.

Eric hung back, letting her explore as he had that first day in the atrium. But this time, she was relaxed, less on edge and worried about the interview.

"We like it here," he said.

She found the source of the water—a small stream running from a rocky outcropping against the wall, across the ground, to disappear beneath a thick layer of ferns. Near the stream a couple of large flat rocks peaked out from the mossy ground covering. They looked like perfect seats for contemplating the bubbling water.

"Is this part of the internal system?" she asked, still leery.

"Yes," he assured. "The entire house has a contained water source. It's beneath this room actually. And this is at the very center of the house."

"It is? I lost track of where we were in relation to the rest of things."

"Another useful trick," he said. "Just in case someone gets past all our security measures and makes it into this area."

"How hard is that to do?"

"You saw the lock. Even finding the panel to get down here is difficult."

"But your cousin could have given the monsters that information."

"Grinluk and Elementals can't fake the biometric security measures, even if they found the panel and knew the code. But I had all the codes changed last night after you fell asleep. Whatever the Elemental knows is old information now."

"That's…reassuring, I guess."

"Still worried about water."

"A little."

"Do you sense anything wrong? Here, with the stream?"

"Not a thing. In fact, my senses are wonderfully quiet at the moment. I haven't felt this calm and settled since arriving."

"So no immediate danger then?"

Oh, she didn't know about that. There was a serious danger standing right in front of her. But Eric wasn't a threat to her life. He was a threat to her heart. And since she'd given in to that eventuality already, her *knowing* had nothing new to tell her.

They wandered through the garden, giving Katie a chance to see most of the room. She had to keep reminding herself they were inside. "This is lovely. I think I'd spend a lot of time down here if I lived in this house. Especially on miserable rainy days. It's like spring, and it's good for my mood."

"Don't like the winter much?"

"Not my favorite season. Though I do like the Christmas holiday stuff. I prefer autumn. Halloween is the best."

He squeezed her hand. "I'm pretty fond of the American way of celebrating that holiday, too."

"Meaning?"

"I like all the chocolate and candy. And I'm good at tricks when I don't get treats."

Her laughter filled the jungle around them.

She was utterly charmed. Just two days ago, she'd been nervous around him. Now she was more comfortable with him than she'd been with anyone in a long time. Even her own family left her feeling a little edgy these days, afraid she say the wrong thing, mention Ana, and drop everyone into a morass of grief. But with Eric, all her muscles had relaxed for the first time in years. Strange, since he'd had her tied up in knots not so long ago. She felt *good.* And she'd missed the simple sensation.

Her level of comfort was at complete odds with the fact that monsters were still after them. Maybe it was the jungle and flower-scented air. Maybe it was just Eric.

She glanced at him from the corner of her eye. He paused and turned to face her.

"What?" he asked.

"Thank you. This…" She waved at the room. "I needed this."

"My pleasure."

Without thinking, she leaned close and touched her lips to his. The shock of excitement was instant, the swell of desire overwhelming. She'd meant to give him a gentle kiss before finishing the tour. But the moment of contact brought back all the unanswered needs of the past few days. In a flash, their kiss went from a gentle press of lips to a deep, desperate exploration.

She found herself jerked up against his body, his arms wrapped tightly around her waist. Clenching her fists into the material covering his shoulders, she molded herself to him, pressing against his full length. She savored the feel and taste of him, letting her tongue twine with his. Oh, she'd wanted this, since last night when she woke beside him in bed, she'd wanted to kiss him. The tension of waiting had tightened her need into a dynamite stick of lust just ready to explode. All it took was one little brush of his lips to ignite the conflagration.

She drew her hands up to his face, cradling his jaw before threading her fingers through his hair. Eric tilted his head and their mouths fused more tightly. His hands stroked up and down her spine, sparking little tingles across her skin and down to her core.

"Katie," he murmured as he pulled his mouth from hers and ran his lips across her neck. "Gods, I want you."

"I want you, too, Eric. I do."

"Not here. Not this time."

"Why?" she panted. He had one hand covering her breast and one squeezing her ass and she had no idea why "here" wasn't as good a place as any.

"The ground isn't as soft as it looks."

She pulled back slightly. "You've got some experience with the ground here?"

"I've heard."

His blatantly false innocent look drove her mad. She tugged his head close and kissed him again. "I love your lips," she said before diving back in.

"I love the way you taste," he answered when he came up for a quick breath.

"More, more, more." She didn't care if the ground was hard. They could find a bed later. She knew once with Eric would be nowhere near enough, so there'd be time for soft cushions and slow passion. Right now, she needed him inside her, and she couldn't wait to get to someplace with a mattress.

CHAPTER TWENTY-NINE

To make her point, Katie reached for the buttons of his jeans. She took a moment to rub the hard ridge of his erection through the denim, then started snapping open the fastenings.

"Katie..." He dropped his head back and groaned when she reached inside to stroke him.

"I owe you," she murmured. She let him take that statement however he chose because she was too busy enjoying the hard feel of him and the way his cock jerked in her palm when she teased the tip with little swipes of her thumb.

With her free hand, she stroked her fingers over the muscles of his abdomen, something she'd wanted to do since last night. He tensed and his hands, where they rested against her waist, clenched tight.

"Take your shirt off," she ordered.

He complied immediately, sending a rush of satisfaction through her. He made her feel powerful and sexy and that fueled her need.

She set her lips against the skin of his chest, just above his heart, reveling in the pounding vibration against her mouth. Flicking her tongue in a quick darting strike, she tasted him, reveling in the flavor of clean, salty male skin. He shuddered and she smiled. Then she kissed her way down his chest, over his stomach, until she was on her knees in front of him, her lips hovering just below his navel.

The sound of his breathing rubbed deliciously against her nerves. She tugged his jeans down over his hips, taking advantage of the move to caress his ass. The muscles bunched in her palms. Once she had his trousers and boxers out of the way, the tempting thrust of his erection waited for her. A quick lick of the tip made him suck in a sharp breath. Humming in pleasure, she took the head of his cock into her mouth, sucking gently. He groaned and the muscles on his thighs tightened under her hands.

"Good?" she murmured, looking up at him.

"Yes."

His voice was deep and gravelly, his gaze heavy-lidded and intense. She licked her lips, watched his pupils dilate further then took the full length of him into her mouth.

She sucked him slowly, setting a steady rhythm, allowing his moans to teach her exactly what pleased him most. He was the perfect size for her, thick and straight, big enough to please without being too large. He was also uncircumcised, and she'd decided in England that she preferred men that way—they were more sensitive and responsive. Her two brief affairs had endeared the male foreskin to her.

Eric's sensitivity was no disappointment. As she fondled and sucked him, she felt his muscles trembling, his stomach clenched tight and his hands fisted in her hair. Giving him pleasure, knowing he was on the edge and she was responsible for taking him there, pushed her own desires to a new level. Each of his guttural grunts of rising excitement sent a shock of lust to her core, making her wet and desperate to feel him deep inside her.

When he finally forced her away from his cock, she was ready to crawl out of her clothing and climb onto him right there. He pulled her to her feet with ease, showing his strength so casually it took her breath away. He sealed his mouth to hers even as he tugged her t-shirt up. She was so eager to be skin to skin, she worked on her own jeans to get them off as quickly as possible. Material ripped, but she wasn't sure whether she'd done the ripping or him. And she didn't care. He barely had her shirt over her head before she was releasing the clasp on her bra. Her breasts spilled into his palms. The sensation was perfect, the rough texture of his fingertips on her nipples a delicious contrast with his gentle pinches. She moaned, but he didn't release her mouth, swallowing her pleasure.

Toeing off her shoes, she wiggled out of her jeans completely, then leaned into him, rubbing her breasts against his softly abrasive chest hair. He pulled back long enough to finish shucking off the last of his clothing, staring at her the whole time. She felt luscious and beautiful under his gaze. And it had been a very long time since she'd felt that way. As he watched, she took off her one last remaining bit of clothing, her panties. His soft growl of approval made her legs tremble.

The instant he was undressed he took her back into his arms. Kissing her hard, his hands moved over her skin. She arched into him, pressing the full length of her body against his, thrilling in the rub of his thighs against hers. She had no idea how they would manage this, short of stretching out on the moss-covered ground, but she didn't really care. As she rubbed her pelvis against his erection, all she could think about was getting him inside her. Now.

Rather than lay down, however, he lifted her off her feet. "Wrap your legs around me," he ordered. When she did, he positioned her just above the jut of his cock.

"Don't you…need something to…lean against." She could barely breathe as he clenched her ass and pressed her against his lower abdomen. So close but not as close as she wanted.

"No," he grunted.

He jerked her hips down, impaling her in one thoroughly satisfying instant. She moaned in relief and clung to his shoulders. She knew he was strong but she was amazed that he could support her full weight like this. She was so pleased with her current position, though, she wasn't about to argue with him.

Clenching her legs around his hips, she rose slowly with his help, then dropped again. They set a slow rhythm, steady and easy at first. She was afraid to hurry, afraid she would come too soon. But the rub of his hair against her clitoris and the need she'd been feeling for days conspired against her. Everything tightened and tightened, built with each thrust, each slow, hard stroke until her orgasm finally broke in a long, body-shaking burst.

She jerked against him and another shockwave cascaded through her system. Each movement extended the sensation until one more orgasm took her. By the time her body started to calm, she could barely breathe. She dropped her forehead onto Eric's shoulder. He was still pumping into her, the friction still felt fabulous, but she didn't think she could possibly come one more time.

Before she could fully recover, he patted her bottom. "Down," he said, his voice harsh and guttural.

She dropped to her feet and then nearly fell because her legs were shaking so much. He grabbed her around the waist and held her while she got her balance. As soon as she could take her own weight, he spun her around and pushed her forward.

"Hold on to the tree."

She hadn't even noticed the palm tree behind her, but she wrapped her hands around the trunk grateful for the support. Eric nudged her legs farther apart, fingered her entrance so that she was fully open to him, and slid inside.

She arched her back and groaned. "God, you feel good." From this angle, she was tighter and he felt thicker and fuller inside her. The point he hit in her changed, and unbelievably, she felt that building pressure coiling in her pussy again.

"So do you," he muttered, already moving. "So damned good. Perfect."

He leaned forward and kissed her shoulder, but his hands remained on her hips as he pumped into her. Harder, faster he moved until Katie could barely stand how wonderful he felt. The sound of skin slapping against skin heightened her pleasure. And when he slammed into her one last time and cried out with his orgasm, she shuddered happily, a last surprise release she'd been certain she wasn't capable of.

He continued to thrust slowly as he spilled into her. She realized belatedly that they hadn't used a condom. She was on the pill so pregnancy wasn't likely. But...well...

"While I thoroughly enjoyed that, down to my toes," she said, with a contented sigh, "we forgot something."

He nuzzled her neck. "Condom."

"Uh, huh."

"I'm healthy."

"Yeah you are." She chuckled and rested her forehead against the palm. "And I'm on the pill and healthy."

"Then we're fine."

"Can you… I mean… Is it hard for your family to make babies?" He had a whole lot of siblings, but he was also over three hundred years old. If babies were easy, wouldn't he have hundreds of siblings at this stage?

"Not hard." He nuzzled the back of her neck. "But it doesn't happen frequently. We live so long if we reproduced as quickly as humans, we'd have overrun the world by now."

Exactly as she'd suspected. She straightened to lean against his chest. He enfolded her in his arms, holding her close, his chin resting on her shoulder.

"But how does that work with people from outside the Families? Or do you…do you only have kids with people from the other six Families? Like say could a dragon make babies with a wolf?"

"It's possible." He chuckled. "Though, I wouldn't put an eagle in the same room with a griffin. And wolves and lions have issues. But it happens."

"How about gay couples?"

"If they want kids, they make arrangements—adoption, artificial insemination—same way same sex human couples have kids."

"And if members of the Families don't want kids?"

"They don't have them. There are enough of us to carry on the Family businesses. And again, because we're so long-lived, the opportunity to have children is a much longer period of time for those who want them."

He lifted away from her and patted her on the butt. The motion made his cock slip out of her. She sighed at the loss.

"This is not the kind of conversation I'd have expected after fucking you against a palm tree," he said. "So much for romantic sweet talk."

She turned and leaned into him, wrapping her arms around his neck. "Wanna talk sweet nothings, or can I keep asking questions?"

He threw his head back and laughed. "As if I could stop your curiosity."

He snuggled her close, a comfortable hug that tightened her throat. How could they be so comfortable? They'd just fucked like sex-starved teenagers in the middle of this beautiful smelling jungle. Her body still tingled from her orgasms—plural. And the feel of his naked skin against hers was like heaven, new and wonderful.

Everything felt so right, so natural. That just shouldn't be possible after so short a time. But she couldn't seem to convince her feelings of that.

She pulled back and studied his face. Was he feeling this connection, too?

He looked satisfied, content. But further than that she couldn't tell. She still couldn't sense a damned thing from him. He was impossible to read beyond what he gave her. So she decided this weird sensation of rightness between them was probably just her. Hopefully, it wouldn't make her life impossible when their time together ended. She'd never felt this way in another man's arms. She was afraid she never would.

"You hungry?" he asked. "I think we'd better eat something."

"Why?"

"Because I fully intend on doing this again very soon. And I need my energy."

She laughed and patted his chest, pulling away when his arms dropped. She bent over to pick up her discarded clothes, heard him growl, and glanced back.

"Get dressed," he said, his gaze growing hotter by the minute. "Or we won't get to the food."

She raised a brow. "You know, you really make a woman feel sexy."

"You are sexy. Get dressed."

"You'd better too," she warned. Then turned her back on him so she wouldn't be tempted.

"Keep asking questions," he said.

She heard the sound of him putting clothes on and got side-tracked by the thought of getting him undressed again. "What?"

"Keep asking questions. It'll keep me distracted enough to get my jeans buttoned back up."

She grinned. "Okay. The Seven Families, they intermarry sometimes, right? Or at least partner up and have babies. But you also take partners and have children with people from outside any of the Families, right?"

"Right."

"So…how does that work exactly? I mean, do you only get a chance at one baby since a human would obviously have a shorter fertility period than you do? Do you marry several people over the course of your life, since they'll always die so much sooner than you do? By the way, I mean the metaphorical you, not *you* specifically." She felt her cheeks heating, but pressed on because he wasn't looking at her so he couldn't see her blush. "What happens in those relationships?"

She worked hard to keep her tone impersonally curious. Her interviewers voice. She didn't want to start convincing herself this thing between them was going to last any longer than the next few weeks. At most. Maybe only the next couple of days—depending on the storm. She definitely didn't want to consider long term and Eric and her all in the same thought.

"Actually," he said, "it depends on the couple."

"Okay. How?"

He was silent. A long time.

She finally turned around to face him. He'd shrugged his shirt on but it hung open. He seemed to be thinking, but he was staring at her so hard she wanted to fidget.

"What?" she asked, suspicious of his expression.

"That is…a complicated area of our lives. Maybe later. When we have more time."

"We have until the storm breaks," she reminded him.

"Not right now. Right now, we only have until I can get us food."

He buttoned up his shirt then nodded toward the front of the garden. "Let's get moving."

His sudden change in mood made her frown. What had she asked? And why was this something he didn't want to talk about?

CHAPTER THIRTY

Katie followed Eric to a small room that looked like a family dining room, and he contacted Geraldine on an internal video communication system. Katie was impressed by the set up and even more impressed at the speed Geraldine managed to get food to them via a dumbwaiter in the wall.

Over lunch, they talked about inconsequential things—travel, plans for the upcoming holidays, even what movie she wanted to see for their date that night—but nothing about his nature or the way relationships with humans and member of his family worked. In a way, though her curiosity was a powerful prod, she was glad they were avoiding the topic. She knew her romantic sensibilities would start conjuring a way to have a future with him. Oh, her practical self knew better. This was temporary. And she knew she'd have regretted missing this with him.

But she also knew she liked the man much too much for so short a period of time. Her liking could all too quickly turn to more. In fact, she was a little worried she was half in love with him already. But he wasn't the kind of man who settled down with one woman. At least, not one relatively ordinary woman like her. She couldn't afford to pretend they might have a future. She sure as hell didn't want to start imagining what that future might be like. If she could just keep in mind that this was a short-term affair, she might not hurt as badly when it ended.

She stared at him across the table, over the remains of their lunch. He was staring back with those dark, heavy-lidded eyes that seduced her so effortlessly.

Too late, she thought. When this ended, she was going to hurt. A lot. And there wasn't a damned thing she could do about that.

They spent the afternoon playing. Katie couldn't quite believe it. But they spent most of the day in the game room playing video games, foosball, shooting hoops, and generally acting like twenty-somethings turned loose at an amusement park.

He made constant excuses to touch her, and each contact left her a little more excited, revving up her desire without giving it any release. The tension was almost unbearable. But it felt so good and fun at the same time. After the events of the last few days, the play was a needed release.

When they walked back upstairs to get ready for their date, she leaned into him. "Thanks. I needed a day like this."

He dropped his arm over her shoulders and squeezed. "We're not finished yet."

He was good at giving promises. He was even better at following through on them.

They watched an old comedy—one of her favorites—and ate popcorn and chocolate-covered raisins. Then true to his word, he whipped up an amazing chili dog and a delicious chocolate milk shake for dinner.

By the end of the night, she started to worry about the calorie intake. She didn't have Rea's metabolism. But when she mentioned that to Eric, he said, "You're going to need the energy."

Sitting on a bench in the little diner in the basement, Katie had to press her knees together to keep from leaping across the table and devouring him. That look, something about the way his eyes darkened, his mouth quirked up at one end, and his nostril flared, left her so damned needy. She'd never been around a man who could do that to her with just a look. But then she was sure there wasn't another man in the world like Eric Logan.

By the time they reached his room that evening, Katie was bursting with anticipation. As she turned to face him just outside his closed door, she remembered not two nights ago doing the same thing across the hall. Then she'd been trying to avoid his kiss. Now, she was worried he wouldn't kiss her soon enough.

"I had a wonderful day, Eric. Thank you."

He wound a tendril of her hair around his finger. "It was my pleasure."

Using the soft hold he had on her hair, he eased her closer with gentle pressure. He held her gaze until only a fraction of an inch remained between their lips, then his attention turned to her mouth. Anticipation made her tingle. He drew out the wait for what felt like ages before finally finally closing the space and touching his mouth to hers.

He kissed her slowly, deliberately, moving his lips over hers in gentle sweeps that kept her tension high. She clutched his shirt in her fists mostly to keep her balance but still ended up leaning back against the door so her weak knees wouldn't drop her to the floor. He followed her but didn't deepen his kiss. He continued to tease her with delicious little nips at her lower lip before soothing her with a gentle touch of his tongue. Each pass was a little more intense, a little more erotic, until a fine tremor rumbled through her body. His was the most delicious kiss she'd ever experienced.

He leaned into her just enough so her breasts just brushed against his chest. Every breath rubbed her nipples into tight little peaks. When she couldn't stand the distance any longer, she used her grip on his shirt to tug him against her. He didn't resist and his weight pressed her hard against the door, even as the heat of his body wrapped around her. The relief of the full body contact was short lived, though, because there were too many articles of clothing in the way. He moved from her mouth to her throat where he continued to tease her. Slow, drugging, toe curling passes of his lips and teeth over the sensitive skin of her neck stole any semblance of coherent thought.

Her hips bucked against his without her permission, a reflex more than anything under her control. The feel of his erection made her stomach dance and she ground herself against him, hoping to relieve some of the pressure building in her.

When he groaned into her neck, she started to pant. "We should… we should go inside now."

Without a word, he reached down and opened the door. His free arm wrapped around her waist, keeping her from falling backward, but with the loss of the solid wooden support, they still stumbled awkwardly into the room. He kicked the door closed as he wrapped his other arm around her and brought her up tight against his chest.

His mouth returned to hers, now more urgent and demanding. She softened against him so every curve fitted to his hard body. The sheer maleness of him thrilled her and she could barely wait to get him naked and explore every inch of his muscled form. Then he lifted her off the floor and carried her to the bed, never releasing her captive mouth.

She couldn't seem to taste enough of him. He was like chocolate and coffee, both addictive and required to make her day good. As the tension tightened, she tangled her tongue with his, fighting for more, deeper, harder.

He set her on her feet at the edge of the bed and wasted no time getting her naked. She'd been afraid he'd take his time and strip her slowly, the way he'd kissed her so languidly at the door. Fortunately, whatever control he'd been exerting earlier had dissolved the instant they entered the room. He didn't waste a minute with his own clothes either. Soon they were both blessedly naked, flesh rubbing against flesh, creating a cascade of shocks and tingles through her system.

He tumbled her back onto the bed and she welcomed his weight. This was what she'd wanted last night but had resisted. Her resistance seemed ridiculous in that moment, with him in her arms. Too late to alter her earlier decision, but she intended to make up for the lost time.

She filled her hands with him, her mouth, learning what made him groan or sigh. And when he growled, that low sound that made the hair on her nap stand up, she shivered in delight.

When he entered her, condom on this time, he held her face

between his palms, keeping her gaze locked to his. The intensity of his stare heightened the feel of his slow penetration until she swore she could feel him everywhere. Wrapping her legs over his hips, she arched up to meet his thrusts, taking him as deep as she could. They danced together, faster, harder, until she could no longer hold his gaze. She dropped her head back against the pillows, closed her eyes and let go. Her orgasm tore through her so strongly she couldn't even cry out.

As the waves of sensation settled, Eric's rhythm increased and he followed her over the edge. His muscles tensed, his head thrown back and his jaw clenched, sweat dripped down his chest and beaded on his brow. He looked out of control and wild. In that instant, she could believe he carried the essence of a wolf.

He settled heavily on top of her and hugged her close. Snuggling her cheek into his shoulder, she hugged back and swallowed a sigh. Damn. This felt too good. She didn't want to give him up.

Especially since she was now sure she was in love with him.

CHAPTER THIRTY-ONE

They spent the next few days playing in the basement, exploring the house, and fucking at every conceivable opportunity. Eric couldn't get enough of her. Just when he thought he was satisfied, she'd glance at him over her shoulder, or flash that mischievous grin of hers, and he'd want her all over again.

The storm outside continued to slash down out of the skies. The Elemental was obviously not prepared to give up easily. Yet they'd seen no sign of the remaining grinluk or experienced any attempts by the monsters to get past the house security. Gregory kept a close watch, and they met each day to discuss any problems. Rea stayed on guard as well, and she and the dogs patrolled the house several times a day. She refused his help, saying he should stick close to Katie. Since that was exactly what he wanted to do, he hadn't argued too hard.

The lull in attacks had him edgy, though, like waiting for the proverbial second shoe. But keeping Katie entertained and her mind off the danger was enough of a focus to prevent him from going stir crazy.

He had daily reports from those of the Family he could reach. No one had any useful information. Whatever the Elemental intended, it had kept the plan carefully concealed from any of the wolf Family. He'd have to approach the heads of the other six Families eventually.

But until he knew more, he hesitated to discuss this with anyone other than his own people. The Elemental might just have a personal grudge against the wolves. In which case, it was their fight alone. The other Families wouldn't get involved. If it was something bigger, however, all seven Families would come together to prevent disaster.

In the meantime, he concentrated on getting Katie to stay with him. He hadn't actually asked her to yet. He wasn't even sure how to pose such a question. She'd stopped asking him about relationships between ordinary humans and his kind, and in a way, that was good. Telling her that part of the story would involve revealing his full nature. He didn't want to do that until she was ready to stay with him. Yet he wasn't sure he could convince her to stay if he kept avoiding the topic of long term relationships. He was caught in a quandary of his own making.

If he spent enough time with her, though, he was positive he could ensure the revelation of his true nature didn't scare her away. The very thought of her leaving terrified him. There wasn't much he could do if she decided she couldn't live with what he really was because he was prohibited from forcing her to stay.

And frankly, now, he couldn't even conceive of forcing a relationship on her. He wanted her to *choose* him. To *want* him. To stay with him because of what was between them, not what an ancient god had decreed. She was his Nam-tar, his destined mate, and she could break his curse, but… But he hadn't been prepared for how much more she'd mean to him than that.

Convincing her to remain in his world… She'd already had to face a graphic example of what he fought on a regular basis. That much, at least, she seemed to be taking in stride. Would she be able to accept the rest so easily?

He needed time. Time the storm was giving him, but he wasn't sure it would be enough. So he spent what time he had in a constant effort to woo and seduce her. The seducing was working out well—to both their enjoyment. He was pretty sure she felt something more than just lust for him, too. There was a flavor in her scent now that hadn't been there before, a sort of hopeful burst of spice that went beyond just sex. He just needed to make sure those feelings turned to love. If she fell in love with him, she wouldn't leave him, even after finding out the full truth. If she loved him, she'd choose him. She'd stay.

On the third day after the grinluk invasion, Eric finally talked her into taking a swim in the heated, indoor swimming pool. She'd resisted, despite his assurances about the contained water supply. But when they continued to pass the days in safety, she gave in to his coaxing.

"I'll have to borrow a swimsuit," she said, staring dubiously at the water.

"No, you won't."

"You said there are cameras in here. I'm not skinny dipping in a place Gregory can monitor."

"First, Gregory would always respect your privacy." He pulled her into his arms. "Second, the camera can be temporarily turned off."

"Is that a good idea? With everything going on."

He nuzzled her neck, knowing it made her more susceptible to his logic. Or maybe it made her less capable of heeding her own. Either way, the move gave him an advantage in their debates. And as soon as he could reach the back of her knee, she'd lose all sense of resistance. Discovering just how sensitive she was there had been one of his favorite parts of the last few days.

"It's your choice," he said. "We can leave the camera on, and have a video recording of our swim, or we can turn it off, and you'll just have to rely on me to protect you."

"I'm not worried about that," she murmured.

Her breathing had deepened and the sound sent a shiver of satisfaction through him.

"I trust you to protect me."

That statement brought his head up. "You do?"

"Of course. You've been doing a wonderful job of it so far. Why wouldn't I trust you? This is your job after all."

"You're more than a job, Katie."

She smiled. "I'm glad to hear that. You know you're more than a job too, right? I mean…the interview… Well, I still have to give my editor something, but this stopped being about that interview days ago."

A rush of excitement swept through him. If she saw him as more than that bloody interview, she'd be able to consider a relationship with him. "Good," he murmured. "And I will keep you safe. No matter what."

"Then I guess we should turn off that camera." Her smile turned sultry.

He gave her a quick, hard kiss because he couldn't resist. Then he went to the internal communication system and got in touch with Gregory, letting him know they were turning the camera off on purpose.

"Yes, sir. Please let me know when you're ready for the camera to be turned on again."

"I will, Gregory. Thanks."

When he returned to Katie, she was staring at him with raised eyebrows. "What?" he asked.

"You do this often? Go skinny dipping with women?"

"Why do you say that?"

"Gregory didn't think your order was particularly startling. He has to know why you want that camera off."

"Of course he knows. But why would you think that meant I did this a lot?"

She paused, as if his way of thinking about the situation hadn't occurred to her.

"Katie, the whole house knows we're sleeping together. Or...not sleeping, as the case may be."

Her cheeks flushed a lovely pink, which surprised and charmed him.

"I know," she said. "It's just a little embarrassing that everyone knows what we're up to."

"Don't worry. They won't spy."

She rolled her eyes and glanced away.

Rather than give her time to over think and change her mind, he simply lifted her shirt up over her head and threw it aside. She gasped but didn't resist.

"Are you sure the camera's off now?"

"Yes." He removed her bra next.

"How can you tell?"

To his pleasure, she didn't cover herself even though she was still worried about the camera. "The blinking red light is off now."

"There's a light? Where's the camera? I didn't know you could see it."

She looked around the room, heedless of her partial nudity, and it was all he could do not to rush to get inside her. To maintain some semblance of control, he pointed out the location of the camera across the room. "See, no red light."

"I never saw the red light to begin with. How do I even know there was a red light?"

"Katie."

She grinned sheepishly and shrugged. "Okay, you're right. If I trust you enough to protect me, I should trust you enough to believe we don't have an audience."

"Exactly. Now turn around."

She did as commanded, facing him again, and he went to work on unfastening her jeans and getting her out of the rest of her clothes. When he was done, he stood back to take in her beauty. The cut on her leg was healing well, the edges had sealed and formed a scab, making the butterfly stitches unnecessary. At this stage, he was sure the chlorine wouldn't sting either, which was good. He was still sorry she'd have a scar. The thought that she'd been scarred under his roof bothered him. But she didn't seem worried, so he tried not to think about it too much. Fortunately, her bruises had also faded to faint yellow splotches. Thank the gods. Each injury only reminded him how close he'd come to losing her, and the very idea made him crazy.

"Are you just going to stare or are we going swimming?" she asked.

Her voice dropped to a seductive tenor which brushed over his skin in velvety strokes. He loved when her voice did that. "I thought I might stare a bit. But don't let that stop you."

"Strip," she ordered. "I want company when I step into that water for the first time."

He complied, watching her watch him as he removed his clothing. The way her blue eyes dilated and her breathing sped and her scent filled with that heady spicy flavor of lust. Her obvious arousal went right to his cock. By the time he was nude, he was also fully erect and more than a little convinced they'd never make it to the water.

She stepped back when he reached for her, though. "Into the pool, big guy. You've promised me it's safe. Now show me how lovely water can be."

He groaned, but happily complied, because he wanted her feeling comfortable and safe. He stepped to the brick-lined edge and dove in, surfacing halfway across the width of the pool. A gentle swing of his arms turned him to face her. She stood at the edge of the water, remaining very still for a long moment. With her gaze locked to his, she stuck her toe into the pool. A moment later, a slow, wicked grin lifted her lips, and she dove in.

She reached him in a single stroke, and he immediately took her into his arms.

"You were waiting to see if your psychic senses sounded the alert," he commented as he pulled her body close to his.

Warm water swirled around and between them. Where skin touched skin, a shock of heat shivered through him. He'd made sure the temperature in the pool was bathtub comfortable—he wasn't planning on doing laps, and freezing water wouldn't have been good for his image—but the heat of their entangled limbs seemed to increase the warmth around them.

"I was," she answered. "Not that I don't trust you. It's just that, well, things happen beyond your control. Like the atrium."

He smiled when she said she trusted him again. Trust between them would be extremely important. He had a momentary stab of guilt that he was still hiding part of his nature, but he pushed the guilt aside. If she trusted him, if she loved him, she'd forgive him for waiting to reveal his final secret.

"I understand," he said. The feel of her body swaying against his made thinking difficult, but he made an attempt. "I wasn't offended. You didn't get a warning?"

"Not even a tingle." Her mouth quirked up at one side and she rubbed her breasts against his chest. "Well, not psychically. I *am* tingling."

The confession broke what little concentration he'd maintained. Tightening his grip around her waist brought her face close enough for a kiss. They met in a hard, sensuous clash of lips and tongues. What was it about her? He never seemed to be able taste enough, feel enough. The brush of her hips against his erection made his spine arch. He dropped a hand to her ass and pulled her hard against his cock, rubbing against her with abandon. The thrill of simply touching her amazed him. Being inside her was heaven. And it was the only place he wanted to be.

He kicked out, keeping her close with one hand as he swam them toward shallower water. When his feet touched the ground, he stood. Only his shoulders were above the surface, but now he had enough leverage. She wrapped her legs around his hips without prompting and rubbed against him. He slid one hand down the back of her thigh to the soft skin behind her knee. She bucked and her legs tightened as she gasped.

"So damned sensitive here," he murmured, drawing small circles in that tender spot. "Could you come just by me touching you here?"

"Maybe. I don't know. Let's try sometime. But not now. Now I want you inside me."

He growled softly and kissed her again. Water sloshed over his chest and arms, a sultry caress along his dancing nerves. He gripped her hips and pulled her down onto his cock in a slow, steady thrust, giving her exactly what she'd asked for. She groaned into his mouth, her fingers digging into his shoulders.

"Gods, I thought the water was warm." He moved his mouth to her throat. "You feel so good, Katie. So hot and tight."

"Eric."

Her voice was breathy and strained. The sound made his muscles clench with need. He pumped into her, steady and hard, making sure the water never splashed up into her face. The rhythm made her gasp with each thrust, and he felt her tightening around him. He shifted his hands from her hips to her butt and squeezed, knowing that little move would excite her further. He wasn't disappointed, her gasps turned to a sharp cry. He leaned back just enough to watch her face. A sexy pink warmed her cheeks, her lips were wet and parted, her eyes narrowed to slits. She held his gaze for a few strokes. But when she started to tremble, her eyes closed and her head dropped back.

He continued to watch her as she slipped one hand between their bodies and caressed her stomach. The move pulled his gaze down. She brushed her palm over her curls until she was teasing her clit with one fingertip. He couldn't look away, the sight of her pleasuring herself even as he moved in and out of her drove him out of his mind.

He pumped faster, answering his own rising tension. When her fingers increased their pressure, he thrust harder. The water around them splashed and rippled until he could no longer watch the show beneath the surface. He looked up to savor her expression again, but his own release was beating against his resistance. Knowing how close she was, he moved hard, faster, and was rewarded with the sight of her orgasm shuddering across her face. The shivers of her climax rippled over his cock and triggered his own orgasm, forcing him to close his eyes as his body erupted with pleasure and release.

Breathing hard, he opened his eyes to see Katie staring at him. He smiled. She smiled back.

And Eric felt his chest tighten. Love was a very strange emotion. One he thought he could get used to.

So long as Katie let him.

CHAPTER THIRTY-TWO

The next morning, Katie woke to bright sunshine slipping in through the curtains. She blinked at the shocking band of light. A full minute passed before she realized why she was squinting. A breath later, she realized what it meant.

"Eric, Eric." She nudged his arm where it rested on her waist. Rolling over in his still heavy hold, she pushed at his chest and stared at the sunshine. "Eric, wake up. The storm's gone."

He woke so suddenly and completely she jumped.

"Gone?" He looked over her shoulder to see the same bright slash of light between the curtains.

"Is that a good thing or a bad thing?" she asked.

"Not sure."

He threw the covers off and rolled out of bed. Katie took a moment to admire his naked butt as he headed to the bathroom, then got out of bed and hunted up something to wear. Thanks to Gregory's constant efforts and a few borrowed pieces from Tanya's closet, she had clean clothing every morning. She was starting to feel a little spoiled. How would she go back to doing her own laundry down at the laundromat after this?

She dressed and traded places with Eric as he came out of the bathroom, still beautifully naked. He headed to his closet saying, "I'll wait till you're ready. Then we'll go talk to the others. I don't want to leave you alone, just in case."

"Just in case…," she muttered as she closed the door. That statement filled her with a sense of dread. Not her psychic dread, fortunately. Just an ordinary sense of unease. She never thought she'd distrust the appearance of sunshine.

When she emerged from the bathroom, Eric was dressed in black slacks and a black button-down, like he'd worn the first day they met, and was pacing in front of his couch. He glanced up when she cleared her throat.

"Ready?"

She nodded. "You're worried."

"Without a storm, I have no idea where the Elemental is. It could have left. It could still be lurking around the house. At least with the rain falling, I knew where the damned thing was."

"True. You think it left."

"No." He took her hand and led her from the room.

They met Gregory and Geraldine in the kitchen. Rea came loping in a moment after Eric asked where she was.

"The storm left a lot of flooding and damage in its wake," Gregory said as Geraldine poured cups of coffee. "I've called emergency services. It will take days to clear the roads—after the flooding subsides. They said that could take at least three days."

"So basically we're still trapped in the house for another week or so?" Rea said before slurping her coffee. She downed a cup before Katie could take two sips then went to the coffee pot for more.

"At least another week," Gregory confirmed.

"Our supplies?" Eric asked.

"We've got plenty." Geraldine waved away that concern. "We could hold up here for months. Even feeding Rea. Made sure of that myself."

Eric flashed her a smile that made the older woman roll her eyes. Katie grinned into her cup. So even Geraldine Patterson wasn't immune to his rare full smiles. Nice to know she wasn't the only one.

The thought of not seeing those rare smiles anymore wiped away Katie's amusement.

But this was no time for sentimentality. Especially when Eric had made her no promises. She expected their affair to end when this situation ended. She'd been given a little more time, but things would end eventually. Soon. And she'd have to deal with that.

Unfortunately, her heart was not listening to rational thought.

And damn him anyway for making her fall in love with him.

As she watched him discuss supplies with Geraldine, she wondered if she'd have done anything differently, knowing what she knew now. The sad, pathetic answer was no. She wouldn't have given up this time with him no matter how much it was going to hurt when it ended.

"Do we risk a survey of the grounds?" Rea asked.

The comment pulled Katie's attention back to the danger. "Is that a good idea? We don't know where this Elemental is. Shouldn't we maybe wait awhile. Until we can be sure it's left?"

"It's immortal," Eric said. "It's concept of time isn't like ours. Even days of waiting won't guarantee it's left." He reached across the table and took her hand. "But we don't want to rush things either. We'll start with a scan through the external cameras. See if they're all working, or if any have been disabled."

"I've already started a scan," Gregory said. "So far, all is in working order."

"Why couldn't we use the external cameras during the storm to locate the monsters?" Katie asked.

"The storm made visual scanning unreliable," Gregory said.

"And even with the cameras, we won't be able to see the monster or the Elemental. They move too fast. Remember?" Eric squeezed her hand.

"Then why bother with them now?"

"Because if something isn't working, that'll give us a place to look," Rea said. "The Elemental would only bother disrupting cameras to hide something."

"And it would know that's where you'd look, wouldn't it?"

"Yes," Eric said.

"Then that could be a trap."

"Yes," he said again. "But at least it would draw the creature out."

"And anything is better than waiting around indefinitely for something to happen," Rea said. "That thing could keep us holed up here for ages. I am not that patient."

"An understatement," Eric muttered.

Rea smacked him none too gently on the arm as she paced past the back of his chair.

"So we use the cameras to find a place to start a physical search?" Katie asked.

"Exactly," Eric said.

"Then I'll take the dogs out to see if we can find anything," Rea added.

"And I'll back her up when and if she needs it."

Katie tensed at the thought of either of them going out to face those things. "Is there any other way? Can't you wait for help, more of the family maybe?"

"We can't afford to risk anyone else," Eric said.

Rea put a hand on Katie's shoulder. She looked up at the other woman.

"If the Elemental wants to kill our Family," Rea murmured, "it'll be harder to do if we're scattered around the world."

"That's what you've decided its plan is?" Katie faced Eric again. "You think it wants to kill off all of your Family?"

"I think it's a good enough hypothesis to keep me cautious."

"Fuck," Katie muttered, twirling her mug on the table with one hand.

"Don't worry," Rea said, squeezing her shoulder before circling to a seat across the table. "Most of the time, there's only one of us around to fight a monster. You've got two protecting you." She winked. "Piece of—"

"Don't say cake!" Katie raised a hand to cut off Rea's comment. "Every time someone says that phrase in a movie something awful happens. I'd prefer not to jinx us."

Rea tilted her head to one side and raised her brows. "I never noticed that before. Guess I'd better rid that phrase from my vocab. Like not saying Macbeth in a theatre around actors."

"Exactly. Just think of me as your friendly neighborhood superstitious journalist."

Rea shook her head as she gulped more coffee. "I can't believe you've got a sense of humor in the middle of all this. Thought I was the only one with that kind of sick humor."

"Believe me, I'm more than a little terrified." She glanced out the massive glass doors making up one wall of the kitchen to the sunny morning beyond. "This is way beyond my usual experience."

Eric lifted her hand and kissed her knuckles. "I promise nothing will happen to you."

"I'm not worried about me. You and Rea are the ones that will be fighting that thing. Have you ever even faced an Elemental before?"

Eric and Rea exchanged looks. "We haven't," Eric said. "But our father did. When he was young. A Water Elemental."

"Did he… Well, he couldn't have killed it. But did he make it dissipate or whatever?"

"Yes."

"Is this revenge?"

"There's no way to know."

"But you've considered the possibility."

"I think revenge is a possible motive. I can't know if this is the same Elemental my father faced. But since this Water was working with my cousin, I assumed the revenge was for Jason's death. Not necessarily anything my father had done."

"Yes, but your cousin arranged your father's murder."

"There are a lot of reasons for killing off the head of one of the Seven Families. I can't assume anything."

"If this is revenge because of what your father did, things are much more personal."

"They've been personal since my father was killed."

She held Eric's gaze for a quiet moment. "Fair enough." Straightening her shoulders, she picked up her coffee mug again. "So we look for places to start hunting the Elemental and the grinluk using the cameras. Then, Rea and the dogs go sniffing around the backyard?"

Rea nodded. The woman looked entirely too pleased by the plan.

"You're enjoying this," Katie accused.

"It is what we do."

"Yeah, but you don't have to like it so much."

"Do you like being a writer?"

"Of course. I wouldn't do it otherwise."

Rea shrugged. "Same."

"Yes, but mine isn't a divinely appointed duty. I thought you *had* to hunt monsters."

Rea's gaze was in her mug when she said, "Well, yes, we do. But that doesn't mean we can't enjoy our work."

Katie snorted. "If you say so."

Rea grinned and propped her legs up on the table, cradling her coffee cup in her hands.

"So, then what? Rea and the dogs go hunting and…?"

"Then we plan around what they find," Eric said.

Geraldine set a plate of eggs and bacon on the table in front of her as she stared at Eric. "You mean you aren't going to have a strategy before sending her out there?"

"The strategy will be dependent on what she uncovers."

Eric forked in a mouthful of eggs as she continued to stare, dumbfounded. "I don't mean to judge. I'm sure you guys know your jobs better than I do. But it seems to me not having any plan beyond, 'wait and see what Rea finds' isn't a very good plan."

"A lot of what we do involves flying by the seat of our pants," Rea said. "It's what works best under certain circumstances." She didn't even bother to drop her feet from the table when Geraldine handed her a breakfast plate. She simply set down her mug, took up the plate and shoveled food into her mouth.

Katie noticed Rea's plate was double the size of hers own and loaded with significantly more food. "I don't like it."

"That's why you'll be staying safe inside with Gregory and Mrs. Patterson," Eric said. "No more running to our rescue."

She frowned down at her plate. "I seem to recall helping last time."

"And giving me several heart attacks in the process." He gripped her hand under the table, his hold tight, and lowered his voice. "If I'm going to concentrate on the hunt, you have to be safe."

She shrugged, not about to make a firm promise, but also not fool-hearty enough to go charging in again unless the situation was life or death.

The problem was, in this game, it was always life or death.

CHAPTER THIRTY-THREE

After breakfast, Geraldine went into the video surveillance room to finish the scans while Gregory went off to some mysterious errand he didn't feel the need to share. Katie stayed in the kitchen sipping coffee while Rea went to get her dogs and Eric to collect weapons.

As she stared at the beautiful green grass and boxes of evergreens and spices outside the kitchen door, she tried very hard not to worry. Instead, she opened herself up to her psychic sense and tried to *know* something. She'd so rarely made an effort to use her other sense. Mostly, the feelings just came over her. In fact, until coming to this house, she couldn't remember ever opening herself up to her *knowing* on purpose.

But now, the situation was too dangerous, the outcome too potentially devastating for her to keep suppressing her talent. If she was ever going to get a psychic flash that actually helped, this was the time to get it.

She settled into her seat, letting her vision blur and her mind wander. At first, she simply tried to assess if she was getting a psychic nudge through all her ordinary panic. When she was sure she could tell the difference between her fear and her *knowing*, she began searching with her entire body for that sense, hunting for something, anything that would help Rea and Eric.

She wasn't sure how long she sat at the table concentrating. She had no sense of time passing. There was just the smell of coffee and bacon, the quiet hum of the dishwasher, the passing of clouds over the sun outside, the gentle sway of greenery in a breeze. Air moved across her cheek, warm and gentle as the heaters kept the kitchen comfortable. Her nerves felt open to and yet securely insulated from the world around her.

Remaining in that quiet place, she hunted for danger in *her* way.

And came up with only a vague sense of dread and unease. Nothing concrete. Nothing to point to the location of the monsters. Nothing that would help keep Eric alive.

"Bollocks," she growled and dropped out of the trance she'd invoked. She took a sip of her coffee. It was cold.

"Are you okay?"

Eric's voice startled a choked "eep" out of her.

She turned to face him, coughing to clear her throat. "I'm fine." She heard the frustration in her own voice and shook her head. "No, I'm not. I'm scared and there's nothing I can do to help. Believe me, I was just trying."

"You were attempting to get a psychic…vision?"

"Yes."

"And?"

"And it didn't bloody work. Of course. Why would it when I really need it? It never has before."

"Katie, you keep saying that, but your psychic premonitions have kept us both from getting killed at least three times since you arrived. You are helping. Your ability is helping."

She blew out a breath and stood to face him. "I want to believe that. I know on some level you're right. The problem is, this thing isn't over and all my previous success will be meaningless if you die in this next fight."

A very slight smile lifted the edges of his mouth. "Then I'll just have to stay alive."

"Please do. I'd really appreciate it."

"Katie."

He opened his arms. She took three steps and sighed into his embrace. The strength she felt coursing through his body helped calm some of her fear. He had been doing this for a long time, she reminded herself. More than three hundred years. And he was still alive. He'd be okay.

"When this is over, we should take a trip," she said. "Someplace warm. Where you won't need to wear a lot of clothes."

He laughed, so hard his body shook. "I was just thinking the same thing," he said into her hair. "Especially the part about us not wearing much clothing."

"Great minds," she murmured and tipped her head back so she could kiss him. She was revealing too much. If he hadn't guessed she loved him, her last comment at least made it clear she wanted this relationship to continue. That was the closest she'd come to admitting the truth to him.

And he wasn't running away or putting off her suggestion. He was embracing it even as he held her. Which meant he wasn't in a hurry to be rid of her.

At least not yet.

But hope was a double-edged knife.

Several hours later, the scans were complete and Geraldine announced several possible places to search. Cameras were down in half a dozen locations around the estate. The problem was, neither she nor Gregory could tell if the malfunction was deliberate or just a product of the storm.

"Gives me a few places to check anyway," Rea said.

Her dogs snuffled against her legs, both looking eager to get outside. The injured one, Bella, seemed to have recovered fully, a fact which amazed Katie. Everyone in this house healed fast except her. And possibly Gregory and Geraldine. So far, they'd been smart enough not to get hurt, though.

Rea pulled the swords from the scabbards strapped to her hips and thighs and whistled to the dogs. They trotted out in front of her, heading toward yet another area of the house Katie was unfamiliar with. Rea waved over her shoulder with one sword and loped after them.

"She seems…relaxed," Katie commented, still confused by Rea's response to the danger.

Eric shrugged. "Rea likes the tension of a hunt. And the dogs need a run. She's always happier when her dogs are happy."

That comment reminded Katie of something. "You said the other day, during the grinluk attack, that she was the only one in the family that could be around dogs? Dogs don't like the…wolf in you, is that it?"

"Domestic dogs tend to be nervous around us, that's all."

"Then why do they like Rea?"

"Rea is…unique."

Katie snorted. "That I figured out."

She glanced down at the sword on his hip. He also had a knife tucked into a scabbard at the small of his back and another two knives inside his boots. He wore olive green canvas trousers and a fitted brown thermal sweater. The combination of clothing and weaponry made him look like an odd mix of modern and ancient warrior. The overall impression was incredibly powerful and, she had to admit, pretty damned sexy.

He didn't look like he was the least bit worried. His expression was composed and calm, as if waiting for the other shoe to drop didn't have any effect on him.

"You're not even the teensiest bit worried about your sister?" she asked.

"Rea is a good hunter. She has excellent individual skills that make her very good at what she does."

"But she's never faced an Elemental before." Katie gestured to the knife at his back. All of his weapons were the special ones needed to fight a Water Elemental, but Rea had only taken a few extra daggers with her. Her swords were the same ones she'd used fighting the grinluk.

"Will it make you feel better to know I'm a little worried?"

She couldn't tell if his tone was condescending, sarcastic, or sincere. "No. But maybe I'd feel less alone in my fear."

He pulled her into a hug. "You're not alone, Katie. Ever."

She settled her head on his shoulder and tried to take comfort in his embrace. Just as his strength started to relax her muscles, however, the radio in his thigh pocket squawked. Eric pulled it out while still keeping an arm around her shoulders.

"Go," he said.

"Found one of the broken cameras." Rea's voice came back crystal clear. "Looks like water damage. Serious water damage."

"Accident or on purpose?"

"Can't tell for sure," she said. "Damage is too subtle. No sign of grinluk, though."

"Keep looking. Stay out of any puddles."

Katie heard Rea's snort before the connection broke with a loud static bark.

"One down. Five to go," Eric said.

"Yeah, and a whole lot of open ground in between."

CHAPTER THIRTY-FOUR

The tension nearly did Katie in. By the time Rea radioed in a report on the final camera, she was stalking through the halls, stopping by the kitchen to check in, then continuing her circuit of the nearby corridors. She stuck to parts of the house she knew so she wouldn't get lost, but she couldn't sit still.

Eric, on the other hand, had remained calmly standing in the kitchen waiting for Rea's reports. When they all came back negative, Katie wanted to scream. Eric remained stoic.

By the time Rea rejoined them, it had been dark for half an hour.

"So?" Katie asked. "Any sign of…anything?"

Rea glanced at Eric and something unspoken passed between them. Then she shrugged and said, "No sign of the Elemental or the grinluk."

Katie frowned. "So what do we do now?"

"We quarter the ground and hunt in sections," Eric said. "They can't and probably won't avoid us for long." He motioned Rea close. She complied and he stared into her face for a long moment. Then he said, "You need food and rest. I'll take the first quarter."

Katie expected Rea to protest. She was no doubt hungry—Rea was always hungry—but she didn't look all that tired. Instead, the woman nodded compliantly. She leaned in, whispered something to Eric, glanced at Katie, back at Eric, and raised a brow. He shook his head very slightly but enough for Katie to deduce he was telling Rea to keep whatever they'd just said between them. Katie's curiosity and annoyance rose in equal measure.

She waited until Rea left before she said, "What the hell was that about? What did Rea whisper to you? Can you read her mind or something?"

He held up a hand. "What makes you say that?"

"The way you were staring at her. It almost looked like you two were talking without talking."

"I have a lot of talents, love, but mind reading isn't one of them. However, as the Family leader, I do have a heightened…awareness of the physical condition of my family members. It's important when sending them out to hunt that I know what kind of shape they're in. And when the head of the Family says you need rest and food, you go get rest and eat. No arguing."

"Okay. That's kind of cool." She shook her head. "But that doesn't tell me what she said to you. What was with that look she gave me? You didn't want her to tell me something. What was it?"

"If I wanted to tell you, I would have."

His answer made her straightened her shoulders. *Now* he was keeping secrets? When this was life or death? And after all they'd been through, all they'd revealed. Hell, she'd told him about her Pulitzer ambitions and she kept that mostly to herself.

She felt betrayed even though the logical side of her brain cautioned that her reaction was excessive. Especially when he hadn't made any promises to her. They might know each other better now, but that didn't mean he was willing to tell her everything.

"Fine," she said, looking at the wall so she wouldn't have to meet his gaze. "Your choice."

"Yes. Besides, you don't want to know."

"Oh, well, that makes me less curious." The sarcasm in her voice couldn't completely hide the hurt.

"Katie…"

She put a hand up to stop him. "Look, I don't have the least clue what's going on with all this monster hunting crap, so you're probably right that I don't need to know everything. I'm gonna go sit down for a bit. I wore myself out this afternoon."

She turned to leave, still without looking at him, but he stopped her by grabbing her hand.

"You're mad at me?"

She shrugged. "I just thought we were past secrets."

He murmured something she didn't catch.

"What was that?" She finally looked at him.

"This isn't about secrets or us, Katie. You want to know? Rea found evidence of two other types of monsters on the property. Both very dangerous. I just didn't want to scare you."

"Another two?" She felt her head go light. He'd said there were a lot of different monsters, but handling the one she'd seen so far had been overwhelming. She pulled in a deep breath and said, "You should still tell me. Even if it freaks me out. It's not safe for me to be in the dark about the situation."

He studied her a moment before nodding. "You're right. I'm sorry. I was trying to protect you. I'd have preferred you didn't find out about all this first hand, and I keep trying to buffer you from the horror of it."

"You're still doing it because you haven't told me what these other monsters are."

His lips compressed in a tight line before he said, "They're bad. Neither are as intelligent as a grinluk, but both are voraciously hungry and relentless when they're intent on prey. One's favorite food is living human flesh."

Katie shivered.

"See. Damn it. This is why I didn't want to tell you. You don't need to know about this right now."

"What do they look like?"

"Katie—"

"What. Do. They look like?"

"Like nightmares. Katie… You don't want these images in your head."

"How will I know what to look for?"

"If you saw an aghris or a chridic, you'd know. I'm hoping you'll never see either one and therefore you won't need to know what they look like."

Given Katie's imagination, she had to concede he was probably right. She didn't really need to know what these new monsters looked like. The images would only add fodder to her nightmares. "Okay. It's enough for me to know there are more monsters to worry about."

"Which is what I was trying to avoid."

"Then you and Rea should have been more subtle. You didn't think I'd notice the looks?"

"I forgot about your powers of journalistic observation." His mouth quirked up at one corner, a charming little expression accompanied by a lifting of the eyebrows.

The looked succeeded. "Right. Okay, you're forgiven. This time. But…" She paused and realized just how little right she had to demand of him what she'd intended to demand. What on earth made her think he would agree to stop keeping secrets from her when they weren't even a committed couple? Her earlier anger seemed ridiculous in light of that thought. "Sorry I pushed you," she said instead. "I'm just scared, and it helps if I have as much information as possible. At least, it makes me feel a little better."

"Fine," he conceded. "I'll stop keeping information like this from you."

"Thanks."

His offer surprised her enough to make her smile. His answering smile made her spine tingle in a good way.

KATIE PACED THE KITCHEN, DRINKING HER WAY THROUGH A POT OF coffee, as she waited for Eric to do his first quarter of the grounds. She continued to pace the kitchen when Rea went out again. Although she suspected Geraldine switched the coffee to decaf sometime during all the pacing because exhaustion dragged at her limbs with each circuit of the kitchen. She tried to eat dinner when Eric and Gregory forced food on her, but she was too nervous to swallow much. She kept staring into the pitch dark night beyond the kitchen doors waiting for something scary to launch at the windows.

By the time Eric went out for his next patrol, Katie was asleep on her feet. She'd always assumed that phrase was poetic license until she found her head bouncing and her mind drifting into soothing darkness while she was still walking. When she bumped off the table one too many times, Rea, Gregory, and Geraldine insisted she try to get some sleep. Rea even accompanied her to Eric's room and did a search just so she'd feel safer.

"Here. This should help." Rea handed her a gun from the weapons closet. "It's loaded."

Katie weighed the Glock 30 in the palm of her hand. The gun was relatively light weight but held a magazine of ten .45 bullets so it had a lot of stopping power. She'd handled similar guns at the shooting range, though not this exact one, and knew she'd have to anticipate some recoil. She didn't care. The high caliber rounds were worth it. The weapon made her feel…prepared, even if not exactly safe.

Still, she wasn't crazy about guns. She hated being in a situation where she felt she needed one.

"Just don't shoot Eric when he comes in later," Rea said.

Katie couldn't even muster up a snort of amusement. She cradled the gun in her palms, wondering if she could sleep sitting on the couch.

"Leave the door open," she said to Rea as the woman started to leave. "I'll feel cut off from everyone if you close me in here."

Rea nodded. After a pause near the door, she came back into the sitting area and handed Katie her radio. "Just in case. I'll get another on my way back downstairs. Keep the volume low so you don't have to hear all the chatter between me and Eric. But keep it close to hand. If anything at all happens, just call for us. We'll be here faster than you can say pizza."

This time Katie did manage to muster a smile. "Thanks. I'm so tired I can't see straight. But I'm not sure I can sleep." She held up the comforting weight of the radio. "This will help."

When she was finally alone, Katie stretched out her senses. She wasn't getting any suspicious feelings. And with the smell of Eric surrounding her, she felt safe enough to crawl into bed. First, though, she turned on the bathroom light. Total darkness sounded like a bad idea tonight. There was just enough glow when the bedroom lights were off to offer a degree of comfort without being too bright.

She toed out of her shoes and socks, slipped her bra off underneath her shirt, but she was too tired, and too nervous, to strip out of the rest of her clothes and put on anything like pajamas. Having clothes on felt safer anyway, just like the bathroom light. And her trousers and t-shirt were loose enough to be comfortable. She was so exhausted she wasn't sure she'd even notice.

Once in bed, she set the gun on the bedside table, afraid she'd shoot herself in the head if she tried to place it on the bed next to her, then she cradled the radio on the pillow by her ear. Her eyes drifted shut and sleep pulled her under without much resistance.

She came awake suddenly. Without a clear idea of what had brought her out of sleep.

Lying perfectly still, Katie listened to the quiet bedroom. That awful *knowing* skittered along the back of her neck. She *knew* she was in terrible danger. She tried to hear and see into the dark room as she reached out for the gun. Her fingers brushed the empty top of the nightstand.

In the next instant, she realized the radio wasn't where she'd left it either.

Shit, shit, shit.

A sound jerked her head toward the fireplace. *Shickashickashickashicka.*

Her breathing turned to a rapid pant. A shiver crawled over her skin. What the hell was that?

Shickashickashickashicka.

She jerked again. Whatever it was sounded closer, to the right near the bathroom.

Swallowing, she edged up higher on the mattress.

Then *shickashickashickashicka* came from under the bed.

She squealed. Her heartbeat pounded so hard it hurt. Fear closed her throat. She swung her head from right to left, trying to find the source of the sound, attempting to look everywhere at once.

The skittering noise again, still under the bed but high, near the headboard.

A scream bubbled into her throat and got stuck.

Rolling to the center of the bed, she crouched on the balls of her feet and jumped in small half circles. She wanted off that bed more than anything, but she was afraid to leap without knowing what was under there.

What if it was a grinluk with those long tentacles?

What if it was worse?

She felt around the tossed blankets, frantically searching for the radio. Maybe she'd just pushed it down the bed.

But in the dim glow from the bathroom light, she couldn't see it anywhere. And if she'd dropped it onto the ground, she sure as hell wasn't going to reach for it without knowing what was under the bed.

A long silence drew her nerves out to the absolute breaking point. She wanted to scream but was afraid everyone was too far away to hear her without the radio. And she wasn't sure her voice was working at any rate.

Fuck. Fuck. Bugger. Bollocks. *Fuck*!

A slight sound made her spin toward the foot of the bed. Nothing. She let out a low breath, her heart hammering as she swiveled back to face the headboard.

And froze. Filled with so much terror she thought her heart might actually stop.

Rising up over the edge of the bed was a creature nearly six feet long. With hundreds of legs along its sides, each roughly half a foot long. Its body was covered in interlocking scales that moved when it shifted. Its head was a set of pincers surrounding a hole filled with row upon row of teeth layering back into the blackness of its mouth.

She couldn't see any eyes, but when she let loose a tiny sound of horror, the head swung toward her. The pincers moved and some of the legs shifted.

Fear unlike anything she'd ever felt consumed her.

And she finally screamed.

Without thought, she launched off the bed, making a dash for the door. She realized too late it was closed and hit the solid wood hard, not giving herself room to open it.

Scrambling at the knob, she heard the *shickashickashickashicka* sound. She glanced over her shoulder, saw the huge thing with its thousands of legs skittering toward her. She screamed again.

Panic shut off her logical thought. The door didn't give way and the thing was getting close, so she scrambled toward the fireplace, squealing in disgust.

Its head and the front third of its body rose off the ground, its pincers moving as it followed her progress. She didn't dare take her eyes off it, so she wasn't watching where she was going and her feet caught on the rug. She fell on her butt, hard.

Animal terror had her up and moving again before the front of the thing's body hit the floor. It moved toward her, faster this time. Thousands of legs skittered over the wooden floor.

Another scream built in her throat. She grabbed out, reaching for a weapon and threw the first thing she came into contact with, not even bothering to check what it was.

The monster dodged aside and the lamp she'd tossed shattered harmlessly beside it. She pushed the coffee table into its path, then shoved the large chair in front of her. Anything to keep space and barriers between her and that thing.

It slithered over the top of the upturned table and crawled up onto the chair. She hit the wall behind her with a thud. The bookshelf was to her left, but throwing books at the monster didn't even slow it down.

Katie attempted to jump to the right, toward the bedroom, but the monster shifted and blocked her path. She dodged another direction and it shifted again.

She was cornered.

It rose up in front of her, only a few feet away. The pincers around its mouth opened and closed quickly. The circular mouth widened and shrunk, making the rows of sharp teeth flex. A sound like the crunching of wet bones gurgled out of the monster's mouth, followed by a low-pitched hiss.

Beyond hysterical with fear, Katie frozen in place, unable to look away as those thousands of spike-covered legs waved and shifted. The ones on the ground moved the monster closer while the ones in the air seemed to be reaching for her.

It inched nearer, the hissing sound vibrating in the air, crawling over her nerves.

Until the scream that was caught in her throat exploded.

CHAPTER THIRTY-FIVE

The bedroom door crashed open. Bringing with it such bright light Katie raised her hand to block the glare.

A roar filled the room.

She blinked in the sudden brightness. Then a huge form blocked her view. She knew without question it was Eric. She caught the flash of a sword around his shoulders, followed by an ear-piercing screech. And a squishing sound.

The thunk and scratching that followed made Katie gag.

Eric turned to face her as she collapsed back against the wall.

"Are you okay?" he asked. "Did it hurt you at all?"

She shook her head but her voice wasn't working. Staring past him at the twitching body of the monster made her stomach turn. She felt as if tiny legs crawled over her skin. Grimacing, she rubbed her hands up and down her arms trying to rid herself of the awful sensation.

Eric looked back at the body, handed her his sword and crossed to the fireplace. She continued to stare at the carcass, afraid that if she looked away it would start crawling toward her again. A flare of light to her left broke the spell and she flicked a glance toward Eric. A huge blaze glowed red and yellow on the grate. Eric returned to the monster's remains and very carefully lifted its blood dripping head in one hand and the body in the other. He picked the body up from the back, avoiding both the blood and legs.

Katie shivered as he carried the remains to the fire and tossed them in. A high-pitched squeal filled the room, stealing her breath. The body thrashed on the fire, but within moments both the sound and the movement stopped.

"Is it dead now?" she asked, her voice choked and quiet. She was going to throw up.

Eric nodded. "You sure you're not hurt?"

She swallowed, glanced at the fireplace then looked away. "I'm fine. How did it get in?"

"Not sure. But they're very good diggers. It may have burrowed in through a wall, or slipped in through one of the chimneys."

"I thought those were secured."

"They are from most things." He shook his head. "Hell, it could have gotten in during the grinluk attack and been hiding. I'll search out its entry point later. I'm not leaving you alone again. The aghrises travel in…swarms."

Katie doubled over as her stomach lurched. A loud thud made her realize she'd dropped the sword. Before she could pick it up, Eric was beside her, one hand on her shoulder, the other brushing her hair back from her face.

"Rea left a gun," she murmured as she swallowed down the rising bile. "I don't know where it is, but would it help?"

"Yes."

He picked up the dropped sword, then took her hand with his free one and led her toward the bed. She resisted, planting her feet and refusing to go near it. She didn't want to go anywhere near that bed when another of those things could be beneath it. Eric seemed to understand because he let her go and went into a crouch to search under the frame.

"No more monsters," he assured her. "And your gun is here." He returned to her and handed her the weapon. "Better?"

"Sort of. I still feel like things are crawling on me." She shook herself hard like a dog dislodging water.

"I'm sorry I wasn't here—"

"Don't," she interrupted. "I'm just glad you heard my screams since I lost the radio, too." She started to lean into him when a sudden sense of dread swept over her.

She spun around. But there was nothing in the room. "What the…?"

The flash of *knowing* dropped her to her knees. "Rea. Eric, she's in trouble. Go. Now."

"I'm not leaving you." He reached for her but she gestured him away.

"Go! You have to go. Now. Or it'll be too late." She stumbled to her feet. "Hurry! I'll be behind you. But you have to go now." To make her point, she shoved him hard.

He barely moved, but her intensity must have gotten through. "Go back to the kitchen and stay with the others."

He kissed her quickly, then was out the door so fast she barely saw him move.

She checked the gun to make sure it was still loaded and ready for use but the safety was still on. Her hands were shaking so much she didn't want to take a chance. Then she hurried after Eric.

Another sense of dread swept through her and nearly brought her to her knees again.

Rea would die if Eric didn't get to her quickly. And even if he reached her, it might still be too late. Just like the night her own sister was killed, when she hadn't been able to reach the street fast enough.

At the thought of another sister dead, she broke into a run. She only knew one way into the backyard, through the kitchen. And she'd never explored the grounds. Didn't matter. Her sense of impending disaster would direct her.

She charged into the kitchen and out the back door before Gregory or Geraldine could get out more than a vague shout.

She spun in a half circle, letting her eyes adjust to the darkness, then took off in the direction her senses pointed.

She wasn't even sure where she was going. She just knew she had to get there. Her feet were bare and cold from the wet grass. But adrenaline kept the rest of her from freezing in the sharp cold.

There was barely enough light to see the terrain in front of her. A sliver of moon overhead and some ambient light from the house gave her just enough illumination to keep from killing herself as she charged across the unfamiliar grounds.

In the back of her mind, she realized more of those millipede monsters could be anywhere. And the grinluk was still on the loose. But her overwhelming knowledge of looming catastrophe kept her moving when fear might have stopped her in her tracks.

Chances were good she was running toward the monsters anyway, so she didn't need to worry about their sudden appearance.

They could just wait for her to get to them.

She heard the fight long before she could see it. The echo of metal whistling in the air. The guttural screams and cries of monsters and people carried across the manicured lawns. She stumbled to a halt when she finally caught sight of the chaos.

Pillars of water whooshed into the air in a random pattern that resembled a fountain display in Las Vegas. But with such force they looked like they would launch a person caught under one into space. In between the geysers, at least ten more of the millipede monsters thrashed and hissed, slithering around the grass. Rea and Eric stood back-to-back in the middle of the storm swinging their weapons as each monster lunged forward.

Beside the aghrises was another skittering creature. A new monster for Katie's nightmares.

It had a round body the size of a basketball and six skeletal legs arching up over its back. The body was covered in a course dark hair, but the legs were pale, and in the moonlight actually looked like bones. It didn't seem to have a head of any kind, but when one launched at Rea's face, Katie saw the underside of the things body and almost screamed.

Suckers lined its belly, and inside each sucker was a small, teeth filled mouth squishing in and out of the external structure like a deadly worm. In between the mouth infested suction cups were an equal number of eyes flickering open and closed even as one of Rea's swords sliced its body in half.

There were at least a dozen of the spider-like monsters scurrying around the fight. Katie, still frozen in place, was sure Eric and his sister would be overrun at any moment. There were so many swishing, writhing creatures jumping and slithering around them.

But as she watched, she realized the two warriors weren't showing any signs of the panic overwhelming her. They fought with a kind of calm calculation that made the battle look easy for them.

She was about to let out a relieved breath when she saw the shadow of grey tentacles rising up on the opposite side of the fight.

The grinluk.

Last time it had taken two of them and the dogs to defeat that monster. And Eric had been wounded. With all the other monsters, they were officially outnumbered.

Swallowing back the bile in her throat, she raised her gun and took aim. Her weapon was no good against the grinluk. But she could take out some of the other things. Give Eric and Rea room to fight.

Her hands shook as she tried to target one of the spider-like monsters. They moved so fast and the night was so dark. She focused on the slight glow of their skeletal legs and aimed for the dark patch in the middle.

The sound of flesh and bone splattering around the grass resonated with the clap of gunfire.

One down. Lots more to go.

A water spout erupted to her right, near enough to make her squeal and jump away. When she looked back to the fight, one of the aghris had broken off and was headed her way.

She wanted to cry as terror sent her heartbeat into overdrive. Without even aiming, she fired three shots at the thing, hitting it once in the face and once along the body. Her third shot went wide.

The thing hissed and waved its pincers at her. Then suddenly disappeared into the ground.

It didn't burrow. It simply moved those hundreds of legs in a rapid flurry and sank into the soil. Leaving a six-foot-long ditch in its place.

Katie did make a noise then, though she was so choked by fear it was little more than a gasp. Suddenly, her bare feet felt incredibly vulnerable. And standing still was impossible.

She lurched around, jumping from foot to foot as she searched the ground. She avoided the things crater but wasn't sure if it moved underground or just remained waiting for a victim in that dirt churned crevice.

As she danced around, two of the spider things skittered toward her. She shot each one, stopping their forward movement. But she used four bullets to do it. The magazine was full before she'd started shooting.

Which meant she had exactly two bullets left. With no spare magazines.

Her hands tingling from firing such a heavy caliber weapon. The craziness of the night affected her aim. But as she glanced up to scan for more approaching monsters, she realized most of the others were dead or gone.

And the grinluk was no longer in sight.

Rea stood with her swords lowered, studying the darkness. Eric stomped to Katie, a very dangerous look on his face.

"Why the hell are you out here?"

He didn't touch her, for which she was grateful. Her nerves were too raw. "Helping," she said. "There's still danger. Where's the grinluk?"

"It ran off when you fired the gun."

"Really? Surprising since the gun can't kill it."

"Maybe it saw what you did to its partner."

For some reason, that thought pleased her in the midst of all the madness. Katie Donavan, big bad monster hunter. She nearly burst into a hysterical laugh and had to choke it off. The knowledge that Rea was still in deadly danger continued to haunt her.

"Something's wrong," she told Eric. "I'm still feeling like Rea's in danger. Like she'll be killed."

Rea glanced back at them. "That what brought you out? You're worried about me? That's sweet, Katie, but this really isn't a good place for you."

Katie exchanged a glance with Eric then met Rea's gaze. "I'm… psychic I guess you'd call it. I get these feelings. No, it's more like I just *know* things. Sometimes I know them suddenly, like a flash. No images. It's not like a vision. I just suddenly know things. And what I *know* right now is that you're about to die. Or at least, you will be killed if we don't stop it."

Rea raised a brow. "That's some pretty serious knowledge."

"What happened to the other monsters?" Katie asked, scanning the dark grounds.

"Dead or scattered," Eric said.

"Where's the Elemental?"

"Right here," a voice said from just beyond Rea.

CHAPTER THIRTY-SIX

They all spun to face the voice. Rea raised her swords but not fast enough. A whip of water lashed out, knocking both weapons away. In the next blink, Rea was engulfed by water, twisting around her like ropes and lifting her off the ground. The water covered her face then uncovered in several slow pumps. By the third cycle, Rea was choking for breath even as she struggled against the bands holding her.

"Stop it," Katie yelled before she could stop herself. Did she really think this powerful creature would listen to her?

"You foresaw her death?" the voice echoed from the bands around Rea, sounding like a waterfall pounding on rocks. "Then it will be. Why try to fight destiny?"

"It doesn't have to be destiny, damn it."

Eric put a hand on Katie's arm, and she realized she'd taken several steps towards the twisted fountain of water holding Rea.

"Let my sister go," Eric said quietly.

The warning was simple and obvious. Katie glanced at him and saw the knife in his free hand. One of the fire daggers. She looked back to the fountain. It transformed into a human shape of shifting clear water with a face she could almost read. The creature held Rea out in front of it, its "arm" around her throat. The position would make a knife throw difficult if not impossible without hitting Rea.

"What do you want?" Eric asked, his hand still firmly on Katie's arm.

"Your Family dead," it said. "We have plans. You will interfere. Therefore, you must be eliminated."

"'We'?"

The mouth in watery face lifted in simulation of a smile, though there wasn't any emotion in the expression that Katie could see.

"I am not inclined to reveal my plans like a dime-store villain, Logan."

"I won't let you kill my sister."

"How about your lover? Will you trade her for your sister's life?"

Eric's grip tightened and he shoved Katie behind him. He moved his hand down to hers and placed her palm at the small of his back. For an instant, she thought he was just protecting her, making sure he knew where she was.

Then she felt the knife hilt just above the edge of his trousers.

She kept her gaze on the Elemental and Rea as she slid the knife slowly from the scabbard. With her hands and most of her body hidden behind Eric, she eased the knife into her trouser pocket, careful not to nick herself with it.

"I won't let you hurt either of them," Eric said.

"Does she know how important she is to you? I do. I know who she is."

Katie felt Eric's entire body go still.

"What's it mean?" she murmured.

"Later," Eric said over his shoulder without looking away from the Elemental.

"She doesn't know?" The creature actually managed to sound amused.

Katie frowned, but she kept quiet. The last thing Eric needed was further distraction.

A sound at their backs started trembles of fear crawling up her spine. She glanced over her shoulder and saw the grinluk rising up behind them, its mouth of pointed grey teeth spread into a smile.

"Eric," she choked.

He didn't even turn. "I know. Stay close."

"You cannot fight us both and still save the women," the Elemental said. "Which will you choose? Your blood. Or your soul."

"You're wrong about Katie," Eric said. "She's not the one."

"Why protect her so carefully? Why bring a reporter into your inner sanctum? Do not try to bluff me, Logan. I am as old as time. I know she's your Nam-tar."

Eric didn't comment, but Katie felt his muscles bunch and release as if he was preparing to make a move. She stood sideways, her shoulder against his back so she could keep an eye on the grinluk. The thing remained several feet away as if waiting for some sort of sign from the Elemental.

She held her gun in the hand facing the grinluk. She only had two bullets left, but it was better than nothing. The fire dagger was hidden in her opposite pocket, the side blocked by Eric.

The Elemental's words nagged at her. What the hell was a Nam-tar? And why would that be important to Eric? This was no time to ask, and an even worse time to be thinking about it, but she couldn't keep her brain from circling the strange word, trying to decipher its meaning from the context of the conversation.

A watery gurgle of laughter rose from the Elemental. "The Logans will not survive this. You are too few in number, and we are too many."

"You're gloating. Why? You haven't won yet."

"You can't use that knife you have against me with your sister in the way. Your sister does not have one she can reach. And the grinluk at your back will move too quickly for you to alter the current status. You have lost. You will all die. But if you like, I will kill your Nam-tar first, so she does not have to witness your death. She has not committed yet. Your death will not be an easy thing for her to see."

"You're not going to touch her."

The growl in Eric's voice made the fine hairs on Katie's arms stand up. The grinluk smiled wider. And she realized Eric was losing his composure—exactly what the Elemental wanted.

She had to do something. She had to stop this. What was the point of all her psychic skills if she just stood here and watched Rea die?

A sudden *knowing* hit her so sharply she gasped. She *knew* what she had to do. With the same clarity that had sent her out into the dark night to face things she could barely comprehend. She knew exactly what her next move had to be.

Eric was going to hate this.

She eased away from his back, just a bit, and he dropped his hold on her, taking his sword in a two-handed grip. He was preparing to fight. That was good because he was going to have one hell of a fight on his hands in a minute. She stepped back just a little further, putting as much space between them as she dared.

Then she fired one shot into the grinluk's face.

The sudden attack startled everyone. The grinluk screeched. Eric half-turned to see what had happened.

And Katie ran toward the Elemental and Rea.

Its watery chuckle filled the night air. Katie shot it in what could roughly be called its face. The laughter died for a few seconds, long enough for Katie to reach Rea. Then the laughter started again as the face reformed.

A whip of water knocked her to the ground at Rea's feet, flinging the gun out of her grip. She looked up as Rea tried to reach for her, but the grip of water bands held her tight.

Eric shouted her name. Katie realized that wasn't the first time he'd yelled for her. The sound of his sword singing through the air confirmed what she'd known would happen. The grinluk attacked in its outrage and pain. Eric was in a desperate fight and couldn't reach her.

She was on her own.

CHAPTER THIRTY-SEVEN

The Elemental's laughter faded into a chuckle before it spoke directly to Katie. The sound of its voice was quiet and almost gentle in the darkness, despite the words that emerged.

"He did not tell you bullets were useless? I am Water. You cannot harm Water with mere projectiles."

Lying on the ground at the "feet" of the mocking creature, Katie kept the fire dagger hidden with her body. She'd pulled the weapon from her pocket in the instant after she'd fired her last bullet. She was never going to hit the wavering mass of water between its "eyes" to dissipate it for long. But she only had one chance at this so she was going to take whatever shot she could get.

She stared up at the Elemental, a creature so ancient, so fundamental, she couldn't even comprehend its nature nonetheless its lifetime. And she tried to show it nothing but fear. That wasn't too tough because she was absolutely terrified.

"For your audacity," it said, "you will watch your lover die. And then you will watch this one die." Water rose up over Rea's face, cutting her off from vital oxygen. "And then, I will kill you slowly. Human."

There was a sneer in its tone, a disgust it hadn't revealed before.

"You think you're superior," it continued. "You think you can do as you please with no punishment. There is a reason Ne loosed his monsters on your kind. En should not have bothered to intervene on your behalf. You," it said in that same disgusted tone, "have never been worth the effort. But that will change very shortly."

"You kill the Logans. Then you kill all humans? Is that it?" The tremble of horror in her voice didn't have to be manufactured. Her heart thumped so hard her chest hurt from the pressure. She rolled, a move designed to give the impression she was trying to move away from the sentient water.

A coil of cold wetness wrapped around her waist and dragged her so close she was touching the base of its human form.

"Do not tempt me to kill you too soon. I would not want you to miss this." It nodded its head toward the fight behind her.

For the first time, she risked looking back at Eric. He was swing at the grinluk's thrashing tentacles, so fast it was hard to follow his movements. But the monster was forcing him to fall back, step by step. A dark stain covered Eric's right arm and liquid seeped down his leg where his trousers were ripped open.

Even though she couldn't see well enough to discern a color, she knew that was blood. And at least some of it was Eric's.

He needed help. The wound she'd inflicted on the grinluk hadn't been significant enough to slow it down. And she had no doubt Eric's attention was divided because of worry for her. She hated that she'd done that to him. But this was the only way.

She *knew* it was.

She looked back at the Elemental, letting tears fill her eyes. "Please. Stop this. Don't hurt him." The tears and the panic were genuine. If she didn't get this right, they were all dead.

"Do you love him?"

The question surprised her so much she answered honestly. "Yes."

"Would you die for him?"

"I…" She swallowed. "I would."

"You're lying. You do not want to die."

"Of course I don't want to die. But I don't want him to die either. And I'm willing to do what it takes to prevent that."

"Even die? Death for you is forever."

"I know. I've lost someone close to me before."

"Then perhaps I will accommodate you."

"Meaning?"

"I will kill you but spare him."

"Now you're the one lying."

Its chuckle made the water around her waist vibrate in a horrible imitation of a spa jet. "So does that mean you are not prepared to die for him?"

"Oh no. I'd die for him." Katie whipped out the fire dagger and plunged it deep into the Elemental's leg. "But I'll kill for him first."

Steam hissed from the area of the knife wound, scalding her hand, but she held the blade in place as long as she could.

And watched as the Elemental's form shimmered, wavered, boiling into a screen of damp heat.

The grip on her waist disappeared. She scrambled away on hands and knees even as a high whining sound filled the air. Rea was thrown to the ground a few feet away. Unlike Katie, though, she rolled gracefully to her feet, picking her swords up as she went, and faced the pulsing wall of boiling water within seconds of being toss free.

The whine hit a pitch that pierced Katie's skull. She cringed and covered her ears. She wasn't sure what she'd been expecting, but she was afraid her gamble had failed. That she hadn't succeeded in destroying the thing and they would still all die.

Then the boiling water exploded.

She ducked and covered her head but scalding droplets still pelted her defenseless arms. The whine cut off abruptly, making Katie's ears ring in the sudden silence.

When the hot rain stopped, she looked up. There was no sign of the Elemental. No evidence that it had ever existed. Even the ground around her was dry, the grass brittle against her hands.

She scrambled to her feet and looked for Eric. He was sprawled on the ground with Rea kneeling over him, holding her hands against this neck.

Katie choked on a cry. Stumbling to his side, she dropped back to the grass and stared at the blood covering Rea's hands as it pumped from his throat.

"Eric, you have to," Rea was saying. "You'll die otherwise. The Elemental was right, she hasn't agreed yet."

Eric shook his head, the gesture feeble. Blood bubbled out of his mouth.

"Eric, whatever she's telling you to do, do it," Katie said, taking his hand. "Please. Please. I don't want you to die. Oh please, you can't die. I love you. Do you hear me? Please don't die on me."

He stared up at her, his gaze intense and steady. She felt something move under his skin and nearly shrieked. The skin over his cheek seemed to distend. What the hell was happening to him? Had the grinluk infected him with some horrible alien parasite? Sunday afternoon sci-fi movies filled her head adding to the absolute terror washing through her.

"Please don't die." She choked on her own tears and squeezed his hand tighter.

"Eric," Rea said, "you're bleeding out. You will die. You have to do it. Now! Before it's too late to make the transition."

His eyes closed for a brief moment. Then he opened them and nodded.

"Katie, step back. He'll need a little space."

She didn't want to move. Didn't want to let go of his hand. But Rea met her gaze and nodded her away.

"He'll be okay," she said.

Reluctantly, Katie let go of his hand but not before he gave her one hard squeeze. When he dropped his grip, she crawled backward a couple of feet. Wrapping her arms around her waist, she sat on her knees, rocking back and forth as she watched him.

At first, nothing seemed to happen except that his body went very still. Then something rose from his chest, like a ghost or a cloud of mist. But the mist had form. It was hard to see in the darkness. The vague outline of what might have been an animal head seemed to leap from Eric's chest. Followed quickly by an actual body. Leaping upward and away from him. An animal. Like a dog.

No, not a dog.

A wolf.

The wolf form was insubstantial as it leapt from Eric's chest. But it solidified more and more as it arched away from him. Becoming substantial. Becoming real.

And then she was staring into the dark eyes of a large black wolf.

She looked back at Eric. Blinked a few times. He looked different now. Very still and somehow wrong. Her gaze jumping between him and the wolf, she eased closer. When she was close enough to see clearly, she sucked in a sharp breath. The body on the ground was solid stone, like one of the statues in the atrium, this one of a gravely wounded soldier in the last moments of his life.

For a heartbeat, Katie couldn't breathe. She looked back and forth from the wolf to the statue to the wolf. Her brain couldn't make sense of what she'd seen, what she was seeing.

"What...?" She touched the statue that looked like Eric and when she felt the cold smoothness of marble, she let out a short, sharp scream. "What is this? Is he dead? What's happened?"

A canine whine drew her attention. The wolf was crouched, its head on its forelegs, staring up at her and making a small, pathetic noise. It edged closer but stilled when she fell back.

As she stared at the animal, she remembered the dream she'd had of a wolf coming to Eric's room the first night she was in the house. A wolf that had sat down beneath the windows to guard and protect her. She'd felt very safe in the presence of that dream wolf.

A wolf that looked exactly like the one before her now.

"Eric?"

The animal nodded. An impossible gesture if it was only a wolf.

Rea touched her shoulder, but Katie jerked away.

"This is what we mean when we say we're the wolf Family," Rea murmured. "The human and animal share bodies and spirits. And when necessary, the animal spirit can leave the human body, taking solid form and bringing the spirit of the human with it."

"The stone?"

"Protects the human body while it's empty. Eric will heal this way. His human body will be good as new by midday tomorrow."

"The artery in his neck was cut. He was bleeding to death."

"Now he won't."

"This is impossible."

"More impossible than talking water and the monsters you've seen?"

The woman had a point.

But this might just be the final break to Katie's tentative hold on her sanity. He wasn't a werewolf. He was something else altogether. Something so foreign there weren't even myths about it. She just didn't know if she could handle any more of this.

The wolf whined again, bringing her attention back to it…him. He remained still, but his head was up and he was looking at her with such a human expression of pleading in his dark eyes.

Beside her, Rea rose to her feet. "I have to go after the grinluk. It's wounded but still alive and still dangerous. Stay with him."

"What? No. Alone?"

"Katie, that's Eric. He would never hurt you. You said you loved him. You told the Elemental you would die for him. You did kill for him. You can sit here with him until Gregory comes out to help with his human body."

Katie wasn't so sure about that, but Rea didn't give her a chance to argue. She ran off with her swords in her hands, following the distant sound of dogs howling. She had just disappeared into the darkness when Katie heard a strange sound, like the snap of canvas. And a strong breeze brushed her hair back from her face.

Frowning, she didn't even attempt to guess what that sound meant. Her fragile psyche had taken all it could for one night. She sat silently, staring at the wolf. It…he stared back, remaining perfectly still.

Finally, she spoke. "Eric, that is you in there?"

Again the animal nodded.

"We're gonna have a lot to talk about tomorrow."

Another nod.

"You're lucky you can't talk now. I have about a million questions for you. But I think I'm too tired to deal with the answers."

He whined quietly and, still in a crouched position with his belly on the grass, inched nearer to her. This time she didn't jump away.

He stopped close but not close enough for her to touch. She continued to stare at him. The idea that the man she loved was *inside* that wolf, that the wolf was him… She glanced at the stone body next to her then back to the wolf.

"At least you were telling the truth when you said you weren't a werewolf." She shifted a little, settling into a more comfortable position on her haunches. She wasn't quite ready to sit—she wanted to be able to jump up quickly if she needed too. Even as the thought crossed her mind, she realized the reason she wanted to remain at the ready wasn't because she was afraid of the wolf. She was afraid one of those monsters that had sunk underground might return. And she'd lost the gun, which was out of bullets anyway.

"If the monsters come back, can you fight like that?"

The wolf nodded.

"As good as when you're in your human body?"

He whined and tilted his head back and forth.

The gesture was strange and she couldn't interpret it. "Does that mean my question doesn't have a simple yes or no answer?"

That got her an affirmative nod.

"Okay, then we'll talk about your fighting skills later. Will the monsters return? That one went underground. Will it come back tonight?"

A very definite shake of the wolf's head had Katie letting out a breath. "Even though you were wounded?"

Another headshake.

"I assume that means they won't come back even though you're wounded?"

Now the wolf nodded.

"This is a very odd conversation." She paused. "But not as odd as I would have thought. It's a bit like talking to a dog. Except you're actually answering."

That comment earned her a snort that sounded suspiciously insulted. She smiled. And realized she felt safe with the wolf. That animal carried Eric with it. In essence it was Eric. And she felt very safe with him.

"I have to tell you some things. While you can't talk and interrupt me. I know, that's not normal for a reporter but…" She swallowed and finally settled into a cross-legged position, hugging herself in an attempt to stay warm as her sweat cooled in the cold night air. "You'll remember everything we talk about now? Everything that's said? I mean, when you go back into your human body?"

The wolf nodded.

"Okay. I was afraid of that. Which means I really do need to explain something to you now. The thing is…" She glanced at his human body, then back at him. "The thing is, this isn't the strangest revelation I've had in the last week. Learning that monsters are real, that was the worst. I knew about the two-legged kind."

The wolf whined quietly and she raised her hand.

"My turn. You can talk when you're human again. What I'm trying to say is that…when you told me your family was the wolf family, and I thought you might be a werewolf—which is pretty fricking strange for a down-to-earth girl like me—I was prepared to believe that. I've heard of werewolves. I've read fiction and seen those cool documentaries about the werewolf myths. I admit I was relieved when you told me you weren't one, but still, I was ready to accept. This… What you really are, isn't all that much stranger. I've never even come close to considering that…" She paused and gestured to his body. "I couldn't have guessed something like this, someone like you existed. But you're not any more surprising than that giant millipede thing that almost ate me earlier."

She shrugged. "This also explains why my 'wolf' dream left me feeling so safe. That was you, wasn't it? Protecting me."

The wolf nodded and edged an inch closer.

"All of this rambling is to say that I trusted you before. Finding out about this part of you… It hasn't changed that. It'll take me some time to get used to it. But…" She stopped and thought back to the first day she'd met him and their tour around the atrium.

"That statue, of you with the wolf leaping from your torso… That's based on reality. Why would you show that to me? Were you…were you trying to prepare me or something? Or did you assume I'd never see this part of you so it didn't matter if I saw the statue?"

She raised a hand even as the wolf opened his mouth. "I'm sorry. That's not a yes or no question. Okay, we'll talk about that when you're back to being human. For now… For now, I just want you to know that this doesn't change what I told the Elemental. I assume you were too busy trying not to get killed by the grinluk to hear, but Rea opened her big mouth already so there's no point in me trying to deny it. And it's probably best I tell you now so you have time to think about what you want to say in return."

She pulled her knees up and wrapped her arms around them. "I don't expect anything," she said quietly. "I'm not telling you this with any illusions of happily ever after. But I love you. It's too soon, and it's too strange, and I will completely understand if you don't feel the same."

She looked into the wolf's dark eyes and realized she could see Eric there. The eyes were different, and yet there was something, some essence that was what she saw every time she looked into Eric's eyes.

"I love you," she repeated. "You know, this is easier to admit when I know you can't answer back. I can't even read your expression really, so I have no idea what you're thinking. That makes this easier too." She cringed. "Though now I'm a little afraid to face you when you are human."

The wolf whined and grunted, the two sounds strange in combination. He edged further forward, this time coming close enough to touch her with his nose. When she didn't move away, he crawled another inch forward and rested his nose on her bare foot.

"Are you trying to tell me not to be embarrassed?"

When the wolf nodded, she chuckled. He scooted even closer and this time rested his head against her thigh. The weight was heavier than she would have expected but also comfortable and comforting. And warm.

"May I touch you, too?"

He grunted. She rested her hand on the top of his head, sliding her palm once across his fur before resettling at the top of his head. "It would feel really weird to pet you, so I'm not going to. But this is nice."

He rubbed his head gently against her thigh.

"Thanks for not licking me in response. That would have been even weirder than petting." She looked at the wolf, into Eric's eyes as he stared up at her. They sat silently in the dark for a bit longer, though how long, Katie wasn't sure. Then a circle of jumping light came into view from the direction of the house.

"Katie? Are you alright?" Gregory called just before he and his flashlight got close enough to identify.

"I'm fine. We're both fine. Sort of. Eric was seriously hurt by the grinluk."

"Yes." Gregory stopped next to her and looked down at the stone statue that was Eric's body. "Are you hurt? Can you walk back to the house?"

"I'm fine. I can walk. But you can't carry him alone."

Gregory smiled, the expression looking strangely wicked in the light from his torch. "Don't worry, miss. I'm much stronger than I look."

He handed her the flashlight, then squatted down and put one arm under the statue's shoulders and the other its upper thighs. Then he stood, lifting the stone with what looked to be very little effort.

"What the hell are you, Gregory? Are you a monster hunting wolf, too?"

She scrambled to her feet as the wolf rose and stepped out of her way.

"I'm not like Mr. Logan." Gregory started back toward the house.

Katie hurried to keep up with him. The wolf trotted off ahead, staying several yards in front of them.

"So what are you then?" she asked again, watching him carry what had to be a very heavy block of marble with ease.

"A…relation if you will. I'm sure Mr. Logan will be able to explain. I imagine there are many things he still has to tell you?"

"Oh lots and lots," she confirmed with an emphatic nod.

"What I am will no doubt be part of that explanation. And since I need my breath to get you all back to the house, I won't waste the effort giving you a half answer."

"Gregory?"

"Yes?"

"You're more evasive than Eric when it comes to answering questions."

Gregory flashed her a brief smile. "Yes, miss."

He continued to avoid answering her questions all the way back to the house.

CHAPTER THIRTY-EIGHT

Eric paced his room, waiting for Katie. She'd remained with him in his wolf form until Rea returned. Then she'd disappeared, and he hadn't seen her since. He sent Gregory to find her as soon as he was able to return to his human body.

As he paced, he rubbed at his sore neck. The wound wasn't fully healed because he'd rushed back to this shape as soon as he was able. A line of lumpy red tissue still covered the area. But he couldn't wait for the injury to heal completely. He needed to talk to Katie.

She loved him.

At least, she thought she did. The very idea made his heart beat faster and a sense of peace washed through him. She loved him. If he asked, knowing everything she knew, she would stay. His curse would be broken. He would never again risk the kind of death he'd faced last night.

But…

The memory of her wrapped in the watery clutches of the Elemental filled his mind. The memory of the monsters turning toward her. The way those monsters had gone for her *because* of who she was to him.

He stalked by the windows, the curtains thrown back to reveal a sunny, bright morning. It was early in the day but Gregory reported the weather stations were declaring the storms over. Even the flooding had abated faster than expected. There were still road blocks—downed electrical poles, felled trees, the remaining flood waters. But Katie's way home would be clear by tomorrow, the day after at the latest.

There was the small matter of her damaged car but that could easily be taken care of. His biggest problem was that he didn't want to let her leave.

And yet…

The sound of her screams when the aghris had attacked her in this room echoed in his head like a bell. He shook his head hard and returned to stalking through the room, restlessness making it impossible to sit.

A hesitant knock stopped his pacing and he turned to face the door as it swung opened.

Katie poked her head around the edge. "You sent Gregory to find me?"

"Come in." He frowned. His tone sounded so formal and out of place given what they'd been through, what she'd admitted last night.

She stood just inside the room looking very uncomfortable, which only made him feel worse. This wasn't starting out well.

"Sit. Please." He gestured to the couch.

Even after she'd settled, though, he was too nervous to sit, so he paced in front of the fireplace as he started. "Where did you go last night? After Rea got back?"

"I figured you needed to sleep alone to heal. I was just next door, in your brother's room. Rea said it would be okay." She blushed and wouldn't meet his gaze when she said, "I didn't want you to feel like you had to protect me or anything. With all the monsters gone, it seemed silly not to give you your space."

"I don't want space from you," he said quietly and stopped to face her. "Did you mean what you said?"

To his relief, she didn't pretend not to know what he was talking about. "Yes. I did. But I understand if you don't feel the same way."

"That's not it. I…I have to tell you the whole story of our family.

Of the Families. Once I've finished…" He took a deep breath and started pacing again. "Story first. You saw what I am last night. The wolf spirit given to my family is a very real thing and an innate part of us. The wolf can leave the human body. When it does, the human essence goes with it. So the wolf is more itself but also infused with me, just as I'm more myself in the human body but infused with the wolf. Does that make sense?"

"Sort of. You're saying you and the wolf are actually two different beings? And you share bodies?"

"Yes. We couldn't survive without each other. But the wolf and the human spirits are two separate entities. It's a symbiotic relationship, one that can't be undone without both our deaths."

"Okay. I get that. I guess. And when the wolf leaves the human body, and the human essence goes with the wolf, your human body turns to stone. Why?"

"To keep the human body safe. When we were formed, turning the body to stone ensured it would be protected from the damages that might befall an otherwise spiritless body. I'm not entirely sure En considered that the statues could be destroyed with a big hammer when he and Pah created that part of our natures."

"What happens if the statue is destroyed?" She sat forward on the couch as she asked.

"We're trapped as the wolf. Until we die. Which isn't very long after the human body dies. The wolf can continue for a week maybe. But it's not meant to exist outside the human body, on its own, for any length of time. Eventually, it will die too."

"Doesn't sound like your gods thought that part through."

"I suspect they thought the need for the Seven Families would end much earlier in human history, before destroying stone blocks became commonplace. They underestimated the staying power of both Ne and his monsters."

She tilted her head to one side. "Is that why all the stone statues around the house? A sort of camouflage?"

"Exactly." He smiled, or tried too. But he was too edgy to make the expression charming. "The Families have been doing that for millennia. There is almost always a sculptor in each generation. If there isn't one in a Family, they'll go to another Family's sculptor for the necessary work."

"Wow. That'd keep a person busy."

"Doesn't happen very often. Usually, each Family can look after their own…camouflage."

She shifted in her seat. "So when your human body is stone, it heals faster?"

"Yes. One of the benefits of the state."

She glanced at his neck and he unconsciously touched the scar tissue.

"You're not fully healed," she said quietly.

"I will be soon. I… I rushed the process a little. We needed to talk."

"You shouldn't have. I would have waited."

That made his heart flip around in his chest. He ignored the reaction. There was still a lot to discuss.

But he couldn't stay away from her any longer, so he took a seat on the couch next to her. She didn't move away, much to his relief. And to his immense pleasure, she actually leaned closer as she asked her next question.

"Is that why you live so long? Because your body can be healed every time you turn to stone?"

"Basically. The wolf gives the human body advanced hunting skills and senses, the human gives the wolf logic and reasoning. And opposable thumbs. The process of moving between forms extends both our existences. It's necessary. It takes time to train a hunter. We don't like to risk death too early."

"Why not? I mean, obviously you don't want to die. Who does? But Rea and the Elemental both said something last night that made me think death was particularly…nasty for your kind."

"I'm getting to that, I promise."

"By all means, continue then." She made a hand gesture and settled back into the couch.

He couldn't help a slight smile. And it felt really good. The smile died, however, when he continued. "What I failed to mention when I told you most of the story of our beginnings was the curse placed on us by Ne. Revenge against En for creating us to hunt and destroy his monsters. To protect humanity."

"Curse?"

He let out a long breath. Then dove in. "We're doomed to a horrific death. If we…take a wound serious enough to kill us, the animal spirit tries to escape the dying human body. But it will fail. And both go through a…through physical torture, stuck together. Unable to separate. The animal corporealizes inside the human body, while the human body turns to stone."

Katie jerked back, her hand coming up to her throat before she dropped it back to her lap. "Wait. Stuck? As in, your spirits don't move on or go away after death? You're not aware and stuck in stone, are you?"

She looked so horrified he was quick to reassure her. "No, no nothing quite that awful. Once dead, we're dead and both spirits are gone. At least, that's what En promised us. I've never died, so I can't be positive."

"Eric—"

He took the warning in her tone to heart and stopped trying to joke. "Every member of the Seven Families is destined to die with the animal symbiote desperately trying to escape, trying to tear its way out of the human body as it becomes stone."

She closed her eyes. He wanted to reach out, to touch her, to reassure her. But she needed to understand this, needed to understand…him.

Her eyes snapped open. "That grotesque statue in the atrium… Oh. That wasn't… Was that…?"

"That was my cousin. The one who had my father murdered."

"That was his body? His…corpse?"

Eric nodded. The gesture felt jerky and awkward. He had trouble meeting her gaze when he said, "I hadn't intended on showing you that. I left his body there as a warning to other Family members. What happened to those who betrayed the Family."

"The silver pole… Was that necessary or just convenient for killing him?"

"Silver speeds up our death. If silver gets into our blood, we die faster. That's only something that works with the wolf Family. The other Families have other…poisons."

"You used silver with your cousin on purpose."

It wasn't quite a question, but he still said, "I did."

"So he would die faster."

He let out a rough sigh. "I was angry enough to let him die slowly. But, in the end… Dying for his crimes was enough. Having the process take longer than necessary wouldn't have served any purpose. It wouldn't have brought my father back."

She nodded, her gaze steady on his face. He didn't look away this time.

"Something moved under your skin last night," she said quietly after a moment. "When you were close to dying. I thought it was some sort of… Well, I was imagining horror science fiction films and parasites trying to crawl out of you." She swallowed. "That was your wolf."

"It was."

"You would have ended up like your cousin. You were close to that, weren't you? Only without the silver to speed things up. I would have watched your animal try to tear its way out of you while you turned to stone."

"Yes."

She closed her eyes again, and a tremor moved through her. He reached for her before he thought better of it and fisted his hands in his lap.

"There is a way to break the curse. We don't *have* to die that way."

Her eyes snapped open. "How?"

"En couldn't undue his brother's spell. But he could give us an out to the curse."

When he stopped, she leaned forward again. "What's the out?"

And here it was. The moment of truth. The point of his salvation. Or doom.

The sounds of her screams last night echoed through his head again. And a small part of him hoped she'd hear this and walk away. He needed her, wanted her…loved her. So much. If she stayed, he was free.

But she wouldn't be. She'd be trapped in a world that had nearly killed her last night.

He forced himself to finish the full story. "En promised us that one day we would meet our true love," he said, quietly. "Our Nam-tar. Our destiny. And if we could convince that individual to stay with us willingly, the curse would be broken. Our deaths after that would be more… Well, if not pleasant, at least not so painfully horrific. The animal and human bodies wouldn't get stuck together in mid-transition. We'd just…die."

Her expression was impossible to read. He could scent some of her fear and confusion, but not well enough to parse out what she was actually feeling, what she thought of the story. One of the few times he might have preferred his wolf's sense of smell in this form. It was all he could do to stay on the opposite side of the couch and not rush her for her reaction.

"Your curse is broken by love?" she said after a moment. "That's very fairytale-ish, isn't it? I mean, in a world of monsters and hunters that seems so romantic and fanciful."

He shrugged. "The gods have an odd sense of humor. En promised us a true love to break our curse. And that's how it's worked for the last sixteen thousand years. When our Nam-tar finally enters our lives, we spend all our energy trying to convince them to stay with us."

She glanced away. "The Elemental said I was important to you," she said slowly, her gaze on the fireplace. "It called me your Nam-tar. You don't think I am, do you?"

He had to touch her when he said this, so he took her hand. She didn't pull away, but she didn't return his grip either.

"Katie. You are my Nam-tar. My destiny. I know it. I've known from the very beginning."

"But you haven't been in love with me from the beginning."

"That's not… I don't have to love you right away, and you don't have to love me in the beginning. Destined couples always end up in love eventually, though."

"Eventually."

"It's part of the promise."

"So if I'm your…Nam-tar, how would I break your curse?"

He swallowed and said, "By staying with me. Of your own free will. By choosing to spend your life with me."

She pulled her hand from his and his heartbeat sped as panic bubbled through his bloodstream. Panic but also a strange kind of relief. He forced down both reactions.

"When were you going to tell me this, about the curse and the other part of your nature?"

"Originally, I was going to tell you after you agreed to stay. I was hoping…you'd fall in love with me and *want* to stay. And you did. You can't tell me now that you don't love me."

"No. I wouldn't take that back. I do. I'm just deciding if I'm mad at you for not telling me this sooner."

"I didn't want you to feel obligated to stay just to break my curse. That actually wouldn't even work. I can't coerce you, even with the truth of my fate."

"But seducing me and getting me to fall in love with you isn't considered coercion?"

"No. It's not."

Her eyebrows rose at his blunt and honest answer. "Okay, then." She went back to staring at the fireplace, not meeting his gaze even though he tried to look into her eyes to see what she was thinking.

"You're going to leave, aren't you?" he said finally, when she'd been silent for longer than he could stand. He was surprised by the punch of both regret and resignation that accompanied those words. Even more surprised by the hint of relief.

She faced him. And he steeled himself for her rejection.

"No. I'm not," she said.

He blinked at her a few times. "You're not?"

"Well, actually, I am for a few days. I have obligations in the city that I have to deal with. But after that… I'll go wherever you want me to and stay with you as long as you want me."

He opened his mouth. Closed it to swallow the lump in his throat. Tried again. "Katie, I'm talking about staying with me forever. For a lifetime. It's not a decision to take lightly."

She smiled. "You trying to talk me out of it?"

Was he? He hadn't intended to but it did sort of sound like he was trying to talk her into leaving.

She leaned toward him, and Eric's skin tingled with a need to pull her close. But he didn't dare rush her.

"Eric, I love you. I faced an Elemental for you. A little thing like you having to turn to stone every so often is not going to send me running away now."

"It's more than—"

She set a hand to his mouth. "I know. I don't care."

"You're not just staying to help me with the curse?"

"No."

She scooted near enough he could feel the warmth of her skin. So close. Not close enough.

"I'd always assumed that our affair would end after I went back to the city. I hadn't expected you to *want* me to stay."

"I do. I very much do want you to stay. And not just because of the curse." He clenched his hand so he wouldn't reach for her yet. "But, you should know, life with me… There will always be monsters I have to hunt. And the Elemental hinted at a bigger conspiracy. My life is going to be extremely dangerous in the coming months. Actually, it's never going to be a safe, calm life."

And that was the rub.

He didn't want Katie to *have* to live that life. Last night, when she'd ended up at the Elemental's mercy, Eric had never been so terrified in his life. And he couldn't get to her. He couldn't save her. He'd felt so helpless and frantic. And because he'd been distracted and frantic, the grinluk had gotten the better of him in their fight. He'd been too desperate to reach Katie. His training, three hundred years of fighting monsters, all that experience… Right out the window when his love was in danger.

He wasn't sure he could take that kind of fear and helplessness again, even if she thought she could. He didn't want her to have to face those threats.

"Eric, after what's happened the last week, the fact that I'm still here should tell you something. Monsters aren't scaring me away."

She closed the last of the space between them and settled her mouth against his. Something in Eric relaxed, breaking open until he thought he might burst. He pulled her into his arms, finally finally allowing himself to hold her. Deepening the kiss when she melted in his arms.

She would stay. His curse would be over.

The sounds of her screams last night echoed in his mind again. He clutched her tighter, trying to ignore that sound, that fear. Trying to ignore his conscious, that small part of him whispering that it wasn't right to force her into his world. She wasn't safe here. She wasn't safe with him.

He loved her. He needed her.

But he needed her to be safe more.

That small, whispering part of him thought being cursed would be preferable to forcing Katie to face the dangers of his life.

For the next two days, he loved her, savored her, gave her all of himself that he had to give. He memorized the curve of her cheek, the way she felt in his arms while they slept, the sound of her laughter, the warmth of her breath against his cheek when she sighed, the rub of her silken hair against his fingertips, the way her body responded to his touch.

And he tried desperately to ignore that whispering voice.

She loved him. She wanted to stay. They could have forever. He could be free.

But she'd never be safe, the whispering voice reminded him. She'd never be safe.

When the roads were finally clear, when she left for the city to take care of her business…

That small, whispering voice won.

* * *

KATIE KNOCKED ON THE LARGE FRONT DOOR TO THE LOGAN MANSION A week later, almost giddy with her need to see him. She hadn't spoken with him since the morning she'd left, taking one of the family's spare cars back to the city. They'd kissed goodbye and she'd promised to return as quickly as she could. But the week it had taken her to get her affairs in order had been torture. She'd barely been able to think straight.

Now she was here and so excited to see him she didn't pay heed to the slight sensation creeping along her neck. It wasn't a hint of danger so she ignored it. She didn't want to *know* anything right now. She just wanted to see Eric.

Even as she waited, she realized this was the first time she'd actively been able to ignore a *knowing*. She grinned as she glanced around the impressive drive and grounds at the front of the house, the trees now in full, colorful autumn attire. She was so much more comfortable with her gift now. There was a level of control she'd never experienced before and a level of confidence in her talent that left her feeling whole for the first time in a very very long while.

When the door finally opened, she was greeted by an unsmiling Gregory. She realized she'd never found out what Gregory was, but she had plenty of time for questions now that she was back.

Then his serious expression sank in. "Hello, Gregory. What's wrong? Is everyone okay?"

"The household is just fine, Ms. Donavan."

Back to using her last name? That was weird. When he didn't step back, she said, "Can I come in? Where's Eric? I thought he'd be here to meet me."

"I'm sorry, Ms. Donavan. Mr. Logan had to leave the country on business."

"He's gone? Did he leave me a message? When is he due back?"

The itch at her nape increased, and Katie had to work hard to ignore the sensation. But the *knowing* was creeping over her, like it or not.

"I'm afraid he left no message. And he is not due back for the foreseeable future."

Katie clenched her jaw as her bottom lip started to tremble. "'Foreseeable future'? How long is that, Gregory?"

"He indicated that he would not be returning to the US for a very long time."

She stared hard at him as the *knowing* finally washed over her. She couldn't avoid it now that the truth was staring her in the face.

Eric had left her. Despite everything, despite claiming he needed her, he was simply brushing her off. He didn't want to see her again and had no intention of committing to her. All his talk of breaking his curse must have been a lot of bloody bullshit.

Even as she thought that, she *knew* better. He was under a curse. A curse she was supposedly destined to break.

Yet even that wasn't enough for him to stick with her.

She swallowed hard. "Okay, Gregory. I understand." Gregory opened his mouth but she held up a hand. "Listen, I'm going to borrow the car for a little longer. Just to get to the train station. I'll leave it in the parking lot there. You can have it collected?"

"Yes."

"Fine. It was very nice meeting you, Gregory. I'm sorry I won't be seeing you again."

"It's been an honor, Katie."

Gregory spoke with such sincerity she wanted to cry. Before she gave in to the impulse, she turned back to the car she'd left in the driveway. The train home was a good idea. With her heart breaking, doing nothing more than sitting and staring out the window sounded about all she'd be capable of for the next few hours.

When she climbed behind the wheel, she took one last look at the mansion. Eric's room wasn't visible from this side of the house, but the library where she'd first met him was. The curtains were open. She could just see the shelves of books inside.

She drove away, roughly brushing away a tear. She could cry later.

She'd have plenty of time for tears. She had a feeling this ache in her chest would be with her for a long time.

Eric waited until the car disappeared around a bend in the drive before stepping close to the library window. He'd watched her bounce up to the door, then watched her slump back to the car with her shoulder's down. He'd held perfectly still, letting her go for her own good.

But it was one of the hardest things he'd ever done.

"You happy now," Rea said from behind him.

"This is for the best."

"No, it's not."

The library door closed with a loud click, but he didn't turn around. He continued to stare out the window. Maybe he would leave the country. Staying so close to Katie without being able to go to her tore at him.

But being too far away would be intolerable.

So he'd stay here. And try to learn how to live without her.

CHAPTER THIRTY-NINE

Katie *knew* she was being followed. She'd known for more than two weeks.

And she was really pissed.

Eric Logan. The love of her life. And the current bane of her existence.

No matter how she'd tried to corner him over the last two weeks, she couldn't make him come out and talk to her. It had taken her the better part of the last three months just to learn to live with the ache of his leaving. She'd gone on with her life. What else could she do? But the lack of closure as much as anything had left her hollow. The fact that she was still desperately in love with him made things infinitely worse. She was pretty sure she would always love him. And that made contemplating her life without him overwhelming.

She'd manage to get on with things, though. Her editor loved the interview so much Katie was allowed to write whatever she wanted now. Her current article involved unsung heroes in child services, a story which gave her great satisfaction to research and write. She finally felt on track toward that Pulitzer. And that made her happy.

But everything felt a little less bright, a little less exciting without Eric.

And now? Now, after months of silence and no contact, suddenly he was here. Following her around the city. Never far away. But refusing to face her.

Why the hell was he here? What did he think he was doing? He had to realize she *knew* he was there. So why avoid her?

Well, she was tired of this dance. And she intended to do something about it. If he wouldn't come out of the shadows of his own accord, she'd force him out. By going into the shadows herself.

Walking alone, late at night, in a part of the city she'd be careful in during daylight. Under streetlights that flickered. With very little traffic passing. And all the businesses and apartments in the area dark and closed.

She turned down a street she was positive held a high level of danger, facing into an icy cold whip of January wind blowing in off the Hudson River. The man hiding in the shadows ahead and to the right, tucked against a closed storefront, would want more than just money from the woman coming toward him.

Katie walked with her face in her purse, pretending to ignore the chill racing over her skin and the knowledge that a mugger and rapist waited just a few hundred yards ahead of her. She could play dumb if she had to.

The dark shape moved out of the shadows ahead, and Katie gasped at his appearance—for affect. In the next instant, Eric stood in front of her. She hadn't seen where he'd come from and had only a breeze ruffling her hair to hint at how fast he'd moved to get into position.

She watched his back with a half-smile, even as the fine hairs on the nape of her neck bristled when he growled. Glancing around his shoulder, she saw the shadow disappear back down the street, hurrying around a corner in the opposite direction.

A few moments passed before Eric finally faced her, so she steeled herself for the sight of him.

When he did spin around, she siwas glad she had. Her first look at him in person for more than three months overwhelmed her. His beloved face, so close. Him so solid and strong, standing only an arm's length away. He was dressed in dark clothes as usual, so he blended with the other shadows. But the sharp lines and angles of his face caught the streetlight, the reality of him so precisely matched to her memory, the ache of it caught in her throat.

It took a great deal of effort not to step close and pull him into her arms.

Even more effort not to snarl and give him a piece of her mind.

His eyes were dark and his expression furious as he glared down at her. She didn't even flinch. She had more than enough of her own anger to meet his.

"What in the name of all that is holy did you think you were doing?" he growled. "How can you not know to stay aware of your surroundings on a dark street at night when you live in this city?"

"Don't be ridiculous," she said, settling her purse over her shoulder and then her hands on her hips. "Even if I was stupid enough to walk through this neighborhood at night with my face in my purse, my psychic senses would have sent me running in the opposite direction long before I turned down this street."

"Then what the hell were you doing?"

"You've been following me for two weeks and still wouldn't come out and talk to me."

"You did this on purpose to draw me out? What if I hadn't come to your rescue?"

"Ah, but I *knew* you would." She gave a little shrug. "Though, if you hadn't, I would have had a great excuse to taser you the next time I caught you following me. Then you'd just be a stalker, and I'd be within my rights to drop you on your ass."

She watched his lip twitch, whether with humor or annoyance she couldn't tell. But the sign of an emotion other than anger was encouraging.

"Now that we've settled that," she continued. "You mind telling me *why* you've been following me around for the last two weeks? I assumed when you dumped me that would be the last I saw of you."

His jaw tightened and he glanced away. "How did you know I was around?"

"Are you kidding?"

"Psychic," he muttered. "Should have thought…"

"Yeah, well obviously you're not big on thinking these days. Eric, damn it, what are you doing here? If you don't want me, why are you pestering me?"

"Don't," he snarled and pointed a finger at her. "Do not ever again say I don't want you."

"You *dumped* me after I was gone for a week. Hell, you didn't even do it yourself. You had your bloody butler do it. I don't think I'm off base in assuming you don't want me."

"You're wrong."

She threw her hands in the air. "Jesus Christ. Will you just bloody tell me the truth? What's going on?"

"I… I was worried about you."

"Why?"

"Because the Elemental hinted there was more going on. Where you stabbed it… It'll be gone for a while. Maybe years. But I didn't want its associates coming after you."

"Then why did you wait so long to start tailing me? Three months ago when you dumped me you weren't worried about the Elemental."

"Stop saying that. I didn't dump you."

"No. Your butler did."

The sound of crashing cans echoed from farther down the street. Eric's stance changed from defensive to watchful in a blink, and he angled himself so he was between her and the sound.

"Can we discuss this somewhere a little less…dangerous?" he asked.

She scowled. "That was a cat. And don't ask how I know. Psychic, remember?"

"I know it was a cat." He tapped his nose. "Enhanced sense of smell, remember?"

She rolled her eyes at his mocking imitation of her tone.

"That doesn't make this particular street any safer," he finished.

"Where?"

"I have an apartment—"

"No," she cut him off. The last thing she needed was to be alone with him in his territory again. "My place. Since you already know where it is."

"Will you at least let me get us a taxi? The subway will take too long."

"Fine." She wasn't one to turn down a free taxi. She hated waiting on the subway platform in January. Too bloody cold. Speaking of cold… She pulled the lapels on her wool trench closed. "Let's get out of here before my fingers go numb."

"The muggers you'll brave, but the cold sends you scurrying indoors?"

"That better not be humor, mister. I'm still pissed off at you for dumping me. Especially after all that bullshit about being your Namtar."

"That wasn't bullshit."

"Bollocks." But she didn't want to discuss all this on a cold city street either. "Taxi first. Talk later."

They walked downtown, along a better lit avenue until Eric flagged a yellow cab. The ride to her tiny Westside apartment was silent, which suited her. She didn't feel like discussing all this in front of the driver. Not to mention the fact that they'd have to talk in code.

When she let Eric into her studio, she dropped her keys on the small table by the door, hung her coat on the wall hangers, and went straight to the kitchen. She didn't bother inviting him in or telling him to make himself comfortable. She didn't want him comfortable. She wanted him to squirm.

"I'm making coffee."

"Thank you."

"For me." She relented with a shrug. "But, obviously, you can have some." She faced him from behind the small counter that separated her cube-sized kitchen from the rest of the room. Her double bed took up one wall. A couple of overstuffed chairs and a small circular coffee table filled the middle of the room. And the world's smallest flat-screen TV on a tiny TV stand took up the other wall. Her "desk", the coffee table, held her laptop, printer, and a few piles of paper—research for her current article. Around the two windows opposite the kitchen, she'd set up bookshelves, which were overflowing, and a small window garden which looked a little neglected. The bathroom door was just off to the right of the kitchen.

She watched Eric take in the small space and wondered if he was comparing it to his own home. Her entire apartment, bathroom included, was smaller than his bedroom.

"Cozy," he said when he faced her.

"Don't be condescending. The rent is good for the location. And I'm saving money. I don't want to waste my salary on a big apartment I can only barely afford."

"I wasn't being condescending. I like your apartment. It's very…you."

She glanced around again and decided her apartment was her. But he shouldn't have realized that. She didn't want him to know her that well. Not when he'd been so willing to let her go.

"Now we're in a nice warm place," she said, "you want to explain why you waited three months to decide I might still be in danger?"

"Still so tenacious when it comes to getting answers."

"A woman doesn't change personalities just because a man leaves her broken-hearted. Answer the question."

"I didn't mean to break your heart. If it makes you feel any better, I've been miserable without you."

"That might help if I wanted it to. I'm not letting you off the hook yet, though. Now answer my question."

"I didn't wait three months. I've had people watching you since the day you drove away from the mansion."

"When I left intending to come back? Or after you had Gregory dump me."

"He was angry with me for making him do that, by the way."

"Good. Which time?"

"The very first time you left."

"I didn't pick them up. Why not?"

"That I can't tell you. I'm no expert on the way psychic powers work. Maybe you didn't want to *know*."

"Or I was too hurt to notice."

"Katie, I didn't want to hurt you." He spread his hands out to his sides, looking helpless and vulnerable in her little apartment.

She would not soften to that look. She would *not*. "But you did. Now you're going to explain why? You were worried enough to have me followed for the last three months. You personally started following me two weeks ago. Why the change? Has something happened?"

The coffee maker gurgled its final drip, signaling that it was ready. She turned her back on him to pour two cups. It was difficult to face him with her emotions so raw and visible. Yet she didn't want to hide. She wanted him to know just how much he'd hurt her. She hoped he felt bad for it, too. Petty though those emotions were, she didn't feel like rising above the pettiness. She'd earned a little guilt from him.

"Nothing's happened. I just couldn't keep away any longer. I needed to know for myself you were safe."

She crossed the room and handed him a mug, his coffee black just as he liked it. Watching his face as she took her first sip, she tried to gage his sincerity. And damn him, he was being as honest with his emotions as she was, which only made her ache that much more. Seeing him, standing this close to him, smelling that lovely soap he used, brought back all the love and anger and hurt and fear until she wanted to choke on it.

Instead, she washed it all down with another sip of coffee and sat in one of the chairs.

Without an invitation, he sat in the opposite chair, but he turned it so he was facing her instead of the TV.

"I've missed you," he murmured.

"Right. That's why you've called me every day and tried to explain why you broke my heart?"

"Katie, I love you."

"Don't do that," she warned, pointing a finger at him. Her hands started to shake so she set the coffee mug down on the wooden floor beside her chair. "Don't you dare say that now."

"It's the truth. I love you. I don't know when I fell. Sometime while I was trying to get you to fall in love with me. But I do love you. And that's why I made you leave."

"That makes no sense." She clenched the armrests to keep her hands still.

Eric set his own mug on the floor, then leaned forward, his gaze so intent she couldn't look away, no matter how much she wanted to.

"My world is dangerous. More dangerous than anything you've ever had to deal with. Even your sister's murder doesn't compare to what you'll have to live with over a lifetime with me. How could I do that to someone I love?"

"What about that curse? The awful death that only I can prevent?"

"I'd rather be cursed than have you in danger."

"I'm in danger all the time anyway, you idiot." She stood up to stalk around the room. "I could get hit by a bus. I could have a fricking plane fly into my building while I'm at the office. Some asshole with a grudge could stalk into the coffee shop where I go for my breakfast and start shooting up the place. The world is bloody dangerous, no matter what we do."

"I know."

His quietly spoken comment brought her up short. She hadn't expected him to agree with her so readily. "If you know, why haven't you been in touch?"

"Because I was an idiot. Because I hurt you, and I didn't know how to fix that. Because I love you so much, I still can't stand the idea of you being trapped in my world."

"But I'm not the only human to come into your world, am I? You said your people found their significant others among people outside the Families."

"Doesn't change how I feel about having you in my world when it's so dangerous for you."

"Then why are you here?"

"Because I can't live without you anymore." He raised a hand when she opened her mouth. "And not because of the curse."

He stood and crossed to stand in front of her, close enough that she breathed in his scent and heat.

"Despite the curse," he murmured. "Despite myself, I can't live without you. I still don't know how to fix things between us. I only know I need to be near you. Even if that means I stay in your shadow and do no more than watch out for your safety."

"That's impossible. You have a job to do, a family to run."

"You're more important to me."

"I should really hate you now." Her jaw muscles clenched with emotions she couldn't begin to name. "You're breaking my heart all over again. And I thought it was pretty well shattered already."

"Katie…"

He cupped her cheek in one large, warm hand. And to her surprise, she didn't jerk away. His touch felt like he should always be touching her. Like a homecoming.

"How am I supposed to trust you?" she said, her voice low. "How am I supposed to believe you won't just kick me to the curb again when things get scary?"

"Staying or going is your choice. Even if I weren't cursed, I wouldn't really have the choice anymore. I couldn't even make it for three months. I don't want to exist without you."

"I am so fucking angry with you." She sniffed and realized with horror that tears were pooling in her eyes. Damn it, she didn't want to cry. She'd managed to spend the last three months *not* crying over Eric Logan. "The worst part was that I never stopped loving you. I couldn't. I will for the rest of my life. And it sucked because you weren't going to be in my life."

"How about now?"

"Now." What about now? Could she learn to trust him? Could she learn to forgive him? She didn't want to spend her entire life without him either. But she was still leery. And she needed him to put that leeriness to rest.

"Now," she said more firmly, "you're going to have to earn me." She straightened her shoulders and the tears dried up. "You want me in your life, you're going to have to prove to me I'll be safe there. And

I'm not talking safe from the monsters. I'm talking about being safe from your damned sense of... I don't even know what to call it. Chivalry seems too nice. Whatever. You need to prove you're not going to up and dump me again just because you get scared."

"I can do that. I don't know how, but I'll do whatever you ask me to."

"Move into the city. Temporarily. Can you do that?"

He nodded.

"Take me out. On real dates. Talk with me. Tell me everything about you. Listen to me when I talk. Seduce me. Win me back. On my terms."

He nodded again and his lips tilted up slightly.

"When you tell me you love me, you sure as shit better mean it."

"I do. With my whole heart."

"And when your curse is broken, you will continue to work at keeping me in your life. No matter how many years I live."

"I swear it."

The formal vow relaxed her stiff spine, and all her righteous indignation drained away. "You mean that don't you. You're going to do what I ask."

"Absolutely. Anything you ask. Everything you want."

The last of her resistance crumbled.

She was sure she was opening herself up to heartbreak again. But she just couldn't say no. Not with him standing there looking so vulnerable and serious. She took a single step closer to him and wrapped her arms around his waist, sighing when he hugged her close.

"Gods, Katie, I've missed this. I've missed you. So much."

He kissed the top of her head, rubbed his cheek against her hair. And when she looked up, he kissed her on the mouth. She gave in to her need and returned his kiss, long and languid and gentle. Savoring his taste, the familiar feel of his lips, the way his kiss felt both new and so so familiar.

She'd missed him, too.

When she finally broke the kiss, she said, "You really love me?"

"Yes."

"Why didn't you say that earlier? When I told you I loved you? You had two days afterward to tell me."

"I didn't?" He frowned a little, blinking as he stared down at her. "I thought I must have."

"Nope."

"I'm sorry. I should have said the words."

She narrowed her gaze and shook her head. "No. If you had and still dumped me that would have been worse."

"Rea and Gregory haven't given me any peace since I let you go."

"Good. You deserved it."

"I know." He smiled, that grin that stole her breath.

"What did they say when you finally decided to come to the city?"

"Rea told me to buy you expensive gifts and flowers and crawl on my knees until you forgave me."

"Well, damn. I wish I'd talked to her about this before I dragged you out of stalking mode. I could have gotten some good loot."

"I'll give you anything you want."

She shook her head. "I don't want stuff. I want a Pulitzer. And I intend to get that on my own." She snuggled closer and tucked her head under his chin, savoring the warmth of his embrace. "No, the only thing I want from you now is your love. And, of course, all the groveling I already demanded."

His chuckle made her cheek vibrate. "Done."

But her smile fell as something just a little depressing struck her. "You've already lived a really long time. Will you continue to live for a lot longer? I mean, are you…middle aged for your people? Young? Old?"

"You could say I'm the equivalent of a thirty-six, thirty-seven-year-old human."

"So you're going to live a lot longer."

"If the monsters don't get me. Yes."

"Don't even joke about the monsters killing you. I don't want to think about that."

"Now you know how I feel."

"That aside, you're going to live a long, long time." She sighed and kept her face firmly snuggled against his shoulder.

"What's wrong?" he said, kissing her on the head again.

"Just thinking it's a shame I'll die so much sooner than you."

"You don't have to."

That made her straighten to face him. "What? How?"

"There's a way. But it requires a great deal of trust. I'm not sure we're ready for that step yet. Not after… Not until I make up for my overzealous attempt to protect you."

"I'm glad you recognize your attempts were over the top. But you still need to tell me how it's possible to extend my life. I'm not gonna let that one go until later."

His hands tightened around her waist a little, like he was afraid she'd move away. "You'd have to stand in front of me, with your back to me, and let my wolf jump through you. Then you'd have to let it return to my human body back through you."

Her eyes widened. "Holy shit. Is that possible? The wolf becomes solid as it leaves you. How could it even get through another person? Wouldn't it just…knock me over?"

"The ritual is really only possible between a hunter and their Nam-tar. The wolf won't solidify into corporeal form until it's finished passing through you, and when it leaps to reenter, it will become incorporeal sooner."

"How does this ritual extend my life?"

"Enough of the wolf is left behind to join you to the Family. You won't have a symbiotic animal spirit that can leave your body, not like I do. But enough of the wolf will be with you to extend your life, help you heal faster, make you stronger—"

"Wait, is that what Gregory is?" she interrupted, excited by the discovery. "Did he go through the ritual? He said trying to explain what he was would involve your explanations to me about your nature and the curse and everything. Is this what he meant? Is he a Nam-tar for one of the Logans?"

"So many questions." Eric hugged her closer. "Yes, Gregory was my father's sister's oldest son's Nam-tar. A close paternal cousin. They met when Gregory took up employment with Abraham's father as a valet and butler."

"How old is Gregory?"

"Old. Not as old as me. But he's been with the Family for many many years."

"And this cousin? Abraham?"

"He died about five years ago. Killed during a hunt."

"Poor Gregory." And poor her, she realized. She could lose Eric at any time to one of the monsters. Suddenly, his reasons for letting her go didn't seem so idiotic. The idea of him dying closed her throat.

"Gregory chose to stay with the Family, in the home he'd always lived in with Abraham. They had many happy years together."

"Why is he working as a butler for you when he's a member of your Family?"

"His choice. He wanted to remain useful. And he's more than just a butler, if you hadn't noticed."

He had her there. "So. He went through the ritual with his Abraham. But now that he's outlived Abraham, what happens?"

"He continues to live and grow old at a slower rate, though his aging has sped up with the passing of Abraham's wolf. Gregory is still very strong, and he heals quickly. But he won't live another few centuries like he might have if Abraham was still alive."

"That's probably good. I don't think I'd want to keep living for centuries without you."

"That's exactly why I had to come see you." He rested his forehead against hers. "I couldn't face the centuries ahead without you. But, Katie, the ritual… It's not absolutely necessary. We can be very happy without it. You don't have to go through that."

"Oh, I intend to do it. Eventually. Not tonight. But I will do it. I want as much time with you as I can get." She leaned back and wagged her eyebrows. "Plus, I'll have all that extra time to work on getting a bunch of Pulitzers."

He chuckled. And then he laughed, hugging her so close she felt a part of him.

The satisfaction and contentment that filled her in that moment left her in no doubt about her decision. She loved him senseless. She'd remain with him for as long as possible, loving him till the end of time. Knowing he felt the same way intensified her sense of completeness. Of finally being home. This was where she wanted to be, where she belonged, held firmly in Eric's arms.

"I love you," she said, rising on her toes to kiss him.

"I love you too, Katie. And I promise, I'll prove it every day for the rest of our lives."

When he kissed her, she *knew* he meant every word.

THANK YOU

Thank you for reading DARKNESS IN STONE, the first in this new paranormal romance series. I hope you enjoyed it, and the horror twist. There will be more of the Logans to come. If you'd like a sneak peek, keep reading for an excerpt from book two, REDEMPTION IN STONE.

This series idea has been a long time in coming. The initial spark of the story started with a statue in the Metropolitan Museum of Art, a piece called *Struggle of the Two Natures in Man* by George Grey Barnard (1863-1938). It's a statue of a man lying on his side and another identical man climbing out of the reclining man. There's even a weird little bat detail on it that no one quite knows the meaning of. I'm not sure why this sculpture stuck with me, but it did. And when I realized I wanted to play with a fated mates idea in a paranormal romance, but not do the usual shifters, I remembered this statue. That was the initial spark that evolved into the Seven Families of monster hunters.

These books have been a long time in coming, too. I had that initial idea, and started the first version of this book, before my oldest son was born. He's fourteen now. So the series has been percolating for a while. I'm really excited to finally be able to bring it to readers.

Look for more books about the Logans coming soon. And if you're interested in more of my paranormal romance, check out my Tiger Shifters series where the mates aren't fated, but they do have to fight for each other. The first book in that series, ONCE UPON A TIGER, is currently available in eBook for free.

Subscribers to my newsletter (https://bit.ly/KatSimonsNewsletter) also get an exclusive Tiger Shifters short story that isn't available anywhere else. I also have all kinds of advanced excerpts, cover reveals, deal announcements, news, and other fun stuff for subscribers, so if you'd like to keep up to date on releases and other news, please subscribe.

Thank you again for reading DARKNESS IN STONE. I hope you enjoyed the novel.

~Kat

REDEMPTION IN STONE EXCERPT

A Seven Families Novel
Wolf Family
Book 2

CHAPTER ONE

Rebecca Logan crept through the woods, studying the ground, the lines barely visible in the dirt. With the night covering the ground beneath the pines in shadows, she needed every ounce of her heightened eyesight to follow the faint path.

The monster was close.

She'd been following it through the mountains for two days now. Rumors of mysterious cattle deaths just the other side of the mountain drew her here to the Cascades. Then trails of dead deer, their bodies torn apart in ways that some accounts tried to write off as bear or wolf killings. One story tried to blame a coyote for the slaughter.

But little details had crept into the news accounts. Little signs of "something not right" with the excuse of ordinary animals, even packs of animals, being responsible for the weird slaughters. Things like the dead carrion birds found near the bodies. The bulging round injuries that looked almost like suction cup burns. The fact that none of the teeth marks could be matched to any of the local predators.

And then, the stories of people seeing a "monster" started to show up in less reputable magazines and newspapers. Seeing something with tentacles moving around the edge of property. Something with huge teeth scurrying through the yard.

No humans believed those stories. They were nightmares. Fictions. Things you found in horror books, not in real life. Must have been weird shadows. Something ordinary looking strange in the dark.

But Becca knew better.

Monsters were real. And it was the job of her family to hunt and kill them.

She'd been fighting monsters her whole life. Almost two centuries training and then hunting them down. Destroying them so they couldn't harm En's precious humans. The job was ordained by old gods and came with a lot of responsibility.

A lot of potential danger as well.

The faint trail she followed started to widen. Signs of something large moving through, pushing down the undergrowth, scrapping pine needles into unnatural lines. The smell hit her next. Faint on the wind, but there. An almost salty scent, mixed with the metallic tang of blood, and a faint hint of something like animal feces. She wrinkled her nose. Not only did the fucking things have to be dangerous. An inordinate number of them stank.

She let out a long, slow breath, settling her shoulders. There was a clearing ahead. A good place for an ambush.

Pulling her sword from the scabbard across her back, and dropping the pack she carried from her shoulder to rested against the thick base of a fir tree, she inched silently through the trees, her full attention now on the very faint snuffling noise ahead. So faint, if she'd been an ordinary human, she would have missed the sound. Maybe confused it for a breeze or the ruffle of a night bird's feathers.

Autumn in these mountains was already getting cold enough to feel the approaching winter. Though it was still early in October, a bite of sharp chill kissed her cheeks as she slipped silently to the edge of the clearing.

She took her sword in a two-handed grip and stared at the beast.

An irgotoc. She could hardly believe it. She'd really hoped she was wrong.

Tiny blade-like talons flicked out from the tips of two dozen brown-skinned tentacles covering the thing's scaled sides. Its bat-like wings rose and fell, shrunken and useless for flight, but the movements created a wisping sound, like canvas shuddering in an ocean wind. Its four thick crocodile-like legs were squatted down low, putting the monster's belly close to the ground. From her angle behind a tree, she couldn't see the beast's tail, but its flat snout was buried in the remains of…something. Hard to tell what that something used to be from her angle.

Two humans had gone missing over the mountains before she'd been able to get here. Their bodies hadn't been found. She very much hoped that wasn't one of them.

Settling her sword more firmly in her grip, she moved out of the trees, approaching the monster at an angle. If it was occupied with its meal, she might be able to get close enough to cut off its head before a real fight erupted.

But irgotoc weren't so easy to sneak up on.

The beast spun around, faster than it looked like it should move, whipping its tail around with a snap, the wicked six-inch barbs covering the tail's tip hit the ground only a few inches from Becca's leg.

Okay. Fight it was.

The tentacles along its side flailed toward her, forcing her to swing wildly at one before jumping to one side and slashing through another. The creature's acid blood leeched into the ground, making the dirt sizzle.

She hated irgotoc. Acid blood was such a pain to deal with.

Another slash along its side drove it back a few feet, but then it charged again, fast on those squat crocodile legs, two side tentacles flicking at her as its barbed tail swung around again. She leapt back a foot, took a swipe at the beast's side, and scrapped her sword over the rock-hard scales.

Those were tricky to get past. But she didn't need to get her sword through its side. She needed to get her sword through its neck.

But getting at the neck with all those flailing tentacles and that spike-barbed tail wasn't a simple ask.

She dove close again, swinging in wide arcs to dislodge the

tentacles. The irgotoc screeched and spun, those short squat legs swinging it around faster than even a crocodile. Moving fast enough to push her into moving faster as well. Her enhanced speed would make it obvious to a human she wasn't entirely human herself, but there were no witnesses this deep in the mountains.

Fortunately. Because she didn't want any humans in danger.

A blur of movement from the side, and she flicked her sword out without looking, the metal tinging against the hard talons tipping the tentacle. Then she dove away as the beast's tail whipped over the top of her head. The whistling sound of those sharp barbs passing close to her hair made her wince.

Coming to her feet a few yards away didn't give her any breathing space, though. The irgotoc charged forward.

She took out a tentacle, the severed limb dropping to the ground with a wiggling thud, the blade shaped talons on its tip churning up the dirt.

To her horror, the severed tentacle started to grow back.

What the hell? Irgotoc didn't have limbs that regenerated.

The beast's little vestigial wings beat the air. And while they were small and useless, the movement sent the noxious smell of its blood and natural shit stench over the top of Becca. She gaged and snarled. One of the times her sensitive sense of smell was a drawback.

She slashed and cut at flailing limbs again and again. Diving beyond the beast's tail. Spinning and lunging forward again. Always aiming for the neck.

Two of the severed tentacles regenerated, but a third remained a lumpy, bleeding stub. The anomaly in the irgotoc's physiology was distracting.

Irgotoc weren't new monsters. The species had existed for millennia. They weren't the oldest of the monsters, but they were still old enough that the Families had all their traits and dangers well catalogued.

But the Families had also managed to drive the irgotoc to near extinction. She hadn't personally fought one in…a very long time. In fact, they'd started to believe the irgotoc was actually extinct.

Then she'd started seeing those reports of dead animals and the two missing people. She'd expected to find some sort of monster in these mountains.

When she'd seen the scat evidence of an irgotoc, she hadn't quite believed her eyes.

There was no denying the monster still existed, though, when it was right in front of her. And it looked like it had evolved.

Which really really sucked.

She dove to the left as it charged, tail swinging, the wicked six-inch barbs covering the tail's tip barely missing her head again. She took two tentacles in one swing, leaping back to avoid the talons as the limbs flew away from the beast.

A piercing screech erupted from the irgotoc. Wincing, she jumped over more flailing limbs, and used a tree trunk to boost herself in a high jump that landed her several feet behind the monster.

She sucked in a deep breath. Sweat trickled down her back beneath her sweater, despite the cold air kissing her cheeks.

The irgotoc spun again, but this time, instead of charging toward her, it lunged into the darkness beneath the trees.

Shit.

Her most basic instincts urged her to race after it. But her training checked the charge. She opened her senses, listening, scenting the air. They were fast, the irgotoc, and more graceful than might be expected for that collection of body parts. But they weren't naturally suited to moving easily in the undergrowth.

A shadowed movement to her left. The sounds of scrapping over dirt and detritus.

She rushed toward the sound, the scent of shit and monster getting stronger in that direction.

But another smell, something weirdly familiar, weirdly nice, brushed her senses. Made her stumble a step. Blinking.

What the…?

Before she could analyze the new smell, the irgotoc rushed out of the trees at her, forcing her into defensive sword swings and retreat to gain some ground. Fuck.

She tripped over a branch, dropping hard onto her ass. With another curse, she stabbed her sword toward the irgotoc's face as it raced to overwhelm her. She skewered one of the tiny black eyes above its bloodied snout.

The beast screeched again and stopped the headlong charge. Gave her enough time to roll back to her feet.

Then a second huge shape lunged between her and the monster.

And that weirdly familiar scent brought her up short again.

Oh no.

CHAPTER TWO

B ecca had a full second to register the stranger standing between her and the monster, one single second to take in the large shadow of him. The blackness under the trees, hid any distinct features. But she got the impression of wide shoulders and height.

Then the large shape leapt away again.

The irgotoc spun, following the moving shadow, its bloodied snout snuffling the air, its vestigial wings fluttering as it shuffled on its crocodile legs to face the stranger.

A weird sort of panic she wasn't used to filled her. Panic that the monster would reach the newcomer before she could kill it.

The strange fear, that pulse of terror, was a distraction she couldn't afford. She hadn't felt *panic* in a fight with a monster since her early years. Why now? Where was the throat-clogging terror coming from?

Whatever it was, the emotion sent her charging toward the irgotoc, desperate to get its attention back on her and away from the stranger.

The monster's distraction worked for her, though. She went right for its neck, able to slide through the still flailing tentacles, slipping past tiny blades, to slice her sword across the thick neck at the base of its round head. No scales here. Nothing to stop the honed edge of her sword.

The monster spun around, tentacles swiping at her, tail a blur of movement. Its acid blood sprayed out with its wild movements, forcing her to leap away, to pull her sword free too soon.

Damn it. Hadn't gotten the head off. And the fuckers just kept moving so long as their heads were attached. Even if only barely.

The shadow that had distracted the monster before charged behind the beast. The irgotoc swung around, its head lolling sickeningly to one side. Becca cursed, pulled the dagger from her boot sheath, and charged the irgotoc again.

Dodging deadly tentacles, slashing at them with both dagger and sword, she tried to work her way back to the monster's neck, looking for an opening. From the corner of her eye, she saw the shadow dart past the back of the beast again, watched the irgotoc's tail whip toward that shadow. She might have screamed a warning, she couldn't be sure. But her own distraction cost her.

A tentacle hooked her ankle and brought her down hard on her ass again.

The irgotoc lunged toward her, its snout open to reveal shockingly thick, sharp teeth. Instinctively, she dropped her weapons and reached with both hands to hold the monster's head back.

She realized in that moment, the neck wound she'd already issued was healing. No more acid blood spit out. Good given her position as she struggled to hold the snout and sharp, snapping teeth away from her face. Bad because she still had to get the head off somehow.

And she'd had to drop her sword and dagger.

Desperately, she reached one-handed for her sword, keeping one hand on the irgotoc. But every time she released her hold, the monster pushed forward, and she had to quickly use two hands to hold it back again.

She was stronger than a human woman, by a lot, but the irgotoc was her match. It pushed those sharp teeth at her, making a high-pitched sound like a snuffle and a whine combined. The sound pierced her sensitive ears, breaking up her concentration.

As she struggled, one of the blades tipping a tentacle cut through the thigh pocket of her cargo pants, only missing skin because the pocket carried a water flask.

Her lungs burned and she realized she wasn't breathing through her gritted teeth. She sucked in a breath, gulping foul-smelling air. The creature's rotten shit smell coating the back of her throat. And where its acid blood had sizzled the soil, that sharp acrid stench stung her nostrils.

She reached for her sword again, only to have to swing back to keep both hands on the snapping beast's head. She needed purchase and a better position. She didn't have any leverage like this. But the irgotoc gave her no room to move, to stand up. And no space to reach her weapons.

A high howl rent the night air.

Suddenly the monster jerked back a few inches. Pulled off of her. Giving her some room to move. Its head swiveled to look at its tail.

And Becca took those precious seconds.

Without looking, she snatched up the closest weapon to hand. Then she thrust her dagger up under the irgotoc's chin into the soft flesh of its neck.

It reared back, releasing another piercing whining screech.

Scrambling away as acid blood sprayed out, Becca snatched up her sword and stood in one movement. Spun. And brought the sharp blade down across the monster's neck. This time severing its head in a single swing.

The head bounced along the dark soil, rolling a few feet away. The body continued to thrash for several seconds, the remaining tentacles groping wildly at the air. Then it collapsed and dark acid blood seeped from its neck to soak the ground.

Becca took a breath. Fucking irgotoc.

She scooted away from the pooling blood and turned her attention to the monster's tail to see what had pulled it off her.

And she realized why the scent she'd caught earlier seemed familiar.

A wolf, twice the size of a normal animal, held the creature's tail in its massive jaws. Black blood dripped from the wolf's mouth, but it didn't let go until the final tentacle lay still.

"Drop it," she said, a little panicky. "Drop the tail. Acid blood. It's burning you."

The wolf dropped its hold and took a step away from the irgotoc. Shook its snout a little, as if to dislodge the blood. Then looked up and met her gaze. Intelligent, glowing yellow eyes stared steadily at her.

There was more awareness in those eyes than there should have been in an ordinary wolf. And that glowing yellow…not just a trick of the night.

She stepped around the monster, carefully, approaching the wolf slowly and deliberately. Worried about the acid burns he must have gotten. She didn't want to send him running away without first assuring herself the injuries were survivable. Especially since the wolf had helped her.

She wanted to scan the trees for the human man who'd jumped into the mix earlier—had he been wounded? Had he run away? Had the wolf hurt him?—but with the huge wolf standing only a few feet away, possibly severely injured, she had to focus on him first. And something about the sheer size of the animal, and the color of his eyes…

"That wasn't a very good idea," she said, keeping her voice low and soothing. "This thing's killed a lot of animals. Probably a couple of humans, too. They're very dangerous. You could have been killed."

The almost sardonic tilt of the wolf's head made Becca certain he understood her. And that he was absolutely more than a wolf.

The absence of the human man who'd first jumped between her and the irgotoc started to make sense.

"Thanks for the help," she murmured.

The wolf dipped his head in acknowledgement. Which confirmed her suspicions.

"No ordinary wolf, then." Not like her either. But not just a wolf.

The instant she voiced the realization out loud, the wolf started to change. His body convulsed and expanded as he rose onto two legs. Hair receded. Tail disappeared. Paws turned to hands. Muzzle retracted. Within minutes, the wolf had shifted. And a human man stood in the woods before her.

Wow.

Becca blinked. He was…not what she'd been expecting.

His eyes were still a little yellow, though not as bright as the wolf's had been, and for some reasons she was insanely curious what his eye color without the shifter glow might be. His hair was a shaggy dark brown, almost black, crowning a ruggedly handsome face. Not pretty, but compelling. The sort of face that would make her miss a step if she passed him on the street. Sharp, wide features. Shadows cutting beneath his high cheekbones. A hard mouth that kept drawing her attention—just to reassure herself the irgotoc's acid blood hadn't done him any serious damage, though, she told herself. That's the only reason she couldn't seem to pull her attention from his mouth.

He was naked after his shift, of course, and was nicely muscled. At least in the parts of him she allowed herself to peek at. She knew shapeshifters didn't worry about nudity the way humans often did. But since he'd helped her in the irgotoc fight, she felt like she should afford him at least a little discretion. Keeping her gaze from dipping lower was more difficult than it should have been, though. Something about him…drew her.

So much so, she took another step toward him.

His scent washed over her then. Not just wolf this time, but…*him*.

Recognition hit like a hammer. The panic earlier in the fight after he'd appeared… That distracting terror that had filled her…

Shocked realization left her breathless for several long seconds. Her heartbeat pounded hard in her chest. Her pulse throbbed in her veins. Was this real? Could this be possible? Here? Now?

She met his gaze.

After all these years. One hundred and ninety years of knowing this moment would come. Hoping this moment would happen. Holding the god En's promise in her heart. That this would come before one of the monsters killed her.

And here he was. Just…standing in the woods with her over the carcass of an irgotoc.

He was the one.

The one man who could save her from the curse that haunted very member of her Family—haunted all of the Families. A curse En had promised would be broken when they found their Nam-tar. Their true love. Their destiny.

After almost two centuries, she stood face-to-face with the one person who would change her life forever.

The overwhelming reality crashed down on her, leaving her speechless. Breathless.

A slight movement from below and to her left caught her attention. She reacted instinctively, jumping backward to escape a last, spasmodic thrash of the dead monster's tail. But she wasn't fast enough.

One of the spiked barbs sliced through her thigh, tearing open her pants and quadricep muscle in one painful cut.

Cursing under her breath to offset the pain, she stared at the wound. Blood oozed down her leg. Thanks to her instinctive reaction, the spike hadn't buried itself in her thigh or caught a vital artery. Still, she needed to bind the wound. Soon.

Amateur move. Letting a dead monster injure her. Not exactly the first impression she'd hoped to make when meeting her Nam-tar for the first time.

She opened her mouth to say something, though what she wasn't sure. Then her vision started to cloud. Black spots danced in front of her eyes. Numbness seeped up her limps. All of it too sudden and pervasive. Not shock. Not just blood loss.

Her heartbeat stuttered, then pounded hard. She sucked in a ragged breath. Glanced at the man.

He took several steps closer, reached for her.

"Oh, this isn't good," she said.

And darkness closed around her.

REDEMPTION IN STONE
Coming March 2023

Don't miss the latest Kat Simons
news, updates, excerpts, cover reveals, and more!

All new subscribers get two exclusive stories.

Mate Run
A Tiger Shifters Paranormal Romance short story

and

When Cary Met Ariel
A Cary Redmond Urban Fantasy novella

Join Now!
https://bit.ly/KatSimonsNewsletter

BOOKS BY KAT SIMONS

The Trouble with Leopard Queens and Shifter Wars

The Trouble with Baby Gods and Vampires

The Trouble with Magic and Faery Curses

The Trouble with Wizards and Old Enemies

The Trouble with Death and Demon Gods

The Cary Redmond Series Box Set Books 1-3

CARY REDMOND SHORT STORIES

* When Cary Met Jaxer * When Cary Met Pickles * When Cary Met Marianne * When Cary Met Lucy * When Cary Met Angie * Cary and Deacon (Try to) Go on a Date * Date Night Take Two * Third Date's the Charm * Cary vs the Goblin King * Dinner with the Joneses * Cary and the Cursed Jack-O'-Lantern * Cary and the Demon Witch * Cary Goes to Hawaii * Cary Holidays * Cary and Dragons and Goblins * Cary's Galentine's Day * Cary at the Haunt and Howl

When Cary Met the Good Guys (Collection 1)

Dates, Dinners, and Other Disasters (Collection 2)

Witches and Weavers and Ghosts, Oh Boy (Collection 3)

DEMON WITCH SERIES

Howling Dreadful

Moonlit Strange

Bone Lantern Witch

Spiderweb Witch

JOAN OF KERRY SERIES

Joan of Kerry: Joan and the Abhartach

Joan and the Leprechaun

Joan and the Kraken COMING SOON

ABOUT THE AUTHOR

Kat Simons earned her Ph.D. in animal behavior, working with animals as diverse as dolphins and deer. She brought her experience and knowledge of biology to her paranormal romances and urban fantasy fiction, where she delights in taking nature and turning it on its ear. She writes urban fantasy, contemporary fantasy, and paranormal romance in series which combine action adventure, the otherworldly, and a frequent dose of sexy romance.

DARKNESS IN STONE, launches the newest paranormal romance series for Kat, following the exploits and loves of the Seven Families of monster hunters. The first trilogy follows the Wolf Family, as our heroes and heroines struggle to win their fated mates while fending off deadly monsters bent on destroying the world.

The latest book in her bestselling romantic urban fantasy series about Protector Cary Redmond, THE TROUBLE WITH DEATH AND DEMON GODS, is also out now. As are the newest stories in the romantic urban fantasy Demon Witch series, including the first "meet cute" for Angie and her demon hunter boyfriend Sebastian in the novella HOWLING DREADFUL.

For something a little different, Kat also publishes fantasy, science fiction, and the occasional hockey romance under the name Isabo Kelly (https://www.isabokelly.com).

After traveling the world, living in places like Hawaii, Germany, and Ireland, Kat now lives in New York City with her family and a library's worth of books.

For more on Kat and her future books

Website: https://www.katsimons.com
Newsletter: https://bit.ly/KatSimonsNewsletter
Bookstore: https://tanddpublishingbookstore.com/

Socials
Facebook Page: https://www.facebook.com/KatSimonsAuthor
BookBub: https://www.bookbub.com/authors/kat-simons
Instagram: https://www.instagram.com/isabokelly/
Twitter: https://twitter.com/IsaboKelly

www.ingramcontent.com/pod-product-compliance
Lightning Source LLC
Chambersburg PA
CBHW061624210726
48287CB00001B/269